Where the Light Gathers

D KATHRYN PRESSMAN

DELPHINE BOOKS

Publisher's Note: This is a work of fiction. Names, characters, places, and incidents are a product of the author's imagination. Locales and public names are sometimes used for atmospheric purposes. Any resemblance to actual people, living or dead, or to businesses, companies, events, institutions, or locales is completely coincidental.

Ordering Information:
Quantity sales. Special discounts are available on quantity purchases by corporations, associations, and others. For details, contact the "Special Sales Department" at the website above.

Where the Light Gathers/ D Kathryn Pressman. -- 1st ed.
ISBN 978-0-578-59339-5 (Paperback)
ISBN 978-0-578-59346-3 (eBook)

Author photograph by Rob Skinner

For my husband, Marty, and my son, Ewen,
with love and gratitude

ACKNOWLEDGMENTS

First and foremost, I would like to thank Christopher Noël, whose thoughtful, precise, and insightful editorial comments led to the expansion of the work and the discovery of additional threads and connections. I am grateful for his sound advice and encouragement throughout the revision process.

I would also like to thank Adele and Padre Joe for allowing me inside the room that holds a fragment of Filippo Lippi's earliest fresco, The Confirmation of the Carmelite Rule. They were both gracious and generous with their time, providing me the opportunity to closely study the work. In addition, I wish to thank Emma Molignoni, who acted as my guide in Florence and Prato. She met my many questions with an in-depth knowledge of the history, people, culture, and art of Renaissance Florence. I would also like to thank Nancy Levy, research librarian at Princeton University, for her helpful suggestions.

Finally, and most importantly, I would like to thank my husband, Martin Pressman, and my son, Ewen Kronemeyer, for their enduring encouragement and support throughout the lengthy process of researching and writing this book.

D Kathryn Pressman

June 2019

SOURCES

Sources for quotations woven into the text:

Alberti, Leon Battista. *On Painting*. Translated by John R. Spencer. New Haven: Yale Univ. Press, 1966. www.yalebooks.com Used with permission.

Boethius. *The Consolation of Philosophy*. Edited and translated by Scott Goins and Barbara H. Wyman. San Francisco: Ignatius Press, 2012. www.ignatius.com Used with permission.

Cennini, Cennino d'Andrea. *The Craftsman's Handbook*. Translated by Daniel V. Thompson, Jr. New York: Dover Publications, first published by Yale University Press, 1933. www.yalebooks.com Used with permission.

Cicero. *Selected Works*. Translated by Michael Gant. New York: Penguin Books, 1971. www.penguin.co.uk Used with permission.

Cicero. *On Duties*. Edited by M. T. Griffin and E. M. Atkins. Cambridge: Cambridge Univ. Press, 1991. www.cambridge.org Reproduced with permission of the Licensor through PLSclear.

Dante. *The Inferno*. Translated by Robert Hollander and Jean Hollander. New York: Random House, Anchor Books, 2000. www.anchorbooks.com Used with permission.

Dante. *Purgatorio*. Translated by Robert Hollander and Jean Hollander. New York: Random House, Anchor Books, 2004. www.anchorbooks.com Used with permission.

Dante. *Paradiso*. Translated by Robert Hollander and Jean Hollander. New York: Random House, Anchor Books, 2007. www.anchorbooks.com Used with permission.

Plato. *Great Dialogues of Plato*. Translated by W. H. D. Rouse. Edited by Eric H. Warmington and Philip G. Rouse. Signet Classics, The New American Library, 1956. www.penguin.com Used with permission.

Plato. *Philebus: A Dialogue of Plato on Pleasure and Knowledge and Their Relations to the Highest Good*. Translated by Edward Poste. London: John W. Parker and Son, West Strand, 1860.

Saint Augustine. *Confessions*. Translated by Henry Chadwick. Oxford: Oxford Univ. Press, 2008. Reproduced with permission of the Licensor through PLSclear.

Seneca. *Moral and Political Essays*. Edited by John M. Cooper and J. F. Procope. Cambridge: Cambridge Univ. Press, 1998. www.cambridge.org Reproduced with permission of the Licensor through PLSclear.

For a complete bibliography, see my website: dkathrynpressman.com

PAINTINGS

List of paintings with links to online images:

Barbadori altarpiece for Santo Spirito, now in the Louvre
https://commons.wikimedia.org/wiki/File:Pala_barbadori_louvre_lippi.jpg

Martelli Chapel *Annunciation*, San Lorenzo, Florence, in situ
https://wikivisually.com/wiki/Martelli_Annunciation (click on image to enlarge)

Sant' Ambrogio *Coronation of the Virgin*, now in the Uffizi, Florence
https://artsandculture.google.com/asset/coronation_of_the_virgin/
FQHAX2kUpkEteg

Fresco cycle, Santo Stefano, Prato
https://www.wga.hu/html_m/l/lippi/filippo/1450pr/index.html
(click on thumbnail images to enlarge)

Adoration in the Forest, for Cosimo de' Medici's chapel, Palazzo Medici, now in the
Staatliche Museen Preussischer, Berlin
https://useum.org/artwork/Adoration-in-the-Forest-Filippo-Lippi-1458

The Madonna and Child with the Birth of the Virgin, tondo, now in the Museo Palatino,
Palazzo Pitti, Florence
https://www.uffizi.it/en/artworks/
madonna-with-the-child-and-scenes-from-the-life-of-st-anne

Madonna and Child with Two Angels, now in the Uffizi, Florence
https://www.khanacademy.org/madonnaandchildwithtwoangels

Fresco cycle, Santa Maria Assunta, Spoleto
https://www.wga.hu.html_m/l/lippi/filippo/1460s/index.html
(click on thumbnail images to enlarge)

Self-portrait of Filippo Lippi with his son Filippino (holding taper), fresco cycle,
Spoleto, detail from *Dormition of the Virgin*
https://commons.wikimedia.org/wiki/
Category:Life_of_the_Virgin_frescos_in_the_Spoleto_Cathedral

The first layer of plaster needs to be rough and uneven or the smoothest layers on top will not adhere.

CENNINO D'ANDREA CENNINI
(*THE CRAFTSMAN'S HANDBOOK*)

PART ONE

THE FIRST LAYER

CHAPTER 1

The year of Our Lord 1433, Mediterranean Sea

S hadows define form, Filippo thought, as he stretched out on the hard, rough bench, his muscles sore and aching. Like sorrow and joy, they fall into subtle gradations from light to dark. His eyes still closed in the first moments of awakening, he searched her tormented face, the new sense of shame traced across her features. Beside her, Adam, head bent, wept into his hands. Both torsos caved inward, stomach muscles tensed around the sudden shock of anguish. There was no return. Masaccio's painting, the expulsion of Adam and Eve from paradise, came alive in his memory. Filippo continued to trace the heft and weight of them who had surely once drifted on air. Bound to the earth beneath their feet, moving forward into their new life with the strained muscles of legs and buttocks, all would now take effort, every step, every experience. Did he himself not know it?

Adam and Eve, rejected, were newly formed of shadow. Where all before had been light, now each fold of glorious ultramarine would cast a shadow, each ray of gold leaf hold separate from all that was not gold. Each of their descendants, earthbound. 'O, earthly creatures! O, thick-headed men!' When striving to know another person, do we not pick through the bare bones, the debris of their life in an attempt to make a sketch of it? But, as such, it is severed from the continuous thread of their existence. What do we know of them? Of their light and shadow?

Filippo yawned and stretched once more. He heard voices and knew the pirates were awake above deck. As he swung his legs around and sat up, a deep rumble unfurled in the sky above.

Only a thin sliver of sky was visible at the sea's far rim. The rest hung heavy with cloud. A snarling wind had picked up and was buffeting the ship, which rolled unsteadily, its boards creaking with the strain of holding together. If the ship were pried apart, they would be sucked into the dark, indifferent sea.

All of the men had now awakened and were ready.

"Drive!" the oars guard yelled out. "Outrun!" But his last words were lost in the din.

The men heaved the massive oars, pulling them back against the raging sea. They worked hard, but the ship was stalled. Filippo, looking up, saw a whirling funnel made of black cloud. As if up-ended in its function, it sucked a stream of water from the sea, the water swirling skyward. They, too, could be drawn into its dark belly.

The oars guard shouted, "We will crash into the rocks! Head into the wind. Drive hard."

This was the opposite of the meeting of sky and sea long ago, so saturated with color, Filippo's eyes so enticed by it that he had never seen the pirate ship coming. Here, now, the sea and sky had become one, closing over them like a trap door.

When rowing became impossible, the oars guard ordered them to stop. Then he climbed the stairs to the top deck, leaving them below.

"We drown with the rats," the man next to Filippo grumbled, his voice barely audible above the roar of wind and sea. By now the waves rose to the full height of the ship. When they crashed against it, the oarsmen were submerged. Tied by chains to the ship's floor, all they could do was hold their breath and hold on until each wave subsided.

Men cried out for the Lord to save them, for Saint Christopher, the protector of travelers. Some cursed. They cursed God, the sea, the storm. "Hold fast!" Demetrius yelled at the moment of each wave's descent.

Filippo, gasping for air, prayed to Mary, mother of God, "Not here. Not now. Let this not be the hour of my death."

"Hold fast," he heard again and gripped the wood of the boat so hard that when he was thrown backward, it rasped his palms, pressing splinters into his skin, his torn skin smarting in the salt water. Two men were swept overboard. They hung from the chains manacled to their ankles, submerged and struggling until another wave battered them against the side of the ship. Stilled now, their bodies floated, tossed by the sea.

Then the wind died down, the sea calmed. The rain continued to fall, but the dark cloud, the funnel, had moved off in another direction. The oars guard returned, releasing the two men who had been lost. Filippo made the sign of the cross and prayed for their souls.

"Pick up your oars," the guard ordered. "We head to land."

As he heaved the massive oar, Filippo wondered why he had not allowed himself to be swept overboard. What had he to live for? Why had he held on with all his strength? The clouds parted, allowing the sun to pierce through, threads of its light reaching the water's surface, shimmering. He had been challenged and had made the decision to hold onto life. It should have been a quick and welcome relief to let go, but a thread like a fragile sliver of gold leaf had held him fast to the darkness that was now his life. It had no longer been about him but about the breathing, pulsing, ineffable mystery of life, his thin, barely discernable connection to it.

The first layer of plaster needs to be rough and uneven or the smoothest layers on top will not adhere. Cennini

The ship had been blown far off course, so that it took two full cycles of day to night to return to the place where the storm had engulfed them. Filippo thought of the marteloio, the chart of numbers used to calculate direction and distance that al-Basir, the old wise man, had explained. He knew that Maumen, the pirate leader, was now using it to chart their course, to find what had been lost.

It was a simple pleasure that had led him to be enslaved on a pirate ship. Filippo was twenty-six in the year of Our Lord 1432, a young man flush with the joy of newly won freedom. Days unfolded before him, unplanned, loosened from the bonds of daily chores and the cycle of prayer. Prior to that, he had lived as a monk at Santa Maria del Carmine in his hometown of Florence. Placed there against his will at the age of eight, he had taken his vows early, at the age of fifteen. But he was also a painter, and the prior, no fool, knew that it was not Filippo's calling to serve God as a man of the cloth. He also realized that the young monk possessed a rare talent, one that could bring honor to the Carmine. So, when he was twenty-five, the prior released him, telling him to go out into the world to study with the great maestros of his craft.

He traveled first to Siena, where he made detailed sketches of Ghiberti and Donatello's works, focusing on Donatello's bronze relief depicting the feast of Herod, created for the baptismal font. Filippo went next to Naples, a great center of culture couched in an idyllic seaside setting. He had finally settled in Genoa where there were more Tuscan artists than in all of Tuscany. Here, he traveled from one bottega to the next, learning his craft.

When autumn arrived, the hills lit up, torches whose flame lulled Filippo, distracting him from work. His energy had always ebbed and flowed, so he had learned how to let go when it waned, to allow it to guide him to a place where thought was stilled, until slowly the desire for action roared within him once again. It was in this state of quietude that Filippo decided to look up the prior's friend, Fra Matteo, who lived in Vernazza, a small village on the Ligurian coast. He took his time, traveling on foot south along the rocky coastline.

Once in Vernazza, Filippo easily found Santa Margherita d'Antiocho, a weathered twelfth- century structure of blackened stone perched precariously above the sea. When he asked the caretaker the whereabouts of Fra Matteo, he was directed to the Olive and Thistle, a tavern located on one of the narrow, winding streets tucked into the rocky hillside. Within its dark interior, he easily found Fra Matteo, who was having his supper with a group of villagers, his laugh ringing out above that of the others.

Fra Matteo's cheeks were round as a baby's bottom. His pudgy wrists grew straight into his hands, no contour differentiating them, his fingers short and wide. The man had a peasant's hands. Had he not been a friar, they would have served him well with heavy farm labor. His dark brown eyes were his most defining feature, etched with lines that fanned out from the corners, the only wrinkles that revealed his age, two decades older than Filippo. This first meeting was not the only time that Filippo would notice the light in his eyes, a light from within, for even in the darkness of night and tavern, there was a spark in them.

Hearing who had sent him, the kindly friar greeted Filippo warmly, clapping him on the arms, kissing him on both cheeks, and inviting him to join them. The friar poured him a glass of wine that was ruby red with a smoky after-taste, the best he had ever drunk.

Matteo toasted the prior and asked after him. "How is my old friend? Not a better man have I met in all four corners of Italy."

"You have not been to all four corners of Italy," one of the group reminded him, drawing laughter from the others. "In fact, I believe you have never set foot outside of Vernazza."

Matteo winked. "Never mind, then. He is a prince among paupers in God's spiritual realm."

"Ah." The man wagged a finger and held up his glass. "He wiggles out of it, for who can question the good friar's knowledge of the world of God?"

"How long do you stay?" Matteo asked, turning his attention back to Filippo.

"Indefinitely," he answered, being in the habit, during these days, of living life with the flexibility of a bird that can drift in any direction so long as it finds food and shelter.

"Well, then," Matteo told him, "we must show you the entire expanse of our little paradise."

A few meters up from the small town that clung to the rocky slopes, an expanse of olive groves rose precipitously, and beyond these, vineyards stretched past where the eye could see, up into the surrounding hills. Vernazza was known for its wines and, as it possessed the only natural harbor of the five villages along this stretch of coastline, it was able to profit from the export of its superior wines to other parts of Italy and beyond.

Vernazza was renowned mostly for its reds, but its whites were also sought after. Matteo showed Filippo how the locals produced a rare wine that he had heard of called sciacchetra. It was a delicacy, requiring ten kilos of grapes to produce a one-and-a-half kilo bottle. The people of Vernazza dried the grapes nearly to raisins on their rooftops just as Filippo, when an apprentice in Florence, had dried cakes of lime and water to make the white pigment that is essential for flesh tones in frescoes.

It was a steep climb up to the vineyards, but it was well worth the exertion. The height gave a perfect view of the sea. Matteo had the habit of softly whistling under his breath when he hiked or was engaged in any occupation other than prayer. He reminded Filippo of his brother, Giovanni, who was also round and plump, his face always with the trace of a contented smile. It was Giovanni's smiling face that peered out at the viewer from the fresco Filippo had painted at the Carmine.

Matteo always chose a spot to rest just above the final line of olive trees, their silver shimmer of leaves dancing in the sun. It was such a quiet, peaceful place that as Filippo sat and stared out over the sea, birds often flew so close past his head that he had to duck. Filippo confided in Matteo during these times, talking to him about things he had never shared with anyone.

He explained that his mother had passed into the great sea shortly after he was born, leaving him with no memory of her. It was his sister, Piera, who became his closest companion and, in spite of her years, a mother to him. There was a deep longing inside of him to know his mother's face, her touch. Four years later, when their father passed into the great sea, Piera was sent to live with relatives, and Filippo's dour aunt, his father's sister, arrived in the home to care for him. Mona Lapaccia was an old widow with no children of her own. She abandoned him to the convent against his will when he was only eight-years-old. When, finally, Fortuna smiled on him, bringing the great painter Masaccio to the Carmine to work on frescoes in the Brancacci chapel there, it was only to turn her smiling face away two years later with his death.

"I learned more from Masaccio in two years' time than in all the remainder of my life," he lamented.

"And it has been such a long life," Matteo laughed.

"I needed to learn more," Filippo said, disregarding Matteo's jibe.

Matteo grew serious. "It may be that you learned all you needed to in that time. The rest must come with experience."

"Masaccio should not have died." Filippo was sure of this. The greatest of painters, he was only twenty-seven, just a little older than Filippo was now, when he was taken by God to His heavenly kingdom. "He was meant to do great things. It is nothing if I am lost, but Masaccio."

"Each person has his story," Matteo said. "If your friend has been lost to the great sea, all the more reason for you, he whom Masaccio taught, to do all that you are capable of doing for this art that you shared. Honor his memory. Breathe life into paint as he said, as he alone could have taught you to do."

Matteo passed a hunk of bread and some cheese to Filippo, who admitted that his work had not been progressing as quickly as he had hoped. Wiping crumbs from his mouth, Matteo said, "It is the way of things. Does not a seed send roots into the earth, at times waiting three seasons before sending up shoots? You must root yourself in occupation, work long and hard in darkness, before the tender shoots of your labor are ready to break through the ground, to be rewarded with the sun's light."

Filippo saw his meaning. As he contemplated Matteo's words, the kind friar continued, "You must get back to work. Genoa awaits you. But, first," and here there was a twinkle in his eyes, "I will show you something of such beauty that you will remember it forever."

That very evening, as the light waned, Matteo proposed that they head out to sea in a rowboat. "I promised you beauty," he said, "and the heavens favor us with clear sky."

The two had just shared a jug of wine. Talking and refilling their cups, they had lost track of the quantity until Matteo, turning the jug over, came up empty. He peered down into the neck. "It was full not an hour ago. Where have you gone, then?" At this Filippo, drunk, laughed and could not stop. Matteo, tickled by the sound of his laughter, joined in until Filippo fell from the bench, which sent them both into further peals of laughter. When they were finally able to settle down, Matteo, wiping the tears from his eyes, said, "Well, then. There is no more wine, so it must be time to head out to sea."

"I have never been in a boat before," Filippo said, looking warily out at the vast sea. It crossed his mind that the common expression for death was "passing into the great sea."

"An adventure, then. All the better," Matteo answered, his smile broad as his belly.

Filippo hesitated. "Can we not enjoy this light as well from land?"

"We can. But, when the sun sets beneath the sea, making its way under Earth's far rim, it spills a light you will never forget, and if you are out beyond land, surrounded by water, you will feel as if you can reach out and touch it."

The painter in Filippo won him over, the prospect of seeing such a light chasing away his fear. He eagerly climbed into the unsteady cavity of the boat, but feeling it rock beneath his weight, one foot yet in the doorway, he hesitated once again. "Is it safe?"

"What true adventure is safe?" Matteo responded with a hearty laugh, but then, seeing the uncertainty in Filippo's eyes, assured him, "Of course it is safe. It is a rowboat. We go out only a short way."

The boat was one of many, tied directly to the façades of the houses. Each home had a front door that opened to the water and a back door that led to the street. As Filippo placed his other foot into the boat and it rocked beneath him, he pushed his fears aside and settled into the comforting motion of rowing. The exertion relieved him of anxiety. When they reached a point well beyond the finger of land that formed Vernazza's natural harbor, they turned the boat parallel to the shore, left far behind now, so that they could sit side by side. They pulled their oars in and waited in silence, attention focused where sky met sea.

The most perfect steersman that you can have, and the best helm, lie in the triumphal gateway of copying from nature. Cennini

The feeling of drift was not new to Filippo; he had often felt as if alone in a vast darkness, untethered. The quiet on the water, however, far from land, was different from that in the countryside. On land, one inhabited the earth with other creatures, who ventured out when they sensed that people were absent. On the water, a chamber of silence, Filippo felt an overwhelming sadness. But then the calm, comforting slap of water against the side of the boat pulled his attention back to the horizon, where the colors had begun to deepen. The lapping sound soothed him, punctuated by the sudden cry of a gull, its call like scraps of hope pealed from his soul and flung out to sea. He felt he, too, soared on the wind.

The sun edged slowly down and spread itself out along the thin ledge of the earth, violet blankets of light swelling upward. At the horizon, liquid light, as if it had drunk of the sea, floated, a rose-gold light of such brilliance, it seemed God himself must be in it. Filippo felt only his breath moving slowly in and out as the light grew. A burst of rays from the central orb, threads of gold, pierced the fabric of sky and sea.

They were sitting side by side, suspended in awe, immersed in the beauty of the light, when Filippo felt himself physically rising, then falling, rising and tilting. When they turned they saw a ship headed in their direction, cleaving the water with its massive prow, creating waves that hove outward, reaching all the way to their small, unsteady craft, and still the boat came on.

"They are headed directly for us!" Matteo yelled out. "Row!" He had picked up his own oar, which he now frantically slapped across the water's surface. Filippo dug his oar deep into the waves, turning their boat around, moving it forward toward land, toward Vernazza. The waves, growing higher and higher, made rowing difficult and finally impossible. A sudden surge and tilt lifted Filippo's stomach, and the boat slipped out from under him. As he reached out to grab it, a rush of water pulled him under. Caged beneath the boat, Filippo flailed, water filling his nose and throat. Instinctively, he blew out. He did not know how to swim. He opened his eyes, but the darkness frightened him. He became aware of a deep pounding in his ears. Panicked, he threw up his arms. A hand clasped his own. Matteo pulled him to the surface, thrusting his body onto the overturned bottom of the boat. As he coughed and sputtered, he heard Matteo say, "More adventure than I had in mind."

The hull of a ship rose above them. Filippo heard it creak as it passed slowly by. He clung with all his strength to the small rowboat. He was about to yell out for help when he saw men lowering a boat over the side of the ship. As they drew near, he noticed the long knives tucked into their waistbands. Initial fear gave way to reason. Sailors would have need of knives for any number of tasks. As he climbed the rope ladder that had been tossed over the side of the ship, Filippo thanked God for being saved and looked forward to soon arriving back on land.

Once on board, Filippo realized that Fortuna, fickle, had spun her globe. This was not salvation. The sailors spoke an unfamiliar tongue. When he turned to ask Matteo who they were, it was his friend, still on the hull below, who had a look of fear upon his face. "Pirates," he whispered, and Filippo followed his gaze landward where, high upon the hill of the promontory, smoke signals billowed from the round stone tower. "The village residents," Matteo explained, "are being called to safety by the caretaker of the watchtower." The church's bell tower rang out.

Filippo planted his feet firmly against the rocking motion of the boat and watched as the shore slipped from view. The bell ceased its ringing.

CHAPTER 2

The year of Our Lord 1432, Mediterranean Sea

They were soon surrounded, hemmed in by a sweaty band of pirates. To steady himself, Filippo focused his gaze on the unusual triangular shape of the sails. One of the pirates, speaking Italian, demanded that they disrobe. The cloth, sagging with seawater, was cumbersome, so Filippo gratefully stripped off his mantello. But, Matteo stayed him with his hand. "We cannot," he said.

The pirate thrust out his arm, striking Matteo across the face with such force that he fell to his knees. A shiver passed through Filippo as he reached down to help his friend to his feet. Straightening up, he saw a lean man, taller than the rest, push through the crowd. A scraggly black beard framed his thin face. His head was concealed beneath a white turban. Beside him stood an old man, small in stature, with a face creased like wrinkled linen. He also wore a white turban, a loose top with wide sleeves, and pants cinched at the ankles, his long white beard fanning out across his chest. There was an all-knowing depth in his dark eyes. This and his relaxed posture seemed to permeate the space around him with a peace and calm antithetical to the harsh atmosphere of the ship.

The tall one fixed his piercing gaze on the prisoners. After scrutinizing them, he spoke. The one who knew some Italian asked why they would not strip to their undergarments.

"We are priests," Matteo explained. "Our religion forbids us to wear anything but our monk's robes."

The man, who appeared to be the leader, looked at the older one, nodded his head, and said something in an authoritative tone. The pirates scattered, except for the old man. He took possession of Filippo's white mantello. Apart from this garment, it seemed that the leader had given permission for them to remain in their robes, which later became more important than Filippo would have guessed. Matteo, in his wisdom, had known that it would allow them to remember who they were when all ties to their former selves had been broken.

At the same time, it interfered with their new occupation, so that they had to strip each morning to their undergarments before it commenced. Their main job was to row the boat, each with an oar the length of a small tree, ten braccia, or arm's lengths, with a weight greater than that of a medium-sized man. Two rowers shared a bench. It was back-breaking labor.

It reminded Filippo of preparing a wall for a fresco. After the mixing and troweling of plaster, a large board, much like the oar, was used to level the plaster from top to bottom along the entire length of the wall. It was so heavy that it required two apprentices to maneuver it. He had cursed the chore at the time, but he now thanked God to have built up the muscle and stamina to endure hard labor. His ability to keep up with the other rowers saved him lashings. Matteo, being older and more used to a sedentary life, drew the oars guard's ire.

Each stroke began with the oar out of the water. The rowers rose in unison, stepping onto a footboard for leverage. Arms straight out, they pushed the blade forward. As they pushed, they stepped with their other foot onto the back of the bench in front and, as the blade entered the water, they strained with both feet and backs, adding their own weight to its thrust. It was only when the oar came up out of the water that they collapsed onto the bench, one stroke completed. The work was staggered since they were able to do only three strokes before requiring a rest for two, and then they began again.

The monotonous sound of the waves slapping the side of the boat was not soothing like the gentle lapping on the sides of the rowboat. It lacked the intervals of silence, was now punctuated by the sting of salt on Filippo's skin. His lips were dry and cracked. And then there was the monotonous rocking. Once a dove, circling, signaled land. There was excitement among the men. Then the slow, steady turn and thrust of the boat sent them past it, back to the limitless expanse of the sea.

They rowed from first matins until just after nones, when the sun, straight up in the sky, made it too hot to continue. Since rowing was confined to the earliest hours of the day, they took a brief morning meal of dried biscuit and beans on the benches. The biscuit caused constipation, the beans flatulence. The words they yelled in unison to coordinate their movements were punctuated by loud bursts of noise from their bodies.

"Trumpets!" Matteo called them. "We make music like angels."

Comments like these were met with laughter. The oars guard seemed to appreciate Matteo's ability to keep the workers happy and soon let up on his lashings.

There was no rest except for sleep. When they were not rowing, Filippo and Matteo emptied the boat of water, for there were always cracks through which water slowly seeped. They worked from dark until last light, with only a mid-day break for rest. The menial tasks that the friars of his order had originally intended for Filippo had at long last become his lot.

The food they received was scant, even by the convent's standards. Their second meal of the day, eaten when they were done rowing, consisted of old biscuits full of worms, dipped in oil, and yellowed water. If they were lucky, there was a small chunk of moldy cheese.

The largest of the rowers, a giant of a man named Demetrius, a prisoner taken from a Venetian galley, laughed at their initial reticence to eat the biscuit. "We eat what the rats eat. You had better swallow it before they do, for you will get no more."

When they hesitated to drink the water, he added, "Hold your nose. Its smell will make you gag."

Just as Filippo filled his mouth with it, Demetrius said, "Rat piss."

Filippo's throat constricted. He sprayed the contents of his mouth onto the deck.

Demetrius threw his head back and roared with laughter. "What do you think happens to water that sits in barrels under the heat of the sun for months? They put vinegar in it to keep it from spoiling. Drink up. Lack of water will kill you faster than the drinking of it."

"And what part of the world does a giant of a man sail from?" Matteo asked him.

"I am from Rhodes," Demetrius said, drawing himself up so that he seemed to stand even taller.

"Do they eat the fruit of a growing tree, these men of Rhodes?" Matteo asked.

"Ha," Demetrius exclaimed, "not all are so tall in stature on Rhodes, but all are strong. The men in my family are colossal. My mother is a sturdy woman, as well. They say I was the size of a full-grown child at birth, twenty stone."

"It is a good place that creates men such as yourself," Matteo said, and from that day a bond was forged.

This dismal hour engulfing my head/came while Fortune favored me/She changed her cheating face.   Boethius

On the upper deck the light was harsh and bright, forcing Filippo to squint. Colors were washed out, as if scrubbed by the sea. The sun's light, straight up in the sky, threw few shadows, created little of contour. Below deck, by contrast, forms were barely visible in the darkness of the hold. Bright or dark, there were no subtleties of color, little distinction between light and shadow. Days lost their mystery.

There was no way to clearly distinguish the time of day that delineated the canonical hours, still Filippo continued his practice since leaving the convent of praying before sleep overtook him. He was so exhausted that his prayers were cut short. He prayed again upon waking, but was soon hard at work rowing.

"I have prayed," Filippo told Matteo. "I have prayed to no avail. I ask God for His help, but I receive no answer."

"God works in mysterious ways," Matteo said.

"As the mystery that carried off so many when the pestilence swept through the convent? Or the mystery that took Masaccio, the world's greatest painter, at the beginning of his life's work? Is it mystery, or is it God's indifference?"

"Filippo, you must not allow such thoughts to take hold in you. It is the devil who senses weakness and moves in to destroy your faith. Without faith, who are you?"

"A man at odds. A man who has lost hope."

"Faith first, and then hope," Matteo instructed him. "It is all part of God's plan."

"It seems not a very good plan," Filippo said.

Matteo laughed heartily, "Well, a sense of humor is a good beginning."

Drudgery and loss of his occupation challenged Filippo's previously held belief that as each day unfolded, the light changed in order to peel back Earth's cover and reveal its treasures. For the first time, he felt a trespasser, cut off from the world's repository of beauty. Dante take his accursed inferno, with its eternal flames, its devouring demons. This ship was Filippo's inferno, his own personal hell.

CHAPTER 3

The year of Our Lord 1399, Florence

Cosimo de' Medici walked through the gate and into the loggia of his family home. He possessed a confident air unusual for a ten-year-old, his shoulders thrown back, his gait swift and determined. He was returning from a long day of study at Santa Maria degli Angeli, where he was one of several young boys from wealthy Florentine families who attended classes.

His mentors thought him mature for his age, self-confident without being arrogant, an unusual combination in one so young. Although he was not as athletic as the other boys, being short and thin, with large, clumsy feet, he did well at sword fighting, a skill taught to all sons of prominent citizens. In fact, Cosimo was fascinated with arms and armour and had already begun a collection. It was displayed in his personal rooms where, still too small to don the armour, he often chose a weapon and feigned an opponent. Not that he was bloodthirsty. It was sport to him, with nothing at stake but a matching of his intellect and will against that of another.

Cosimo felt fortunate to have a father who was not only a prominent man in the city, but a well-respected one. His mother was a member of one of the oldest and wealthiest families in Florence, in spite of which, she was gentle and unassuming. Even more rare among his classmates was the fact that his parents so loved each other that it was evident to him in every glance and gesture that passed between them. Theirs was a calm and nurturing household. Most boys did not have two such loving parents; many, in fact, had no mother at all. Some had lived through two subsequent mothers. Childbirth was dangerous, and when the pestilence swept through the city, it took many parents with it, at times entire families. Fortuna had smiled on Cosimo's family, compelling him to believe that they were meant for greatness.

Although he was considered to be one of the brightest students at the monastery, Cosimo did not possess a gift for rhetoric. In fact, he was parsimonious in speech. He struggled with languages, doing best in Latin, which he loved. He found German, French, and the smattering of Hebrew, Greek, and Arabic that were taught difficult to master. Cosimo did, however, possess keen insight, and he was able to parse the most challenging tenets of philosophy, to comprehend the many subtleties of mathematics.

Excellence is never an accident. Aristotle

Cosimo was obedient, conscientious, and well behaved. Overall, he excelled in his studies. For these reasons and others, he knew, his parents were proud of him. This knowledge imbued him with the feeling that he could do anything if he truly put his mind to it. The one thing Cosimo had to work on was not allowing this confidence to run unbridled. "Arrogance," his father often said, "is the fruit born of ignorance."

After passing through the loggia and climbing the stairs to the second-floor apartments where the family lived, Cosimo went straight to the grand sala where artisans were at work covering the walls with frescoes. Although his father, Giovanni di Bicci de' Medici, was not a cultured man, he appreciated the arts enough to spend some of his hard-earned money on this unusually opulent form of decoration. He also splurged in this particular way, Cosimo knew, in order to please his wife, whose senses were more refined. The house itself was a modest one for their social standing. Ostentation, in Giovanni's view, only invited envy. He taught Cosimo and his little brother, Lorenzo, this valuable lesson.

Cosimo watched intently as the artisans, high up on their scaffolds, painted in the cartoon drawings that had been traced earlier with a ponce bag on that day's section of wet plaster. It was late so that the light was beginning to wane. The artisans quickly finished and began to clean up while Cosimo continued to contemplate their work.

Along the top section of wall, panels contained three different sets of recurring tree motifs, although they did not look like real trees. They were flat, more like ideas of trees. One design was a huge green mass above a trunk over which branches and leaves webbed their way in a pattern of silver lines. Although no leaves ever looked like that, it gave a pleasing effect. On the other side of the room, a worker was beginning to paint a garland of olive leaves that was more realistic. What was that, next to one tree? A bird suspended in mid-air, as if hanging from an invisible string. Cosimo knew it was meant to be flying, but its stick-legs dangled straight down and its wing was barely lifted at a right angle to its body. Cosimo knew enough about momentum to recognize that this bird was going nowhere. Still, painting was a magical skill that he, himself, would never possess.

It was nearly time for dinner, so Cosimo raced to his room to ready himself. As he entered, he was distracted by a suit of armour. He stood before it, transfixed, imagining himself encased in it, sword in hand, battling a foe. He feigned. He thrust. There was a knock on the door. Annoyed—he had been about to slice through his opponent's arm—he called out, "Enter."

A maidservant had arrived to announce that his mother requested his presence at the table. The evening meal was always a happy time for him. It was a chance to talk about the day with his father, his mother, and Lorenzo. On this particular night, the feast of San Giovanni, the patron saint of Florence, one of the dishes was to be lamb, a delicacy not often served, and usually cut up in stew. Not tonight.

When the meal was nearly done, Cosimo and Lorenzo both reached for the last piece of meat left on the plate. They stopped, hands extended above it, eyes locked. Cosimo imagined his father saying, 'And, what, my sons, does one do when there is only one piece of meat left and two brothers?' He cut the meat in two, placing one half on Lorenzo's plate, disappointed by the fact that, since a bone cannot be cut, no one would enjoy gnawing into it. His mouth watered as he thought of it being tossed into a soup pot.

Let parents bequeath to their children not riches but the spirit of reverence.   Plato

Cosimo looked up to see his father smiling at him. "Well done. It is better not to have than not to share. Sacrifice teaches us what we value most."

CHAPTER 4

The year of Our Lord 1432, Mediterranean Sea:
remembering 1414, Florence

One day while, side by side, Filippo and Matteo swabbed the deck together, Matteo said, "I grow bored. I am in need of a tale to pass the time. Tell me about this old aunt of yours. I am certain there is a good story in her."

"Hers was a dour personality," Filippo began. "If she possessed a smile, no one saw it."

He explained that she was a dark presence in his life, her black hair pulled severely back from her face, revealing its uncomely shape and features. Her black eyes were set alight only by the occasional glint of anger. She dressed in black, as if to confirm the somber tone of her spirit. Her front teeth protruded so that, like tusks, they were always visible just beneath her upper lip. The crease between her brows gave her the look of being perpetually vexed, while the squint of her eyes seemed to compensate for the fact that they were placed too close together, surely hindering perfect sight. Apart from that, no emotion seemed to last long enough to imprint itself upon her features except for two deep lines that ran lengthwise down the center of each cheek to her jawline, etched there by an inflexibility that easily leads to anger.

One day, while cleaning, she had knocked a vase from the mantle. It crashed onto the floor with such force that Filippo, repairing a broom, jumped from his seat. The vase was a possession she had brought with her, an ornate piece. She cried out, and then knelt down and picked up the largest of the shards. Holding it up reverently, she muttered, "Stupid. Careless. Beyond repair." She picked up another shard. "Stupid. Stupid. Clumsy." Surely because he was the only other person in the room, she turned toward him and said, "A gift from Pappa." Then she grabbed the broom from his hands and began sweeping up the hundreds of pieces that had once been the vase, all the time spitting the words, "Stupid. Careless. Clumsy."

This was the first but not the last time he would witness such a scene. Mona Lapaccia was in the habit of breaking the things she most valued.

Four years in her care did not reconcile Filippo to her kinship. He could not remember her touch except in anger. She was as unlike his father as the creator could have imagined. How they had come from the same parents was a mystery to Filippo, whose memory of his father, though blurred, was that of a smiling man with green eyes like his own that had held a glint of light as if all of life were there for his amusement. He had been big in girth and possessed a hearty laugh. Filippo also remembered with longing his crushing hug.

One summer day while Filippo sat in the stifling heat of the kitchen, where the shutters were always shut tight, shelling beans, Mona Lapaccia entertained her one friend, Mona Angelina. Mona Lapaccia was in the habit of talking about Filippo in his presence, as if he were not there. He often wondered if she believed him to be deaf.

"I thought the boy would be easier," Mona Lapaccia was saying. "They say that boys are easier, so I sent the girl to live with relatives. The sale of the business will provide her, too, with a small dowry. But he is like a beggar's child, no discipline, a weed growing in my garden. I give him occupation, and he leans on shovels, stares off into space as if without a thought in his head. Or I find he has run off to loiter in the streets."

"I feel sorry for him," Mona Angelina said, sipping her wine. "He has lost both father and mother, his sister far away. So young to lose all that is familiar."

"Am I not familiar?" Mona Lapaccia retorted. "Has he not eaten his meals in my house these four years?"

"Yes. That is true," Mona Angelina agreed, although the house did not belong to her. "I only meant that, having lost so much within these walls, perhaps he feels more at home outside."

"Well, then, let him stay outside," Mona Lapaccia spat angrily. "Ungrateful little beggar. I keep a home for him. I cook for him. My life was quiet once."

"I did not mean to imply that he was ungrateful, only that—"

"I cannot take much more of this," his aunt complained. "I am too old, and he will not be a child in need of care much longer."

Filippo was staring at a long, thin line of light that had crept in through the top of the shutters to rest on the hearth. He had come to recognize that the last light of the day was golden. He was drawn in, here to a world of shadow, there to a world of crimson, indigo, or gold, which then cast its light over objects nearby. Now the color of the brick sparked as if ablaze with fire. When his gaze was rapt, as it was then, caught up in watching a shadow or the way the light changed a color, he moved in slow motion. The golden light burnished the brick; the brick was burning with light. A rude smack to the side of his head brought tears to his eyes. His aunt's voice rose in anger. "Do you see? Do you see?" She had no tolerance for slowed movement.

She walked back to her seat, grumbling, "It is like washing an ass's head." She said this often, but it was a long time before Filippo came to know its meaning, that she was wasting her efforts on him. "He will find himself in the hands of the monks soon enough," she predicted.

Filippo had often thought about running away, but where would he go? If he stayed in the city, she would find him, and there would be a beating to pay. Outside of the city walls, a child had little chance of survival and was defenseless against roaming bands of thieves.

She was right about one thing. Bored, Filippo often wandered into the streets. There was much to see, and he knew a group of boys older than himself. They played games of chance with stones. The loser, which was always Filippo, paid the price by stealing fruit from one of the vendors for the others to enjoy.

One day, squatting in the dirt, throwing stones, thinking this time he had a chance of success, Filippo suddenly felt himself yanked up by the collar and watched as his friends scattered. Mona Lapaccia turned him around and stuck her face into his. "Ruffian!" she yelled. "And only eight. Does Antonio know where you are?" Antonio was a local she paid to do heavy work around the house, the only servant she could afford. Filippo searched for an answer, not wishing to get Antonio, who was kind, into trouble.

Before he could answer, she said, "I thought not" and trudged off with Filippo in tow, her head down, her long strides capable of leaving him in the dust, or any man for that matter, had she not been digging her fingers into his arm.

"I am a small boy!" Filippo yelled out.

She threw him a look that made him shiver. If they had not been out in public, he was sure she would have struck him.

When they arrived at the house, they found Antonio where Filippo had left him, working in the small patch of vegetable garden. Mona Lapaccia thrust Filippo toward him. "I found him squatting disgracefully in the street. Playing a game of chance. Did you not know that he was gone?"

Poor Antonio, bewildered, blinked several times. "I was tending the garden," he softly stammered, holding the hoe aloft as proof, "and Filippo was a great help to me," he lied. "He must have slipped inside for refreshment."

Mona Lapaccia would have none of it. "You are as much of a pigeon head as the boy. I do not know why I keep you on. I send you outside to teach him to tend garden, and on my return from market, I find him gambling with boys twice his age. He will know

the arm of the law before he is nine," she predicted, "and you"—
she wagged her finger in his face—"you are done. Finished."

Poor Antonio needed every soldi she gave him. He did not seem
to know what to do next. Dropping the hoe, he held his hands together as if in prayer and begged, "No, please, Signora. You will
see that I know how to put the handle on a shovel."

"You, useful?" Mona Lapaccia scoffed. "You cannot even use a
shovel once it is made."

She did not dismiss him, however. It was difficult for her to find
workers. Filippo felt sorry for Antonio and helped him as best he
could for the remainder of the day. Afterwards, he continued to
spend every chance he had in the streets, avoiding only the main
thoroughfare, where Mona Lapaccia might again cross his path.

Not long after this transgression, while Filippo was sweeping the
floors, his father's brother Aniello arrived. After greeting Mona Lapaccia
and tousling Filippo's hair, he said to his sister, "We must speak."

Mona Lapaccia grabbed the broom from Filippo's hand. "Go
outside. See what help Antonio needs in the garden."

As he walked from the room he heard his uncle say, "You keep
him well occupied."

"It is the only way," Mona Lapaccia answered.

"This is the subject about which I wish to speak," Aniello began,
lowering his voice, which grew muffled with distance. Filippo's
steps had echoed down the tiled hallway. He now opened and
closed the door without stepping through. He took off his shoes
and snuck back to the closed door. At the first sign of movement,
he would have to be quick. If she caught him eavesdropping, there
would be the devil himself to pay.

"The largest of the properties...." And here his uncle's voice
lowered so that Filippo, however much he strained, could not make
out the words. "As you know," Filippo heard him say, "I have been
unfortunate. My debts and those of my brothers."

"You have been reckless," Mona Lapaccia admonished.

"Yes. Well," Uncle Aniello stammered. "You will benefit. What
does that make you?"

"Grateful," Mona Lapaccia said.

"We wish to sell," Filippo heard him say, but again the final word was lost. Sell what?

His uncle continued, "It will pay all of our debts and, even then, leave a small sum."

Mona Lapaccia's tone took on an edge of suspicion. "And since his sons inherit, and one is already in the Carmine, I will receive additional funds. Yes?" she demanded more than asked.

His uncle hesitated, and then said, "That is the other thing about which I wish to speak." His voice lowered to a whisper. Filippo only caught the words "He is" and "We think it best" and "You will be able to stay on."

Mona Lapaccia said, "This does not disappoint me."

Uncle Aniello was taking his leave. Filippo flew down the hallway, his feet barely touching the tiles, and slipped through the doorway, startling poor Antonio, who almost dropped the pot he was carrying.

"Quick," Filippo said, "give me something. She comes." That was all he needed to say.

Antonio pointed. "See where I was weeding."

"Thank you," Filippo said, running to the spot where a small pile of weeds lay on the path. Kneeling, he bent over and quickly began pulling at them just as Mona Lapaccia came through the doorway looking for him. Her shadow loomed over Filippo and a large swath of the garden, like that of a giant bird of prey.

"That is an herb," she screamed, "you imbecile!" Filippo flinched and ducked, but her hand caught the back of his head. "Give me these," she said, grabbing the small handful he had pulled. "Get back inside and finish sweeping. That is all you are good for."

Stars, cloud-concealed, shed no light. Boethius

The Carmine had cast its shadow across his path from birth, its bell tower blocking the sun from their garden for half of each day.

Their house was on a quiet street that backed onto the Carmine's property. The area in which the house stood was known as Canto della Cuculia because of the cuckoo birds that frequented the gardens there. Filippo found the birdsong soothing, but he snuck down the cobblestone street and along a narrow alleyway to the mercato in the Piazza Santo Spirito as often as he was able. The day after his uncle's visit, he made his way stealthily down the narrow street.

Today was the day. All Filippo had to do was convince his friend, Giuseppe. He hugged the walls of the houses with his body so that Mona Angelina, who was prone to peering out of her windows to the street below, would not spy him. Safely arriving at the corner, he glanced back at the archway above the narrow street on which his house stood and then turned and strode to the corner of Via Sant'Agostino and Via de' Serragli, heading in the direction of the stalls of the open market. He was not quite eight, but he knew that the other side of the Arno was different from the one in which he lived.

He was not long in finding Giuseppe, who was helping his mother set out the last of the day's plums. This task completed, Mona Stefania gave her son leave to play. "I have heard the streets are wide," Filippo began, "and the avenues even wider. New buildings rise up everywhere."

"My mama will whip me." Giuseppe wiped his butt with his hand at the thought.

"It will be worth the beating," Filippo countered. He could see that Giuseppe was giving it thought, so he added, "Your mama has seven children. She will beat you, and she will forget about it tomorrow."

"Well," Giuseppe considered, "she does not like to hit me. It does not hurt that much."

Filippo turned up the pressure, seeing that he was close to a win. "There is only one of me. When old squint-eye beats me, the sting lasts for days. She uses a wooden spoon."

Giuseppe winced at the thought. "But," Filippo concluded, throwing his manhood into the argument, "I think it is worth it."

"Well." Giuseppe hesitated. "Allore. But we have to be back before vespers, or Mama will be worried."

They were about to do something Filippo believed no other eight-year-olds had ever done; they would cross the river to the new Florence. Giuseppe turned in the direction of Santo Spirito.

"No," Filippo said, "not the Ponte Vecchio. Shops are closing for the mid-day meal, but it will still be too risky. It is the busiest place in all Florence. We will cross over the Ponte Nuovo."

"But that is the one that collapsed," Giuseppe protested. "Hundreds died."

"That was more than a hundred years ago," Filippo reminded him.

"But they were watching Dante's Inferno on the river below." Giuseppe seemed to shiver at the thought.

Filippo was exasperated. "It was not the play below that made the bridge collapse. It was that there were too many people on it." He had heard his aunt say as much when her friend, Angelina, voiced this same superstition.

"And," Giuseppe persisted, "years later it was washed away by flood. It is a bad bridge. No good can come to anyone who crosses it."

"Giuseppe." Filippo shook his head in disbelief. "People have been crossing Ponte Nuovo for hundreds of years. Nothing bad has happened to them. And it is not the only bridge to be washed away. There are no shops on it. At this time of day people will be home for the mid-day meal, so it will be empty. We do not want to be turned back before we ever get across the river."

"Well." Giuseppe hesitated.

"There is no room for superstition when one undertakes an adventure," Filippo said authoritatively, surprising himself with his grown-up words.

"Well. If we run across," Giuseppe conceded.

After crossing at breakneck speed, they stopped at the end to catch their breath. Filippo, feeling that the since it was his idea, it was his responsibility to be the navigator, said, "This way, I think." In truth, he had no idea which way to go. They headed in the direction of the Ponte Vecchio but immediately turned down a side street. Not long into their wanderings, they came upon a vast piazza.

"Piazza della Signoria," Filippo guessed, noting the massive building that was surely the palazzo about which he had heard. His eyes took in the blocks of grey stone, the square shape of the structure, the double-paned windows on the top floors, and the tower. "The men who make the laws stay here, and the men who make sure they are followed."

"What if they catch us?" Giuseppe asked, looking suspiciously round.

"Look." Filippo pointed to the tower rising high above them. "That is where they keep prisoners."

Giuseppe's eyes grew wide, and Filippo could not help teasing him. "The worst are put in a cell at the very top so that no one can help them escape. I have heard that they throw them from the battlements above, and they go splat on the ground."

"Ugh." Giuseppe covered his ears with his hands. "Stop."

Just then a group of men exited the building, and Filippo punched Giuseppe's arm. "You had better run like a chicken or they'll chop your head."

Filippo ran as fast as he could, Giuseppe right behind him, down a narrow side street and out of sight. They did not stop running until, careening around a corner, they came to a full stop in the Piazza del Duomo. They were stunned into silence by the sight of the immense duomo, sprawling and soaring. It was a mountain, as if the builders had taken Filippo's own street and the one next to it, and the one beyond that, as well as the Carmine and made it into one building that reached to the sky. "All of the city could fit inside," Filippo said.

The two boys walked around it, examining the building from all angles, its shape shifting as they did. Who had conceived of this greatness? They found themselves at the bottom of the bell tower, so high above them that its tip seemed to pierce the clouds above.

Workers began to filter back in small groups. All around, deep holes were dug in the ground for foundations, and scaffolding swathed newly built structures. Beneath the scaffolding, Filippo picked up the gritty scent of dust not yet settled, the smell of industry. Reluctantly, he grabbed Giuseppe's arm and pulled him down another side street. "Great mother Mary and all the saints," Giuseppe said, rubbing his eyes and glancing back at the duomo just visible now between the buildings.

Filippo agreed. "It is a sight worth crossing the Arno to see. Wait. What is this now?" he asked as they rounded a corner.

They had come upon a building with tall niches every few feet along its outside walls. Some niches were empty, but others held larger-than-life-sized statues. "This is Sant' Giovanni," Filippo said. "See his staff." The building opposite blocked some of the light so that a shadow fell across the saint's right shoulder, then down his torso and right leg. Since his left knee was bent, his left foot exposed, it appeared as if he was walking out of the shadows.

They headed around the corner of the building, where they passed a Madonna and Child, the deep azure background surrounding them patterned with gold stars that glistened in a shaft of late afternoon light. At the next corner, they came upon a statue so lifelike that Filippo stopped and stared in awe. "Who is this, then?"

"Look." Giuseppe pointed to each of the bottom corners of the niche on which the statue stood. "The crest of the linen workers' guild. It is Sant' Marchio."

Filippo had never seen such a statue. The saint's right leg stood firm and solid, the folds of his garment draping it like a fluted column, while his left leg, knee bent in forward motion, rustled the fabric of his robes with delicate, mere traces of line. He was certain that if he could reach high up where the statue stood, the saint's garment would feel like real cloth. Filippo became lost in contemplation of the nails on the tips of the saint's long fingers, the fine lines etched on his hand and along the top of his foot. The movement of this massive figure was so well defined that it appeared as if he might walk from his niche at any moment and hover over them.

Suddenly, there was a loud creaking sound. Startled, Filippo peered around the corner, where he saw that a large, wooden door stood open. From behind it a short, pudgy monk waddled out. The door slammed shut and, his head lowered, the monk strode in the opposite direction. He had not locked the door behind him. "We must go inside," Filippo said. "Think what must be in there if these statues are left outdoors."

"I am afraid," Giuseppe hesitated. "What if they catch us?"

"We can run faster than any monk," Filippo scoffed.

It took two of them to pry open the heavy door, which, with even greater effort, they closed softly behind them. Inside was a massive space, dark as a dungeon. There were two naves, which was odd because all churches have one, but there was no doubt that this was a church. Benches were lined up along both naves, facing tabernacles, one of which was the size of a small building. Filippo made his way quickly down the aisle to investigate this structure. The tabernacle, large as his bedchamber, was made of intricately carved ivory. It was a miniature building of lace, gilded and inlaid with colored glass and precious stones. The glass glistened in the candlelight, a deep lustrous azure and crimson. Filippo sucked in his breath. In the center of the tabernacle, encased in latticework and surrounded by carved figures, a painting of the Virgin Mary and the baby Jesus shimmered with gold leaf. Two lions carved from ivory stood guard, one on each side.

At that moment, Giuseppe tilted his head back to examine the frescoes painted on the ceiling. "Look." He pointed. "There are four iron rings in the ceiling, right in the middle of the figures painted there. The rings were there first. I am going to look around."

Giuseppe wandered off, but Filippo was transfixed. He had never seen anything so beautiful. The transcendent spirit of the piece was enhanced by the light filtering through stained-glass windows of varying shapes and sizes in the wall behind it. He slowly walked around to the side of the structure, and then behind, taking it in from all angles, before coming upon a plaque at the rear of the structure. Even the back of this wonder hid a treasure. The carving depicted the dormition and ascension of the Virgin Mary.

Just then, Giuseppe called out, "Look. There are bits of something falling through those grates. You can see in the sunlight. It is gold dust. God is sending gold dust from heaven."

Filippo peeked around the corner and saw that Giuseppe was standing in the wide-open space beyond the naves, which was quite large and appeared to have no purpose. He was pointing to the ceiling and the windows high up on the walls, through which the afternoon light was sifting. Filippo joined him.

Although he clearly saw something illuminated in the light, he was not fanciful and did not believe that God would send gold dust from heaven. To what purpose? He reached up with open palm into which particles fell. Looking down into his palm, rubbing it with the fingers of his other hand, he noticed a fragment of chaff. This made no more sense than that gold fell from the grates, but Filippo knew grain. He had once poured a bag of it on his head, and that was not something he was soon likely to forget. "It is grain," he told Giuseppe.

"It is not!" Giuseppe insisted, his voice loud and echoing up into the high rafters.

The sound of footsteps rushed toward them.

"What are you boys up to?" someone yelled.

Filippo raced to the front of the church, Giuseppe close behind. Fear seized them as they struggled again with the massive door. They squeezed through, a voice yelling, "Come back here!"

They did not stop running until they had turned several corners. When they stopped to catch their breath, they looked behind, but no one followed. Filippo was about to say, "See. I told you" when the bells of the duomo rang out for vespers. Giuseppe whined, "You promised." Yes, he had promised to get them home before vespers, but as he looked up and down the streets, he realized they were lost.

"Soon it will be dark," Giuseppe was crying. "We will be out after curfew. They will lock us in the dungeon at the top of the tower!"

"Stop wailing," Filippo demanded. "I will find our way home."

He knew that he sounded more confident than he felt, but one thing was certain. Standing in place was not going to get them home. Filippo chose a direction and began his search. On nearly every street they walked down new houses were being built where old ones had once stood. Gaping holes awaited foundations; the forms of buildings, not yet solid structures, were traced out in footings and beams. As the shadows lengthened and Filippo navigated the deserted streets, he took in the sacrifice of the old for the new. He loved the activity, although quieted now in the hush of early evening, how it bustled with energy throughout the day, swept away what no longer served a purpose. Houses had once been built like battlements, niches and rings on upper floors positioned to secure bridges so that neighborhoods could be defended without exposure to the dangers of the streets below.

"We must hurry," Giuseppe was saying. "The bridges across the Arno are haunted when it grows dark."

Filippo remembered his aunt and her friend telling the stories about each bridge. "There is a goblin that guards the Ponte Vecchio," he said, warming to the topic. "An old miser haunts the Ponte alla Carraia. He sold himself to the devil for money, and then he hid his money in the arch of the bridge even though he had relations who were poor. He left nothing to nobody. And, so, he cannot rest in peace but is seen at night on the bridge as a goat that breathes fire."

"Stop," Giuseppe said. "You are scaring me."

"Then there is the girl, betrayed by a friend, who threw herself from the bridge and drowned." Just then, Filippo turned a corner, Giuseppe in tow, and came upon a large, open piazza surrounded by columns, beyond which he could see the stone wall that edged the Arno. He turned to look back one last time at the north side of the city and said, "I will live here one day." Then he grabbed Giuseppe by the arm and broke into a run. Once past the buildings, he was able to see that off to their left stretched the Ponte Vecchio, deserted now, the shops shuttered.

"Once over," he told Giuseppe, "we will be in Santo Spirito. You will be home soon. No goblins tonight."

Filippo was happy that they had come out close to Giuseppe's house. He felt guilty about having gotten his friend into trouble, and he himself would catch no worse of a beating either way. He stopped halfway across the bridge to admire the reflection of the setting sun on the water below. The Arno was ablaze, a flowing river of light.

Darkness was descending when he reached the door to his house, but when he tried to pull it open, it held fast. It was locked. He sucked in his breath and knocked. After several minutes, his aunt opened the door, her white dressing gown ghostly in the darkness of the interior. She did not say a word. Filippo squeezed in past her expecting to feel the iron grip of her fingers on his shoulder, but she remained motionless. He made his way to the stairs, the heavy sound of the door creaking shut behind him. When he reached his room, he expected his aunt to follow him in, but she walked past his door to her own, which he heard snap shut.

This was worse than a beating. Filippo knew she was angry, and the anticipation of what she had planned for him made his heart beat like a rabbit's hunkered down in tall grasses, hoping to escape the attention of the hawk. Although his stomach growled, Filippo stripped and got into bed, but the light coming through the slats in the shutters drew him to the window. He opened them and saw that the moon was full, casting its light on all below. The Carmine, just on the other side of the walled garden, was so tall and wide that it blocked a view of anything beyond, its round bell tower looming into the night sky. Filippo shivered as much from the cold as with the fear of anticipation, but then his mind wandered to the day's activity. He thought of all he had seen, resolved once more to be a part of forging the new, to work, when he was older, where possibility opened endlessly, to live on the opposite side of the Arno. He had not felt this excited about anything since before his father had passed into the great sea, when he was certain that one day he would be a butcher and work alongside him. Filippo shuttered the window and crawled back into bed, but he had a fitful sleep.

When he awoke the next morning, Filippo stared at the ceiling, loath to face Mona Lapaccia. Normally, he would spend a few extra minutes in bed, not yet quite awake, reviewing the sights and sounds of the previous day, absorbing every detail. Upon waking, he always indulged this vision, integrating the day before with the one to come, the subtleties of form, color, and tone offering themselves up for his consideration.

But this morning the dark cloud of his return home in the night swept across the vision. The fear of what was to come drove him from his bed. He took his time getting dressed, washing his face and hands more methodically than usual. As he entered the kitchen, he saw his aunt's dark form standing before the fireplace, where the wooden spoon hung.

He stiffened, but her hand did not move in the direction of the spoon. Meat and cheese, bread and grapes were set out on the table. Hesitantly, Filippo sat down. This was unlike her. Mona Lapaccia left the room.

Something was not right, but as he ate, Filippo tried to convince himself that there would be no punishment. Perhaps Mona Lapaccia had given up. This would free him to do as he pleased.

But, when Filippo had finished his breakfast, Mona Lapaccia reentered the room and said only, "Come." They made their way under the arch but, at the end of the street, turned in the direction not of the market, as Filippo had expected, but of the Carmine. They continued on past the church steps. When Mona Lapaccia made her way to a door in a wall at the side of the church, Filippo froze. But Mona Lapaccia, thin as a stalk, had the strength of a man. She seized him by the arm, almost lifting him bodily off the ground, and pulled him behind her. At her knock, a small window in the door opened. "We are here to see the prior. He is expecting us," she said.

Filippo attempted to wrest himself from her grasp, but she held firm and pushed him through the open doorway. When it had closed behind him, Filippo threw himself at the door, beating it with his fists and screaming.

"As you can see…" He heard Mona Lapaccia's voice raised against his screaming. "…he is possessed by demons."

They waited until Filippo had spent himself. Mona Lapaccia again grabbed his arm, almost yanking it out of his body and, holding it upright at an angle, dragged Filippo across the courtyard and down the long, vaulted loggia to the door of the prior's office.

Not a single drop of blood remains in me that does not tremble.   Dante

The prior was a portly man with a large, red nose. Immediately, Filippo disliked him. "We will take good care of the boy," he said.

"Well, you will have your hands full trying," Mona Lapaccia warned.

"You may visit him whenever you wish."

"I think," she interrupted, "it is best that I not visit. It will only remind him of the outside world, when his focus, surely, should be inward."

"Well, prayers and study will be a part of each day, but knowing he is cared for." Looking up, Filippo thought he saw kindness in the prior's eyes.

"Prayer," she said. "Prayer and penance. I trust you will take good care of him." She wheeled abruptly, brushing past Filippo, and then, as if remembering herself, stopped and turned. "Be good for the kind monks," she told him, with a feeble attempt at a smile that resembled a snarl, then bowed her head for the prior's blessing and departed.

"I was not sad to see her go," Filippo ended.

"I imagine not." Matteo puffed out his cheeks and expelled a long breath. "She is a personage to freeze the blood. A story that does not disappoint. Well," he summed up, "old saber-tooth has managed to dump you. All is well with her." He placed his arm around Filippo's shoulder. "But what of you, my ruffian friend? I wish to know. You had a bit of the mischief in you, mercilessly teasing poor little Giuseppe. But, the sensitive painter's eye as well. For which your aunt had no appreciation. The fact remains that you are a painter, and so what happens to you in the convent, I wonder? And, you are such a good storyteller. But, our work here is done. We will leave it for another day, then."

CHAPTER 5

The year of Our Lord 1406, Florence, and somewhere outside of Pisa

For the first time in seventeen years, Cosimo was angry with his father. Why could he not travel to the holy land with his friend Niccolo? His excitement at the prospect of so daring an adventure quickly gave way to rage at being prevented from setting off. He ruminated as he made his way to Santa Maria degli Angeli, where his father suggested he go to cool down. He often visited his old school in order to discuss readings with his former teacher Fra Ambrogio Traversari.

As he entered the loggia, Traversari was waiting for him. They greeted each other warmly, the pleasure of seeing the kind old man putting Cosimo's anger to rest. But, while sitting in Traversari's cell discussing his translation of Dionysius the Areopagite, Cosimo's mentor said, "You seem agitated, Cosimo. Not yourself. Is there something about which you wish to speak?"

"My father holds me back," Cosimo blurted. "I have planned a trip with Niccolo to the holy land, to hunt down antiquities, lost manuscripts."

"When do you leave?"

"My father strictly forbids it."

"I see," Traversari said. "Well, it is a dangerous undertaking. Seas can be treacherous. Pirates take prisoners. Thieves lurk about roadways."

Cosimo scoffed. "I am able to handle myself. I am no longer a boy."

Trying a different approach, Traversari asked, "Why is this journey of such importance to you?"

"All that we have studied," Cosimo said, appealing to Traversari's love of knowledge. "Imagine what we might discover. Manuscripts lost for centuries that we might bring back."

"I see. Yes. But must it be you who unearths it? If a manuscript is brought back, will not the reading of it be of the greatest importance? Leave the digging to others. Once a manuscript has been uncovered, Cosimo, it is you who will sponsor the translation of it. You who will benefit from the reading of it. It is the knowledge that is important."

Cosimo knew that Traversari was right. There was ego involved in wanting to be the adventurer. But there was youthful enthusiasm as well. What was wrong with that? "I feel as though my wings have been clipped before I have flown."

"There are many ways to fly, my son."

A mind without instruction can no more bear fruit than a field, however fertile, without cultivation. Cicero

Not long after Cosimo's disappointment, war broke out between Florence and Pisa. If Florence won, Pisa would provide the Republic with its own port. This was of paramount importance. Cosimo was surprised when his father decided to send him, along with two other boys, to join the effort. As the son of a prominent Florentine citizen whose bank was critical in subsidizing the conflict, Cosimo was not there to fight but to learn strategy. A boy of seventeen, he showed great aptitude and passion for the subject.

The sinews of war, a limitless supply of money. Cicero

The night before his first battle, Cosimo made his way from the captain's tent to his own. Before going to sleep that night, he knelt beside his cot to pray. It was not only with anticipation or with the chill in the air that he shook. They would be far removed from the fighting, but battles were unpredictable. He did not want to die here, too young to have accomplished anything. Although he did not yet know what it was, he felt certain that his destiny and that of Florence were intertwined. He must live to see the promise fulfilled.

Slowly, Cosimo's prayers began to comfort him. His fears stilled, confidence reestablished itself. He was certain that he was meant to do great things. God would see to it that he survived.

Early the following morning, as the sun burned the mist from the hills, the captain of the guard approached their party. It consisted of Cosimo, the two other boys, and six men at arms sent by their families to protect them. "Do you see that line of trees just now visible north of our position?" The line of trees stood high on a promontory, a good vantage point, and one far from the action. "Position yourselves on that hill, well behind the trees," the captain continued, "and watch how it goes. If the battle lines shift, head back to camp. There is no predicting where it flows. Whatever you do, for God's sake, do not get captured."

As they watched the battle from just behind the trees, to Cosimo's satisfaction, it was unfolding as strategy had predicted. The infantries of both armies had met mid-field and were jumbled together, battling it out. Cosimo watched for the wedge. That would be the signal for the cavalry to rush in. Horses were saved until the very end. Although they provided an advantage, they tired quickly. The infantry continued to drive an opening. Soon the cavalry would be able to push through it. Then, quite suddenly, the wedge began to disappear as the Pisan infantry, instead of retreating, leveled their lines out at two ends and pushed forward. The shape of the battle had shifted. Now long and thin, it stretched all the way to just beneath their position on the hill.

Cosimo's interest was piqued. He was now unable to predict the next movement.

"We must go," he heard a companion yell.

Cosimo held up his hand. "One moment." This was a perfect position from which to study all possibilities, but the pounding rhythm of hoofbeats retreating into the distance broke his concentration. The others, apart from the two men assigned to protect him, were gone. As he watched, a bulge formed at the edge closest to them. Quite suddenly, it began to swell up the hill in their direction. Cosimo could not remain there alone. Reluctantly, he raced after the others.

They were less than a third of the way back to camp when they were ambushed. Surrounded on all sides, Cosimo dismounted and unsheathed his sword. He felt a swell of energy with the chink of metal, the heft of his sword, the strain of thrusting it, of bending it against another's will.

He was not the strongest of lads. The soldier he now fought held that advantage. But, faced with a foe, he spurned defeat. The other man's thrusts were swift, his blows heavy. Cosimo, light on his feet, dodged, thrust, beat back, dodged again. He kept the other man moving until he slowed, grunted with the effort of lifting his sword. As the man raised his sword high into the air, Cosimo ducked beneath his reach, thrust his blade, and hit his mark, a space between breastplate and groin. His adversary fell to the ground. Another came on.

Whatever one has, one ought to use.   Cicero

Confident now, Cosimo was turning to meet his opponent when he was struck a sudden blow from behind and tumbled. Before he could scramble to his feet, a blade was wedged between his breastplate and helmet. He felt the cold trickle of blood at his neck.

A horse reared up beside him, the soldier on it yelling out, "Take them alive! They are worth a kingdom in ransom." It was the rider's lance that had been his undoing. It might have pierced him through but had side-swiped him instead, where it had landed now smarting with pain.

Sweating and breathing hard, Cosimo was chained together with the others and led away. They were taken to the enemy's camp where they waited, helpless. While negotiations were underway, they were moved several times until, after two cycles of the moon had passed, a ransom was paid and they were set free. Although Florence had won both the battle and the war, the boys' freedom had been bought at a hefty price.

Ultimately, it had not been the clever battlefield strategy that won the war but the slow starvation, over thirteen months, of the citizens within the walls. Cosimo learned much from the experience. He learned that intellect, agility and, most importantly, a strong will were a match for brute strength. He also learned that his passion for knowledge could cloud his judgement. More than anything, he now knew that there are better ways to win a war than to fight it, and that he would never again allow himself to be caught off guard, to be held helpless in the grip of his enemy.

CHAPTER 6

The year of Our Lord 1432, Mediterranean Sea

On the ship, Filippo initiated the games of chance he had learned as a boy on the streets of Florence before he had entered the Carmine. They helped to pass the time. One day, just as he was about to throw the dice, he looked up to see the wizened old man in the turban watching him from above. Filippo wondered that he was not too old to endure the privations of the ship. He had noticed that the man spent much of his time alone. He seemed to be the only one who enjoyed a comfortable relationship with the pirate leader, and it was he who communicated the leader's commands to the men. Filippo again noticed that the look on the old man's face was at odds with his surroundings. If pressed, he would have described the man's countenance as devotional.

Since the day of their arrival, Filippo and Matteo had only seen the leader of the pirates from a distance, which was fortunate, for although he had granted their request to retain their robes, they could see that his men were afraid of him. A remote figure, he occasionally stood at the bow, hands clasped behind his back, looking out to sea. When he appeared on deck, although he did not interact with the men, all banter ceased, and they bent their heads to their tasks.

Once, while Filippo and Matteo cleaned the deck, a pirate was accused of stealing. The leader parted the crowd, much as he had done when Filippo and Matteo had boarded the ship. He listened to all accounts of the story, made a pronouncement, and the pirate, screaming and struggling, was thrown into the sea. The man's screams sent a chill through Filippo's body as he labored under the scorching sun. What man could dispatch a soul so decisively and turn his back on the sound of its terror?

One afternoon, the old man sat tying knots in several lengths of rope. Filippo focused on the man's hands, sketching them in detail on his robe with his finger. This imaginary sketching had become a habit of his. He began by sketching the brute features of the pirates, as he had his classmates at the Carmine. It was not long before places filled with people unraveled on the folds of his robe, worlds emerging from his fingertips. While engaged in his daily regimen, he could not wait to get back to the realms he created. They drew him back to Florence's palazzos with intricately tiled floors, its loggias and gardens, its bustling piazzas. Without these imaginary worlds, Filippo himself would disappear.

And let the helm and steersman of this power to see be the light of the sun, the light of your own eye, and your own hand. Cennini

The old man looked up. "What is it that you do?"

"You understand Italian." Filippo was astonished.

"And Greek, and Hebrew," the man informed him. "The men believe you to be crazy." He tapped the side of his head with his finger. "But"— he pointed his index finger upward—"I watch the steady focus in your eyes. What is it that you do with your finger on your robe?"

"I sketch what I see," Filippo explained, thinking that if he admitted to sketching what he did not see, his madness would be confirmed. The man looked puzzled. "I trace the likeness of what I see."

"Ahhhh," the man said, "I have seen this. We do not create like-nesses. We leave creation to God. He does it best."

Filippo, frightened, wondered if this activity would bring him trouble. But, seemingly satisfied with his explanation, the old man held up the knotted rope for his inspection and asked, "Would you like to learn?"

Filippo stood and walked closer. The old man, as was his habit, sat cross-legged. This appeared to be comfortable, so Filippo sat and curved one leg inward, tucking his foot in close to his body. When he reached out to grab his other foot, he noted the amuse-ment in the old man's eyes. As he pulled his other foot inward, intending to cross it over the first, his body rolled backwards until he could see the sky directly overhead.

The old man laughed in a delighted, childlike way while Filippo rolled from side to side. Then he jammed his elbow into the ship's floor. This maneuver twisted him so that he lost his grip, and his foot shot from his grasp. The old man had to lean backwards to avoid being kicked. Filippo gave up and fell onto his back like a stranded turtle. When he managed to right himself, he saw that the old man was wiping tears from the corners of his eyes. Filippo shook his head and grumbled, "It looks easy enough."

The old man said, "I have not been taken by laughter so com-plete in a long time." He then handed Filippo a length of rope, and they began to work.

The man's name, he learned, was al-Basir. Although Filippo had never done well at his studies, his powers of observation were keen and, once he saw something, he never forgot it. For this reason, he was quick to learn the different ways of tying a knot. His aptitude impressed al-Basir, and Filippo's new skill was put to immediate use. This relieved him for intervals of time from the harder work of bailing water and cleaning the deck.

But Filippo's main job remained the onerous one of rowing. When he grumbled about it, the old man chastised him, "It is es-sential." When Filippo complained about being taken prisoner, al-Basir asked, "What have you learned from it?"

"Nothing," Filippo replied, angrily.

"When you lost sight of land, how did you feel?"

Filippo considered. "Frightened."

"You have not been within sight of land for three phases of the moon. How do you now feel?"

Filippo realized that his fear was gone.

"A man can get used to anything. Is that not worth learning? All experience has value. How far along the path of learning a man travels is determined by the strength of his soul."

Over these months, Filippo had thought less and less about the state of his soul. "If my father had lived," he said, nursing an old wound, "I would now be a butcher."

"You are not a butcher. It follows that you were not meant to be one."

"If I were, I would not now be held prisoner."

"You would be a prisoner. Where and how do not matter. There is a lesson in it for you alone."

"What lesson?" Filippo asked, thinking that if he knew, he could get it over with.

"It is your lesson, not mine. Once you have learned it, you will be free."

Every kind of fortune is completely good...since it is either just or useful.

Boethius

Filippo did not know if al-Basir meant his figurative or literal freedom, but either would be a blessing. There was much to contemplate in what the old man said. What was such a wise man doing here, on a pirate ship?

One day as they worked, Filippo asked.

"I was drawn to the sea," al-Basir said. "Where there is land, there is war."

"If you set out to sea for this reason," Filippo asked, "how did you come to be on a pirate ship?"

"A man must go where he is needed," al-Basir said.

"And how is it you are needed here?" Filippo asked.

"Restraint," he said, "is the most difficult thing for a man to learn, a man with power most of all."

"You speak of the leader of the ship."

Al-Basir stopped work and looked at him. "Do you know what they say of the pomegranate?"

"I do not."

"It is life sustaining and, as such, has attained from out of this mystery the power of symbol. It is said that one seed in each comes directly from heaven." He pointed upward. "He who eats of it is filled with the light of paradise."

"Do you believe this?"

"I believe it to be a symbol of a greater truth. Within each person is a seed of light that comes directly from heaven. It is this seed that connects one to the divine light."

"A beautiful image."

"It is more than an image. It is the source of all life, the thread that connects us to God and to each other. When we stray from the path of light and creation, seduced by the power to destroy that we possess, we enter the dark wood. It is then that we begin to extinguish this internal light. I have seen men enter the dark wood and never return."

"What happens to them?"

"Eventually? Death."

"And after death?" Filippo wondered if hell played a part in al-Basir's beliefs.

"Darkness," he answered. "A man takes with him all that he has done in life. If he has chosen to destroy, that which he destroys most is the seed of light within himself."

"There is a darkness inside of me," Filippo said. "Not the darkness of destruction. But there is a deep well in me that admits no light."

"Ah, but it is a kind of destruction," Al-Basir challenged him. "Is it not true in your religion, as in Islam, that to take a life is the gravest of sins?"

Filippo assented.

"Why, then, would you wish to annihilate the life inside of you? Your task is to find the promise that lives within and, through all obstacles, nourish it. It is the seed of light that connects you to the divine."

"Like the pomegranate," Filippo said.

"God gave us a simple fruit," al-Basir said, "in a hard casing, containing seeds that provide us with all the nourishment we need. It is not unlike the body we possess, a casing to withstand adversity. Some see only the casing. They knock on the hard shell and decide it is empty, never discovering the treasure within. The seed of light within each of us provides the illumination we need to travel life's path."

Inside clings truth's seed, submerged in the soul. Boethius

CHAPTER 7

The years of Our Lord 1414 – 1415,
Florence, and Constance, Germany

Cosimo was about to knock but hesitated, hearing his parents deep in discussion on the other side of the door. He did not mean to eavesdrop, but their words filtered through.

"But he is so young," Piccarda, Cosimo's mother, protested, "not yet twenty-five."

"We will wait one year," his father relented, "but no longer. I hear what young men get up to. At his age, I toiled day and night to build a business. Today, the family fortune made, many sons are left idle. That is why, when he was yet a boy, I sent Cosimo on missions to represent the family. He and Lorenzo are kept busy learning the business. Now Cosimo must wed."

"Perhaps it is too soon," Piccarda persisted. "To wait another three years cannot hurt, surely. He would then be twenty-eight as you yourself were when we wed."

Hers was the art of gentle persuasion, and Cosimo expected the same this time, but it seemed the man's mind was made up. "The Bardis will make a good alliance," he said. "An old and venerable family who will accept our offer because their wealth is not what it once was. If we do not act, they will accept another offer. Cosimo is ready. Young men get up to mischief. If he is to spill his seed, he may as well—."

His mother gasped. "Giovanni."

"I am sorry, my dear, to be so indelicate, but we must face facts. He may as well do so legitimately, with a wife, and produce an heir."

"He is so young," she lamented, "so unsteady still."

"A family is forever stained by illegitimacy," his father said. "Such an easy thing to avoid. A family's reputation is paramount."

Cosimo would not go against his father, and did not protest the match. He saw marriage as a duty to family and to the Republic, as much as going to war was, or learning the family business. He approached everything with the same sense of obligation, so that a few months after their lavish and well-attended wedding, Contessina was found to be with child. Cosimo was not physically attracted to his new wife, but she was a woman, and in bed his desire found quick release. He did not know how she felt, but he could see that she was proud to be carrying a potential heir.

Before she had given birth, Giovanni called upon Cosimo to again represent the family, this time at the Council of Constance. Chafing within the confines of domesticity, he was more than ready for an adventure. Still, how would Contessina feel about his absence at the moment of birth? He sought her out in order to inquire. "If you prefer that I wait until you have given birth," he offered.

"I will send word when the child arrives," she said. "If that is all?"

Arrives, Cosimo thought. She makes it sound as if it were a bale of linen cloth to be delivered. He would have stayed on until after the birth had she implored him. But her abruptness did leave him free to set out without a sense of guilt. Many men traveled for years at a time, and most children did not survive to the age of three. His own twin had not lived more than a day, and other brothers had been lost as well, how many he was uncertain. It was unwise to become too attached early on.

Sitting astride a handsome chestnut horse that was draped in the finest of silk cloth, Cosimo felt regal but, being his father's son, he fought this impulse. His servants, too, were well liveried in matching silk, all in the Medici colors of white, green, and red. They entered the city of Constance, in Germany, as part of Pope John's entourage. Bishops, abbots, university masters of law and theology, as well as representatives of princes and nobles were arriving from every Christian country in Europe. Horses and attendants were liveried without regard for expense. Cosimo had never seen such an array of silks. Masters, servants, horses, and slaves were adorned in matching colors, many much more elaborate than those of the Medici.

The purpose of the council was to solve the problem of the three popes, among other issues. However, the schism was the overriding reason, and it was Pope John XXIII, his father's friend and confidante, who had called it into being. Cosimo had been sent as a representative of the Medici family but also as a representative of the bank for, as his father told him, "With crowds arriving from all over Europe, there will be a fortune to be made in exchange." Perhaps most importantly, he was sent as an aide to Pope John. "Events," Cosimo's father had warned him, "could turn dangerous."

As he looked around, Cosimo was struck by the fact that trade had the ability to bring all humankind together. He could also see that his father had been right about the monies to be made in exchange. In addition to the entourages of dukes, princes, and prelates, merchants of all types had arrived to sell their wares, some from as far as the Orient. Artisans had flocked to the city in hopes of obtaining commissions. There must have been forty thousand horses alone, so that there was a constant threat of a skittish mount creating a stampede. So much commerce was taking place that a fixed price was applied to all foodstuffs and tariffs applied to merchandise. Business would, indeed, prove to be profitable. Never had so many from all parts of Europe and beyond convened in one place at one time.

Making his way through the streets, Cosimo surveyed the abundance of goods. He stopped at the stall of a merchant from the

Orient who sat among piles of the finest silk in colors of every shade and hue, where he bought several lengths in a deep sapphire blue to send home to Contessina. Feathers plucked from exotic birds seemed to bloom from jars at the man's back. Beaded necklaces of jade and exquisite pearls were spread out on a table before him. Other merchants along his path displayed beaten metal platters, intricately woven rugs, and radiant gold bangles. There were carved and painted cedar chests, gracefully executed tapestries, and gleaming, stone-encrusted swords. He would need to return when he had more time to peruse the cross-bows and blades.

Cosimo was jostled by venders hawking their wares, required to sidestep crowds bulging out around jugglers and acrobats, and pressed to the walls of buildings to avoid being trampled by musicians trailing festive revelers behind them. The atmosphere of the streets was one of a great fair in full swing, but inside the proceedings it was solemn.

Cosimo went every day to check on the progress of the council. While milling about, he met international bankers, men of business, and other esteemed personages. Each day provided the opportunity to cultivate these relationships, contacts who would become guarantors for bills of exchange, credit notes, and commercial transactions. This council was proving to be beneficial for more than immediate business dealings.

Not long after their arrival, during one of the council's first sessions, its representatives took a firm and ominous stand. Cosimo had expected the first few months of proceedings to be ceremonial and of little value, like those at the previous, unsuccessful, council at Pisa. As it turned out, events were so surprising that they prompted a letter to his father, sent in haste: The council, early in its proceedings, has claimed supreme authority. It will not first elect a Pope, as was done, most appropriately, at Pisa. The council will make decisions regarding reforms prior to debating the schism. The council has set itself up as the ultimate authority, including with reference to the matter of how and why a Pope may be disciplined or deposed. This action portends censure or worse.

Years earlier, when Cosimo had fought in the battle at Pisa, he had known fear, but with sword in hand and skill to draw on. This was different. If they were rounded up, a sham trial and execution awaited. He would be attacked with his hands chained behind his back, as he had been when he was a prisoner of war. There was nothing that frightened him more than being helpless in the face of danger.

[M]y will would be content if I could know what fate draws near, for the arrow one expects comes slower.   Dante

An answer was swift in coming: Keep eye and ear well trained. Should a wind pick up from an inauspicious direction, risk not, but flee.

Reading this, Cosimo knew that, as much as his father's advice was intended for him, it was also meant as a message for another. He quickly tucked the letter inside his breast pocket, threw on his mantello, and made his way to the pope's apartments.

CHAPTER 8

The year of Our Lord 1432, Mediterranean Sea:
remembering Florence, 1414 – 1417

Since Filippo spent much of his time helping al-Basir, he did not often have the opportunity to work alongside Matteo, except when they rowed and the exertion left no breath for conversation. One day they happily sat side by side bailing water. "We find ourselves with the perfect opportunity to continue your story," Matteo said, rubbing his hands together. "I am all ears. Well, perhaps mostly blubber, and then ears that have been waiting to hear the tale of the convent."

"That first night," Filippo began, "I found myself in a large dormitory filled with beds, where I lay awake, staring at the ceiling."

He wondered, Who were these boys, asleep in other beds, and why must he share the intimate space of sleep with them? They were thrown together, each bed the same, no personal possessions, no differences among them. Filippo had never felt so alone. Who cared about boys left to fend for themselves, without families to protect them? He broke down and sobbed. The more he did, the more he felt as if he would suffocate. The image of a coffin came into his mind and, clutching his throat with both hands, he gasped for air. Choking, he fell out of bed onto the hard, stone floor. He beat it with his fists. Someone placed a hand gently but firmly on his back. He looked up to see his brother Giovanni leaning over him.

Filippo knew that Giovanni, six years older and already a novice, was shut up in this place, but he had not seen his brother since his father had died. Giovanni hushed him, warning, "You must be still now. The friars need their sleep. They will be up soon for matins. Here. Get into bed. I will sit with you while you fall back to sleep." After that night, his brother continued to sit with Filippo until he drifted off.

Convents, as a rule, did not like to take in orphans. Filippo was received because his family had a long-standing relationship with the Carmine. His father, Tommaso, had supplied them on the rare occasions when they ate meat. He had also served as witness for important convent documents, and as an arbiter on their behalf. For generations, Filippo's family had been members of the Confraternity of Sant' Agnese, a lay group that did good works for the district and met in the Carmine to sing lauds. This confraternity was also responsible for the important Ascension play, which was well known throughout Florence and beyond. Giovanni, his brother, was a willing novice, as well as the organist. The friars said that when he played the organ, the music was so beautiful that the angels came down from heaven to listen. Altogether, there were seven boys and ten novices living at the Carmine.

The dining hall was housed in a dark, damp room, part of a structure that had been built in the 1200s. It had been constructed from large, rough-hewn stone blocks that had blackened with age. There were no windows in the structure, the only light emanating from candles placed in sconces high up on the walls, making it a world of shadow with a lurking musty smell. It looked as if the stone wept. Filippo soon learned not to dwell on his surroundings, but to eat quickly. The insufficient time allotted for each meal and the meager fare meant that he was never full, and it would be a long time before he ate again. If only he could get leave to step outside of the walls, to drink his fill of the sights and sounds of the city, he would not feel so hungry.

Lessons were difficult for Filippo. He struggled with reading and writing. He had a penchant, though, for noticing details, and accurately sketched the likenesses of people on paper. Nothing escaped his notice. He gave, over time, names to each of his fellow students. Antonio, whose bones, discernable under his thin skin, jutted out, his shoulders stooping a little forward, head slung back, and a thin, beaked nose, with a decided lack of chin, reminded Filippo of a chicken. He called him Poultray, a variation on the name that he found amusing. Poultray was a kind boy, and Filippo likened the nubs of his shoulder blades to the buds of angel wings. Another boy, Jacopo, had narrow eyes that darted back and forth. He was stealthy. He was also mean and vicious, often mocking the other boys. Filippo called him Lupino after the roaming packs of wolves that made travel treacherous. He drew both boys, and his other classmates, in his workbooks, becoming more precise with each rendering.

Before coming to the convent, the world had been Filippo's classroom. The monastery, enclosed within a high wall, kept the world out. How was he to learn? His eyes remembered everything. They took in round, soft, ridged, straight-edged, latticed rows of fruits gleaming; street vendors calling "fresh lemons, sweet figs, ripe tomatoes, rich olive oil"; women carefully picking through piles, to squeeze, hold items up for review in sunlight; children, ragged, playing in the dust of the streets, their high-pitched screaming; important men swaggering past, three and four abreast, mantelli flapping behind like wings, talking and gesturing, not looking to either side but straight ahead, as if conversing with the world as they traversed it. Filippo could still see the transformation of light as it plumped up each shape, singed each color, and later filled them slowly with shadow, the light progressing from a gentle white gold that softened and made colors pale and watery, to a heated white that washed them clean, until, at day's end, the deep indigo of shadow blossomed in the amber farewell of the sun's departing rays.

What ditches or what chains did you encounter across your path to make you cast aside all hope of going forward? Dante

One day the boys were kicking a ball around in the dirt just outside of the convent's south wall. Filippo scooped it out from under the foot of Lupino and kicked it to Poultray. Lupino, angry at losing the ball, taunted, "Filippo, idiot! Every village has its idiot." He mimicked Fra Paulo, their teacher. "Would you read for us, Filippo?" By then the boys had gathered around. "Uhhh. Uhhhh. Pa, Pa, Pa. t, t, Pt." Lupino stuttered. Filippo felt his face grow hot. Lupino again imitated Fra Paulo's voice. "'Pater noster,' Filippo, 'Pater noster.'" The boys reeled with laughter. Only Poultray did not laugh. He placed his hand on Filippo's arm and said, "Come. Let us kick the ball around. What do you say?"

Soon after, Fra Paulo began keeping Filippo back every day between classes and vespers. He explained his intention to have him fill an entire workbook with one letter, until he could fill it without a mistake. Filippo began with the letter 'a'. Several days and several workbooks later, Fra Paulo towered over him to examine his work. The friar, though large, was kind, not menacing. Finally, with grave concern in his eyes, and in answer to the pleading question in Filippo's own, Fra Paulo shook his head. Filippo felt tears of frustration begin to well, but held them back.

"Again," Fra Paulo instructed Filippo, as he swept the charcoal away, readying the page for the next exercise. "Slowly. Form each letter carefully, exactly like the letter that precedes it. Say to yourself, 'Line, up, circle back' as you write," and then he added, kindly, "Do not lose hope, Filippo. See. You have gotten nine rows right this time." Out of one hundred, Filippo thought. "We will get through this," Fra Paulo promised. "You will learn how to write." As he turned to head back to his desk, the rough cloth of his habit scraped Filippo's cheek. He knew he was not an idiot, and yet even Gennaro, who was considered a real blockhead, was able to read and write. Why did letters elude him, march off in all directions like armies of soldiers dispersed in a skirmish?

Since Filippo's brother Giovanni was a novice, his time was taken up with his studies, duties, and prayer, as well as with practicing the organ. He rarely saw him, but Giovanni sought him out whenever he had the chance. One day, while the other boys played, Filippo sat on a bench in the courtyard staring at the high wall that separated the Carmine from the garden of his father's house. Just as the Carmine had towered above that little patch of garden, casting its dark shadow across the length of it during the earliest hours of each day, it now shadowed his life, cut him off from all but dull routine, the dark abyss of endless servitude.

Filippo turned and watched a small group of friars walk around the perimeter of the yard, arms folded above their bellies, hands tucked into their sleeves. Their black robes and white mantelli were devoid of color, like life in the convent, lacking the verisimilitude of earthly experience. He knew that if he called out, and if Antonio happened to be working in the garden on the other side of the wall, the old man would hear him. He missed Antonio, but what good would it do? He could do nothing to help.

Giovanni sat down beside Filippo. "You cannot go back, you know." He was right. Filippo did long to go back. There seemed wisdom in what Giovanni said, of course, but he had trouble accepting it.

"Why could I not have gone to live with Uncle Aniello? He likes me." Filippo remembered the kindness in his uncle's eyes when he tousled his head.

"Filippo, you are here because of him."

Filippo was stunned. "But he liked me. I could see that he did."

"It was not your little adventure that landed you here, although it well might have."

"What then?"

"I overheard the prior talking to the sub-prior. Our father did not have much, but he did own a few houses and some property. Uncle Aniello amassed large debts and wished to sell some property to pay them off. This property would have passed to you, Filippo. But, since a monk cannot own anything. Well. That is why you are here."

Filippo thought back to the conversation he had overheard between his aunt and uncle. He had only been able to hear portions of it, but coupled with this new piece of information, he realized that Giovanni must be right. So, his fate had been decided before he had ever crossed the Arno. "Well then, it is good that I risked crossing the Arno. It was well worth it." He had seen something of the world before being shut away from it and had now learned more of the world as well—that a man was not always who he seemed to be.

"Is it so bad here?" Giovanni asked.

"Yes," Filippo answered with conviction. "But one thing is good. I am rid of old squint-eye."

"Squint-eye?"

"Mona Lapaccia. I hate her."

"Hate, Filippo," Giovanni began to lecture his brother, but Filippo had turned away. He was not listening. "Pappa did not like her either."

This drew Filippo's attention. "How do you know?"

"Pappa would say, 'She comes to visit us today, my sister,' and roll his eyes."

Filippo laughed. He could see the rolling of the eyes as something his father might do. "And?"

"He would say, 'I wonder what new faults she will find with us on this most beautiful day.' She did nothing but complain, even when Mama was alive."

"What did Mama say of her?" Filippo was hungry to know anything about his mother.

"Mama was kind to everyone. She would say, 'We must be charitable. She lives such a sad little life.'"

"What did she mean by that?"

"No man would have Mona Lapaccia."

Filippo shuddered to think of the poor man who might.

"She lived with her father, Pappa's stepfather. She took care of him until he died, a very old man."

"So, she is not Pappa's sister."

"She is his half-sister."

They sat together in silence. The longer they sat, the more it dawned on Filippo that he was sitting, silently, staring at a wall. It was then that Giovanni's words echoed in his mind, the truth in them clear as the stroke of a bell: "You cannot go back."

On paper you may draw with...lead....And if you ever make a slip, so that you want to remove some stroke made by this little lead, take a bit of the crumb of some bread, and rub it over the paper, and you will remove whatever you wish. Cennini

When he had given up on the desire to be somewhere else, the present imposed itself more clearly on his senses. Later that day, Filippo was making his way around the loggia when his footsteps startled a bevy of small finches, who burst from the center of a cypress tree. When he stopped, they settled back in. As he enjoyed their soothing music, Filippo's eyes were drawn to a color. It was not the white, black, or gray of buildings, dress, or birds, that had only been broken until now by the deep, severe green of the cypresses at each corner of the loggia. This was a color to stop one, the pale gold flowers of a rose bush he had never noticed. The gold was so brilliant that it looked as if the flowers had drunk in the light of the sun. It surely had always been there. How had Filippo missed it? As he moved closer, he saw that the center of each flower deepened until it held at its core the rose color of its life's blood. The sun seemed to illuminate the skin of each petal from within. In that moment, Filippo wished that he, too, could swallow the sun.

Then, in the year of Our Lord 1417, three years after Filippo had entered the Carmine, the pestilence swept through Florence. It arrived in April, with Easter not yet upon them and the heat of summer imminent, a welcome home for the disease. Its siege would be long and drawn out.

At first, the boys knew only that certain of the friars had disappeared. They were told that God had taken them to be with Him. The first of the boys to fall ill was Alberto. The others watched with horror one day as his robes were pulled back to reveal lumps under his arms the size of oranges, oozing puss. He was taken away to the infirmary.

One day, while the boys played, Filippo, who was being pre-pared to do menial tasks since he struggled with reading and writ-ing, was asked to deliver a bucket of water to the infirmary. As he entered through the doorway, he saw Alberto in a bed across the room, delirious with fever, naked to the waist, blackened lumps now spread across his torso.

A sinister figure stood beside him, wearing a hood and mask with cut-outs for eyes and a long cloth beak that hung to his waist. The horrible figure leaned over the boy. Was it the specter of death? Filippo was rooted to the spot, unable to turn away from the grotesque sight when, suddenly, Alberto turned with a violent, wrenching motion and vomited blood. Filippo dropped the bucket, splashing water over himself and the floor. The specter looked di-rectly at him and, pointing a finger, began to speak. Filippo did not wait to hear what it said. He fled through the doorway and down the stairs.

When the others were ushered to vespers, Filippo still stood, his back pressed against the wall of the loggia, his hands glued to it in fear. The rough stone dug into his palms, stinging them, providing a grounding sensation. The other boys stopped short upon seeing him and gathered around. "Alberto's sores cover his whole body," he told them. "They are black as soot, with puss running out. He leapt and jerked his body as if he wrestled with the devil, and then. And then, blood poured from his mouth."

Filippo felt his own fear spread through them like fire. As Fra Paolo approached to disperse them, Filippo became aware for the first time of the stench of urine surrounding him. Fra Paulo urged the others on to vespers and took Filippo off to wash up.

He was humiliated, worried that the other boys might tease him. Seeming to sense his anxiety, Fra Paolo said, "Do not worry, my son. The others will not have the inclination nor the time to taunt you."

The friar's contemplative gaze rested in the direction of the doorway to the chapel through which the other boys had filed in silence after Filippo's revelation. Filippo had noticed that Fra Paolo's emphasis had rested on the word time. He wondered, knowing all too well the endless round of canonical hours that droned from day to day, how it was that time could be in any way different in this place. "Time never changes here," he said aloud, tying the heavy string that girded his new robe.

As if thinking aloud, Fra Paolo said, "Circumstance can change time forever."

Quite suddenly, Fra Paolo jumped up, hurrying Filippo along. "Come, come along now. We will miss all of vespers. And if ever there was a time to pray…"

Later that evening, before the candles in the dormitory were snuffed out, the boys were told to pray for the soul of Alberto, who had passed into the great sea. Remembering the boy's convulsing body, Filippo wondered at the violence it took to wrest a person from this life and usher him into heaven. Perhaps the pain of this world needed to well up, burst through them, to compel them to let go. One thing was certain: if we entered the great sea, it took the crash and drag of a monumental wave to sweep us there.

Consider that this day may never dawn again.   Dante

Only two days later, Filippo awoke to find that his friend Poultray had fallen into a fever during the night. His face flushed, his head rolling from side to side, he was carried away. Filippo tried to go to him, but Fra Paulo pulled him back. "It is time for lauds, my son. We will pray for him."

Filippo prayed in earnest. If there ever was a boy who deserved a miracle, it was kind-hearted Poultray. Filippo was certain God would see it that way. But, when the boys returned to the dormitory that night after vespers, they were told that God had decided otherwise; he had taken Poultray to his kingdom in heaven.

Stunned, Filippo stood beside his friend's empty bed and

reached an arm out to touch the last place he had seen him. His arm was roughly wrenched backward. He turned to see Giovanni, eyes ablaze with anger. "Are you crazy?" his brother yelled.

He pulled Filippo out through the doorway. "I will take care of you, Filippo," he said. "I will speak with the prior. Beseech him for permission that you may sleep in my cell."

Giovanni, who had just turned seventeen, had been recently ordained and now lived in his own small room, a space large enough for a cot and a kneeling bench. The frati who were left had been quarantined, taking meals in their rooms, where they devoted their days to silent prayer.

Giovanni received permission and soon settled Filippo in, giving him his cot. "I will sleep on the floor," he said, throwing a straw mat down. "They have provided an extra blanket."

Filippo protested, the floor being made of stone, insisting that he would return to the dormitory. Giovanni grabbed him by the arms and shook him. This was so uncharacteristic that it frightened Filippo. "This is the pestilence," Giovanni screamed. "Do you not understand? Thousands will die."

When the pestilence ended, fourteen of the twenty-one frati had passed into the great sea. Filippo's kind teacher Fra Paulo was gone. Of the seven young boys in the cloister, only he had survived. Even little Pepo, who was six years old, had been taken. Five of the ten novices had perished. Afterwards, there were four new novices, and three new boys who had been orphaned. A wave of boys lost, a wave of boys washed in.

Filippo and Matteo sat in silence for some time, bent to the task of bailing water. Finally, Matteo let out a soft whistle. "The pestilence. Such a terrifying experience for one so young. I shiver to think of what you saw, my friend, and now understand how you might question God's plan." After another silence, Matteo said, "But this story's path has a propitious bend in it as well. Old squint-eye did you a favor by dumping you in the convent, did she not? Giovanni saved you from the pestilence. Far more than she would have done, no doubt. And, you have become a painter. So there is more to this story at the convent that we will need to hear. Then, there is the struggle to read and write. Well now, humility is a good lesson."

"Humiliating," Filippo countered.

"Humility," Matteo insisted. "The same Latin root—humili—low, base. Think of it as meeting up with the base of your being, the vulnerability inside of you. When you are brought low, it can feel humiliating, but if your vulnerability awakens you to the vulnerability inside others, well, then. It nurtures our compassion, does it not? The struggle within the soul."

CHAPTER 9

The year of Our Lord 1416, Constance, Germany

Five days prior to the feast of the Annunciation, while Frederick, Duke of Austria, was holding a fine and lavish tournament, Cosimo and the pope, along with most of his retinue made their move. John chose noon, the most unlikely of times, but the height of the activities that drew crowds of thousands to the tournament, to make his way out of the city. Cosimo, following close behind, his belongings tied to an ass, pulled the hood of his unlined homespun brown mantello down to his brow, bent his head, and hunched his shoulders. As he passed the guards and made his way through the gate, he shuffled his feet in the way his father's servant Jacopo had done.

If they were discovered they would be brought before the council. An attempt to escape would be seen as an admission of guilt to the charges brought against John. It was the pope, disguised as a groom, wearing a homespun gray mantello, crossbow slung from the saddle of a sad little mare, who took the greatest risk. But, if he stayed, he risked imprisonment and possible execution.

Council decisions that threatened Pope John's safety had

begun to be introduced shortly after Christmas, with the arrival of Emperor Sigismund of Germany. Although Sigismund, Cosimo knew, had been the one in whom Pope John had placed his trust and hope of success, the emperor's presence seemed to turn the tide against him. In early February, the pope received another blow. It was decided that each country represented at the council would have the strength of only one vote. This was meant to undermine the eighty Italian bishops and doctors who supported John and would now possess one vote altogether. Cosimo could see that John grew uneasy. Finally, in early March, a tract was introduced before the council that brought charges against John, and he was forced to resign. Matters had become perilous. "They will dispose of all three popes, one by one, before this is over," John reasoned.

Pope John, Cosimo wrote to his father, had also been closely watching another matter before the council, that of Jan Hus, who spoke out against clerical abuse, including the sale of indulgences. The council had accused him of heresy because he challenged the authority of the pope's office and the cardinals. Hus maintained that they were not the Church; the Church had existed long before they had. His logic on this matter agreed with Saint Augustine, who was revered, but no logic found its way into council proceedings against him. Although the emperor had guaranteed Hus safe passage, he now rotted in a dungeon and would, no doubt, be burned at the stake. Politics at the council had become so complex that "Not even your father," John told Cosimo, "a master of diplomacy, could prevail. My decision is made."

Choice, not chance, determines your destiny. Aristotle

Passing through the gate and starting down the road, Cosimo tensed, waiting for the guards to shout out for them to stop. Nothing. He slowly released his breath. When it was found that they were missing, probably some time the following morning, they would be pursued. For now, Cosimo let out a deep sigh of relief and allowed his body to relax.

Up ahead, Pope John seemed to be enjoying his role as a groom of no standing. He strode along, looking from side to side and smiling as if this were a jaunt. He appeared to be more comfortable dressed in homespun cloth than he had been in the finest of Florentine wools and brocades. Cosimo was reminded that he had been a soldier first and even, some said, a corsair for a time. Given that, he had filled his role as pope with an energy of purpose seldom seen right up until nones that very day. He was a resolute and courageous man.

They would travel together for the remainder of the day and the one following, after which their paths would diverge. John was headed to the castle of a duke and close friend in Schaffhausen. There, he could conceal himself until the council adjourned. Cosimo was headed to the branch of the family's bank in Bruges. Once they went separate ways, Cosimo would be safe. The council did not care overly much about the pope's entourage if they were not caught all together, only about the person of the pope himself.

CHAPTER 10

The year of Our Lord 1432, Mediterranean Sea

Filippo enjoyed working side by side with al-Basir, who often talked as they worked. One day, he told Filippo that the ship they traveled on was called a qarib. It was light and fast, its design making it highly maneuverable, a necessity when targeting a merchant galley, which was large and cumbersome by comparison. The qarib they were on had been enlarged in order to hold more cargo.

"And the sails?" Filippo asked. "Why are they triangular in shape?"

"They allow us to sail into the wind."

The shape of the sails had caught Filippo's attention when he had first boarded the ship. The other thing he had wondered about since then was the pirate leader. "You have explained what led you to this life, but why did the man who leads not become a legitimate trader in goods?"

Al-Basir did not answer at once. He considered. "I will tell you of the man, but a brief outline of a life does not, in truth, tell us who he is."

Filippo agreed, thinking of al-Basir himself, and of the much less inscrutable Matteo, who had continued to be the buoy of the men's spirits. The friar's faith was clear and straightforward, the joy he took in life, even in their current extremity, sincere. "A man is always part mystery."

Al-Basir began, "His name is Ab' dul Maumen, but this is not the name given him at birth. It is a name received from the Sultan. But we will get to that. Maumen was born 'Umar Ibn al-Hasan, 'Umar, son of Hasan.'"

"How did you come to know him?" Filippo asked.

"I knew his father, a great man," al-Basir said in a reverential tone. "He told me once that, when 'Umar was a little boy, he was interested in how things worked. Tired of carrying sacks of flour and jugs of oil home from market, he built a little cart on wheels." Al-Basir smiled as if he could see the little boy pulling the cart. "That is how he earned his name, 'Umar al-Gani, 'Umar the self-sufficient."

"When did you meet 'Umar?"

"Ahhh"— al-Basir smiled at the memory—"his father brought him one day to the port to purchase cloth. I worked on the ship of a silk merchant with whom he did business. 'Umar was a clever boy. I could see it in his eyes. Aware, curious, he did not miss a thing. His father introduced him to me as the boy who loved mathematics and how things work."

"'Ahhh,' I told 'Umar, 'then you must learn how to travel a path at sea, how to regain it when it is lost.' 'Umar was excited. Was this really possible?"

"On a small scrap of paper, I drew a square, dividing it into sections, and filling each section with a series of numbers. On the back of the paper I drew a circle and divided it into eight sections, the eight directions. I took a bowl, poured a small quantity of water into it from a jug, and placed a magnetized metal arrow in its center. As we leaned over it, watching, the arrow moved. 'Umar sucked in his breath. When the arrow stopped moving, I said, 'The arrow always finds north. That is your starting point. Now, you must memorize the chart of numbers.'"

"Umar's mouth dropped open. 'But there are hundreds of numbers,'" he said.

"'You will accomplish this,' I told him, knowing that my certainty would seep into 'Umar's bones so that he, too, would believe that he could do this."

"'If you learn this,' I told him, 'you will never be lost. And now,' I said, 'I will teach you how to read the wind.'"

"Where is his father now?" Filippo asked, wondering why Maumen was not selling cloth with him.

"He left this world, may God bless him. An infection that did not heal. Maumen, then a young man of fifteen years, having also lost his mother seven years before, sold everything they owned and came to the port, where my ship had arrived the day before. I think, perhaps, at a time when he felt most alone, my words spoken years before came back to him."

Filippo did not understand. Al-Basir explained, "'If you learn this,' I had told him, 'you will never be lost.'"

When you do not know what harbour you are aiming for, no wind is the right wind. Seneca

"He, too, was orphaned." Filippo said.

Al-Basir eyed him for a moment without speaking, then said, "It is important to have a friend of advanced age. For you, without a father, more so. Once you find that person, stay close. Do you have such a one?"

"Fra Matteo," Filippo said, smiling at the thought of his benevolent friend.

"Ah, the old priest. Stay close by his side."

"And what," Filippo asked, "does the elder derive from such an alliance?"

"To be able to give as he once received. To continue to see the world anew."

"If this is true, you surely would not have recommended that Maumen choose this life. How did he come to command a pirate ship?"

"I taught him well," al-Basir said, his voice tinged with sadness, "perhaps too well. He became known as the greatest captain to pilot a ship. This brought him to the attention of the Sultan. 'Umar found great favor there. When the Sultan decided that it was unfair to tax his people, he gave 'Umar a new name and a new job."

"Could he not have declined the offer?" Filippo asked.

"One does not say no to the Sultan."

CHAPTER 11

The year of Our Lord 1417, Florence

Unwilling to relinquish his freedom, Cosimo had decided to visit various cities where they might open branches of the bank, and where he could also search for ancient manuscripts. He had set off for Bruges and then London and Lyons. Contessina wrote often, chiding him "not to be chary with paper and pen," but the trivial nature of her letters—Did you receive the clothes I sent? The linens? The almonds? Did they survive the trip? Do you need warmer clothing?—at the same time forgetting to send the books he had requested, did not invite response. During his absence, Contessina gave birth to a son. Cosimo was delighted but piqued that his wife had written to ask his opinion about the boy's Christian name. Tradition dictated that he be named Giovanni after his paternal grandfather. Cosimo assumed that Contessina would see to it given that her own father shared the same name. Consumed with business, he left it in her hands. When he finally found time to answer her letter, he learned that his son had been christened Piero. Cosimo was certain that his wife had chosen this name out of spite both for his absence and his silence. They would simply need to have another son.

When more than a year had passed since his departure, Cosimo's father ordered him home. His son Piero had survived his first year of life, his father wrote. Did he not wish to see him? Cosimo reluctantly complied and started out for Florence, taking his time. But, the closer he drew to his beloved city, the more excited he became, realizing how much he had missed it. He was looking forward to seeing his son, although he was also frightened at the prospect. He felt not much more than a boy himself.

Arriving at his house on Via Bardi, Cosimo dismounted and handed the reins to a servant. There were twenty people, he calculated, who sat on benches in the loggia waiting to speak with his secretary who, he knew, was within the offices. What a boon to them that he had arrived home that day. He would get to work as soon as he washed the dust off and greeted his family. Exhausted, he turned, ready to cross the courtyard and bound up the stairs to their private apartments. There they stood at the bottom of the stairs, Contessina, plumper than he remembered her, the boy holding her hand.

Cosimo was startled and unsure what to do. He walked over and stiffly placed his hands on Contessina's arms, giving her a perfunctory kiss on each cheek. "Piero," he said, reaching down to tousle the little boy's head. The soft wispy hair beneath his palm sent a jolt through his arm that came to rest somewhere in his chest. This was his son. He was struck by the wonder of it. He was a fine-looking boy, perhaps a little thin, with whisps of light-colored curls and wide brown eyes.

"Piero," Contessina said, her voice ringing out clearly in the open space of the courtyard so that all could hear, "this is your father."

So, he had been right about her. She was spiteful, Contessina, and appropriately named, little countess.

CHAPTER 12

The year of Our Lord 1433, Tunis

When Filippo and Matteo boarded the ship, it had already been out to sea for several cycles of the moon. The pirates raided merchant ships that sailed far out at sea, far from aid, and the hold was filled with treasures: gold, silk, rare spices, including pepper and saffron, and allum, goods that would bring a high price at market. Al-Basir told Filippo they were headed to land, to Tunis, a bustling port on the coast of north Africa that was Maumen's home.

After arriving in Tunis, the oarsmen's wrists were tied with rough cord, and they were shackled together at the ankles. As they shuffled single-file through the crowded port, Filippo heard many dialects of Arabic, Spanish, French, and Italian. He wondered to whom he might yell out for help but knew it was futile. What stranger would pay for their release?

They continued through back streets until they reached a market. Filippo luxuriated in the many colors and textures. There were vessels of clay and beaten metal, ostrich and peacock feathers like those used for the angels' wings in the Ascension play. His eyes lingered over silks of many colors stacked in piles and luxurious carpets in deep, rich hues, of intricate design.

As they passed by, street vendors scoffed at them. Men glared. Women averted their eyes. The children taunted them, dancing around and picking up handfuls of dirt from the street to throw at them. Filippo was not bothered by their antics, thinking that he had been as much of a ruffian once and would have done the same. But Demetrius puffed out his chest and roared. This sent the boys scattering in all directions, and the prisoners had a good laugh.

Filippo thrilled to the bustle of the streets, the sights and sounds of this exotic place. Strings of peppers hung from stalls. The smell of spices drew Filippo's eye to where they were piled high in baskets, vermillion, gold, and ochre. Their scent made his mouth water, his head light with hunger.

Just when Filippo thought he could stand it no more, he was distracted by the fluid lines of a script that danced across many of the buildings. Having struggled in school with reading and writing, he was attracted by its loops and swirls, struck by the art of it. Design more than word, it mimicked song, life as continuous flow. It was the distillation of thought into word and meaning as not merely musical notation, like the forward march of Latin letters, but as the swell of the music itself.

Once out of the market, and down a few narrow, winding streets, the oarsmen were placed in a small, cramped cell that, protected by taller structures from the sun, nevertheless was hot and would soon be putrid with the smell of them.

"Ah, Filippo." Matteo smacked him on the back. "This exotic place is filled with gifts for the eyes, a blessing for a painter such as yourself."

"Did you see the hills of spices?" Filippo asked. "The piles of silk cloth and carpets, the writing like song."

Just then servants arrived with bowls filled with a kind of grain, the pieces of which were as tiny as grains of sand, filled with chunks of turnip. "And now, a gift to fill up our traveler's bags," Matteo said, slapping his stomach appreciatively.

Afterwards, they were given small green figs. "Praise God," Matteo said, "to be on land once more, where food is not scarce."

There were two small, barred windows high up in one wall, too high even for Demetrius to see out of and too high to relieve the stench.

The next morning, Demetrius said, "Climb onto my shoulders, Padre, and I will lift you up." He knelt to allow Filippo to straddle his broad shoulders. "What do you see?" he asked after lifting him, the tone of his voice not betraying any strain although Filippo was sturdily built.

"A walled garden. I see ornamental trees at its far end, a small section of greenery and walkways. There are fig trees full of fine ripe figs. Baskets hang, from which cascade a viney plant covered in small white flowers."

"That is all?" Demetrius asked.

Filippo imagined the fountains, sculptures, and flowering trees that must exist there as they had in the gardens of Florence's palazzos, and he began to describe them from memory. Before long the cell had fallen silent except for his voice. All of the men listened as Filippo filled their imaginations with the sights with which he had once filled panels. Then, someone walked into the garden. "A woman has appeared. She glides with grace. She is covered from head to toe in blue silk the color of the sky, edged in fine gold threads that glint in the sunlight and embroidered with white flowers. She reaches out, exposing a thin wrist, a small hand that caresses a vine. She brings it up close, a white-flowered tendril. She holds it long and breathes in its fragrance."

"What else does she do?"

"She turns and leaves."

"No. She cannot leave."

"She is gone."

"What else do you see?"

"Pomegranate trees."

As Filippo climbed down, Matteo said, "You prove that reality dwells in the mind, my friend. But, now your story is ended, an overwhelming aroma seeps back into my senses. Thrusts my attention once again to our cramped quarters."

"We stink like hogs, Padre," Demetrius agreed.

"Ah, but with a scent as of little flowers to God's nose," Matteo assured him.

"God must have a wondrous nose that can mask the stink of the likes of us," Demetrius countered.

"Well said, Demetrius. Wondrous, indeed."

The following day, when Filippo was raised to the window, the men asked after the young woman in blue. "Is she there today? She was there yesterday. She must be. She comes every day. She must." It seemed all it took was the mention of a woman, the merest of details about her, for each man to feel as if he knew her.

Filippo, used to the deprivations of the convent, did not share their obsession, although the woman's beauty did pierce his heart. More so, the gardens, so like those in Florence, reawakened in his breast the desire to paint. He felt as if he might split his chest in two, allowing his life's blood to flow out, to seep across panel after panel, dispersing there into hues and shades, shapes and contours, creating scenes in rapid succession.

Maumen passed by the windows when he left his dwelling, which was, as al-Basir had intimated, magnificent. The garden in the distance belonged to him. In this place, Maumen dressed like a prince. He wore brilliant white robes and an outer garment of saffron silk, on which gold threads blended with the color of the cloth, but shimmered. He wore a clean white turban that was held together in front with a single emerald set in gold. His everyday sword was replaced with one on which handle and scabbard were inscribed with a fluid design, encrusted with rubies and sapphires.

The oarsmen were informed that foul weather threatened travel and that they would stay in this place for one full cycle of the moon. Filippo calculated that it was now close to a year since he had been captured. He was in no hurry to head back out to sea. He only wished that he could explore the city, feast his eyes on the many colors and textures of this new land.

When the men, much rested and healthier than at any time since their capture, were shackled together once again and led through the market, the port, and back onto the ship, they lamented the loss of the woman, as she had become known. She had only appeared twice more during their stay. As they filed out of the cell, they wondered, "When he brings us back in a year's time, will she still be there?" Of the answer, some were certain: "We will never see her again."

"Ah, but I have no doubt that you will," Matteo assured them, winking at Filippo.

Filippo's spirits sank at the thought of another year out at sea, only to return to Tunis. How many times would he live through this cycle? Once back on the ship and his old duties, he was told that al-Basir was staying behind in Tunis. Without word from the old man himself, there was no way to know the reason. Perhaps it was his advanced age, that he no longer possessed the stamina for the hard life aboard a ship. When Filippo saw that the pirates had loaded large barrels of pomegranates onto the deck, he read it as a message from the old wise man, "one seed in each comes directly from heaven," imploring him to remember his connection to the divine.

Filippo was drawn to the fruit's deep rose color in this world of ink and wash. He could read gradations of color in the same way that his brother, Giovanni, read music, each variation in hue a different note, the whole creating a distinct melody. Human character, in a similar way, revealed itself in faces, with almost imperceptible changes of expression.

"If my father had lived," he had told Matteo, "I would have been happy to have spent my days by his side, a butcher as he was." But would he have?

"Perhaps," Matteo had said, "but would there not still have been this gift inside of you, making its presence known when you looked upon the work of another? A promise unfulfilled?"

"I would be contented that my father lived."

"His path had been fulfilled," Matteo countered. "God also has a path for you."

"Where does it lead?" he had asked, looking around disconsolately.

"God is the inception of all paths. Ultimately, all paths lead back to God, who will want to know, what did you do with this path I laid out for you?"

Al-Basir had said much the same. He had also said that the seed of light within provides us with the illumination we need to travel life's path.

The open barrel of pomegranates gleamed in the sun, beckoning. A simple fruit. He reached out and took one in hand. Holding it, he could almost taste its color. But, as he gave praise in his heart, he was struck from behind with a club and then beaten. Afterwards his body ached, but his soul ached more, the deep rose color within reach but elusive. If he ever escaped from the ship, he would suffuse his paintings with a light tinged by the color of this fruit.

"The pomegranates are not for us," Matteo told him later on, as they settled down to sleep for the night.

"Your advice comes late," Filippo complained, rubbing the back of his neck with one hand, the bottom of his back with the other. "I only wished to touch it."

"Demetrius told me that those who travel great distances prize the pomegranate," Matteo explained. "It can mean the difference between life and death."

Filippo shared al-Basir's story about the pomegranate.

"I do not know about that," Matteo said, "but it travels well, lasts long, and staves off disease. It comes from their part of the world. They know its worth."

"Well," Filippo agreed, "I have learned it too. I do not think the theft of a gold florin would have brought such a beating upon my head."

"They will not share the pomegranate," Matteo said.

CHAPTER 13

The years of Our Lord 1419 – 1420, Florence

P ope John had been betrayed and was wasting away in the dungeon of a castle in Germany. "We do not abandon our friends," Cosimo's father told him. It took nearly three years, and when negotiations had ended, Giovanni had paid 38,500 gulden to procure John's release.

When John arrived in Florence, Cosimo was shocked by his appearance. Emaciated, stooped, his eyes sunken, he was a beaten man. Once brilliant, confident, awe-inspiring, he now barely uttered a word.

Giovanni was livid, appalled by the condition of his friend and by the treatment he had endured. He convinced Pope Martin, who was elected at Constance after the ouster of all three previous popes, to appoint John Cardinal-Bishop of Tusculum. But, six months after arriving in Florence, his spirit broken, John passed into God's hands.

Giovanni, still smoldering over the way in which a great man had been mistreated, was determined to honor his friend in death. A magnificent tomb would be built for him in Florence's Baptistry, a rare and significant honor. Donatello and Michelozzo were commissioned to do the work.

When the tomb was completed, there was the question of what to inscribe on the scroll held by angels. Without hesitation, Giovanni decided, "Joannes quondam Papa XXIII," Latin for, "John, the late Pope XXIII."

"Are you certain?" Cosimo asked, surprised that his father, usually so circumspect, would do something to challenge the church and to anger Pope Martin. "Should it not say cardinal? Will the pope not read this as an affront?"

"Quondam," Giovanni said, "means 'former' as well as 'late.' Former pope, late pope, either way, it must say pope, for that he was."

It was Pope Martin's turn to be livid, which was made more troublesome by the fact that he had been living in Florence for some time. Giovanni rode the wave of the pope's anger with equanimity.

In bad times, Fortune reveals which of your friends are sincere, and which changeable. Few are sincere.   Boethius

During the first few years following his return Cosimo found himself avoiding the company of his son Piero. He was afraid to draw too close. The physicians all agreed that the boy would not live to adulthood. Sometimes when he looked at his son his heart ached. What had the child done to deserve such a fate?

Contessina, who had since suffered two miscarriages, doted on the boy. Now four years of age, his light wisps of hair had darkened and, like his mother, he tended toward corpulence. His dark brown eyes were heavy-lidded as if it took great effort for him to keep them open. But, he possessed a fine intellect and shared his father's passion for arms and armor. Slowly, Cosimo softened. He began spending more time with Piero. Together they poured over his vast collection of intaglios, cameos, and ancient coins.

One day Piero reached out his pudgy little hand and pointed to an ancient Roman intaglio. "This one is my favorite," he said. The image of Fortuna was intricately incised into an oval of carnelian.

Winged, she stood on one foot atop a globe and held a wheel aloft with both hands.

"What is it about this particular intaglio?" Cosimo asked.

Piero thought for a moment. "Well. It is nicely carved, and the stone is a pretty color."

The carnelian was a stone that usually ranged in color from deep red to orange and, like most of those spread out on the cloth before them, opaque. The one to which his son now pointed was pale orange shot through with gold and transparent, with a singular clarity.

"You have judged it well," he concluded. "The artist possessed unparalleled skill. His design and execution are striking, and the stone itself brilliant."

Cosimo took his son's small hand in his own and turned it palm upward. He gently placed the delicate stone in the boy's cupped hand. Piero's eyes opened wide, and he let out a deep breath.

"Can I trust you to take good care of it?"

The boy looked up at him and blinked, then slowly nodded his head.

"There's a good boy," Cosimo said, smiling. He took down a small cloth bag from a shelf above, scooped up the stone, and placed it inside, handing the bag to his son. "It is yours."

This tender moment filled his heart with love, but it also pained him to consider the irony of his son's choice in the fickle figure of Fortuna. Perhaps if the boy took good care of her, in return she would be kind to him.

Soon after, Cosimo determined that Piero should learn to use a sword. Why not? The exercise would do him good, as well as the flights of imagination it would inspire. Perhaps the physicians were wrong, in which case it was a skill he would need. He held out this hope, but it was often dashed by the boy's frequent illnesses. Still, each time Piero rallied it rekindled his belief that the boy would live. As his relationship with his son deepened, Contessina grew warmer toward him.

CHAPTER 14

The year of Our Lord 1433, Mediterranean Sea

Remembering Matteo's words, Filippo was surprised when one day his friend whispered to him, "We must steal one of the pomegranates. To sustain us."

"If they catch you," Filippo warned. Had they not seen a pirate thrown overboard for stealing? He could still hear the man's terrified screams. "Reconsider," he said, but they were called to work, and Filippo did not see his friend again until late that night, when Matteo pulled the rose-colored fruit from beneath his robes. Even in the dark, by the light of a full moon, it was beautiful. Filippo cupped it in his hands.

"My monk's robes made the stealing of it easy," Matteo was saying. "Glory be to God." He raised his eyes heavenward. "Now, friend, the real test is in the opening." He knocked on the fruit. It made the dull thump of wood.

"But how?" Filippo asked, now alarmed.

"Shhhh." Matteo motioned for him to be quieter. They waited in silence, listening, but no one had stirred. The rowers, praise be to God, slept soundly on the hard benches.

Filippo's eye fell on the metal ring holding the oar in place. He smashed the fruit against the metal. A deep red juice squirted out. He pried the pomegranate open. They licked the seeds from their fingers, their mouths puckering at its tartness.

"I thought, from the beauty of its color, that its taste would be sweeter," Filippo whispered.

"We must steal one a month," Matteo said when they had finished. "Not enough to be noticed, but enough to sustain us."

They threw the empty shell into the sea, where it was left far behind, in the wake of the ship, long before sunrise.

After one full cycle of the moon, Matteo asked Filippo to steal another. "I do not have enough opportunity," he said, "not being on the upper deck as often." Filippo, it was true, was called upon to help with the rigging, but he hesitated, feeling a coward as a shiver passed through his body. Matteo had risked his own life without hesitation.

"Tomorrow," said Filippo. "I will try to steal one tomorrow."

Filippo was no novice at theft. As a boy, he had practiced the skill on the streets of Florence. In fact, it had been fruit, the easiest item to lift, fitting nicely in the palm of his hand, that he had stolen from the vendors in the mercato along the Piazza Santo Spirito.

The following day, when Filippo was asked to help above deck, the hair prickled on the top of his head. He found no opportunity while he worked, always being in the company of one or another of the pirates. But, when the pirates took a break from work, the heat having grown too oppressive, he found that he would be passing an open barrel on his way back to the bottom deck. Filippo slowed his pace as he approached. Most of the pirates slept beneath the shade of one or another of the sails. One pirate, close by, sat with his back to Filippo, whittling a piece of wood.

Filippo thought of the price he would pay if he were caught. He could simply tell Matteo that no opportunity had presented itself. He could tell him that they must be storing the pomegranates in the hold because he had not seen any. Matteo would believe him without question. But how could he take advantage of his friend's trusting nature? Filippo pushed all further thought from his mind.

Loosening the front of his robe to ready it, Filippo quickly glanced around. Then he took a great leap forward like a bird of prey taking flight and, just as the bird whose glide above the earth must bring all it surveys into a kind of slowed movement, so he felt his stride lengthen, sound hush, his heart drum. One more furtive look before he reached out, grabbed a fruit, and stuffed it into the inside pocket of his robe. He raced below, where he took a deep breath and made the sign of the cross, his prize safely concealed.

That night, while smashing the pomegranate open on the metal oar ring, Matteo's hand slipped and he slashed the side of his palm on a jagged edge. He used his robe, now filthy and threadbare, to stanch the bleeding. "I shall have to be careful not to get it wet," he told Filippo. "Salt water stings like the devil."

They again threw the emptied halves out to sea when they were done. Watching them bob away by the moon's light, they washed the telltale red juice from their faces. Just as Filippo cupped his hands, filling them with seeds that had fallen into the puddle of water at his feet, Demetrius awoke. Rubbing his eyes, he said, "You dream, Filippo." Filippo froze, his hands filled with seeds and water. "The boat does not fill with water," Demetrius assured him. "There is no need to bail."

Filippo feigned surprise. Then, throwing this last handful of water and seeds over the side, he stretched and yawned. "It is a dream then?"

"Go back to sleep," Demetrius grumbled, turning over and closing his eyes.

Filippo and Matteo exchanged a glance. They would have to be more careful, especially when the full moon cast its light. Although Filippo would have liked to share the pomegranates with Demetrius, the more people who knew, the more likely their theft would be discovered. And, as they were all chained at night, and Demetrius two benches away, it would have necessitated the exchange of the fruit in daylight.

Drifting toward sleep, Filippo felt good about having faced his fear that day. But, then, he remembered stepping into the rowboat, how he had wrestled his fear into submission. Had he, instead, given in to his fear, he would not now be a prisoner. Having twice faced his fear, he wondered, would he get into the habit? And, if so, would it cause him no end of trouble?

The following morning, Matteo struggled to lift the oar. When they had finished rowing for the day and were eating the mid-day meal, he was unusually quiet. One could always count on Matteo's good cheer, yet today he was withdrawn, lethargic. "Are you tired today? Did you not sleep well?" Filippo asked.

"Sleep? Yes," Matteo answered without looking up, gnawing away at a moldy biscuit. This was an unusually cryptic response.

"Matteo, what ails you?" Filippo asked, his eyes falling on the man's left hand. It was red and swollen. "You are in pain."

"What is it you say?" Matteo, listless, looked at Filippo as if not quite seeing him.

"May I see your hand?" he whispered, taking it in his own and pulling Matteo's sleeve up. There was a long festering red line running from the gash halfway up his arm. Frightened by what he saw, Filippo quickly pulled Matteo's sleeve back down and looked around. No one had noticed.

"You must rest," he said. "I will make an excuse. I will say you did not sleep last night. Yes. I will say that Demetrius kept you awake all night with his snoring." At this, Matteo smiled, but he seemed far away. "I will go with you down to the bottom deck."

They slowly made their way below, where Filippo settled Matteo on his bench to sleep. Filippo did not know what to do about the gash that was oozing puss. He gently wrapped it up in Matteo's sleeve. "There now. Rest. You will feel better tomorrow."

Before first light the following day, Filippo was awoken by the sound of a cavernous moan. Matteo was hot with fever. Filippo, frantic, tried to lift him. An oarsman who was unable to row was in danger from more than disease. As Filippo struggled to prop him up, Matteo placed a hand on his shoulder. Looking into his eyes, Matteo said, "It is no use."

"You must rise" Filippo insisted.

"Pray with me," Matteo said, the look in his eyes now pleading and weary. His breathing was uneven, his forehead covered with sweat. It seemed to be a great effort for him to focus.

Filippo relented and, along with Matteo, made the sign of the cross. "In nomine Patris, et Filii, et Spiritus Sancti."

Then, Matteo began the prayer to Mary, mother of God, and Filippo joined in. "Ave Maria, gratia plena, Dominus tecum."

When they came to the end of the prayer, Filippo was struck into silence as Matteo asked Mary to "pray for us sinners, now, and in the hour of our death."

Filippo joined in again with, "Amen."

As they finished the prayer, Filippo heard voices. The pirates were stirring.

Matteo whispered, "Promise me, Filippo, that you will escape."

When their eyes met, Matteo's were filled with resolve. In that moment, Filippo knew great courage, but not within his own breast. "It is impossible," he said, thinking that, as death approached, Matteo had lost touch with reality.

"Nothing is impossible," Matteo said with conviction. "You must be the great painter that God has meant for you to be." Filippo heard in his words an echo of those Masaccio had spoken to him three—four?—years earlier. He had lost track of time.

Matteo continued, "You must turn this suffering of ours into paintings of such beauty that all who see them will be moved by the experience. It will please me to know that you do this. Promise."

"I will escape," Filippo promised, though he did not know how it would be possible.

Then Matteo seemed to gain strength. "I had meant to have you hear my confession, but for the life of me"—and here he laughed but soon winced with the effort—"I cannot think of what to confess."

Filippo could not imagine, either, what sin Matteo might have committed, but then, Matteo was saying, "No. Wait. Remember that devil of a man, Arigho? You met him at the Olive and Thistle. Yes. The man is stingy as a raisin is shriveled. Well, he invited me to supper one evening, and the rascal brought out a bottle holding at least three kilos of sciacchetra. Do you know that he showed it to me and then placed it back on the shelf without offering so much as a sip? I did a bad thing, Filippo. When he went out to get more wood for the fire, for it was a frigid winter's night, I poured two full glasses of the stuff and downed them. They warmed my body on such a night." He smiled with the memory. "And then I accidentally knocked the bottle off the shelf so he would never know I had drunk of it."

"Matteo!" Filippo was astonished that his friend could do any wrong. But, then, it was such a small transgression.

He thought it wise to remind Matteo, "I am no longer a man of the cloth. My blessing will not fall on God's ears with the weight of one who is truly devout, who lives the life of one ordained."

"It will have to do," Matteo said, giving him a weak smile.

Filippo made the sign of the cross above Matteo and said, "God hopes that you will never do such a thing again."

"Not likely," Matteo answered. Then, composed, with serious intent, he asked God for forgiveness.

"May God absolve you of your sins," Filippo said, taking a handful of salt water and blessing it. He dipped a finger into the water and anointed first Matteo's eyes, then his ears, nose, mouth, hands—being careful to avoid touching the gash there—and legs, saying each time, "Through this holy unction and His own most tender mercy, may the Lord pardon thee whatever sins or faults thou hast committed by sight, hearing, smell, taste, touch, walking."

"Now that I have received the Lord's blessing, I remember perhaps my gravest sin," Matteo said. "It is my fault, in chasing beauty, that we are here."

"Do not blame yourself," Filippo said, not wanting his friend to feel remorse, "I also chased the beauty."

"What is it I said?" Matteo asked. "Ah, we go out only a short way. God showed me, did he not?" He winced with pain. His mind was drifting.

Filippo, intent on Matteo's needs, did not hear the approach of footsteps. There was a sudden flash of steel, and a sword plunged into Matteo's heart. "No!" Filippo heard a faraway voice yell out. The tiniest of gasps, and Matteo was gone, like a bird flushed out, with the snap of a wing, disappeared into the heavens.

Filippo looked up, expecting to see Maumen, but it was the interpreter who stood there, sword resheathed. All was still, save the gentle flap of the sail. Beyond the interpreter's head, where Matteo's gaze rested, the sky, a deep blue, cloudless, was pierced by the sun, its rays split by a three-sided sail.

The interpreter turned away, allowing a group of pirates just behind him to move forward. As they lifted Matteo's body, Filippo boiled into a sudden rage. He raised both arms and let out a roar like that of a wounded animal.

Grabbing the pirate nearest, he lifted him from the ground and threw him, crashing, to the ship's floor. He was blind but for flashes, a surprised eye, a body tumbling, a thick-set forearm. All movement slowed, each image of what was happening broken apart from the whole, individual shards of a broken vessel. He grabbed and threw, beat with his fists. As he raged, he was struck from all sides until he was brought down. Bleeding and spent, he lay in a stupor and drifted off into darkness, wishing never to awaken.

Take the pieces of your broken dishes or goblets, and, even if they are in a thousand fragments, fit them together, putting this cement on them thinly. Let it dry for a few months in sun and wind, and you will find those dishes stronger, and more fit to stand water, where they are broken than where they are whole. Cennini

The next day, his body bruised and aching, his face swollen, Filippo rested at mid-day. He rubbed the back of his head, wincing where it smarted at his touch. He might have killed a man. He had awoken to a part of himself he had not known existed. He must never again allow himself to fall into a blind rage.

Filippo was soon joined by the interpreter, who stood above him. "You have the rage of the warrior in your blood. Ab'dul Maumen asks if you will join him in the next raid."

Filippo was struck by the humor of this request. Laughter welled up in him, erupting in gasps until he had to wipe the tears from his eyes.

The interpreter placed his hand on the hilt of his sword, pulling it halfway from its sheath. "Ab'dul Maumen's words are not cause for laughter."

This sobered Filippo. "No," he said, "I will not join you." He had fallen from grace, and he knew that he had not the excuse that he acted in defense of his friend, or out of anger for what they had done to him. It was not a heroic deed. He had not been motivated by the instinct to protect, nor was he moved by revenge, only by the thought that he would be next. Take me now, had been his one and only thought. You sons of whores, he had raged inside. Not with time to think, to wait. Now. Battle ready. Quick. In the rage that blocks out fear.

Then the interpreter said something unexpected. "Come, we send your friend to his rest. Ab'dul Maumen requests that you pray for him."

When they reached the upper deck, Filippo was surprised to find that Matteo's body had been carefully wrapped in a makeshift shroud that he recognized as his own mantello. He knelt beside his friend and silently prayed for him. Then, making the sign of the cross above Matteo's head, his lips, and his heart, Filippo prayed aloud. "Eternal rest grant unto your servant, Fra Matteo, O Lord. Let perpetual light shine upon him. May he rest in peace. Amen."

They lifted Matteo's body and delivered it to the sea. Filippo, still kneeling, hands folded, eyes closed, heard the splash.

He did not know how long he had knelt there, lost in prayer, when they roused him. With difficulty, he rose from his knees, stiff and bruised from pressing into the wooden boards of the ship. He hobbled to the lower deck, nearly pitched down the stairs, caught himself, made it to the bottom and dropped onto his bench where it hit him anew. Matteo was now an empty seat beside him.

That night Filippo awoke with a start. The old familiar fear, the empty well within, now threatened to engulf him. It was a feeling he had always known, this sense of being alone in the world, as if he floated in a dark space, not at sea, for even the sea on a moon-less night caught light enough to seem a living, moving thing. This was a vast empty space devoid of light, without a ripple of move-ment. The shard of broken moon above was the same moon that rose above Florence. It looked down on both, while he lay helpless, listening to the monotonous creek of the boat he did not steer.

It was already the time of day which makes travelers at sea think back with longing. Dante

Afterwards, with the coming of each day, Filippo felt newly scored within, a cross-hatching of the desperate attempt to heal sewn with the threads of despair. What more could he have done? This was the question that echoed inside of him. He experienced a deep sense of guilt, as if he had held Matteo's hand while his friend hung from a high cliff, held it against all pressure of time, all oppos-ing force, until he had slipped from his grasp.

During the daytime, Filippo performed his duties in a daze. At night, he had trouble sleeping. Each morning, there was a moment when he opened his eyes to a new day and thought it a day like any other, a blissful moment. Then he remembered. It was worse than the shock of the initial pain, numbed by disbelief; this pain was coupled with the longing to go back, back to the moment that existed before his friend's death, the futility of the desire entwined with hope like a vine choking a new-grown plant.

He had leaned over his father's bed and kissed his sweat-soaked brow. He longed to go back. He had sat on a bench beneath the wall separating the convent from his father's garden and had longed to go back. His brother Giovanni had taught him the futility of this longing, its destructive force. He had felt Masaccio's man-tello brush his cheek, had seen his arm raised in farewell, had heard his booming voice echo through the rafters. He longed to go back. He had placed his foot into the belly of the rowboat and stepped into captivity. To recapture. To go back to the moment before. Why could he not? It should be so easy. But he was a son of Adam, of Eve. There was no going back, no return. Instead, the moment of recognition each morning. But it was the blissful moment of first waking, the one before that of recognition, that turned out to be the cruelest moment of all.

CHAPTER 15

The year of Our Lord 1421, Florence

When Contessina gave birth to another son, Cosimo said, "We shall name him Giovanni. May he possess the wisdom of his grandfather."

"Grandfather*s*," Contessina corrected him.

"Of course," Cosimo assured her, but secretly he wished for his son to inherit the attributes of his own dear father. He knew that his wife held his family in disdain. The Medici were an old and important family in Florence, but one whose fortunes had ebbed and waned until his own father had pulled the Medici back up, placing them on a solid foundation. Cosimo's father had begun with next to nothing, his own father not leaving much wealth when he died, and that divided among his wife and five sons. With acumen and sagacity, Giovanni had made them the wealthiest family in Florence.

Contessina's father was a member of one of the oldest and wealthiest families in Florence, but they were bankers who had lost much of their wealth. They had loaned unwisely and had left various branches mismanaged. Their downfall came when they loaned in a profligate manner to the Kings of England and Naples.

"Never trust a king," Cosimo's father had taught him. "They do not repay their debts. Loan sparingly after first determining that you can afford to lose it all."

The Bardi bank had gone bankrupt. Let Contessina look on the Medici with disdain. Of what use is old family wealth if one did not have the common sense to hold onto it? It is better to create from nothing than to inherit and lose all.

Cosimo's father was a shrewd man of business but also one who understood men. Cosimo hoped that his newly born son would inherit his namesake's good judgement. It was important that he did so since his brother Piero remained a sickly child.

Shortly after Giovanni was born, their father called Lorenzo and Cosimo to his office for a meeting. "Now that my long-time partner, Benedetto, has passed into God's hands, may the Lord bless and keep him, I have come to a decision. My sons, it is time for me to retire. I leave the business in your capable hands."

Cosimo was surprised and a little fearful. He felt unready. "Father, we are honored that you entrust us with this responsibility, but will you not stay on a while longer?"

"Do not doubt your abilities, Cosimo. And do not worry. I will be here to answer any questions you may have. Do not hesitate to seek my counsel. Now, as to the restructuring. Lorenzo, you will stay on here in Florence to oversee the totality of operations. Ilarione will come here from Rome to take over as general manager. Between you two, all will be well provided for here in Florence, which makes it possible for you, Cosimo, to be absent for an extended period. You are already familiar with Rome."

"I am," Cosimo agreed.

"I send Bartolomeo di Bardi to take over there as branch manager," Giovanni continued. "As you know, although we lost our position as papal banker to the Spini when Pope John died, Rome continues to provide more than half our profits. We do not want to lose the confidence of the cardinals and prelates, who search for a secure place to privately invest their money, while we await a return to our former status. Bartolomeo is untried. We do not want another Michele di Baldo on our hands, borrowing from outside sources to hide the results of poor management. It is a long set of instructions that I send with Bartolomeo, with which you will familiarize yourself. They detail who should not be extended credit, who should be discouraged from taking on more loans, and who should be coaxed toward repayment. The pope, himself, has borrowed profligately and should be dissuaded from seeking more funds. A delicate business, all. You see how diplomacy is required, at which you excel."

"Thank you, Father."

"A mere statement of fact. Bartolomeo will benefit from your counsel. He has a good staff in place. Antonio Bertini, his main assistant, is experienced and will prove helpful. In fact, keep an eye trained on Antonio. I consider sending him to the Geneva fairs to represent us, as well as to determine whether we should open a branch there. You will let me know if you think he is up to the task. Finally, and most importantly, Cosimo, I wish you to oversee our secret deposits in Rome. For the many cardinals and prelates who earn interest on their investments we have set the system up to stay just within the bounds of the church's rules on usury. These rules must be strictly followed. Even Cardinal Dwerg, the pope's confidante, and the pope's nephews have investments with discrezione. A last word, Cosimo. Do not trust Romans. They promise but do not deliver."

Cosimo was relieved to see that his father was having difficulty loosening his grip on the reins of power. They would all need time to adjust to this change. He was also excited to be off on another adventure. He missed the carefree life of a traveler. Once settled in Rome, it would be easy to find excuses to extend his stay.

CHAPTER 16

The years of Our Lord 1422 – 1423, Rome

When Cosimo arrived in Rome, he found that rooms had been procured for him, complete with a Circassian slave woman to care for his domestic needs. Sylvestra was a healthy virgin, unobtrusive and efficient, he was told, hand-picked by the bank manager in Venice. This much he found to be true. He also found that his eyes wandered in her direction.

Sylvestra's movements were deft and graceful. She was slight in build but full-breasted. Her luxurious dark hair was set off by pale skin that had a pearl-like radiance and blue-grey eyes, a stunning medley of contrasts. There was a strength of purpose in her that flowed outward like an invigorating autumnal breeze.

One day, while making an insignificant request of her, Cosimo placed a hand on her shoulder. He felt a jolt at his core. She froze. He had been impertinent. "I am sorry," he stammered. One did not apologize to slaves. Flustered, he noticed the long curve of her neck, delicate, vulnerable. He quickly turned and left.

She unnerved him, he thought as he made his way to the rione di Ponte quarter, where the bank's offices were located. Sylvestra was intelligent. She managed the household with a shrewd eye. Merchants and vendors who attempted to cheat her were cut to the quick. It cost far less to maintain the household than he had budgeted for, whereas at home in Florence, Contessina was lax. He suspected that the servants stole from the storeroom, and he often complained that his family wore the most expensive clothing in all of Italy, not by their worth but by what was paid for them. Only two years in Italy and Sylvestra was fluent in Italian. He must stop thinking about her.

Once he arrived at the bank's offices, he lost himself in the minutia of finance, politics, and commerce. He began taking his evening meals at an inn and often arrived home so late that he fell right into bed. In this way, he harnessed his attention.

Then one day, she fell ill. He arrived home earlier than usual to find Sylvestra feverish, sipping a murky liquid from a cup, and trying to go about her duties. He sent her to bed and called for the physician. Cosimo watched as the physician questioned Sylvestra and then shut tight the windows and closed the curtains. "We will need to drain your excessive humors," he told her, removing a small, sharp-pointed, two-edged knife from an ivory case. Cosimo winced.

"Out!" Sylvestra commanded, pointing to the door.

The physician turned to Cosimo, who shrugged.

"Out!" she again shouted.

"I think you must leave," Cosimo said. He, himself, was not at all sure that bloodletting did any good.

The physician left, grumbling as he went, "Let the slave die then."

Sylvestra staggered across the room, where she parted the curtains and threw open the windows. Grabbing onto furniture to steady herself along the way, she collapsed into bed, drew the covers close, and slept.

Cosimo, not knowing what to do, decided to let her sleep. He went to the kitchen in search of food where, curious, he picked up the cup of liquid. Its foul stench turned his stomach. "What devil's brew is this?" He tossed it. Then he sat down to some cured meats, cheese, and bread. He could have gone to an inn for supper, as he usually did, but he was afraid to leave her alone. What if she were to die? He needed to check on her. He took a long draught of wine to steady himself.

Sylvestra was consumed by fever now. She tossed and turned, occasionally babbling a few words in her native tongue. Cosimo went back to the kitchen and filled a small bowl with water. He found a clean cloth. When he arrived back in her room, she was shivering. He stoked the fire and tucked the covers up under her chin. Later, when she threw them off, sweat beading her face, he patted it with the dampened cloth. As he did, he was struck by her beauty, even in illness. One leg was exposed, and her camicia revealed the swell of her breast. He gingerly pulled the cover over her.

At some point, he must have fallen asleep because he awoke with a start to the sounds of the street coming alive with the morning's activities. Startled, he nearly fell off his chair, which awakened Sylvestra. She opened her eyes. With a look of confusion, she brought her hand to her forehead and then, seeing him, her eyes widened and she pulled the covers to her chin.

"Nothing," Cosimo stammered. "Nothing. You were ill. The physician." He could not help but smile. "You threw him out. Decidedly. How do you feel?"

"I am well," she said.

There was an awkward silence.

"I will leave you, then," he said and hurried out.

What foolish thing had he done? Now there was an intimacy between them, one that drew him with a cosmic force. He arrived home early that evening. Curious, he asked Sylvestra about the foul-smelling liquid she had been drinking.

How is virtue to rule pleasure if she follows it? Seneca

"Herbs," she said. "It is what brought on the fever."

"You induced fever?"

"If one can withstand it, this is how the illness leaves the body. Not in the barbaric way of your physician."

Cosimo smiled. His Circassian slave was calling the most prominent physician in Rome a barbarian. Perhaps she was right. She had recovered, after all, and everyone knew that physicians killed more people than they saved. He would be sure to call for Sylvestra should he himself fall ill.

"Share this evening's meal with me," he offered.

CHAPTER 17

The year of Our Lord 1433, the West Coast of Italy

T he pirates sometimes rowed out from the main ship to raid coastal towns. Matteo had once explained to Filippo, "In Vernazza, there are underground tunnels that allow the people of the village to escape to the countryside, and there are many clever hiding places for prized possessions." Filippo and the other rowers stayed on board at these times with a skeleton crew.

Depleted by their fight with the monstrous storm, two lives swallowed by the sea, they put in at a cove somewhere on the western coast of Italy. The entire crew went ashore this time, including the oarsmen. At the mid-day meal, they were given hardened black bread that was not moldy or bug infested. It had been pilfered from a nearby farm along with ripe olives, peaches, and pears. A tent was erected for Maumen, and a large fire built, beside which Filippo and the other rowers were chained for the night.

Staring into the fire was a relief after so much water. Filippo felt a desire to walk into the center of it, to disappear, leaving only clean, dry bones. He would rather do this than go back onto the ship and out to sea. Beside the light and warmth of the fire, Filippo drifted off to sleep and, for the first time since Matteo's death, he slept through the night.

He dreamt that he walked through a dark forest with rugged stone outcroppings. Then, quite suddenly, the trees burst into flame, crackling and splintering all around him. Fear seized his heart until he realized that the fire had burned a hole in the world he traversed, opening a space into a new world into which he now stepped. It was much like the one from which he had come, the forest as deeply draped in darkness, but in this world, as he made his way forward, he noticed that some of the massive oaks had been felled and split for use. He continued on, feeling less alone, discarded tools giving evidence of the presence of life besides his own, of industry and purpose. Quite unexpectedly, he came upon a clearing filled with light. There, on the ground, he saw the baby Jesus lying on a carpet of wildflowers, looking up at his mother, who knelt before him. They were bathed in threads of golden light that streamed from above. Voices crashed in on this peaceful scene, and Filippo felt his body jostled. Halfway between dream and wakefulness, as he reluctantly left the wood, he heard in his mind the words "singed by faith."

The slaves were unshackled so that they could work. While raking the remnants of the fire, Filippo reached down and picked up a charred piece of wood. The substance, like charcoal, blackened his hands in a familiar way. He rubbed it indulgently between his fingers. Instinct drew him to the tent wall, a white space crying out to be filled. He began to sketch, as for a fresco, the life-sized, powerful figure of Ab'dul Maumen, the man who had stolen his freedom, the man responsible for his friend's death. Filippo worked at a feverish pace. He released his anger with every stroke, along with his terror and his pain. He embodied it all in the figure of Maumen.

No one stopped him. Perhaps the emergence of their leader in startling clarity made the pirates hesitate. Filippo drew him alive with power, imbued with an energy that made him appear as if he were about to emerge from the tent wall. When he finished the drawing, he stepped back to take it in, as Fra Arrigo, his first mentor, had taught him to do. It was only then that he was struck on the head from behind.

When he came to, Filippo was being dragged through the opening of the tent. The interior was sparsely furnished but as comfortable as any room in Florence. A fine vermillion carpet, traced with intricate designs, covered the sand. Here, Maumen sat cross-legged beneath burnished multi-tiered metal holders upon which hundreds of candles flickered. Maumen, although tall and thin, was built like a soldier, fit and muscular. His dark eyes seemed to pierce through Filippo's skin, to read his soul. It would be impossible to be evasive, to hide anything from this man. Filippo's head ached from the blow. His palms were sweaty.

The interpreter sat beside Maumen. "How do you do this?" the interpreter asked, sweeping his arm in the direction of the side of the tent upon which Filippo had drawn Maumen's likeness, the faint outline of which could be seen on the interior cloth of the tent.

"This is the work that I do," Filippo said, not knowing how else to explain.

"Is it magic?"

"It comes from God," Filippo answered, speaking his true belief.

"It is not you who are the source of this magic?"

"No. It is God who is the source. The work I do is for the glory of God and His creation."

"Maumen says you have been given a great gift. You are young, but you have been favored. You will eat with us this evening."

That evening, the walls of the tent were suffused with a warm orange glow cast from the many thick candles. The pirates had hunted during the day, and there was game, freshly caught. Many moons had filled and emptied since Filippo had eaten meat. He nearly choked in his haste to fill his stomach. Wine, too, he had not had in as long, and he gulped down several cups. The interpreter cautioned him, "Pace yourself, or you will be sick."

With difficulty, Filippo ate more slowly. "How is it," he asked the interpreter, "that you come to know Italian?"

"I am Italian," he said, surprising Filippo, who did not know what to make of it. "Captured from a Genoese galley. Many captives become pirates. More than half of the men on the ship are Italian or Greek. This is not unusual. We share in the spoils and one day will be freed. You might have joined us."

That would have been good to know, Filippo thought, when he had been asked to take part in a raid. They would be freed one day. But could he have wielded a weapon for any other reason than to save his own life? The food was cleared, Filippo's eyes following it with longing. Then something was given to him more precious than food.

Maumen nodded his head, and the interpreter said, "It is time to make images. Maumen requests that you trace his likeness."

Filippo's hands trembled as he picked up the pen. He teared up at the familiar feel of it in his hand. Sheets of paper were provided, along with ink.

You may sometimes just draw on paper with pen. [W]ork up your lights, half lights, and darks gradually, going back to them many times with a pen. [I]t will make you expert skillful. Cennini

"Did you know," asked the interpreter, "that, when you draw, you look like a man possessed?"

"I do not know how I look," Filippo said, astonished by this revelation. "I know only the peace that I feel when I work. It is like no other."

Filippo smoothed the paper with his hands, luxuriating in its texture. He dipped the pen in the ink, twirling its tip along the rim of the pot, breathing in the deep, musky scent.

While Filippo drew, the interpreter facilitated a conversation with Maumen. "My men are superstitious," Maumen said. "They believe you have captured my soul and that I will now die. I am not a superstitious man. But our belief is that only God can create. It is not for man to do."

Filippo tensed. Was Maumen toying with him? He remembered

al-Basir saying much the same thing. He recalled that in Tunis he had seen only geometric shapes, the artistry of the written language. He had not seen any representations of God's creation. "I did not know," he said, and bowed his head.

"You are of a different faith, but a man of the Book," he said, referring to the Bible. "I, myself, lost my faith the day I lost my father. I have not regained it. Not from the heart. Belief must blossom from within, al-Basir says." Here, Maumen struck his breast with a tight fist as if force might make faith sprout forth.

"Al-Basir is a wise man. He is not with us on this journey," Filippo said.

"He is no longer able to endure the hardships of this life. He must rest."

As Filippo continued to work, Maumen stroked his beard. "It is strange. It is markings on a flat piece of cloth, and yet, it rises up, looks me in the eye, shakes its fist." He shook his own fist. "And I think I have walked out of myself."

"It is a mere likeness," Filippo repeated, although he, too, was awed by it.

"It is more. It has captured me. This is why my men think it sorcery. But, I am a skeptical man."

Filippo worked quickly, without thinking. As he drew Maumen, the mystery of line creating form, taking shape beneath his hand. He fell into an old rhythm. "You are educated," Filippo conjectured.

"By my father. Also a wise man. Wise and good." As Maumen looked off into the distance, his features changed, softened. He was thinking of his father. Filippo worked quickly to capture this change.

After a long pause, Maumen said, "I have not his goodness."

"I, too, struggle," Filippo confessed.

"You?" Maumen asked. "But you are a priest of your people."

"And yet, I struggle."

"You are honest," Maumen said. "That is good. It is important to discover truth. The gift that you have. Why would God give it to you if not for use? For the glory of God, you say? How so?"

Filippo explained, "When I paint a story of Jesus' life, or that of a saint, it helps the people, many of whom cannot read, to feel as if they have stepped into that story. To better understand the story and help people emulate the virtues embodied in it."

Maumen considered. "My father often spoke of Averroes. Do you know of him?" Filippo did not. "Averroes taught that if any passage in the Quran contradicted reason, then it must be subjected to interpretation. The Quran says, 'You, who have eyes to see, reflect.' All knowledge must pass through reason. The Jewish scholar Moses Maimonides also taught this, that the intellect, the ability to reason, is that part of us made in God's image. These two agree with Plato and Aristotle, who believed the intellect is where the human soul resides. My father said that if great minds from different places, different times and traditions, agree on this point, then there must be truth in it."

"Your father sounds learned and wise."

"He was." Filippo once again detected a change in Maumen's eyes as they shifted to the left, stared into the distance, a flame burning at their center. He captured this fleeting emotion that passed across the man's face like the shadow of a bird's wing.

The more they talked, the more comfortable Maumen seemed to become in Filippo's presence, and the more candidly he spoke. Working once again with pen and ink was like the return of someone dearly loved. Filippo absorbed this miracle that might never be repeated, keeping Maumen talking so that he might continue to sketch.

"Why did you take us prisoner? We were of no value to you. We had no money and could not be ransomed. We were not fit. We were barely able to row a small boat."

"Two plump sheep sitting in a rowboat in the middle of the sea," Maumen agreed, smiling. "The lion does not pass by the innocent prey. It is not in his nature."

Filippo thought of the pirate who had been thrown overboard. "Must your justice be so harsh?" he asked. "You are smarter than your men. You know how to regain a course that has been lost. How to lead a raid. Will they not follow you for these reasons?"

"On land man has the luxury of mercy, but the sea herself can swallow a dozen men in one gulp. Each man has a job to do that all others depend upon. There will always be one man who thinks that he can better run a ship." Maumen swiped his hand as if to swat away a fly. "He cannot." His posture was relaxed with the ease of a man used to being in control.

"In my country, there is instability," Filippo agreed. "Fear of war is a constant concern."

"That is why one man must take control. The man who does not hesitate, the one of decisive action, is the leader of men. But he must not give in to the illusion of his own power. He must continue to learn or his power will be lost."

"Broad strokes," Filippo said, remembering the advice of Masaccio, the best of all painters.

"Broad?"

"Someone long ago, a great man, told me this also."

Maumen asked to see what Filippo had drawn. He slowly studied each rendering until he came to the one in which Filippo had depicted a change in his features, a softening. Maumen brought it close. Then he peered at Filippo, who held his breath. Had he gone too far? How? In what way?

There was anger in Maumen's voice. "You draw my father. And yet, you did not know him."

Surprised and frightened, Filippo assured him, "It is you that I drew."

Maumen looked to the interpreter, who bowed his head in ascent. After a moment of silence during which Maumen continued to study the rendering, he said, "I will tell my men that you are a magician. They will be frightened and happy you are not returning to the ship. Sleep well. You will be released in the morning, and you have a long journey ahead."

Not as long as the one behind, Filippo thought as he left the tent.

CHAPTER 18

The year of Our Lord 1425, Rome

From that day forward, Cosimo arrived in time for the evening meal. In fact, he looked forward to it since Sylvestra now shared his table. It was not unusual, he reasoned, for slaves to eat meals with the family.

One night he asked her how she managed to spend so little on the household expenses.

"I begin by knowing the price of an item," she explained. "I fix in my mind the amount I am willing to spend. Then the merchant tells me the price. It is always greatly swollen?" she asked. "Is that how you say?"

"Inflated," Cosimo corrected. He was enjoying this.

"Inflated," she repeated. "Inflated, yes. After this, I offer him a price much reduced from that which I am willing to pay. The merchant becomes angry."

"No doubt." Cosimo smiled.

"Then I—do you have the saying?—rip off his head and breathe fire down his throat?"

"No," Cosimo said, laughing, "but we should."

"That is when he learns that I knew the price of the item all along, and that I will be happy to pay a reduced price since I purchase a large quantity, unlike his other customers."

"You should work in my bank," Cosimo said. "You negotiate better than my manager does. Ha."

At the end of his long days, Cosimo looked forward to conversation with Sylvestra. She quickly learned his preferences and prepared his favorite foods. She took great care with the washing of his clothes, and she drew his weekly bath. He gave her lists of the rare manuscripts he wanted searched out, and she delivered them to the bookseller. He began reading his favorite books to her after the evening meal. Although uneducated, she had a quick mind and provided fresh perspectives. She found Boethius bleak and sad, even when attempting to give hope. She said Cicero had some interesting counsel but that his rhetoric could put one to sleep faster than a banked fire and an abundance of wine.

One night they rose from the table still deep in conversation. She said, "This Cicero is so severe. He has good ideas, but he is relentless as the driven snow. He pelts one with lessons. I do not understand his insistence on reason above all else. The answer to every question is to be found in reason? What of feelings? Do we not possess them for a reason?"

"Ha," Cosimo laughed, "a nice play on words."

Sylvestra persisted. "Do feelings not provide us with important guidance?"

"Feelings," Cosimo explained, "happen to us. They are not to be trusted because they are difficult to control. It is only through reason that we can see clearly, can discern truth."

"Feelings happen to us, but can they not also lead us to truth? Otherwise, what purpose do they serve? You speak of God. Perhaps these feelings that come to us unbidden—just as being able to imagine what does not yet exist—perhaps these are the ways that God speaks to us. God's voice inside of us."

"An interesting concept," Cosimo agreed. "But all philosophers agree that the ability to reason is God's greatest gift to us. Feelings are a base part of our natures that would have us place pleasure above all else. It is only by subduing our emotions and employing reason that we are led to the ultimate truth."

"'Reason commands, and impulse obeys?'" she asked, quoting Cicero. "And happiness? What of happiness?"

"When one seeks truth and finds it, one has discovered the greatest happiness."

"Cicero does not sound happy. I would not wish to know the man. He must walk stiff as a rooster."

Cosimo laughed aloud. He could picture the great man on stick legs, stiffly strutting about. They laughed together. He found himself standing close. His cheek brushed against her hair. Grabbing her, he pressed his lips hard against hers, then pulled away to look at her. Their eyes locked. It was done. Sylvestra did not yield; she met his passion full on.

From that day, they lived together like man and wife. When, on occasion, Cosimo visited Florence, he sorely missed Sylvestra. His indifference to his wife did not go unnoticed by Contessina. She complained that if he continued to be cold and distant, they would not be able to bring more sons into the world. He knew, did he not, that most children did not survive to adulthood? In fact, Piero was sickly. They must have more children. She was right. Cosimo made a great effort, but bedding his wife was now difficult. He strained to find arousal. Then, quite by accident, he discovered a way. He closed his eyes and pictured Sylvestra.

A happy life is one which is in accordance with its own nature. Seneca

One night, while lying in bed with Sylvestra, he told her, "You are Italian now. You need an Italian name. A name that flows off the tongue with ease." He thought of her soft touch, her intense passion. "A name with both soft and strong sounds." He thought of her graceful movements. "A name that is musical. Maddalena. Shall I call you Maddalena? Do you like it?"

"Maddalena," she repeated. "It is strong and soft. Yes, I like it."

He had never before been overwhelmed by passion. He had always been in complete control. This feeling of release was new and, what? Beautiful? Yes, it was beautiful. There was Contessina, a woman of high birth, bound by duty as by chains. And, here was Maddalena, a slave, but the only truly free woman he knew. He wanted her to be able to meet his love freely with her own, so he granted her freedom.

As time went on, Cosimo found that he could not get enough of her. Maddalena was a glorious creature. They tumbled together across the bed, he on top, she beneath, then she on top, he beneath. He loosened her hair so that, like a luxurious black mantello, it hung about him, enclosing them both in a tented world all their own. He had never felt so at ease, so totally engulfed, so free and desirous of intimacy with another. And she now carried his child.

"I must be off to Florence," he told her, sweeping her hair back so he could better see her face.

Her eyes darkened. "When do you leave?"

"In the morning. I will return as soon as I am able. It is my father who calls me home." He did not want her to think that it was Contessina he wished to see. He pulled her face close and kissed her. "I will miss you every moment I am away."

"And I you."

He rolled her off and onto her side. Curled up beside her, he caressed her face. Was he gazing into his own eyes or into hers? Was there any separation between them?

CHAPTER 19

The year of Our Lord 1433, the West Coast of Italy

As the sun began its ascent, Filippo was released with a loaf of bread and a sack of wine. Maumen told him, "You are close to where we found you. If you walk north along the shore, in less than one day's time you will reach the church on the hill. Head inland, and never return to the sea."

There was no path from this small stretch of sand to the road above the rocky cliff. The sea beat against the rocks north and south of where he stood. Filippo would have to climb. He sent a prayer up to Sant Phillipus, his namesake and, placing his sandaled foot on an outcropping, heaved himself up by his hands. He carefully picked his way, zigzagging from foothold to foothold, slipping several times and scraping his shins. But, calming his fear and catching his breath, Filippo found a place for his foot each time, however much he had to spread his body like a spider to hug the cliff. It crossed his mind that his capture had begun with the placement of his foot into the cradle of a boat, and now his liberation was dependent on the placement of his foot upon rock, holding his entire weight, the only thing between him and a cataclysmic fall.

When he reached the top of the ledge and scrambled to his feet, Filippo saw that the ship was heading out to sea. He knelt and sent up a prayer of thanksgiving for his safety. Then he prayed for Demetrius, a friend left behind, for Matteo, a friend lost, and for Maumen, the illusion of Filippo's drawings uniting them and setting him free.

How calm the sea seemed from this height, the cerulean blue like an echo of the eternal. How different it had appeared in the hold, the thrust and charge of it like the turmoil of circumstance, all blackened waves and raging froth, as Filippo drove an oar through its center. Viewing the sea from a distance, as now, life spread out before him once again in this radiance of light, this celestial hue.

Somewhere out there Matteo's bones drifted. Although Filippo was certain that his friend was now in heaven, he knew Matteo was also a part of him, not his bones, the stuff of the flesh, but fragments of his kindness, the compassion that had made up his soul, informing Filippo, expanding his view, the meaning of his own life, the essence of his soul. He imagined Matteo, the cock of his head to one side, his mischievous smile, saying, "It is not wise to take yourself too seriously, Filippo. Waddle off, now, little pigeon."

Filippo laughed to think of it, his laughter welling up from a place deep inside. It flooded over until tears streamed down his face. He raised his arms triumphantly. "I am free!"

CHAPTER 20

The year of Our Lord 1426, Florence, and Rome

Giovanni di Bicci was sitting at his desk when Cosimo entered the room. He looked up from his accounts. "I am disappointed."

This was devastating for Cosimo to hear. He searched his memory for a single mistake he had made since taking over the bank in Rome. He could think of none. "I am sorry," he said, accepting his father's word as truth. "What have I done to displease you, Father?" He held his breath.

"You do not know? You bed this slave woman?" His father's face was flushed, his eyes glassy with anger.

Relief flooded through Cosimo's body. So, he had not made a mistake after all. His father's silence begged a response. Cosimo bowed his head. "Yes."

"Do you think you live in ancient times? You cohabitate with her in Tivoli like a Roman emperor? You will dismiss her. At once."

Cosimo bit his lip. "She is pregnant."

"What?" his father exploded.

Cosimo had never seen his father so angry. In fact, he had rarely seen him ruffled. "What would you have me do, Father?"

"Do? I would have you walk backwards all the way to Florence from Rome to atone for your sin."

"I love her," Cosimo admitted.

"Love? Nonsense. Love. She is a slave."

"I freed her."

"A slave nonetheless. A Circassian. These women know sorcery." He pointed his finger at Cosimo. "She has bewitched you."

"She has not."

"You cannot know if she has bewitched you."

His father turned and walked to the window, where he stood, hands clasped behind his back, fingers twitching in agitation. Quite suddenly, startling Cosimo, he turned and strode forward, pressed his fingertips into the surface of his desk, his knuckles white, and leaned toward his son. "You will dismiss her." He held up a hand to silence Cosimo's protest.

Sadness dissolving the anger from his voice, Giovanni predicted, "You will pay for this mistake for the remainder of your life."

Cosimo knew that his father's words were prescient, but he loved Maddalena and wished to spend the rest of his life with her.

His father was saying, "Find this woman an apartment in Rome, not too expensive, but in a good neighborhood, not tawdry. This will be her home for the rest of her days. You will pay all of her expenses." He hesitated before delivering the final blow.

"You must never see her again. If I hear that you have seen her"—he pointed his index finger upward for emphasis and to silence dissent—"you will be dismissed from your position with the bank. Once you have despatched this slave, you will return to Florence. When the child is weaned, it will be brought here to grow up in your household, with your own children. If a girl, she will be a woman of the cloth. If a boy, God help us, he will take vows as well. This child will not contribute to the Medici lineage. Now, go. Tell your wife of good family, who has been a faithful wife to you, of your indiscretion. Do all in your power to make amends. Please God, she will forgive you." He sat and bent his head to his work.

Cosimo's father had never before been dismissive of him. He also could not have been more accurate in his appraisal of Contessina. "I am a Bardi," she said when he told her, a haughty tilt to her chin. "Have I not been a good wife to you? A good mother to our sons?" This was true, Cosimo told her, and, in truth, he was fond of her for that reason. But she was a woman who pushed forward like a ship, creating a wide berth around her. Her conversation did not stretch beyond the household.

Cosimo had often wished that his wife were more like his mother who, quieter and more reserved, spoke in an unassuming but confident manner. When she spoke, his mother's words, well thought through, held import. Then there was Maddalena, his dear Maddalena, who although a slave and uneducated, had learned the Italian language with ease. She possessed an innate intelligence. Cosimo came to depend on her perspective, which could be counted on to cut through with a simple clarity, to reveal a problem's core, the hidden center of it.

After Cosimo confessed to Contessina, they never spoke of it again. From that day forward, however, with a cold wind of indifference, she attended to his needs. He was not surprised when she shut him out of her bedchamber. In fact, he suspected that she was relieved to have a reason to do so.

We shall conserve honorableness...if we apply some limit and order to the things with which we deal in our life. Cicero

As he made his way back to Rome, Cosimo imagined his father unburdening his heart to his wife. He remembered the conversation between them that he had overheard just before his betrothal. She had known from the beginning, and his father had not listened to her. What was he saying now? One can attempt to avoid a thing too much? His mother would comfort him as she always did, but where did it all leave Cosimo? It pained him to disappoint his father, whom he loved and revered above all others. And he knew his father was right, was always right. But he loved Maddalena deeply. The thought of losing her cut like the thrust of a rapier. If he was honest, however, in weighing his choices, on one side there was Maddalena alone. He had been reckless in his pursuit of her. All was held in the balance, not only his father, but his career, the Medici bank, his standing in the community. He had never been so torn in two directions.

Once back in Rome, Cosimo acted quickly. He requested that Maddalena visit him in his office since he could not trust himself to be alone with her in his apartments. When she entered, he moved from behind his desk and stood in the center of the room, his arms held out in a gesture of helplessness.

"Maddalena, I must send you away." His throat constricted with the words. His hands felt cold and clammy. He balled them into fists.

He discerned fear in her eyes. "Until the baby is born?" She looked down at the swell of her stomach, her hands cradling it protectively.

He could not bring himself to answer her question directly. "You will be well provided for. For the rest of your days."

She said nothing. Her hand moved up and down as if caressing the baby within. Cosimo realized in that moment, for the first time, what she would have to give up, what this would mean for her. The silence was too much for him to bear. Since he could not avoid it, he must be done with it. "Maddalena. The child, our child, will grow up in my home, as my own. If a boy, he will be educated with my sons."

She did not comprehend. "Our child is also your son."

Cosimo's breath caught in his throat. "You know it is a boy?"

"Yes."

He did not doubt her. She was Circassian. Who knew what magic these people possessed? Her words pained him. It would be easier if it were a girl. She would grow up separately from Piero and Giovanni. She would not need to be educated, and at an early age, eight perhaps, she would be sent off to a convent where she would never be heard from again. A boy could rise to heights in the church. In fact, Cosimo would feel obligated to help him do so.

"Yes, he is my son" he said. "That is why he must grow up in Florence." There, he had said it.

Maddalena gave out a gasp, then recovered herself and said, "I will not allow it."

"It is best," he told her, "for all involved."

"No," she said, shoulders thrown back in defiance. "How can you do this to us? To me."

"I must," he said.

"You would betray all that we have shared together?"

Cosimo was willing to make sacrifices for his mistake, but what right had he to demand that she do the same? And yet, he knew that this was best for the child.

"It is best for the child. We knew. We knew this could not last forever."

"My son," she said, her hand now resting on her stomach, "will need me."

"My life is in Florence" was all that he could think to say. "My family. You knew that."

Her eyes filled with tears. Why, he wondered, was he accusing her at the same time as he was hurting her? There was more she needed to know.

She walked toward him.

"We have found you an apartment," he blurted. "You leave today. Whatever you need." He paused. "We will not see each other again."

She froze.

"I will think of you every day," he said, knowing that this was true. Her hands dropped, her eyes narrowed. She did not believe him.

"You will know," he assured her. "You will feel me thinking of you."

He rushed forward. Crushing her in a tight embrace, he pressed his lips hard against hers. For a moment, nothing else existed. Then he released his grip and pushed her away from him. "You must go," he said. Before it is too late, he thought.

Reason commands, and impulse obeys. Cicero

CHAPTER 21

The year of Our Lord 1433, Vernazza, and Genoa

Many hours later, Filippo came upon Vernazza just as the call to vespers burst forth from the bell tower. At the familiar sound, he fell to his knees. The next deep sonorous tone rushed through him, filling him with love for this place, this life, this peace. He pressed his forehead to the ground, nearly swooning with the scent of sunbaked earth. He scooped it up in both hands and breathed it in. The people of Vernazza were being called to prayer. He would say his own right here, on this path, the entrance back into the life he knew.

And then we emerged to see the stars again.   Dante

Filippo had lost much heft, but for his chest and arms, the muscles of which had grown in size by half. The good friars gave him a new robe to wear. They urged him to stay through March, until after the feast of the Annunciation, when the wind and rain would cease to whip and chill travelers to the bone. But Filippo could not stay so near the sea, where he could hear Matteo's words of encouragement as he stepped into the small boat, "You have seen nothing until you have seen the sun set behind the sea. It spills a light you will never forget." The sunset, the last light Filippo had seen before the darkness, the light he remembered thinking must be the love of God made manifest, the likeness of it in the pomegranate, which in the dark world of the ship was life-giving, one seed in each directly from heaven. Filippo would never forget that light. He wished to recreate it in his paintings. It was as Thomas Aquinas had written, "Beautiful things are those which please when seen because they are felt to be rays from God's mind."

Filippo was ready to return to Genoa. He had work to do. But, before he left Vernazza, he sent off a letter to his brother, who was certain to be worried about him, not having had word for more than a year. He did not reveal much about his time on the ship. Instead, he spent most of the letter assuring Giovanni that he was safe and none the worse for his experience.

As Filippo walked from Vernazza, each step reminded him that he was again on solid ground. Once back in Genoa he became like a man possessed, as he had been under Masaccio's tutelage, working each day until well after the waning of the light. This straining to see to the end, until the last rays of the sun receded, became a habit in him.

Filippo decided to stay on in Genoa for a while. He was known in the city and was able to find employment. He needed to regain all of the skill he had lost from disuse. Until this time, Filippo had continued to wear a monk's robes because it had made him feel safe, having been the only life he knew. But, his experience as a slave had stripped him of identity. Back in Genoa, he felt as if he had walked out of the shadows, stepped into a cartoon drawing that provided the outline for a fresco, and filled it with form, all the possibility of who he might become.

When he had made enough money, Filippo purchased a new robe and a mantello, all made of a fine black wool. The cloth was not as expensive or ostentatious as cloth dyed crimson, but morello black was costly and of a luxurious, deep hue, the wool finely woven and soft to the touch. Filippo also had a hat fitted, black wool, shaped like a round of cheese, as was the fashion. In his new clothes, he looked and felt like a well-respected citizen.

Soon Filippo would head to Padua. There was a maestro there, a teacher called Squarsccione. While in Genoa, he had come in contact with a few painters from the North. In Padua he would have the opportunity to see more of their work, to discover their techniques through close observation. One day he would return to Florence, but not until he himself was a maestro.

[A]lways follow the dominant lighting; and make it your careful duty to analyze it, and follow it through, because if it failed in this respect, your work would be lacking in relief, and would come out a shallow thing, of little mastery.

CENNINO D'ANDREA CENNINI
(THE CRAFTSMAN'S HANDBOOK)

PART TWO

THE DOMINANT LIGHTING

CHAPTER 22

The year of Our Lord 1433, Genoa and the Road to Padua:
Remembering Florence, 1418 – 1428

Filippo arrived back in Genoa shortly before the feast of the Annunciation. At first, his progress was slow, but then, as when the Arno floods its banks, all of the knowledge he possessed rushed through him until he had surpassed his previous skill. Not long after the feast of the Assumption, he had fulfilled the terms of his last contract.

During all of this time, Filippo had not once thought of Lunetta, the prostitute he had regularly visited during his first days in Genoa. Now that he was ready to move on, it occurred to him that he might want to see her, to say good-bye. He procrastinated. The more he thought about it, the more it seemed unnecessary. He was surprised by his ambivalence. Here was a woman whose bed he had shared for months, moreover, a woman for whom he felt tenderness. And yet, the time they had spent together felt so decidedly a part of the past. The only thing, in fact, that felt real, that connected Filippo to the present, was his work. It was odd that after all the years spent chafing under the restrictions of the cloister, he now found himself singularly unfit to forge any kind of relationship with a woman. There was intimacy, and then a distancing that he could no more control than he might control the force of the sea.

Filippo stayed in Genoa long enough to celebrate the feast of Mary's Assumption and then, saying farewell to a few friends, he started on his way. It was a long walk to Padua, north as far as Alessandria, then east through Piacenza, Brescia, and Verona, and south to Este and the Euganean Hills. After Filippo's long confinement on the ship, it seemed that he could spend the remainder of his life walking and never tire of the feeling of freedom.

There were other routes, but this path kept to well-traveled roads. Thieves more regularly roamed deserted byways. For the trip, he again donned his friar's robes. A man of the cloth met with goodwill and, at times, a free meal from innkeepers. More importantly, it persuaded thieves that he was poor and not worth the trouble.

[A]lways follow the dominant lighting; and make it your careful duty to analyze it, and follow it through, because if it failed in this respect, your work would be lacking in relief, and would come out a shallow thing, of little mastery. Cennini

Prior to his experience on the ship, Filippo had been a mere outline of himself, a rendering without light or shadow—what might be—candle light and close scrutiny revealing trace marks, suggested form, but little else. It was as if, after this experience, he had walked into himself.

Filippo was ready to take on his own commissions. First, he would have to make himself known in Padua. His release from captivity, based on the strength of his drawings, had instilled in him a new confidence. It filled him with wonder that the subtle differences in Maumen's features and eyes that he had detailed in his renderings had changed the man's appearance enough to make him see his father in them. Thinking about his father had so filled Maumen with the lessons he had learned from him that it had changed the character of his face. Filippo wished, not for the first time, that he had known his own father long enough to be able to experience the same transformation. It was a long walk, providing much time to reflect.

Filippo's thoughts led him back to the pestilence that had swept through the convent and then drifted away by early winter. This was when his training as a painter had begun. That spring, Fra Arrigo d'Arrigo had arrived from Germany to replace Fra Paulo as their permanent teacher. In his native land, he had also been trained as a painter, although he was not particularly gifted in this work. One day he stood behind Filippo watching him draw. Filippo was so absorbed in his work that he did not notice. While the other students held their breath, Fra Arrigo waited. He was a patient man.

Filippo, sensing the silence, looked up. This was it, he thought. He would be banished from the classroom and made to dig in the earth with a shovel.

Fra Arrigo towered over Filippo, who now bit his lip to keep it from trembling. A moment of silence passed that seemed an eternity, and then Fra Arrigo pointed to the drawing of himself. Filippo winced and readied himself for the swat across the head.

Taller than any other man who stood beside him, Fra Arrigo possessed an elongated head, an odd feature that appeared, even on a man so tall, to be twice a head's normal size, and it was bald as a bottom. Filippo had deftly rendered this characteristic. "This drawing, in particular"—Fra Arrigo pointed to the portrait of himself—"is an almost perfect likeness." Filippo froze. "However, the nose is a bit too short, do you not think?" he asked. A smile played around the corners of his mouth. "Pay attention, Filippo, yes?" And he had moved on, continuing with his lecture. Filippo let out a sigh of relief.

Not long after, Fra Arrigo requested permission to have Filippo help him with minor art projects at the Carmine, like the painting of an old wooden cross from which the original paint had worn away. He was the first person to call Filippo's pictures not "little scribblings" but drawings. When the friars visited faraway convents, Fra Arrigo took Filippo to see the works of art in other cities. He taught Filippo, who was voracious to learn, how to look at paintings and sculpture. It was Fra Arrigo who saw the beginnings of some talent in his little scratchings.

Fra Arrigo taught Filippo about the illumination of manuscripts. The first day of his instruction, Fra Arrigo unfolded a laudario before him, one of those used by the Confraternity of Sant' Agnese. Apart from providing service to the community and staging the illustrious Ascension play, its members sang lauds in praise of the Virgin Mary once each week in the Brancacci Chapel of the Carmine. The illuminator of the laudarios, Pacino di Bonaguida, who created them in 1340, nearly one hundred years before Filippo sat together with Fra Arrigo to study them, had departed from the accepted way of illuminating.

Rather than set the scene within the first letter of script, Bonaguida had created diptychs that scanned two pages when the laudario was opened, each narrative unfolding from left to right. Bonaguida, Fra Arrigo told him, had left monastic life in order to further pursue his work. Filippo spent hours each day examining and copying the placement of figures, the use of architectural detail to frame a scene, a landscape within which to place it, the means of moving the viewer's eye from one scene to the next.

Finally, one day, Fra Arrigo told Filippo that he was ready to practice the application of pigment and gold to parchment. But, first, he would teach him how to make his own pigments from nature because, he said, it was important to intimately know one's materials before using them.

Filippo learned how to make vermillion by placing mercury and sulfur in a fluted jar sealed with clay, how to heat it above a flame until it began to emit a blue vapor, finally bursting with the sound of "two uniting."

When he told Filippo what the sound was called, Fra Arrigo gave him a sidelong glance. Filippo blushed since, indeed, he understood the sexual connotation of the term. Although exposure to the outside world was limited, the vernacular of the streets made its way inside the walls, and boys have a way of finding the answers they seek.

Fra Arrigo taught Filippo how to make charcoal black from grapevine twigs, how to boil the color from cabbage, elderberry, leek greens and, even, as he had learned in his native Germany, from rhubarb, a secret, he said, not known in Italy. A beautiful rose pigment could be had from boiling shavings of brazilwood in lye, then soaking them in hot lye. To achieve a more translucent color, this pigment could then be mixed with powdered alum. But, although brazilwood produced crimson lakes, as they were called, it was impermanent and only used for underlayers, along with the less expensive madder lakes, which were a less appealing red weakened with a yellowish tint. Kermes, extracted from the insect found on scarlet oaks, provided a dark mysterious hue resembling blood, but was too expensive to purchase. It could occasionally be had if one chanced to obtain a piece of silk dyed with the color, which was easily extracted through boiling. Pigments were then mixed with egg yolks for binding.

Filippo loved the process of grinding pigments as much as the colors they produced. He did not mind that it took an entire day or more of grinding for the pigment to reach the desired saturation. It gave him time to watch the movement of the sun's light across the room, the casting of shadows, time to study the way light and shadow changed forms, enlivened or deepened colors.

He learned to apply pigment to parchment, darkening vermillion with brown, making it lighter with orpiment, known as King's yellow. He mixed vermillion with white lead to make rose and darkened it with more vermillion. Terre verte, or green earth, was used for the underpainting of flesh and, ultramarine being too expensive, he used azurite to make cool flesh tones.

There was the use of gold leaf, which necessitated a precise placement on the page and, after drying, the removal of excess with a soft brush. It was applied sparingly because of its cost and was so fragile as to require great skill in its use. Gold leaf had a subtle ability to bring a painting to life. This was not the world of ideas, invisible to the eye. It was the careful crafting, the building up, step by step, of the tangible.

Fra Arrigo continued where Fra Paulo had left off, but with more success. Filippo learned to read and write under his tutelage, although his words were often misspelled. He also learned a smattering of Latin.

The year that Filippo turned fifteen, two years earlier than was customary, at the instigation of Mona Lapaccia as she lay ill and dying, he was ordained. He knew that, unlike his brother, he was not meant for this life. Although he believed in God, and that belief was important to him, he had a difficult time accepting all that happened as God's will. Deep in his heart, he searched but could not find certainty. He lacked faith. At the same time that he was bound, not of his own will, to God's service, he was set free to leave the convent for four hours each day to apprentice with Neri di Bicci, whose bottega was in the Oltrarno district, on the same side of the Arno as the Carmine. It was Fra Arrigo who made this possible because he, himself, was on his way to Pistoia to serve as prior for one year.

Filippo made his way each day to the bottega of Bicci di Lorenzo and Neri, father and son. It was not a true apprenticeship, during which he would have spent the entire day, seven days a week, for several years studying with a maestro. Fra Arrigo had only been able to convince the prior to release Filippo for a few hours each afternoon.

Filippo was accompanied to and from the bottega by Fra Bernardo who, with his long strides, often left the boy far behind. It was not only the older man's length of limb, however, that left Filippo lagging, but his own interest in all that he saw around him. Often, he was roused by the scolding tone of Fra Bernardo's voice. "Filippo! Come along. It is indecent to stare at a lady."

Filippo was never aware of how long he studied a face. "I commit it to memory so that I may later sketch it," he explained.

"You will get yourself arrested, or worse," Fra Bernardo warned. "A brother will not be so understanding. Nor a husband."

Filippo could not help himself. An interesting face, or a beautiful one, were all the same to him. He was capable in a short time of tracing a visage in his mind, of committing it to memory so that he could reproduce it faithfully the next time he put charcoal to paper. Exactitude was essential.

In Maestro Bicci's bottega, Filippo was placed under the tutelage of Neri, the son. He first learned how to prepare a panel. The maestro took him along to the lumberyard, teaching him how to choose the best poplar, which they stacked and carried back to the bottega. Filippo learned to glue the pieces together vertically, to buttress them with crossbeams behind to further protect against warping, and then to sand them smooth, making sure afterward to brush away every speck of dust. He loved the sweet smell of the wood, alive with purpose, loved the feel of it beneath his palm after it had been sanded to a smooth, even finish. He then brushed it with gesso, creating a blank white ground for the work. Filippo thrilled to the endless possibility offered up by the blank white space.

Filippo next learned how to mix the paints by first grinding pigment to a fine powder, a chore with which he was familiar, then mixing it together with water on a marble slab until it gained the consistency of a fine paste. The most important responsibility of the job was in the measure. He had once made a quantity that was not enough for the day's work. This was not as bad as making too much and wasting the precious material, but he had been embarrassed by his mistake.

Now, Filippo transferred a portion of the paste into one of three oyster shells used to hold the finished product. He added titanium white to create the tint. Then he cracked an egg open over a bowl, allowing the clear liquid to drain. He placed the yellow center on a piece of blotter paper and gently rolled it from one end to the other to relieve it of any excess liquid that yet clung to it. He carefully held it above the shell and pierced its casing with a pin. The yellow liquid ran into the shell of paint. Filippo added an equal amount of water and stirred. In the second shell, he added black to make shade and followed the same process. In the final shell, he added both white and black to create the middle tone.

When Filippo had placed the three shells beside the panel, the maestro strode over, brush in hand, and peered into the shells. He then picked one up, looked at the panel, and back into the shell, where he swirled the paint. "Well done," he said, handing the brush to Filippo, who swelled with pride. It had not been easy to learn how to create the correct amount of paint, but he was confused by the maestro's gesture, and awkwardly stood holding the brush.

Seeing his hesitation, Maestro Bicci explained, "You will paint the mountains in the background." Filippo felt a rush of fear and excitement. His teacher instructed, "Begin with the underpainting. Work from those farthest away forward to those closest. I will check your progress."

It was during this time that a young painter by the name of Masaccio was at work depicting the consecration of the Carmine above the doorway that led from the cloister into the church. Every day, when Filippo returned from Maestro Bicci's bottega, he stood below it and studied that day's work. New people would have appeared in the crowd since morning, flowing outward from the central scene. Masaccio was depicting all of the prominent citizens of Florence who had attended the consecration, as well as the Carmelite monks. This depiction of real people had never before been done. Filippo was anxious to try his own hand at such work.

One day, Bicci di Lorenzo, the father, took Filippo to the small nondescript church of San Pancrazio, where he had been commissioned to paint a panel for one of the side chapels. At the same time, Fra Lorenzo Monaco was at work in the same church, commissioned by the Petrucci family to paint an altarpiece. Bicci di Lorenzo allowed Filippo, for the first time, to paint the details on the architecture in the background of the panel.

Maestro Monaco stopped by at the bottega and watched as Filippo worked. His own apprentice had been home in bed with an illness for two days. "He is not bad, Bicci," Monaco said. "Do you mind if I borrow him for a few days while my Francesco convalesces?"

"This is an honour," his teacher whispered in Filippo's ear as he followed Monaco to his own bottega.

Below Maestro Monaco's altarpiece, one section of the predella was to portray the story of San Benedetto receiving food from San Romano. The maestro instructed Filippo on the painting of groves of trees in the background of the predella, on how to reveal the sun's rays shining upon the leaves. When Filippo had completed this work, Fra Monaco was pleased and further instructed him on the painting of rocky cliffs in the foreground.

His next great opportunity arrived in the spring of the following year. Two of the greatest painters in all of Florence, Masolino and the young Masaccio, were commissioned by the Brancacci family to create a fresco series in the family's chapel at the Carmine.

Although his name was Tommaso, he was called Masaccio because he was big and messy, not caring that paint stained his clothing and formed permanent rings beneath his fingernails, or that it could also be found smudged on his face and streaked through his hair and beard. Filippo had first met him while studying with Neri di Bicci, for Masaccio had also apprenticed there and visited on occasion. He had come to Florence from his native Arizzo to join his brother, who was also an apprentice in Bicci's bottega. Masaccio, unlike his brother, soon left, having learned all he could of the maestro and, in fact, having far surpassed him in accomplishment. Masaccio joined the painter's guild in the year of Our Lord 1422 and soon proved to be a great maestro.

Filippo was on friendly terms with Masaccio's younger brother, who was called Scheggia, or "splinter" since he was as thin as his brother was large. Scheggia was kind and well-meaning but possessed inferior skill as an artist to that of his brother. It was from him that Filippo learned about their childhood. Scheggia and Masaccio had also lost their father. In 1406, the year of Filippo's birth, their father had passed into the great sea. Masaccio had been five years old at the time. Filippo was four when he lost his own father. Although Filippo had met Masaccio only in passing and they had never exchanged many words, he felt a kind of kinship with him.

Broad shouldered and muscular, Masaccio was built more like a stone mason than a painter. His bold, sweeping gestures created powerful figures that possessed a tangible sense of movement. A viewer was swept into the action of his work, as if becoming a living part of the scene. Filippo drew feverishly in imitation, Masaccio and his work his inspiration. Masaccio was young, vibrant, and he painted with the same gusto with which he lived. Filippo recognized for the first time the living link between a man and his work.

The prior asked to see Filippo. "In Maestro Bicci's bottega, have you learned to prepare a wall for fresco?"

"Yes, Prior," Filippo said, bowing his head.

"Good. You will assist in the preparation of the walls in the Brancacci chapel. None other than Masolino and this newcomer, the young man named Masaccio—but, as we have seen, his work does not reflect his name, thank the Lord God above. Ha. The two have arrived to execute the commission. We will offer your services to do the necessary mundane chores."

These chores were more to Filippo's liking than those he had previously performed for the convent. "Thank you, Prior."

"You come along well, Maestro Bicci tells me," the prior continued. "Bene. Molto bene."

These days were some of the happiest of Filippo's life. The prior, seeing his zeal, soon allowed him to skip his chores in order to watch and draw after the maestros. There was much to learn from Maestro Masaccio, who worked at a frenetic pace, as if chasing images. He was unlike any other painter Filippo had ever watched. Astride the rickety scaffolding, his arm extended to its full length, his other hand pressed against the wall to steady himself, he would reach across to the wall opposite, the one Masolino worked on, in order to illustrate how the beggar's right leg bent at the knee, rested at an angle, how his crippled left foot twisted beneath him. He then painted the man's arm extending upward, beseeching, his hand open to receive San Pietro's miracle. Filippo was certain that Masaccio could balance on his head and paint a work that moved and gestured as if alive, all set in motion by the play of light and shadow.

Take pains and pleasure in constantly copying the best things which you can find done by the hand of great masters. You will find, if nature has granted you any imagination at all, that you will eventually acquire a style individual to yourself, and it cannot help being good; because your hand and your mind, being always accustomed to gather flowers, would ill know how to pluck thorns. Cennini

One day, Masaccio noticed Filippo, singling him out from among the boys drawing in a semicircle behind him. "Ah," he boomed, his voice echoing in the vaulted ceiling, "I see you have a passion for the work. The marks you make speak the truth of it. And your dedication. You remain every day well past the waning of the light, straining to see to the very end." From that point forward, when his day's work was done, Masaccio looked over Filippo's drawings and gave him instruction.

As Filippo toiled away one day, focused on the minutiae of the structure of a hand, Masaccio's voice boomed from behind him again. "It is not hands or feet, Filippo. It is the expression of the face, the gesture of the body, that are the voice of the soul."

"Here," he said another day, "not like this. See, how to draw like this you must be cramped." And he imitated for Filippo the body posture necessary for the making of his inferior little drawings, a result of all of his work on miniatures. "If you would have movement," he illustrated, "you must make sweeping gestures. Do not hold back, Filippo. Put your whole body into it, your soul. Push past your fears. Once past, you will see that there is nothing to fear."

When Masaccio was commissioned to paint an altarpiece for the Carmine in Pisa, he took Filippo and a handful of other apprentices along with him. "It is a massive work, twenty-four panels in all," he said. "I will need much help to bring it to completion."

Having little experience, Filippo did the scuttle work, the sweeping of floors, preparing of panels, mixing of paints, but he was also able to study the maestro as he worked and to draw after him. Then one day, when the work was nearly completed, Masaccio handed Filippo a panel. It was a tall, thin section to be placed at one outer side of the altarpiece. Filippo feared he had not prepared it well and blanched.

Masaccio smacked him heartily on the arm. "I wish for you to paint the sub-prior of this place. Your first work. Do not look so worried. I will help you."

Masaccio did help, and when Filippo was finished, stepping back to view the painting, he knew that he had created a good likeness of the sub-prior. There was something else as well, a light that suffused the figure, that seemed to emanate from his flesh.

Masaccio said, "There is something of your own in this. Do you see it?"

Filippo could see, his work placed alongside that of the other apprentices, a mere glimmer of something wholly his own.

"This," Masaccio was saying, "cannot be taught."

It was merely a figure, nothing more, but it was his figure. It had been done with much help, to be sure, but he, Filippo, had brought it to completion. He was given another panel of the same height and width to be placed on the opposite side of the altarpiece. On this he was to paint the prior of the Carmine in Pisa.

After returning from the trip to Pisa, Filippo began imitating Masaccio's stride and mannerisms, his way of phrasing sentences, as much as his technique and style. His brother Giovanni began teasing him, calling him "little Masaccio." When the maestro was called away to Rome on another commission, Filippo was devastated. The day the man was to leave, sensing Filippo's disappointment, he handed him a brush. "Here. While it is yet wet. Do not be afraid. You cannot ruin it. There is no mess you can make that I cannot fix. Be bold!"

Filippo tentatively dipped the brush in azure paint and brushed over a spot already painted by the maestro on the robe of Sant Pietro, a figure in the background kneeling and reaching toward a fish.

Watching him, Masaccio chided, "Like a little old lady," his laughter booming up to the rafters. "What is this?" He imitated Filippo's feeble attempts with a brush by tucking his elbows close into his sides and dabbing at the fresco with short, jerky stabs. This was the most instructive thing he could have done. It showed Filippo to himself, his timidity, his myopia, his circumspection.

"Try again," Masaccio demanded, and thrust another brush into Filippo's hand. "Choose a bolder color. Perhaps it will inspire you to be bold."

Filippo saturated the brush in a deep crimson paint and, with sweeping gestures, highlighted the folds in the garment of Jesus himself. When he stepped back, he was astonished at the result.

Again, Masaccio laughed. "You see, Filippo. It takes commitment and courage. Above all, an artist must have courage. Do not fight what is inside." And here he beat his breast with his fist. "Do not secret it away, Filippo. Allow it to burst forth. Never hesitate. Bring all you have to bear upon it. Bring the urgency of your soul. Big and broad, so that it soars."

Masaccio assured Filippo that he would be back. He had frescoes to finish. "Keep working," he said, cuffing the boy on the shoulder, "and by the time I return, perhaps I will use your help with the painting of the fresco." He laughed at Filippo's look of surprise.

"You will be a great painter one day, Filippo. This is what God has intended. Keep up the pace; do not slacken. Painting is like breathing. Remember, with every breath"—he breathed in and, as he breathed out, drew phantom strokes in the air— "breathe into your work, and it will live. Upon my return...." And out he swept through the door.

CHAPTER 23

The years of Our Lord 1428 – 1431, Florence, and Siena

One day, little more than two months later, Filippo sat in the Brancacci chapel, working on the rendering of drapery over the human body after Masaccio's style. His heard Masaccio's name uttered by someone in the main transverse. There was great urgency in the speaker's voice. He is here, Filippo thought, jumping up. As he rushed around the corner of the chapel to greet the maestro, his brother Giovanni nearly ran headlong into him.

"Filippo," Giovanni said, placing his hands firmly on his shoulders as if to steady him. There was a hush in the vaulted space, where the merest whisper echoed like thunder. "My brother"—Giovanni took Filippo by the arm—"sit."

Filippo sat down, fear seizing his heart. What could make the usual dancing light in Giovanni's eyes go out, sadden them so that Filippo noticed for the first time the deep creases of age that crept out from their corners?

"Masaccio," Giovanni began, again reaching out to touch Filippo's arm, hesitating.

"He is here?" Filippo asked, his hope fading.

"No, brother. Masaccio has…" Giovanni hesitated. "Masaccio, may God bless him, has passed into the great sea, may his soul rest in peace. In Rome. Word has just arrived."

Filippo could not speak. They sat together in silence. And then, he was seized quite suddenly with anger. "No!" His rage thundered into the rafters. Then, pleadingly, "It is not true."

Why would God take such a great man? At the age of twenty-seven? A painter such as Masaccio had not been seen in one hundred years or more, and he had only just begun his life's work. Filippo refused to believe that he would never again see his great hulking frame rush from one section of fresco to another, hear his booming voice.

"I will sit with you," he heard Giovanni say, seemingly from a great distance. It was as if a door of immense proportions had been slammed shut, and Filippo now sat in utter darkness.

After the news of Masaccio's death, there was a silence in the convent for many days, as if all of life had been sucked from the world along with him. The loss hit Filippo the hardest. He did not draw for weeks. He felt as if he had been kicked in the stomach, the breath knocked out of him. By the end of the month, he had fallen into a deep depression.

To move him out of this melancholic state, the prior, in concert with Fra Arrigo, decided that administrative duty would be best, necessitating as it would the interaction with parishioners. Fra Arrigo agreed to leave Siena at the end of November, freeing his position in that city as sub-prior. Filippo was to replace him, a job for which he was ill suited and a time that would prove to be trying for all involved.

When asked to provide counsel, Filippo was at a loss. What did he know of life, sheltered within four walls, praying—forever praying—and never knowing the love of a woman, the comfort of a family? He wanted to say, "Be happy with what you have, know its value, take great care with it." But they wanted more, always more.

People treated each other with a meanness that startled him;

they shouted the most callous of insults, the most injurious of rebukes, and then wondered why their relationships were not harmonious, why they were not happy. One woman called her husband "the ass of an ass," and then wondered why he did not desire her. A son called his father "an old fool unworthy of respect," and then wondered why his father did not visit him.

Filippo was not the most understanding of confessors, or the most demanding. A man said to him, "I stole from my supplier because my son was sick, and I was in need of money to pay the apothecary. My guilt gnaws at me. But if I tell this man that I cheated him, he will never trust me again."

Filippo could not say, "You must confess. God will only forgive you if you prostrate yourself before this man and ask his forgiveness." This might lead to a rupture of their business arrangement, to a loss of income, which would then result in his family's suffering, all from one mistake. Is God really so unkind? "Repay him," Filippo said, "with a generosity in kind now that you have no need of extra funds." But he could not stop himself from adding, "And, next time, do not be such a fennel-head. Tell him your circumstance, strike a deal beforehand, and guilt will not be laid a perfect pathway to your door."

It was so much easier to paint.

The prior told Filippo that he lacked patience, that he should pray to God for patience. He tried, but God did not answer his prayers—or perhaps could not hear them, for all the infernal complaints he was pestered with each day. Finally, in August of the following year, by which time it had become apparent that the plan was not working, he was called back to Florence.

In the meantime, his brother Giovanni had spoken to the prior about him. "Fra Filippo," he told him, "does not recover from Masaccio's death."

"It is a blow," agreed the prior. "Orphaned so young, and now this. I have come to believe that he is not meant to be a man of the cloth." Giovanni stifled a smile. "Your aunt," the prior continued, "who brought him here, sought only to rid herself of her responsibility toward him. She was, well, she was not the most generous of women, may her soul rest in peace. We will release him."

Giovanni had not expected this decision, and he was concerned that Filippo was not ready. "Prior, may I suggest?" He hesitated.

"What bothers you, my son?"

"Might we wait? He needs time...and God's help. Perhaps a fresco of his own."

"We will pray for him. And we will give him the time he needs. And yes, why not? A fresco."

Not long after Filippo's returned to Florence, on the day marking a year since Masaccio's death, shortly after terce, he sat alone in a wooded area outside the city walls. Behind him the sun's rays were high enough to penetrate the thick foliage of oak and pine so that spots of light and shadow danced on the forest floor with the swaying of the leaves. Filippo was downcast, his mind wandering, when suddenly his eye fell upon a small opening of amber light. It was visible through the dark center of a cypress, shining through a space in the structure of the tree where no needles grew, a dead space of gnarled branches, the sparse remains of matter long dead and decayed. Yet, all around, his eye took in the light through other trees that fell across leaves, yellow and yellow green. This deepening of light at the tree's dead center, this amber presence, opened a space inside of Filippo to answer it, and Masaccio's words flooded back. "You will be a great painter some day.... Push past your fears.... Breathe into your work and it will live."

Something shifted inside of Filippo. Afterwards, he dove into his work with renewed energy. All in Florence began to call him "little Masaccio," saying that the soul of the maestro had entered into Filippo's body. In fact, his gait and his gestures, more sweeping, a newfound volume and confidence in his voice, all echoed the character of his former maestro. It was as if something had opened inside of him, some part of himself, hidden until now, flooded with light. Filippo did feel as if Masaccio had left a part of himself behind, not so much to inhabit Filippo as to guide him. If Masaccio were not to be granted more life, then Filippo would not waste his own.

You, therefore, who with lofty spirit are fired with this ambition, and are about to enter the profession, begin by decking yourselves with this attire: Enthusiasm, Reverence, Obedience, and Constancy. Ceninni

Filippo labored on until he had mastered the human form in motion, the illusion called perspective, the making visible of emotion on faces, and the intricacies of composition. One day the prior called him to his office and asked that he paint a fresco commemorating the confirmation of the Carmelite Rule, when the order moved west. He was to paint the Mount in Jerusalem to pay tribute to the order's origins in the Holy Land and the final mitigation in Rome. It was to be executed in the cloister adjacent to the fresco depicting the consecration of the order that had been completed by Masaccio.

The placement of the fresco was not an idle choice. The prior was hoping to help Filippo reconcile his grief over the loss of his mentor with the creation of his own first major project in close proximity to the Sagra that Masaccio had created above the doorway. Filippo paid much attention to the composition of the narrative. He created a scene in which monks were employed in various occupations and meditation throughout the landscape surrounding the Mount. In the center of the composition, all eyes were raised as the prophet Elijah, from whom the Carmelite order had been born, rose in a fiery chariot to heaven. As the narrative continued, some members of the order could be seen journeying west where, now in Rome, they took their place among the mendicant orders.

Filippo worked slowly, methodically, losing all sense of time. The friars recognized themselves in the fresco. He placed his own brother Giovanni in the center of the scene on the Mount. Sitting on a rock, surrounded by activity, his languid eyes met those of the viewer, his smile contented, as if he had nothing to do but whistle with the birds.

When he had finished the fresco, Filippo was well pleased. But, the following morning, as he approached it, his heart sank. His eyes fell upon two thin red lines, the rooftops of buildings. They were set at opposing angles, which, although technically correct, surrounded as they were by mud-colored buildings and drab desert landscape, jutted up against each other like two red javelins about to be entangled in a joust. Filippo's eyes were drawn back to them again and again. From a distance, he continued to study his work. The grouping of figures seemed natural, the faces clearly those of friars who now resided in the convent, but then his eye rested on the figure of Fra Angelo. The monk's head was silhouetted in a black rectangle that represented a window in a building behind him. This juxtaposition made his head stand out in an unnatural, awkward, and static way. Filippo's stomach turned with anguish, his face burned with embarrassment, when a voice behind him said, "Not bad for a first fresco."

Lost in contemplation, he had not heard Fra Arrigo's footsteps as he approached. Filippo said, "There are mistakes."

"Ah, my son." Fra Arrigo clapped him on the shoulder. "If it were perfect, it would not be art. Art and life."

"It is flawed," Filippo admitted, as much to himself as to Fra Arrigo. "Masaccio taught me. You taught me. I have failed you both."

"You have grown as a painter and will continue to grow," Fra Arrigo assured him. "I, perhaps, taught you too well to be a miniaturist. Masaccio had too short a time, may his soul rest in peace, to expand your view. Close up to this work, Filippo, one sees its careful execution, its detail, its truth. But it is no miniature. Quite the opposite, eh? When working tall, you must remember to step back, to view the whole. As in life."

Filippo nodded, taking in Fra Arrigo's words, which were always wise.

"We are proud of you, Filippo," he continued, "proud of your work."

Fra Arrigo was always able to make Filippo feel better. His encouragement was something he could count on and for which he felt deep gratitude. But he could not shake his disappointment. "I am no Masaccio," he said.

"No, you are not," Fra Arrigo agreed, and Filippo's heart sank even further. "Nor will you ever be." He inwardly flagellated himself. "You must," Fra Arrigo continued, "find who you are," and here he tapped Filippo's breast with his forefinger. "In here. It will be different from Masaccio, but it will possess the seed of a talent as brilliant, as all-encompassing, and it will be yours alone."

Filippo felt hope rise in him again. Fra Arrigo explained, "We teach you technique, my son. To break free from mere exactitude takes a leap of faith, to travel to the place where miracles are born, to dip your brush into that mysterious well."

In his mind, Filippo pictured the well outside, the one in the center of the courtyard into which he had so often dipped the bucket, down into its inky depths in order to haul up clear water. He imagined the paint he might find there. He wanted to learn how to render the soul. He wanted to journey into the depths, the darkness with which he was so familiar, in order to reemerge with luminous images, dripping with color and light.

CHAPTER 24

The year of Our Lord 1431: remembering Florence, and Genoa

The fresco completed, the prior called Filippo to his office once again. Filippo thought perhaps there was some small job he wished him to perform but hoped for another substantial project.

"Filippo," the prior said with a kindly smile, "I have called you here today to tell you that I have entered you in the annals of the Carmine as 'Fra Filippo Lippi, painter.'"

Filippo was astonished. "This is a great honor, Prior. Thank you." He bowed his head. "I will work hard to prove worthy of it."

"You have labored long and hard, Filippo, and you have earned this distinction. Masaccio himself told me that you possess a rare talent."

Filippo was taken by surprise. Masaccio had spoken of him to the prior? Had believed him to possess talent? With trouble, he drew his attention back to the prior, who was talking about this talent of his.

"Filippo, not all are called by God to be men of the cloth. I believe He has placed you on this Earth to make great works in honor of His glory." The prior hesitated. "I know," he continued, "that you are not happy here. You were brought to us by your aunt because she no longer wanted to care for you. Before she died, may her soul rest in peace, she forced one last injustice on you, the taking of vows too early and without your consent. She went above me," he confided, "or I would not have allowed it. Filippo, you are not meant for this life. You must go out into the world, even as Masaccio did, whose work you continue, in order to paint as no one has painted before you."

"But," Filippo began to protest, fear rising in him. He had rarely ventured outside of Florence—in fact, rarely outside the convent walls.

"You will bring great honor to Santa Maria del Carmine, to the Carmelite order," the prior assured him. "I have an old and dear friend, a good man, Fra Matteo. He is rector of Santa Margherita d'Aantiocho, in a village called Vernazza on the Ligurian coast. If you should visit him upon your travels, please send him my greetings."

It was a boat, this information, provided to Filippo as he was about to enter a vast, unknown sea, as if the prior had guessed his fear. Should Filippo find himself frightened and alone, he had only to make his way to this village by the sea, and there he would be warmly welcomed. At this, the anticipation of travel began to drive his fear away. "Prior"—Filippo knelt before him—"thank you."

"You will always be welcome here, my son," the prior said. "But you must go out into the world to study and to witness the great works being done by others. God be with you." Filippo bowed his head to receive the prior's blessing. He was free to leave.

Before he did, Fra Arrigo told Filippo that he must stop at Maestro Bicci's workshop to say good-bye. Early the following morning, just after prime, he set out. Instead of leaving through the front doors and across the piazza, Filippo found himself tracing the steps of his youth, through the dirt yard on the south side of the Carmine. Here was the play area where he and Poultray had many times kicked a ball back and forth. At this early hour, it was deserted, and in the quiet, he could hear the crunching of stones beneath his feet. He looked up at his father's house. Greenery cascaded over the stucco walls from the rooftop garden. Below was the high wall that enclosed his father's back garden, the rear of it bordering on the Carmine. The bench where he had often sat with Giovanni was still there. Antonio, his aunt's gardener, had long since passed into the great sea. Even his aunt was many years gone now. Filippo turned the corner and stood for a moment in front of the house. Cousins from his father's side now lived there. The green shutters were thrown open. He heard women's voices and the clatter of activity coming from the kitchen.

He continued under the archway, following the same path to the end of Via D'Ardaglione that he had taken on that fateful day years ago, when the urge to explore the other side of the Arno had gotten the better of him. At the end of the street, he turned right toward the market. When he reached the corner, at the tabernacle of the Virgin and Child, he blessed himself before continuing. In the mercato, venders were beginning to set up their wares.

When he reached Bicci's workshop, he was welcomed with hugs and slaps on the back. They gave him a gift of some sable brushes, charcoal sticks, and sheets of valuable paper to take with him on his journey. After bidding everyone farewell, Filippo felt the urge to retrace the steps that he and Giuseppe had taken. His duties as a friar being over, he was in no hurry.

Standing beneath the high tower in the Piazza Signoria, he smiled, remembering the look of horror on Giuseppe's face when he had told him that prisoners were thrown from its top to the ground below. He had not known if this was true, but it seemed a good story at the time. Filippo had heard that Giuseppe, along with two brothers and a sister, had perished in the pestilence that had also taken his friend Poultray.

Filippo continued on to the duomo, still awaiting its dome, and finally to Or San Michele. He now knew that long ago it had been a grain market. When a painting of Mary that hung on a wall there performed a miracle, a church was built around it. Surplus grain was still stored in the rooms above. He had been right on that day long ago. It was grain that they had seen drifting in the sunlight.

Statues had been added since he was a boy and, although some niches remained empty, most had been filled. Filippo walked around the building, saving the best for last, Donatello's San Giorgio. In what had been an empty niche on that day long ago, there now stood the imposing figure of the soldier saint, dressed in armor, holding a shield before him. His left foot strode forward and his right hand clenched his sword as if he could hold back no longer, was ready to step any moment off the platform, raise his sword, and with dispassionate gaze lay waste to the dragon, the embodiment of evil, perhaps to challenge Filippo himself and every evil that lurked inside his own heart. This sculptor Donatello was a maestro beyond compare.

Before crossing back over the Arno, Filippo turned to take one last look at his city. As a boy, a truant, he had on this very spot promised himself to one day live and work this side of the river. The following day, his hopes had been crushed. In the years that followed, many people had passed into the great sea, and yet here he was. God had blessed him, and now he was released from the convent. He would return one day when he was a maestro to live and work here, where day after day all was made new.

We settled down to rest, facing the east, where we had begun our climb, for often it pleases us to see how far we've come. Dante

The hardest of all farewells was that with Giovanni. But his brother's excitement for him eased their parting until he began to cluck over Filippo like a hen. "You will not have me there to take care of you, little brother, so please be cautious. Be careful in your choice of friends. And about what you eat. Avoid sausages, for they have a reputation for bringing on illness if not properly prepared."

"Giovanni, I am no longer a child as I was when I arrived. I appreciate your concern, but I am a man now."

"When did that happen?" Giovanni laughed. "Indeed, look at you. I will miss you, brother. Write to us."

"You know it is not my strength. My letters will be brief."

"Brief let them be, but let us hear from you."

"I will." They embraced, and then Giovanni tousled his hair as if he were a boy.

It was with a little fear and much excitement, a loaf of bread, and a sack of wine that Filippo left the convent. With the prior's farewell blessing, and only a few soldi that they could spare for him, he set off on a fine spring day, the first of May. Filippo had arrived with nothing, and he left with nothing. Although the prior had released him from his obligations to the order, he felt it wise to wear his friar's robes so that thieves, from afar, would surmise his state of poverty. Filippo headed west.

After walking through the gates, leaving Florence behind, and climbing into the hills, Filippo turned to watch as the mist slowly rose, like a curtain drawn back from the sun to reveal all of Florence spread out before him. He had never felt so free, as if the gentlest of breezes could lift him and, like a puff of smoke from a candle, he would float into the air. He was young and free to go wherever adventure called.

His final destination was Genoa, a bustling port filled with Tuscan artists but also with artists from the North. Fra Arrigo had traveled back to his home and had described their work. Filippo was anxious to see it for himself. Fra Arrigo said that it was so realistic one was tempted to reach out and smell a flower to prove that it was fashioned from pigment and not by God, to pick up a grape and eat it, to smooth a piece of velvet. There was so much to learn. By journey's end, he would be ready to accept his own commissions.

In Siena, Filippo went first to see the baptismal font. He copied Ghiberti's carvings, the human form in motion, the dance of life. In Donatello, he studied the depth of space that the sculptor had achieved by varying his carving from a full rounded volume to lines so shallow as to appear to be drawn rather than carved. Filippo marveled at the man's depiction of the feast of Herod. These were real people engaged in real activities. This was what Filippo wanted to achieve with paint.

While in Genoa Filippo's newly won freedom became intoxicating. Engrossed in work, he quickly lost track of the canonical hours until he was sleeping through matins and prime, working through terce and sext, taking a break to eat, working again through nones, and drinking with friends through vespers. At first it bothered him to realize that this link had been broken, and he made a sincere attempt to remember. Failing this, he gave up, instead saying prayers each night before he slept and each morning upon waking, offering up his work as his most heartfelt prayer.

He drank overly much in the company of his fellow artists, and his eye was now liberated to drink its fill of women as well. One night, he and his companions, weaving and singing through the streets, made their way to the candlemaker's shop, above which was an establishment of prostitution.

Filippo stood in the center of the bedchamber while Lunetta, her back to him, untied her camicia. As it fell past her shoulders, he was drawn to the soft curve of her exposed neck. It was a musical note in perfect pitch, traced by the light falling through the shutters. Before she could turn, he surprised her with a kiss at the nape of her neck. She startled at his unexpected touch, which roused him. As she arched her back, he pressed his body into her. He kissed her plump, round shoulder and nuzzled his face into that most tender of curves, her neck, wishing to get lost in her.

Afterwards, a state of calm descended upon him, a sense of peace and forgetfulness. He felt larger than himself, expansive, as if spread out over the countryside. When this feeling subsided, he became aware that he was still lying atop her and that his weight might be crushing her. He rolled off. Lunetta covered herself discreetly with the sheet, an unexpectedly chaste gesture.

Filippo felt ashamed to realize that he did not know her; in fact, she could have been anyone. She, as a person, was not integral to his experience. Unparalleled, overwhelming as it was, it was his alone, and she, a mere vehicle. The next time he visited, he brought her a vial of lavender essence, and thereafter took to bringing her small gifts without fail.

Once when he visited, Filippo was told Lunetta was busy but that he could have another. He was startled, and then horrified. He had grown fond of her. He never knew if that was her real name, for although he confided much to her, she refused to speak about her life outside the walls of the room where they met, or of what her life had been before. She was of large heft, with a comely face, the most beautiful feature of which were her deep brown eyes, which spoke of her warm nature.

She most loved salted almonds, a delicacy, and an embroidered purse he had brought her but, apart from these preferences, she remained an enigma. She taught Filippo much about bringing a woman pleasure, and the physical joy he brought to her increased his own. He gained, most of all, a state of peace, and wished he could give her the same. Years later, he would think of her when with the prostitutes of Florence, who kept strictly to the more traditional code of conduct, no pleasure for the provider of services.

CHAPTER 25

The year of Our Lord 1429, Florence

This was the day Cosimo had dreaded. His father lay dying. Giovanni's skin had grown pale and mottled, his breathing shallow. Cosimo's mother sat beside the bed, her hand draped over that of her husband.

Cosimo and Lorenzo had been called to their father's bedside so that he might share some parting words. Given Giovanni's state, Cosimo was surprised at the clarity of his thoughts, spoken in little more than a whisper so that his sons had to lean in close to hear.

Giovanni began by reminding them that envy was a weed in one's garden that should never be watered. He said, "I am proud of you, my sons."

Cosimo choked back tears.

Giovanni's voice now strengthened. "Avoid political controversy. Do not show pride when many votes are cast your way. Remember Cicero, 'The more we excel, the more humbly we should behave.' Always be careful in your speech. Go to the Palazzo della Signoria only when called upon, and then do whatever it is that is asked of you. You are a servant of the Republic. Never forget that. Never go against the people's will unless you are certain that they are gravely mistaken. Be kind to all men, no matter their station. Do not give offense to those who are wealthy and strong. Be kind to the downtrodden. Be charitable so as to relieve some of the misery of those who are poor. Most importantly, in all that you do, increase commerce and promote peace for the sake of Florence. In this way, you will bring honor to your city and to your family."

He closed his eyes, weary with the effort. When he opened them again, they rested on his wife. "Picarda," he said, drawing out the saying of her name as if tasting it. His eyelids slowly slid closed, and he rested once again. His wife spread her arms across his body and buried her head in his chest.

Tears clouding his vision, Cosimo turned to leave. Behind him sat a scribe who had been recording his father's words. It is a great man, indeed, Cosimo thought, whose every word is cherished to the last.

He was forty-two, no longer a young man. He was a father himself. Not many were fortunate to have had such a wise man for a father, and fewer yet to have had a father for so long. Knowing this did not diminish his grief. The world would seem an empty place without his father in it.

There was no one else upon whom Cosimo could rely so completely. His father's good judgment had been steady, his discernment subtle, his calculations true. Now Cosimo was on his own. Had he been a good enough student? Had he learned all he would need to know?

Anything that is granted to a man who is good and grateful bears fruit both in him, and also in others. Cicero

CHAPTER 26

The year of Our Lord 1433, Padua

Filippo's journey to Padua was coming to an end. He had been through much, had questioned life itself, and yet here he was walking toward Padua. All of the experiences that had left their mark, etched themselves into his being, he captured in his work, not as they had felt at their inception, but later, after they had become part of the whole, had been sculpted into who he was. In the end, there was beauty. He had consumed images, woven them into his memories until he had expanded into a sea of patterns. Perhaps it was the seed of light within that had served as his North Star. Perhaps there was a marteloio of the soul.

Filippo had set out before dawn, hoping to reach his destination by the end of the day. As he rounded a corner, whistling, a new habit of his, a clearing between trees revealed a landscape flooded with early morning light. He stopped to take it in. Banks of undulating green hills rolled away before him, and then rose in gentle waves to the topmost peaks. Coarsely ground malachite, he thought, the only pigment to capture the depth and brilliance of this land. The sun shone with singular grace, in concert with the landscape, as if with the sole purpose of revealing its vital shade of emerald, its gentle flow of shapes, its swatches of cultivated land, incised squares checkered along the waves of its slopes. He had reached the Euganean Hills.

It was late in the day when Filippo arrived in Padua. He crossed the Bacchiglione River, which surrounded the city like a moat, passing along a wooden bridge and through one of the gates cut into the stone wall. He made his way first to Sant' Antonio to give thanks for his safe passage. Since it was past the hour of nones, Filippo continued on, walking north and exiting through another gate, to reach the Scoletta del Carmine. This building housed members of the brotherhood. Having been a Carmelite friar, he would be welcomed, although this was a lay confraternity only that was affiliated with the Carmelite order.

From the Scoletta del Carmine it was an enjoyable walk to the city center. The Bacchiglione reminded Filippo of the Arno, with houses built along its banks. Apart from this similarity, however, Padua did not remind him of his hometown. Florence was a crowded city bustling with commerce. Padua was peaceful. In this place, solitude seemed to swell from the earth itself.

For two days, Filippo rested. Then, after a mid-day meal, with a letter of introduction from the confraternity, he visited the Scrovegni Chapel to see Giotto's masterpiece, the fresco cycle that Masaccio had so praised. As he approached, the plain façade of the humble chapel burned with a pale rose glow, its brick soaked in the now-lengthening light of day that swept low across the land. The chapel, small and plain, was bordered on the south side by the ruins of an old Roman arena. It was attached at the north to the Scrovegni palazzo, which towered above it and sprawled out from its side, northward, in an imposing arc.

Well, Filippo thought, remembering the story of the Scrovegni, the son did not learn much from the father's demise. Reginaldo had been a wealthy banker with a reputation for corrupt business practices, so corrupt, in fact, that in his Inferno, Dante placed Reginaldo in the most wretched circle of hell. How much worse could it be than to be placed in a fictional hell by the legendary Dante? When the father died and the son, Enrico, built his palazzo, he thought it wise to add a chapel, thereby ensuring the release of his father's soul from hell, as well as his own perhaps, for Enrico was also a banker. It was obvious to Filippo that Enrico had spent much more on his own comfort than on this small and unassuming chapel.

Entertaining these thoughts and smiling to himself, he approached, enjoying the tranquil setting on the outskirts of the city. When Filippo stepped inside, he was overwhelmed. He could almost hear the voices of angels lifted to heaven, which surely resided just beyond the star- studded evening sky spread across the vault that arched above.

Three cycles of frescoes, from top to bottom, encircled the interior. Filippo walked once around the room, taking in the stories as they were intended to be experienced. Then he began a second, slower journey, studying each one with a painter's eye. Here was Joachim and Anna meeting at the golden gate to Jerusalem, knowing they will have a child. They are old and painfully childless, but they have separately been told by angels that Anna will conceive. They look lovingly into each other's eyes, their two heads and halos merging, two people becoming one. Anna's hand cradles the back of Joachim's head, her other hand caressing his face. His arms encircle her. There is a long-lived intimacy expressed in their gestures, in their gaze. This humanness was new when Giotto lived and worked, more than one hundred years earlier.

In the betrayal, the look in Jesus' eye as Judas kisses him is one of resolve and recognition. It is as if he is saying, "I knew it would be you." No surprise, no anger, only sorrow. Filippo stood longest before the lamentation, a masterpiece of design. Mary cradles her dead son on her lap as if he is again her baby. One hand rests on his shoulder, her other hand reaching out, as if to pull him back.

Gestures, Masaccio said, bring the viewer in, reveal emotion. Although Giotto's figures did not possess volume, and their faces did not appear to represent those of real people, Mary's brow is wrinkled, her mouth twisted in grief. She is a human mother who has lost her child. Sant' Giovanni leans forward and throws his arms back, helpless. Mary Magdalene gently holds Jesus' feet in her lap. Each person grieves alone, Filippo thought, each in a different way. Masaccio had taken this to even greater heights, but it began here, with Giotto. Filippo could not wait to share his discovery with his brother Giovanni. He would write to him that very night.

The waning of the light, making it more difficult to see, roused Filippo from his intense study. He reached out in order to lean up against the wall where he stood, expecting the smooth, cold feel of marble, but it was not stone that he touched. He peered more closely at it. The marble look of the wall had been frescoed onto the plaster. This demanded further study. He must learn how to make plaster look like marble.

Filippo left the Scrovegni Chapel with the decision to return the following day but in the early morning. He had not even had time to look at the Last Judgment, in which the giant blue devil sat eating sinners, and usurers hung from their bags of money. Enrico Scrovegni would have walked out of the chapel beneath this looming reminder of his potential fate. He had not done so badly, after all, Filippo thought. The chapel was like a person; it was difficult to imagine what existed inside of it.

"Fra Filippo Lippi," he told Squarcione, "of Santa Maria del Carmine, Florence." Although he was long accustomed to being a lay member of the community, Filippo felt that this introduction would serve to better explain his background. Squarcione was a tall man of solid build with graying hair and an easy, if gruff, manner. He smiled and clapped Filippo on the arm. "Welcome," he said.

Filippo quickly summarized his early training with Fra Arrigo, Neri di Bicci, Lorenzo Monaco, and Masaccio. He then spoke about his more recent work in Genoa. Finally, he confided in Squarcione his desire to see more of the work of Northern painters.

"Well, you have come to the right place," Squarcione assured him. "We have everything in Padua."

Filippo took in the room before him. It was large and empty of furniture except for a long wooden table that stretched the length of it, stools scattered along either side. Its top was littered with drawing implements, ink, brushes, and paper. Two young students sat at the table copying the plaster cast of an antique statue. The cast was carefully positioned on the tabletop so as to be bathed at an angle in direct sunlight entering through a side window. The plaster was similar in property and color to marble but brighter, with a sheen like that of alabaster. The sun caressed its volume and cast defined pools of shadow in the concave valleys of its form, throwing its elongated shadow onto the tabletop. Highlights and shadows were more discernable with no color to distract.

Filippo's gaze then swept across the walls, lined with two levels of shelves. The shelves contained more plaster casts, architectural fragments, and vases. His eyes rested on one shelf in particular. It held magnificent casts of antique statuary.

Squarcione followed Filippo's gaze. He pointed. "This shelf of statues I sent back from Greece, on a merchant ship through Venice."

Nailed to the walls were drawings of yet more antique statues in various poses, some containing two or three figures in concert. Filippo guessed that the drawings must have been done by Squarcione himself. The figures appeared stiff, like rock. Although the forms were adequately depicted, there was no movement, no life in them. Even the hair appeared to have been chiseled. No wind ruffles those curls, Filippo thought, smiling. And yet, he saw the value in making studies of the casts, in order to better understand anatomy.

Squarcione was chastising one of his students. "Where do you see this?" he asked, pointing to a section of the drawing, and then to the corresponding section of the statue. "What do you see? Draw only what you see." He pointed to his own eyes, opening them wide.

"You have an impressive collection," Filippo said. "I will give you ten soldi a week for space in which to work."

Squarcione smiled. It would have been generous of him, Filippo thought, to waive the fee since he was not a student but an accomplished painter, as well as a man of the cloth. In fact, Sqarcione was sure to learn much from him. He must be a stingy man at heart. Then he thought of his brother Giovanni. "Patience, Filippo," he heard him say. "Be generous of heart toward others." Perhaps Squarcione had come into his life to teach him generosity, even toward those who are miserly. Surveying the man, he intuited that it would not be an easy task.

CHAPTER 27

The year of Our Lord 1433, Florence

They climbed the circular stairway, making their way to the topmost cell of the tower. At regular intervals, a narrow rectangular opening provided a view of the city below. Each time they arrived at one that faced north, Cosimo stopped to catch his breath, resting his eyes on the duomo. Silently cursing Brunalescchi, he complained aloud, "There it is again, the duomo. The dome needs completion."

"You have already said so," his jailor reminded him.

"My thinking grows circular," Cosimo retorted. When the jailor laughed, Cosimo grew hopeful. Here was a man with a sense of humor, one who might prove open to friendship. "What is your name?"

"Federigo," his jailor answered, now stopping to catch his own breath. "Federigo Malavolti."

"Well, Federigo Malavolti, if we do not get to the top soon, you will have no need of throwing me off. I will have died from exhaustion."

This comment drew yet another laugh from his jailor. Yes, Federigo Malavolti could prove to be useful.

Earlier that day, Cosimo had been summoned to the Signoria. Making his way to the palazzo, he had stopped halfway across the piazza, his heart gripped by fear. This is where he would be hanged for all to see. A shiver passed through his body. They had it in for him, the current members of the Signoria, but they never would have done a thing while his mother lived, out of respect for her. She was gone barely five months and already they pounced. He knew they feared his power, but more than that, the fact that it derived from the popolo minuto. His enemies, the Albizzi, held a majority in the current Signoria, as well as power over the Gonfalonier, and would use it to advantage. They had, no doubt, brought trumped-up charges against him. If Cosimo's plans failed, if his enemies proved to be more powerful, if God did not grant him success but placed even one fateful turn of events in the hands of his enemies, all would be lost.

He took several deep breaths to steady himself. Thoughts of his father were what finally settled his nerves, bringing him back in touch with his Medici strength. It lay in the certainty that when all else failed, faith would sustain one. He sent up a prayer to God, to his own patron saint and that of the city. When he entered the building, instead of being led to the chamber where the Signoria met, the captain of the guard was now leading him to a cell. As he had suspected, they did not wish to consult with him. They wished to imprison him while they debated his fate.

The following morning, when Federigo entered his cell with his meal, Cosimo was standing at the window, looking out through the barred grate.

"How do you like your accommodations?" Federigo asked jovially.

Cosimo turned. "I have the best view in all of Florence."

"Ha. Indeed," Federigo agreed.

Cosimo turned back to look out once again. "The red-tiled rooftops stretch out, all the way to the Arno, which threads its way like a silver snake through the land. The wooded hills rise beyond. My city. There is no better in all the world."

Federigo placed a tray with bowl and cup on a stone bench covered with straw matting that stretched the length of the wall opposite the window. In the closet-sized room, it was the only furnishing. "Here is your meal, then. Let us hope you enjoy it as much as the view."

Cosimo did not turn from the window. "My sustenance lies without."

"Suit yourself," Federigo said. "One cannot chew with one's eyes."

When Federigo returned several hours later, Cosimo's meal was untouched, as was the next meal, and the one after that. He no longer stood at the window but, now grown weak, curled up in the corner of the stone bench.

"You must eat," Federigo coaxed. There was genuine concern in his voice. "You will starve. Why do you not eat?"

Cosimo met his eyes with a steady gaze but said nothing.

Federigo understood. "It is not poisoned," he assured Cosimo. "You have a few friends in the Signoria. They yet debate what to do with you."

Cosimo did not move. "Look," Federigo said, taking up the plate of food. "May I?" He indicated a desire to sit.

"It is your jail," Cosimo said.

Federigo sat and ate several spoonfuls of a thin brownish broth, tore off a piece of stale bread, and gulped down a mouthful of wine. "See?" He shrugged. "I am still alive."

He pushed the bowl toward Cosimo. "Well?" he asked when Cosimo still made no effort to pick it up.

Cosimo answered, "You are a big man. I will wait."

"Ha. Alright then," Federigo said, and smiling, he leaned back. "What shall we discuss?"

"It is your jail," Cosimo said again, settling back against the wall.

Federigo asked, "What is it that you admire so much about Florence? It is a city like any other."

"No," Cosimo said, "Florence is what we, the men of the city, make it. It is a Republic."

"Ah." Federigo nodded. "But it is what a few wealthy families make it, not all citizens."

"There is some truth in what you say," Cosimo admitted, "but the Signoria is made up of representatives from all walks of life. All citizens have a voice."

"But not of equal value. What of the Ciompi Revolt?" Federigo asked. "Why, after triumphing, after obtaining what was fair and just, did the working class not succeed in maintaining their majority rule? They are a majority of the populace."

"A member of my family," Cosimo said, "was a prior at the time. As you know, my family was sympathetic to the cause. Afterwards, however, there were far too many people in charge. They bickered over petty details, placed personal complaints and demands above all others. What was good for Florence, which must supersede all else, was forgotten. They were pigeons milling about in circles. Nothing was accomplished. No taxes collected. No structures built. The courts were stalled. The treasury empty. No decisions made. It was well we were not attacked while in this weakened state. We would have been overrun while the pigeon heads fought over whose cousin was to oversee the cleaning of the streets in his district. We would now be an occupied city, not a great one. Our freedom from foreign influence is our greatest treasure."

Federigo sat quietly contemplating Cosimo's explanation. "The trouble, then, was that there were too many men in charge, not that those who are wealthy are better rulers than those who are poor."

"If you saw some of the wealthy blockheads who rule, you would not pose this question. No. Several yards of crimson cloth is all it takes to make a new citizen."

"Do you think so?" Federico smiled. This man was unusual for one of his class.

"Shall I tell you a story?" Cosimo asked. "One day, the council was in session, a vote proceeding, when Chiari droned on and on. Eyes drooped. Lethargy descended. I looked to the man sitting between myself and Chiari. He was holding the box of cast votes. I pointed to it and signaled him to pass it along, hoping Chiari would see that the vote must proceed and stop his yammering. The imbecile hit Chiari in the head with the box. I said, 'Why did you do such a thing?' And do you know what he said? 'You told me to.' I explained that I meant for him to move the box along, the idiot, not accost a council member with it."

Federico laughed so that tears ran down his cheeks.

Cosimo continued, "And to think, he did not for a second question what would have been a ludicrous request. We could do with some new blood."

"Will you?" Federico asked, growing serious. "If you survive this trial, will you ensure that new families be added to the borse bag? Families from the popolo minuto?"

"I will," Cosimo promised.

From that day forward Cosimo and Federigo shared every meal. Federigo told Cosimo that Albizzi's son and his armed men guarded the piazza in order to prevent the popolo minuto from rising up in his defense. One morning when the bells of the palazzo, directly above his little cell, began their deep, sonorous tolling, he rushed to the small barred window. The crowds swelled onto the street below, but something was wrong. The Signoria, Cosimo knew, would be calling for a balia, a group of citizens to sanction decisions made by the Signoria in an emergency. The emergency this time was his fate. As he watched, he saw armed guards forcibly preventing the flow of citizens into the piazza. When all was over, the balia accomplished, Federigo told him that there had only been twenty-three citizens allowed into the piazza to vote. Albizzi could now do what he wished.

Cosimo could wait no longer. He and Federigo were becoming friends, so when he asked if he might receive visits from his confessor, Cosimo's old teacher and close friend Traversari, Federigo readily agreed to bring his petition to the Signoria.

As Federigo turned to leave, Cosimo said, "Tell them that Pope Eugenius will surely insist upon this small allowance." The fact that the pope was in residence in Florence added weight to this request.

The wise man sees ahead and has his course of action at the ready. Seneca

Cosimo and his brother, Lorenzo, had spent many nights in Traversari's cell at Santa Maria degli Angeli, deep in discussions of a philosophical nature. Traversari was a brilliant philosopher. He was also someone Cosimo could trust.

When Traversari arrived the following day, Cosimo turned to Federigo and humbly, bowing his head, requested, "May I have privacy in which to make my peace with God?"

Although the Signoria had ordered that Cosimo never be left alone in the cell with another person, Federigo had come to greatly respect the man and complied without question. As they heard his footsteps retreat down the stairway, Cosimo whispered, "Have you brought paper and pen as I requested?" Traversari dug inside his robes and pulled them out.

"We must be quick," Cosimo said, searching for a flat, level place to lay the paper. Finding none, he sat Traversari down and used his broad back as table. He speedily composed a letter to his brother, asking Lorenzo to begin a process of negotiation by offering Guadagni, the Gonfalonier, five hundred florins to bring the vote around to exile. Five years would suit. If Guadagni felt unable to accomplish this himself, he should, for the same amount of money, feign serious illness and step down from his position as Gonfalonier. This would allow the Medici to wrest some control in the form of the vote for his replacement.

"That should suffice for now," Cosimo said when he was finished. Traversari concealed both pen and paper, and the two began to pray in earnest just as they heard Federigo's footsteps returning up the stairway.

Cosimo felt greatly relieved. He had taken the first logical step toward securing his freedom, not by force or violence, but with the kind of action, an appeal to a man's greed, that might actually bring forth results.

CHAPTER 28

The year of Our Lord 1433, Padua

Filippo arrived early every morning at Squarcione's workshop. He soon discovered that the man had the habit of leaning over people as they worked. The scent of onion and garlic broke Filippo's concentration, pulling him quite suddenly from the study of light revealing form to the stark realization of where he was and what he was doing. Now, as he worked, the smell of stale onion assaulted his nose. He turned abruptly. "Are you in need of something?"

Startled, Squarcione jumped back. "No. No. I marvel at the ease and grace with which you render my little casts."

Flattery did not fool Filippo. He liked Squarcione, who was amiable enough, but he understood that he was paying the man for the privilege of teaching him. This rankled. Just as Filippo was about to explain that he was unable to work with someone peering over his shoulder, the door burst open.

"You are late," Squarcione admonished.

Out of breath from running, his student, Bartholomeo, disregarded the anger in his maestro's voice. "Florence is going crazy," he said, panting. "They have arrested Cosimo de' Medici. News races through the streets. They have charged him with treason!"

"Mother of God," Squarcione exclaimed, blessing himself.

"Will they?" Filippo exchanged a glance with Sqarcione, who tilted his head to one side and pulled upward on an imaginary rope with the other.

"They will hang a Medici? Impossible," Filippo concluded.

"For treason, yes," Squarcione assured him.

The Medici were one of the most powerful families in Florence. Like all Florentines, Filippo knew the name as well as he knew the names of the saints whose feast days were celebrated. Hanging was a cruel fate, reserved for the lowest of criminals. It was an insult. Filippo vowed to pray for the poor man.

Later that same day, as he worked, he again felt Sqarcione's breath on his neck. He swung around, angry words at the ready. Squarcione held out a piece of tracing paper to him. "I have received a commission," he said, "from the Podesta. Would you be so kind as to take a look at my design? I would be grateful beyond words."

Filippo grabbed the paper from his hand.

"What do you think?" Squarcione asked anxiously.

Filippo softened toward him. The drawing was adequate, but uninspired. "What are their requirements?"

He redesigned the panel, working within the specifications, but bringing innovation to the whole. Squarcione was so impressed that he asked him to work on the project with him. This was Filippo's first major commission.

Soon after the project was underway, he found that he would be doing most of the work. Squarcione often made excuses about having to attend to his pupils or some other urgent business. In spite of this, Squarcione took the largest share of the payments, doling out paltry sums to Filippo, as though he were a journeyman painting only the insignificant background areas and figures. Still, Filippo luxuriated in having full latitude to paint as he wished, and Squarcione took him along when he bought supplies, introducing him as a painter from Florence, which would hold weight in the future. In addition, Squarcione's students worked as apprentices on the project.

It was an invigorating walk each morning to the Palazzo del Podesta. As he traversed the piazza, Filippo thought about the letter he had recently sent off to Giovanni. It had begun as a tirade against Squarcione, but as he wrote he imagined his brother's uproarious laughter at the chronicled events. Squarcione did make for a good story. He smiled up at the sun that, beginning to ascend, draped the shoulders of shopkeepers who set up tables and stretched awnings above their wares. Filippo strode between pork butchers and chickens, ducks and eggs. He stopped to purchase a pear from a fruit vender before turning back to make his way through the gold and silver smiths, around the Palazzo della Ragione to enter the Piazza del' Erbe. Just as he was winding his way through the wine and vegetable stands, Bartholomeo ran past, almost knocking Filippo over in his haste. "Late again?" Filippo called after him, laughing.

Hearing Filippo's voice, Bartholomeo stopped and ran back to share his news. "Cosimo de' Medici is coming."

Filippo did not understand. Had this Medici not been arrested? "Is he not to be hanged?"

"He has been exiled," Bartholomeo explained, "to Padua."

Was this possible? An illustrious Florentine was to be living in quiet little Padua? "Well," Filippo said, "you have saved your hide once more. The only thing Maestro Squarcione values more than punctuality is a good piece of gossip. Off with you now."

More than a fortnight after news of Cosimo's exile had reached Padua, Cosimo de' Medici had still not arrived. He had decided, it was rumored, to stop in Ferrarra, where he was being lavishly entertained. The Paduans were on edge with anticipation. It seemed that only the Florentines were unaware of the man's distinction.

The virtuous man, calm in his orderly life, stares Fortune in the face, and drives proud Fate beneath his feet. Boethius

Filippo stopped every morning at the Podesta to stand beneath the place where his painting would reside, above the entryway on the interior of the building. He envisioned the completed work, studied the light, how it would fall, from what angle, with what intensity, making final decisions about the position of the figures, where a hand would rest, how a knee would turn, a head incline. When Filippo arrived at Squarcione's workshop, he lifted the curtain from the section of panel on which he worked, transposing all he had seen while he had stood staring at the empty wall.

As was his habit, Squarcione flitted from one student to the next, making himself busy, but Filippo knew that he had arrived early that morning to pour over the work Filippo had done the day before. As long as Squarcione did not stand behind him while he worked, he did not mind. Here was a man, he had discerned, who did not have the skill or the patience to duplicate what he saw.

Intent on his work, Filippo became vaguely aware of a commotion in the room but heard nothing more distinct than a cacophony of voices. Then, Sqarcione was yelling something in his ear. Filippo moved further away, down the tunnel of concentration, waving his hand as if to bat away a noisome fly.

Some time later, he stepped back to examine his work from a distance. The hush of his surroundings slowly crept into his consciousness. He looked around. Where had everyone gone? Just then, the door opened, and Squarcione, followed by his students, poured in, all talking at once.

"You missed it," Squarcione said. "Filippo, you should have seen. The crowd of dignitaries on horseback, dressed in their finest wools and silks, lined up just inside the gate, followed by distinguished university professors along each side of the road. Then all of the mendicant orders. Crowds gathered beyond. The whole city was there." He paused. "But for you."

"Where?" Filippo asked, distracted by a shadow on Sant' Antonio's face that needed fixing.

"Did you not hear me?" Squarcione asked. Receiving no answer, he said, "To greet Cosimo de' Medici." This news grabbed

Filippo's attention. "He wears robes of the finest wool, expertly tailored." Squarcione held up his hand, rubbing the tip of his thumb against his middle and forefinger. "They are the color of the most exquisite Florentine oricello, a deep, rich crimson." His voice drifted off as he remembered the color. Then, abruptly, he added, "He is shorter than I expected," as if Cosimo had purposefully disappointed him. "He is off to the Dominican monastery, his new home, but he will want to visit the university first. They say he is a learned man, who enjoys the companionship of great scholars."

"Ah," Filippo said, "that excludes me."

"Ha!" Squarcione laughed. Then, he walked over and leaned in close to survey Filippo's work. "Or, perhaps not. They say he also appreciates architecture, sculpture, and painting. There are artists in his retinue."

This information was of interest. Florentine artists? Here, in Padua?

"Well, we will have to attract him to our little workshop," Squarcione was saying, still eyeing Filippo's painting, which Filippo was certain would soon be used as bait.

When more than one full cycle of the moon had passed since Cosimo de' Medici's arrival in Padua, no one in the city had seen him again. Filippo continued to work on the panel painting for the Podesta. Since it was intended to hang above the doorway, it was massive in size and necessitated the use of three panels that would later be joined together. Filippo had never worked on so large a project before, and he had underestimated the time it would take. This was something at which he would need to improve in order to be able to meet deadlines stipulated in contracts. Although it was taking longer than anticipated, Filippo did not mind. He was absorbed in it and would be sad to see it go.

Filippo was contemplating the finishing touches on the first of the panels when the door burst open, and Squarcione announced in a voice loud enough to wake a corpse, "And here is my humble workshop, where nobles' sons come to study the proper drafting of human anatomy from the finest antique statuary recovered from Greece and Rome." He swept his arm around as he spoke to encompass the entire room.

A slender, olive-skinned man, whose head reached only to Squarcione's chest, stepped authoritatively into the room. Behind him stood a small group of companions. He walked over to one of the shelves where, running his fingers along the contours of a statue and then rubbing them together, he concluded, "Plaster."

"Well, yes," Squarcione said, flustered, "they are casts of the finest statuary in Greece and—"

"And Rome," the man said. "What else do your students learn?"

"The principle of a plane? To place figures on the…uh, plane," Squarcione said, looking uncomfortable as Cosimo's eyes scanned the room.

Short and slight in stature though the man was, Filippo noted that he had a commanding presence. He was dressed in the finest crimson wool, expertly tailored, leading Filippo to conclude that this must be Cosimo de' Medici himself. Suddenly, Cosimo's eyes landed on Filippo's painting. He crossed the room, intent on the panel, with long strides, his large, flat feet pointed out in either direction, torso bent forward, arms clasped behind his back, the right hand clutching the left forearm as if to prevent it seizing the most impertinent, foolish man in his path and shaking him.

Cosimo glanced at Filippo and then at Squarcione. "This is Filippo Lippi," Squarcione said, "the painter from Florence about whom I spoke."

"I am honored," Filippo said, bowing slightly. He was sure he detected a glint of humor in Cosimo's eyes.

Cosimo inclined his head. "It is a pleasure to meet you. Maestro Squarcione has sung your praises." He looked once again at the painting.

"It is not finished," Filippo said, seeing all that yet needed attention.

Cosimo's black eyes seemed to see straight through to Filippo's soul. "Who was your maestro?"

"Neri di Bicci, Lorenzo Monaco," Filippo said. "And Masaccio."

"Ah," Cosimo exclaimed. He leaned in close to examine the painting and then stood well back, rubbing his chin with his fingers. As he did, the sleeve of his robe dropped, revealing the thin wrists and smallish hands of an adolescent boy. Dark hair stuck out above his ears, from beneath his hat. Filippo sensed that his long, beaked nose was as sensitive to a man's disposition as that of a dog. His chin was strong, the largest bone in his body, evidencing a toughness, a firm jaw with which to meet life's adversities. "I see it," he said. "Masaccio's influence."

Cosimo looked Filippo up and down as if approving of him based on his work. Then he pointed at the painting. "The composition, the narrative playing out. Masaccio. The draperies that reveal the bodies beneath. The solidity of the figures. The emotion in the faces. Masaccio." All the while, he continued to gesture toward the painting, using hand movements that encompassed the story, moved with the drapery as it flowed over the body, held up the solidity, caressed the faces. This man truly did appreciate art. "And there is something more," he added, tapping his forehead with his finger. "Ingegno. The power of the intellect and of the spirit, by which one discovers that which one has not learned from another."

Ingegno. It was what Masaccio had discerned in Filippo's work all those years before in Pisa. This banker knew something about painting.

"Please, join us tomorrow for the mid-day meal," Cosimo said.

Before Filippo could answer, Squarcione was saying, "We would be most humbly honored to be your guests."

Cosimo looked at Sqarcione as if seeing him for the first time. "Hmmm," he said, "yes." Then he turned to Filippo. "Until tomorrow then."

The following day, Filippo and Squarcione sat to either side of Cosimo at the table, along both sides of which gathered the great man's entourage. After each course, the tablecloth was changed for a clean one. First, they were served pork loin, squab, and rabbit. Next came sturgeon, eel, leeks, and broccoli sautéed in olive oil, followed by black cherries preserved in wine, and dough shaped like pine cones that were soaked in honey and rose water. There were almonds, anise seeds, and pine nuts, and an assortment of cheeses served with grapes and muscat pears in tiny cups. Everything was well seasoned with an assortment of herbs and rare spices and washed down with a never-ending stream of wine.

Enjoying his meal, Filippo only half listened to Squarcione's monologue about his adventures in Greece, although Cosimo seemed to be fully absorbed in his stories. Travel had lost its appeal for Filippo. Squarcione went on to explain that his school was "a new idea. Watching a maestro is important, but should not there also be time to draw directly from forms with no intermediary? To hone one's skills, to develop one's own style?"

Convenient, also, Filippo thought, since they cannot learn by watching Squarcione. He had to admit, however, that the disciplined drawing of figures in different poses led to facility and allowed for the development of a personal style. Sqarcione's methods seemed to work. "Yes," he said aloud without intending to, and everyone turned to him for the first time. He realized he would have to say more.

He hesitated. "Discovering. Your breath, I mean. It is different. From that of others."

The silence that followed assured Filippo that no one had understood. Cosimo alone, a grape dropping from his fingers to his plate, looked interested. Everyone else appeared to be confused. He was not good with words.

It was the architect Michelozzo, a kind man, who came to Filippo's rescue. "We all breathe," he said. "And who is to know if we breathe exactly the same way?" There was some nervous laughter. "We do know," Michelozzo continued, "that we all see the same object," and here he pointed at his own eyes and then at his wine goblet, back and forth. "It is the same object, of that we can be sure. Why, then, does one artist depict it in one way, and another artist in another? Yes. Filippo draws our attention to a mystery."

Filippo had thought that he was explaining the mystery, but he was eternally grateful to Michelozzo, and he knew that he would never be able to properly explain himself, so he smiled and nodded.

"I have petitioned the Signoria to allow me to finish out my exile in Venice," said Cosimo. "The university here in Padua is excellent, of course, but at this time does not possess the talent it once did. Sarzana wrote to me not long ago saying as much. He mentioned that the teachers are now second rate. Not even Languschi remains to teach rhetoric, and he himself is not of the quality of Bruni or Barbaro. Carabello, who is now the chair of rhetoric, lulls me to sleep."

"Ah, but there is more than rhetoric at our university." Squarcione pleaded. "There are painters, sculptors, architects. They come to us from Florence as well."

Pushing his chair back from the table, Cosimo said, "Indeed, there is much to be said for the city of Padua. Well, this has been a most enjoyable evening. Thank you for coming, and for the conversation we have shared."

As they rose to leave, Cosimo held Filippo back, whispering, "Return in three days' time for the mid-day meal. Alone."

The next time Filippo dined with Cosimo and his retinue of followers, the meal was no less sumptuous. Afterwards, he was invited into Cosimo's antechamber. Seeing the collection of books that lined the shelves, Filippo hoped that Cosimo would not wish to discuss them. He would be found sorely wanting. But, after motioning for him to be seated, and settling into a chair himself, Cosimo said, "Now, tell me about this Masaccio. His work is of perfect measure, but also possesses ingegno. What kind of man was he?"

Filippo could see Masaccio as if he stood before them, tall in stature, wide in girth, his hands impossibly large, the gusto with which he ate and drank, his love of life so huge that one would have thought he would live forever. "Brave" was the only word he could think of, and in truth, there had been no fear in the man.

"An odd word to describe a painter," Cosimo said, "Tell me more. Fra Angelico always prays first, and when he works he appears to be overcome with devotion. Masaccio's work is such that

I imagined, when he painted, he must, too, have looked like a man overcome with divine inspiration."

Filippo tried to explain. "He looked like a man working at a feverish pace as if to catch an image before it disappeared. It was as if he could see it, but it was always a little ahead and moving quickly."

"Strange how each man's approach is different. Does it reflect his character, I wonder?" Cosimo mused. "And 'brave,' you say. Why brave?"

"Fear, he taught, is the enemy," Filippo said. "A man must shed his own skin, like a mantello, and leave his fears behind, in order to create."

"And you?" Cosimo asked. "What does it look like when you work?"

"I do not know how it appears," Filippo said, remembering what Maumen had told him, "but it is the only time I feel at peace."

Cosimo nodded as if to agree, smiling. "And why," he asked, "have you been gone a long time from Florence? Where have you been?"

Filippo hesitated to share his story, but the interest evident on Cosimo's face as he leaned forward, coupled with his piercing yet compassionate gaze, led Filippo, in fits and starts, to relay his story. It had been less than one year since Maumen had released him, and the events were fresh in his mind. Cosimo prompted him at every turn with a probing question, an understanding comment, until Filippo had revealed all, whereupon Cosimo sat back and slowly let out his breath, his hands forming a triangle, the upper point of which he gently tapped against his nose.

"Extraordinary," he finally said. "An extraordinary story." Then he leaned forward and asked, "Oedipus at Colonus. Do you know it?" Filippo shook his head. "You must read it. Sophocles writes: 'I come to give you something, and the gift is my own beaten self; no feast for the eyes, yet in me is a more lasting grace than beauty.' What would we be without our trials? A great loss, your friend. But a miracle that you were saved." He sat back in his chair. "He was right. God saved you for a reason."

"My work," Filippo said.

"When I was imprisoned," Cosimo said, "in the top-most cell of the tower and gazed through the barred window to the streets below, I knew that not only was I cut off from the life that teemed there, but that I faced death itself. It was that fool Folelfo—you know him?—who used all of his rhetorical skills to spread stories about me throughout Florence. There his skills met their height—in the crafting of malicious gossip. At which he proved to be quite good." And here, oddly, the corner of Cosimo's mouth curved upward as he restrained a smile. "You know, he once said that I placed my family crest"—a shield, Filippo knew, with seven spherical discs denoting coins—"on everything I paid to have built. Even"—and here, Cosimo grimaced with the attempt to stifle laughter—"even, he said, the monks' privies were emblazoned with my balls."

Filippo roared with laughter, and Cosimo, not given to outbursts, joined in. As they wiped tears from the corners of their eyes, Cosimo once again grew grave. "Folelfo pushed for my head upon a pike."

"You have far too many friends for that to have happened."

"Friends?" Cosimo shook his head. "I own their debts. But their intervention was useful. It helped to stall the process."

"What then?"

"Bribery."

"How? You were imprisoned."

"They could not keep my dear friend, the devout and kind monk Ambrogio Traversari, from visiting with me. As my holy advisor. As the representative of Pope Eugenius. He passed notes to and fro. Under his robes."

"I know well the advantages of a monk's robes for concealment. Whom did you bribe?"

"The most impecunious of the lot. When they wrangled a confession from Niccolo Tinucci on the rack, poor man, and I was charged with treason, my brother decided to amass an army. Another was assembled at Cafaggiolo, and Niccolo da Tolentino was on his way from Pisa with mercenaries. This did not seem a good strategy. Many a prisoner's head is lopped off as the armies surge."

"What happened?" Filippo asked.

"I had observed during visits to my Careggi that, although I was the master of the place, my dogs gave me no heed when the Tartar servant who feeds them was near. To dogs, he is the master of the villa. And so, with the Gonfalonier and the priors chosen by the Albizzi. I fed them. The first to fall was the Gonfalonier himself. The Albizzi had had to pay his debts to make him eligible for office, and he was fast running up more. I had hidden vast sums of money at monasteries within Florence before answering the call of the council. Bernardo Guadagni was Gonfalonier, do you know him? A useless man. He accepted my first offer, a trifling sum. I was delighted. Why, he could have had ten times that amount. More. This little success offered me much satisfaction in my dark cell. They call it the 'little inn,' you know. I call it 'Barberia.'When I return to Florence..." Cosimo began but, lost in thought, did not finish.

"It is a long exile," Filippo said, "but there is an end to it." He thought of his own enslavement, which had had no end in sight.

"Yes. Omnia bona in tempore: all good things in time. But I will return before the ten years has elapsed," Cosimo said, surprising him. "They will soon need me. I prepared by sending money from my bank in Florence to branches in other cities both inside and outside of Italy, greatly depleting funds that could be confiscated." He smiled. "And I am told by my spies that no other bankers will lend so much as a pistachio nut"—he pinched his thumb and forefinger together—"to the government of Florence."

CHAPTER 29

The year of Our Lord 1434, Padua, and the road to Florence

Filippo had waited too long. Instead of leaving for Venice, he would now have to catch up with Cosimo's party as it headed back to Florence only one year after his exile from the city. But, how could he have reneged on the opportunity to work on a fresco project for the chapel of the Podesta in the basilica of Sant' Antonio? It was his first major commission, and it was obtained without Squarcione's intervention. He was now a maestro. Thankfully, he had completed the project when news of Cosimo's return to Florence only one year after his exile raced through the streets of Padua. Now, having received full payment for the commission, Filippo would be able to rent a good, sturdy horse. He packed his few belongings, said his good-byes, and made his way to the southwest gate of the city and the stables located there.

The proprietor was as wide as he was tall, with a slow, waddling gait. He squinted and leaned forward to scrutinize Filippo as if already having decided he was a criminal.

"I will want a well-rested horse," Filippo said.

"All do," the man replied in a monotone.

"I am in need of catching up to a party of riders who passed this way last evening," Filippo explained, impatient to be on his way.

"The Medici."

"Yes. So, I will want the horse, as I said, to be well rested."

"All of my horses are rested," the man said, his jaw tilted at an angle. "What kind of a business do you think I run?" He spat in the dirt and waddled off to untether a horse. He returned, slowly leading it out of the stable. Squatting with difficulty, and with much huffing and puffing, he examined each of its hoofs.

"I will return the horse at Borgo San Lorenzo," Filippo told him. "In Florence."

"The Medici," the man said, "Florence. Who would have guessed?"

He was the first rude individual Filippo had met in Padua. He concluded that it must be a symptom of the trade. "I am in a hurry," he repeated.

"Ah, yes," the man said, slowing his pace.

Once on his way, Filippo raced through the Euganean Hills. If they had been beautiful when he had first encountered them, the sight now filled him with euphoria. He had enjoyed his stay in Padua, and would always remember it fondly, but he was anxious and more than prepared to return to Florence, a maestro and an acquaintance of Cosimo de' Medici.

Filippo expected the procession that marched into Florence to be triumphal, with horns blowing to announce Cosimo's arrival, banners bearing his family's crest held high, and people lining the streets to cheer and welcome him back. When Filippo arrived at Careggi just after nones, he hoped he had not missed the event since Cosimo's country villa was more than an hour's walk from Borgo San Lorenzo, where he had returned his horse. But, as he approached, he saw a long line of people walking slowly along the road that led to Florence.

Recognizing Michelozzo, Filippo came up alongside him. "Ah, Lippi," the man said upon seeing him, "you never did make it to Venice."

"I was on my way," Filippo said, falling in line beside him, "when I heard."

"It was sudden," Michelozzo explained. "As soon as word came, Cosimo raced off. He knew he would be less than ten years in exile. But one year? Even he was taken by surprise."

"What changed?" Filippo asked.

"The Albizzi left town."

"That is all?"

Michelozzo shrugged his shoulders to indicate the ease with which the exile had been overturned.

"They will be back, the Albizzi," Filippo said.

"The war has already taken place," Michelozzo explained. "They have been beaten. With the help of the pope."

Filippo looked around, searching here and there for any sign of Cosimo. No crimson mantello draped any of the figures ahead.

"Cosimo stays on at Careggi," Michelozzo informed him.

"Rush to wait," Filippo said, seeing the irony in the dash to return.

"The Signoria has requested that Cosimo enter the city unobserved," Michelozzo explained. "To maintain order. He will be ushered through the gate tonight, when residences are shuttered and all inside are asleep."

"Why did Cosimo comply? Did he not want to arrive in triumph?"

Michelozzo laughed. "You do not know the man. He said, 'If I ride into Florence in triumph today, I well may be tossed outside its walls into a shallow grave tomorrow.' He is a patient man."

They walked on in silence until, from the top of a hill above Florence, the small band of exiles caught sight of the red-tiled rooftops burning beneath the sun's lengthening rays. A cheer was taken up, crested like a wave, and slowly subsided. They were home.

Filippo and the others entered the city through the Porta San Gallo. Florence was as he remembered it, but with new buildings sprouting up, some already completed that were not there when he had left. He was swept up in the sense of urgency, the industry. No one stood idle, not even the merchants at their stalls. They hawked their wares with loud voices, nearly reaching out to grab passersby.

Filippo said goodbye to Michelozzo, arranging to meet with him the following day. He was on his way to the Oltrarno and the Carmine to see his brother, Giovanni, and the other friars. As Filippo rounded the corner and came upon Santa Maria del Fiore, he was overcome with emotion. She was more majestic than he remembered. He could have fallen to his knees and wept with joy. Even without its dome, not yet completed, it represented his city, the grandeur of its aspirations, the solidity of its foundation, the ingenuity of its design, the strength of its God-given means of attaining such beauty. He blessed himself, gave thanks for arriving home, and continued on his way.

When he had set out from Florence, he was a confused, frightened young man. Deprivation had taught him what he could endure. The loss of his art had set him adrift, its return placing him again on firm ground, giving him a feeling of control that was entirely new.

Giuseppe, the caretaker, who was now older and more bent, opened the outer door to him. He did not at first recognize Filippo. Then, he exclaimed, "Look at you!" and grabbed him by both arms. "How you have grown. A boy when you left us. Now a man."

Filippo had forgotten how the year and a half of rowing had chiseled not only his soul, but his body. When he entered the loggia, he was struck by the chattering of birds, taken back to a day long ago when, as a boy of eight, he had stood on the same spot and released his anger, his stubborn desire to return to the past. He stood for a moment to take it all in, the well in the center of the courtyard, the cypresses at the four corners, the single rosebush, now past its bloom. There were other, more beautiful places, but none where he felt so at peace.

After meeting with the prior, Filippo asked after his brother. Giovanni, he was told, was in the duomo practicing the organ. Filippo entered from the cloister, through a side door at the back of the Brancacci chapel. He closed the door gently, not wishing to disturb his brother. Music filled the immense space, echoing up into the rafters. Filippo sat on a bench and rested his eyes on the amber, azure, crimson, and emerald light thrown across the grey stone by the stained- glass windows. He tilted his head back, allowing the music to fill him like an empty vessel with its golden liquid until he was brimming. The friars were right. In his brother's music, he felt the presence of angels.

That night Filippo sat with Giovanni to catch up with all of the news since his departure. Then Filippo told the long, at times painful, story of his own wanderings. When he came to the end, Giovanni sat in silence. Then he embraced his brother. "Thank the blessed Lord you are safe and home once more," he said, and then, holding him at arm's length, asked, "What are your plans, my brother?"

"I meet with Michelozzo at Donatello's bottega in the morning. Michelozzo has promised to introduce me around the city. I will give Cosimo time to settle in. Then I will go to see him. I hope to receive a commission through his intervention. I will need to rent a house, to open my own bottega. But I will first need to acquire work."

Giovanni smiled. "Listen to you. 'Cosimo' he calls the Medici. My little brother, you have done well."

"Not yet," Filippo cautioned.

"Well, you will stay here for as long as you have need," Giovanni assured him. "You are always welcome here."

An odd home, Filippo thought, but he was comforted. An odd home is better than none.

The following morning, Filippo and Michelozzo made their way to Donatello's bottega on Via Cocomero, across from the Convent of San Nicolo. "He is irascible," Michelozzo warned, "but do not allow his bark to fool you. He is as good a man as he is a sculptor, and of sculptors he is the best."

Michelozzo and Donatello were old friends and partners. Years earlier, they had traveled to Rome together to study antiquities. By the time they returned to Florence, they had decided to go into business, Michelozzo providing the architectural designs and construction, Donatello the decoration. Now that he was returning from exile, Michelozzo was anxious to take up where they had left off.

Donatello and Michelozzo greeted each other warmly. "You old horse's ass!" Michelozzo said, embracing his friend. "You are looking as rough as ever, I see."

Filippo had to agree. Donatello wore a filthy, threadbare robe of uncertain color, and the sandals on his feet revealed them to be black with dirt. His hair was matted, and he looked as though he had not washed his face in a month. Florentines, conscious of cleanliness, gave their bodies a thorough washing every Saturday.

"If I am a horse's ass," Donatello was saying, "then you must be his balls, you ugly son of a whore." Just then, Donatello noticed Filippo standing in the doorway.

"This is Filippo Lippi," Michelozzo introduced him, "a Florentine we found in Padua. A most excellent new painter."

Donatello's eyes, foxlike, sparked with interest. "A new painter? You must show me, then, what is new in painting."

Michelozzo pointed to a statue in the center of the room. "Are you still working on Zuccone? It has been more than five years now."

The bald, elongated head of the man portrayed in the statue, for he was real, not idealized, did look like a large squash. His wide, flat nose and gaping mouth emphasized his ungainliness, as did his stooped posture and the long, limp arms hanging at his sides. He was unattractive, but so lacking in grace as to invite compassion. Every vein in his strained and drooping neck, every crease in his face was chiseled with intimate attention to detail. Life burst forth from a block of wood.

As if to concur with his thoughts, Donatello said, "I wait for him to speak." And then, addressing the statue, he demanded, "Speak, damn you. Speak."

While the two old friends conversed, Filippo walked over to have a closer look. It took more than mere skill to create such a sculpture. It transcended the shifting world, buildings torn down, new buildings erected, people dying, others being born, crops failing, crops thriving. There was an aura surrounding Donatello's work that defeated the flowing, rippling tide of existence, that touched on the immutable.

One of Donatello's apprentices walked over to a hanging basket and reached in. With the sound of chinking coins, the youth pulled out a handful, counted, replaced a few, and left the shop. "Donatello cares not about money," Michelozzo said. "But, I say, a man who places money in a basket for all to take is a man who can well afford it." He winked at Filippo, who was shocked by this practice.

Donatello shrugged. Then he asked Filippo, "So, what is new about this painting of yours?"

Filippo considered. "The narrative unfolds in the space around it. I attempt to render, not a large man with brown hair, but Michelozzo, with broad forehead, sloping nose." He knew he could draw on a skill he had begun perfecting as a boy of eight in the convent, scrutinizing faces and rendering them in detail.

Donatello laughed. "I like your passion," he said. "And, Michelozzo, old goat, who will he be in your little drama? One of the thieves, I venture, who hang on the cross."

"Old goat?" Michelozzo said. "That surely describes you. Emaciated and ragged, you must be Lazarus raised from the dead."

Ignoring him, Donatello asked Filippo, "And how do you accomplish this?"

Filippo attempted to be exact. These men were artists who would understand what he was trying to achieve. "I allow space for figures to move through, for landscape to recede into the distance. A story unfolds like a play, from one scene to the next. The use of light"—he pointed to a window—"from a single source, so that figures and objects emerge from shadow." He pointed to Zucone. "You see how the light folds into shadow, a gradual rounding from shadow to light so that bodies hold weight, gestures and faces reveal emotion. I want the person standing before the painting to feel that by taking one step, he could enter their world. I want to accomplish in paint what you do in reliefs."

This is no easy voyage for a little bark, this stretch of sea the daring prow now cleaves.   Dante

"Perspective, yes," Donatello said. "One light source. But in a relief light folds, as you say, into shadow because it is raised from the surface. How do you propose to accomplish this on a flat surface?"

"The harmony of colors that creates depth, the blending of light and shadow," Filippo said. "The eye follows colors into the distance. Color creates light in a painting, the slow gradations into shadow. Color does much of the work. The eye does the rest."

"Ambitious," Donatello said. "And where did you learn this?"

"Masaccio, and I have since, through experience, discovered more," Filippo said.

"Masaccio? Why did you not say so at once?" Donatello asked, evidently excited by this news. "His *Holy Trinity*"— he shook his head as he thought about it—"a work that praises its craftsman. Brunalescchi helped him, of course, with the perspective, but Masaccio. What a painter. A pity. But he has left us a pupil." Here, Donatello clapped Filippo on both arms, leaving traces of marble dust all over the sleeves of his black robe. "Where have you been all this time?"

Filippo said, "Here and there. I have lived through much."

"Never," Donatello said, gazing into his eyes, "allow life to come between you and your work."

Filippo was grateful to have met two older and accomplished maestros.

"We hear that, as we made our way home, the city was poised for war," Michelozzo said, changing the subject.

Donatello grumbled. "They fight, they exile, they return, they fight, they banish. What is it to me? I have work to do."

"And the others? Brunalescchi?" Michelozzo asked.

"Ha," a voice from behind them exclaimed. They turned as a tall, fit, well-dressed man walked through the doorway. "Brunalescchi. He complained that he was too old, and who?" Here the man raised his arm, pointing his index finger upward, and wagging it for emphasis. "Who will complete my dome?"

They all laughed. "Alberti!" Michelozzo embraced the man. Then, he turned to Filippo to explain. "Brunalescchi is brilliant, all concede, but he does think much of himself. He believes he alone is capable."

"And perhaps he is right," Alberti said.

"You must have taken up arms," Michelozzo said.

"Indeed," Alberti answered. "We had organized and supplied reinforcements, were readying to march to the piazza, believing the battle to be underway, when word came that Albizzi was holed up with the pope, his fine friends having deserted him. How important it is to choose faithful friends."

"Hmmmph," Donatello grunted, not looking up from his work.

Filippo was developing affection for the irascible Donatello.

"I am famished," Michelozzo said and, addressing Donatello, asked, "You do eat, do you not? Or have you given up on that as well?"

"Now and then," Donatello said, without much commitment.

CHAPTER 30

The year of Our Lord 1434, Villa Medici at Careggi, and Florence

At Careggi, Cosimo spent the afternoon pruning his vines. He had awoken early, before the others, eaten a light meal, and then read while his entourage departed for Florence. Although he was secretly disappointed that he, himself, would have to slip into the city in the dark of night, he knew it was the wisest choice. He had left Venice in such haste that he had not had time to think.

If Cosimo were to admit the truth, Careggi and not Florence was his favorite place in the world. He felt sunk into the earth of it, grown, as much as his vines, from its soil. Exiled, he had not known when he would see Careggi again. Cosimo stepped back now to examine his work. His favorite activity, apart from banking, was pruning. There was something in the simplicity of it that reminded him of numbers. There was no mistaking what needed to be trimmed to promote growth.

The pleasures of farming…the bank…in which these pleasures keep their account is the earth itself. It never fails to honor their draft, and when it returns the principal, interest invariably comes too. Cicero

Late that night, a mace-bearer arrived from the city. Cosimo, his brother Lorenzo, and a loyal servant followed the emissary to Florence, entering through a small gate near the Bargello. With each click of the horses' hooves against the cobblestones, Cosimo reminded himself that his troubles had only begun. But, while pruning earlier that day, he had devised his plan. He had won the game; his enemies would be vanquished. Exile was not enough. They, and their families, would have to be banished.

A room in the Palazzo della Signoria had been prepared for Cosimo for the night. As he settled in, he remembered that the last time he had entered the palazzo, his accommodations had been significantly less hospitable. Omnia bona in tempore: all good things in time. Cosimo lay awake, running through his plans, anticipating all possible reactions to his return, and deciding how best to deal with each.

Early the following morning, he went to the monastery at Santa Maria Novella to thank Pope Eugenius for his help. It was the pope's support that had been the deciding factor in the overthrow of the Albizzi. Florence had braced for battle with Albizzi and his five hundred armed men, who were readying to attack the center of government power, the Signoria and the Bargello. The government's own troops occupied the piazza and marched through the streets. Districts readied reinforcements. Then, suddenly, Albizzi's fortunes turned. His friends among the prominent citizens, those with the wherewithal to provide money and men at arms, abandoned him first. His troops began to desert. He was, nevertheless, willing to place the city at risk, Peruzzi and Barbadori at his side. And then, the pope sent for him.

Pope Eugenius, Cosimo knew, an intelligent and learned man, was nobody's fool. The pope kept up a discussion throughout the night and well into the morning hours, understanding that Albizzi's men at arms, like bulls scratching at the ground and blowing wind through their nostrils in their zeal for a fight, would not wait forever. Their energy dissipated by the lengthy wait and much wine, most lost interest and went home. Cosimo smiled. It is best to win the war without a fight.

He knelt and kissed the pope's ring. "Your Holiness," he said, standing, "I came straightaway, having returned to Florence only last night, to thank you for your support of my efforts during this unfortunate business. Your handling of the matter, I understand, was characteristically astute and diplomatic."

"Have a seat." The pope motioned for Cosimo to take one opposite him. "I was happy to be able to help, the matter, as you say, being most unfortunate. The affair was seen not only by most of the citizens of Florence, but by all of Rome and Venice, as you know, as most unjust."

"You have saved Florence from unnecessary bloodshed and destruction," Cosimo said. "And you have secured my return, for which I am most grateful. If there is ever anything I can do to repay your kindness...." And here Cosimo thought of his bank and its expansion in service to the Papal Curia.

"There is something," Pope Eugenius said without hesitation.

Ah, Cosimo thought, his Holiness's assistance came with a price in mind.

"I have, myself," the pope began, "had a bit of trouble with the Colonna family. Pope Martin's people. An unruly and demanding lot. Most ungrateful. Well, it seems that I am unable to return to Rome at present. The Venetians have offered military aid, but how to pay the army."

"Do not say another word." Cosimo stopped him so that he would not have to ask. "Consider the Medici bank at your service. I will have my manager stop by later this afternoon to make the arrangements. Since I transferred large sums to my branch in Venice when this trouble began, there will be no need to post funds in order to move forward."

"Thank you."

The pope appeared to be weary, so Cosimo bowed his head, saying, "It is my pleasure," and took his leave. Every man has his worldly troubles, he thought, even the pope. For his own part, he was able to repay a debt and, at the same time, forge deeper bonds with the Curia, a boon for business.

As Cosimo made his way home to the Palazzo Bardi, people called out to him, welcoming him home. He humbly bowed his head to each. He was his father's son. The people of Florence had not given up on him; he would meet their faith with conviction.

When he arrived home, he received a decidedly more lukewarm reception from Contessina, who kissed him perfunctorily on each cheek and said, sounding a bit disappointed, "I had not expected you to return so soon." Then she asked, "Will you be sharing the mid-day meal with us?" When he said yes, she turned abruptly and went off to make arrangements. Watching her go, Cosimo noticed that she had gained in corpulence while he was away. She had always, he noted, possessed a healthy appetite for food.

It was with much more excitement that his sons greeted him on their return from school. They ran to him, embraced him warmly, and tripped over one another to tell him about the war that almost was. All in all, Cosimo was happy that things were back to normal. It was good to be home. Routine calmed him.

CHAPTER 31

The year of Our Lord 1434, Florence

Filippo made his way to Cosimo's palazzo, where a servant relayed the message that the great man was busy and wished for him to return in a fortnight. Filippo worried that he had been forgotten, that perhaps Cosimo would not help him find employment after all. When he voiced his concerns, Michelozzo assured him, "Cosimo is a man of his word. He does not engage in idle chatter. If he promised help, he will give it."

The fortnight passed slowly. Filippo made his way once again to the palazzo where he, along with dozens of other petitioners awaiting their turn, lounged on one of the benches that lined the loggia. After a lengthy interval, he was ushered into Cosimo's office. Upon seeing him, Cosimo smiled. "It is good to see you. You never made it to Venice. A pity."

"I was preparing to leave for Venice when news arrived of your departure for Florence."

Cosimo poured wine for each of them, and then, sitting opposite Filippo, raised his glass. "To our return home."

Cosimo took a sip, placed his glass on the table, and wearily rubbed his eyes.

"You are busy," Filippo said. "I will not take much of your time."

Cosimo looked up. "It is this business about what to do with those who attacked the city. They would have laid waste to Florence to hold tight to power. People cheered me only a few weeks hence, now they grumble in the streets. When people talk about you, it is never to praise."

Filippo had heard the gossip. "They only say that you have swept the streets clean of prominent families. They wonder who will run the businesses, who will be elected to the Signoria, if all of the eminent citizens are banished."

Cosimo swept his arm as if to brush the idea away. "Nine yards of crimson cloth makes a new citizen."

Filippo could see why the popolo minuto, the lowest class, loved this man.

Cosimo jumped up from his seat. "Walk with me."

Once outside, they headed in the direction of San Lorenzo, the Medici's' own church.

"I, myself," Cosimo said, "am content to run my business and prune my vines."

Filippo doubted this was true. It seemed to him that Cosimo loved the game.

Acknowledging each passerby with a nod, and allowing an elder commoner the inside path, Cosimo continued, "My city is in need of a firm guiding hand, however, and it seems that I am the man to provide it. For the good of the city. For liberty. 'Beware the desire for glory,' Cicero warns, 'for it destroys the liberty for which men of great spirit ought to be in competition.' I have begun by keeping my promise to my jailor. Each year one hundred new families will be added to the borse bag, given voting rights, and eligibility to hold public office."

"People grumble," Filippo said, "that one powerful man has banished all of his enemies."

"The enemies of the city," Cosimo said indignantly.

"Entire branches of families."

"My expertise in pruning." Cosimo smiled. "It is not for myself, but for the health of the city that the diseased branches must be trimmed close. In Milan? In Naples? Traitors are executed."

"Palla Strozzi." Filippo remembered his name being mentioned more than any other. "They love the man. They say it is unfair, that he did not ever truly support Albizzi. Yet, he is banished."

"He is weak," Cosimo said. "Weak and flush with money, a dangerous combination. When next someone gets it into his head to overthrow the government, to place his own interests above those of Florence, into whose ear will he pour invective? Whose money will he use? Palla Strozzi. I am fond of the man, but he has no aptitude for politics. The life of a retired scholar suits him well, and he will find it at the university in Padua. I do him a favor. I envy him."

Filippo was not so sure.

"A commission," Cosimo said. "The reason you have come. I have two. My wife, Contessina, is in need of a small devotional panel for her bedchamber. She wishes to stare at the Annunciation while she prays."

"Ah," Filippo said, envisioning the project, "I will place the scene in your own loggia."

"I am sure you will do a fine job," Cosimo said. "My manager has drawn up a contract with specifications. See him before you leave."

"And the other?"

"Yes, the other," Cosimo began. They had circled, turned the corner, and were just arriving back at the Medici palazzo when they heard voices raised in anger. As they entered through the gate, they saw Donatello in the middle of the courtyard, gesticulating wildly. A young, handsome apprentice stood by his side holding a bronze bust. Donatello was screaming obscenities at a stout man wearing a crimson, ermine-trimmed mantello.

Cosimo stopped just inside the entrance. "You have poked your stick into the wrong cave, my friend. You will have the bear to deal with." Then he turned back toward Filippo. "We are done?"

Filippo thanked Cosimo for his help.

"Yes. Yes. I get the commissions. It is up to you to complete them to satisfaction. I must deal with this business."

But instead of departing, Filippo followed Cosimo into the courtyard. "Now, now, what is the trouble?" Cosimo asked in a conciliatory tone.

Filippo soon discovered that, on Cosimo's advice, the man, who was a wealthy merchant from Genoa, had commissioned Donatello to make a bust of him. The specifications were singular. Not wishing to carry a heavy piece back with him, he wanted it to be light and yet sturdy so as not to break "should a clumsy servant drop it."

Having completed the work, which was on view before them, a life-sized head in bronze, Donatello stood ready to collect his fee. The merchant refused to pay the agreed-upon price.

"But look," Cosimo said in an attempt to mediate, "what an excellent likeness Donatello has rendered. It praises its maestro."

"It is not worth what he charges," the man complained.

"A bean counter," Donatello scoffed.

Coming between them, Cosimo suggested that they carry the bust upstairs to the rooftop in order to better see it in the full light of day. They all, including Filippo, who would not miss this for the world, made their way up the stairs to the roof.

When they arrived, Cosimo had his servants place the bust high up between the battlements surrounding the courtyard. "See," he said triumphantly, "the finest of detail. Who else could render such a likeness? And thin as parchment so as not to be heavy. This is beyond the capabilities of any other sculptor. A magnificent work of art."

The man seemed not to have heard a word Cosimo said or to have seen what he could easily, in this light, have beheld. Although inferior to other works Filippo had seen by the maestro—perhaps, he thought, Donatello had not warmed to his subject—it was, nevertheless, expertly executed, capturing the haughty tilt of the man's head, the sneer that tightened his lips, and his cold stare.

The man was agitated. He puffed himself up in such a way that his chest ballooned, and he appeared to be about to stand on his toes. "The work took only one month to complete. At that rate, well, it adds up to more than half a florin per day."

"You see?" Donatello raged. "He is used to bargaining for pig feed, not works of art. A bean counter." Before anyone could reply, Donatello had turned and stalked over to the place where the bust rested. "And in one hundredth of an hour I can spoil the labor and the value of an entire year's worth of work." He reached out and shoved the bust over the side of the building. They heard it crash onto the street below.

All present stood speechless until the merchant begged Donatello, "Please. I will pay you twice what you charged to make another bust."

Without a word, Donatello turned and strode off. Afterwards, not even Cosimo could convince him to recreate the work.

CHAPTER 32

The year of Our Lord 1436, Florence

It was impossible to deny that the structure represented a magnificent feat of engineering. From whichever direction one entered the city, Brunelleschi's dome drew the eye, beautiful to behold. In scope, it matched the man's opinion of himself, Filippo thought, but it was also a fitting tribute to Florence. Pope Eugenius, who yet resided in the city, was to consecrate the duomo, with its newly completed dome, on the feast of the Annunciation. The entire city made ready to celebrate. Filippo was grateful to have arrived back home in time for the event.

Brunelleschi, not one to disappoint the popolo when it came to pageantry—had he not engineered the machinery used in the Carmines' play that lifted Jesus up into the clouds as if by magic?—was now constructing a platform on which the pope would walk all the way from Santa Maria Novella, his lodgings, to the duomo. It stood two braccia in height and spanned four braccia in width, its full length covered in exquisite tapestries. Columns had been erected at intervals, between which benches were set and hung with the heraldic colors of the papacy and various coats of arms, all festooned with boughs of cypress, pine, myrtle, and laurel.

On the day of the ceremony, Filippo was invited to join the Carmelites who, along with the other mendicant orders, would wait just outside the duomo for the pope's arrival. Standing with his brothers at the entrance, he felt fortunate since otherwise he might not have been able to see a thing. The streets were teeming with people. Every citizen of the commune was in attendance, along with visitors from the surrounding provinces, and from as far away as Pisa. As they stood waiting, a rumble like thunder barreled toward them, the roar of the crowd. Above on the platform the Patriarch of Jerusalem and his attendants made their way to the duomo and through the front entrance. The sound subsided, only to grow once again, a new swell that nearly lifted them physically, and there above was the ambassador sent from the Holy Roman Emperor, followed by diplomats sent by the kings of France and of Aragon, along with representatives from Milan, Venice, and Genoa. The wave receded and then grew again as archbishops and bishops strode past, followed by the members of the Signoria. Finally, the prominent citizens of Florence made their way along the platform, all except for Cosimo. He had confided to Filippo that he did not wish to appear before the popolo as a man using a solemn event for self-aggrandizement. Cosimo had carved out a humble, and yet more important role for himself in the proceedings. A sudden surge of sound erupted that threatened to burst the very sphere of heaven, and there was the pope himself surrounded by cardinals. As he approached the entrance, the choir greeted him, their voices lifted in song.

Only then did Filippo and his fellow Carmelites make their way through a side entrance where, along with the other orders, they filled the rear of the duomo. The choir took up a motet, *Nuper rosarum flores*, written for the occasion by Dufay, the esteemed head of the papal choir. Their voices rose into the dome above with such solemn beauty that tears filled Filippo's eyes.

At the end of the ceremony, Cosimo stepped forward, knelt

before the pope, head bent in supplication. Then, looking reverently up at his holiness, he pleaded on behalf of the people of Florence for extra indulgences. The pope granted them.

That evening at the Golden Goose, as Filippo and Donatello shared supper, Donatello said, "It is amusing, do you not agree? All of the prominent citizens of Florence taken by surprise. They call Cosimo a cunning old fox. Years from now no one will remember who strode down the length of the platform, but all will remember the additional indulgences procured for them by the intercession of Cosimo de' Medici. Ha! Cunning, indeed."

CHAPTER 33

The year of Our Lord 1436, Florence

Cosimo and his brother Lorenzo had always been close but, since their parents' deaths, their bond had deepened. They depended on each other, and Lorenzo was the only person in whom Cosimo placed complete trust. No one else had grown to manhood under their father's tutelage. For this reason, there was much that did not need to be said between then. Lorenzo was the one to whom he turned when he wished to air his views before coming to a decision.

As they sat in his antechamber drinking wine, Cosimo thought aloud about his recent decision to invite Francesco Sforza to Florence. "You cannot trust the lying Venetians. The Papal States, though more trustworthy under Pope Eugenius, are only as stable as any pope's most recently satisfied itch for a land grab. It is an uneasy alliance, forever teetering, with Milan and that crazy, unpredictable bastard Visconti always threatening from the north."

"This is why you invite Sforza?"

"He is touted as the best military leader in all of Italy," Cosimo explained. "He has already taken land in the Romagna away from the pope for his personal use. Now, that takes a set of balls."

"So, you will charm him into fighting on behalf of Florence should the need arise?"

"That is a need that always arises sooner or later," Cosimo concurred.

"He is courted by the Duke of Milan at present. If the duke is angry you invite Sforza it is nothing. But will the pope not be enraged?"

"It is worth the gamble," Cosimo reasoned. "I think farther ahead than the possibility of war."

"I discerned as much. What then?" Lorenzo asked.

"Sforza will make a powerful friend. Why, they say even his mercenaries revere him and are loyal. Mercenaries!"

"Yes," Lorenzo agreed, "that is something. The man is a leader. But, Cosimo, this is a risky business. You may end up angering not only our enemies but our allies."

Governments cannot do without a splendid reputation and the good will of their allies. Cicero

"I wish to realign the powers, Lorenzo, to create a balance that will enable Florence to remain at peace. If it works, it will be my greatest achievement. If it does not...."

"...You stand to lose everything." Lorenzo slowly sipped his wine. "So, as I understand it, you befriend the most feared condotiere in Italy in order to obtain peace."

"Yes."

Cosimo was curious to meet this man whose chosen name, Sforza, meant "force." He stood on the roof of his palazzo, peering out from between the parapets, in order to scrutinize Sforza as he arrived.

Astride his horse, Sforza turned from side to side, watching as people averted their gaze, some out of respect, others out of fear. Cosimo noted the unease on his face. He seemed to be uncomfortable with this show of deference.

When the two men sat down to talk, Sforza's attitude was not commanding, but relaxed. He had steely eyes and the prominent nose of all great men. The thin line of his barely discernable lips evidenced a level of self-control and determination. Sforza was not much of a talker, and when he did speak he was a bit awkward.

"I hear rumors," Cosimo said, "that you have ambitions to marry the Visconti's daughter. Do your ambitions extend, then, to the dukedom of Milan?"

"Yes" was all that Sforza could muster, his ambition implicit in his restraint.

This was another fact that made Sforza an important ally to cultivate. Watching him, Cosimo discerned that this most feared condottiere wanted to be liked, to be treated as any other man. "Have you read Cicero?" he asked.

A look of confusion passed across Sforza's face. "No."

"Ah, the great Roman orator and statesman," Cosimo explained. "He warns that 'Arms have little affect abroad if there is no counsel at home.' He will teach you much about how to rule as duke."

Cosimo stood and perused his shelves, finally pulling one and then another volume down. He handed them to Sforza. "Read these, and we will, through correspondence, discuss them."

Sforza raised his eyebrows in surprise, but then he smiled. He was pleased. Cosimo had read the man. Sforza wished to be taken seriously, his designs clearly focused on the mountain's highest peak. Cosimo determined to provide him with guidance.

CHAPTER 34

The year of Our Lord 1435, Florence

C ontracts stipulated dates of delivery for the finished work, and although artists often missed these dates, they risked being sued when they did. Painters and sculptors, when pressed, relied on what had become a common retort, "It will be finished when Brunelleschi's dome is completed." Still, they were often sued. Filippo knew that one day he, too, would be caught up in litigation, but for now, as a newly arrived artist of little standing, it would be better for him to avoid the courts. For this reason, Filippo worked simultaneously on two commissions.

One of Cosimo's friends had requested a painting of Saint Jerome in penitence, in which the saint commands a young monk to remove a thorn from a lion's paw. Filippo took great care to bring about a subtle gradation from light to shadow in all of the forms and figures. He was able to endow even the darkest shadows with a translucent quality. The figures of the young monk and the lion were alive with gesture and emotion. One could feel with what fear and trepidation the monk reached out his hand toward the lion's paw, the lion's face fierce with pain. But, when he was finished, Filippo was disappointed.

Although he had rendered the rocky landscape as realistically as he had been taught years earlier by Fra Monaco, it did not quite recede into the background. The figures, although appearing to move within the space around them, were awkwardly positioned against the lines and contours of the landscape, reminding Filippo of that day long ago at the Carmine when he had stepped back to view his fresco, only to notice the head of a monk stiffly framed within the dark shape of a window in a building behind him. This integration of a scene with its background was a skill that Filippo would need to perfect.

He was more satisfied with the Annunciation for Contessina, Cosimo's wife. Filippo had decided against the common pose, Mary looking up from her reading, the angel kneeling before her. He, instead, allowed the viewer the experience of turning a corner and coming upon an event as it transpired, the angel walking into the room and beginning a bow that would end in genuflection, Mary, one hand at her heart, the other thrown back, startled, taken by surprise, having just entered through the doorway behind her. Filippo paid close attention to his use of color in this painting, warm colors echoing warm, cool colors echoing cool. Cast shadow was so focused that every surface, even the tiniest folds of skin, Mary's eyelids, were modeled from light to shadow in gradual gradation. One source of light shone upon all. Although it was a simpler, architectural background, Filippo had also managed to accomplish the feeling of depth that had eluded him in the Saint Jerome. He was well pleased.

When he presented it to Cosimo, his patron gave it high praise and commissioned Filippo to paint a devotional panel for his son Piero's private chambers. This time Cosimo, as he often did with artists who worked for him, offered Filippo a room at his palazzo, where he would be fed and his needs attended to as he worked. A workspace was set up within Filippo's chambers.

After settling in, Filippo painted as he always did, for four good hours in the morning. He then took a break for the midday meal and worked for another two hours, after which he was done for the day.

Cosimo's secretary, Michele del Giogante, complained. "He does not work from sunrise to sunset as other artisans do. How are we to pay him? Are we to compensate him for hours not worked?"

"Sit with him," Cosimo said. "Not in the way of being intrusive, but so as to gently sway him toward longer hours."

Filippo burst into Cosimo's offices. "I cannot work with someone hovering! Impossible!" So, the secretary was sent away, but later that evening, when Filippo turned the door handle to head out to the local inn for a few glasses of wine and the company of his fellow artists, he found it fastened from without. Filippo banged and hollered, but there was no response. "Am I a dog?" he yelled.

This was unheard of. He had been locked in, as if bondage were all he needed to aid him in his work. Was he a slave? He thought of Maumen. Even the pirate leader recognized the freedom this gift to create required and released him. Was he a pet? Even pets roamed free. Locked inside, Filippo would go mad. It soon became obvious that all were instructed to ignore his pounding and entreaties, for he wasted his fists and lungs in protest. He could not break down a door so heavy. Filippo looked around. The only other entrance to the world outside was the window.

Although high above ground level, since the bedchambers were located on the uppermost floor, it allowed access to the street below. Filippo had no choice. He now thanked al-Basir for teaching him to tie a sturdy knot. He used a single loop knot to secure the end of one sheet to the bedpost, then fastened one sheet to the next with a double overhand knot to hold fast. Hoping that his knots would be strong enough to hold his weight—no small requirement—Filippo threw the length of it over the sill. He made the sign of the cross, said a quick prayer to the Virgin Mary of Humility, and climbed out through the window.

As he hung halfway to the street, the sound of tearing cloth drew Filippo's eyes upward. His knots held fast, but the fabric itself was giving way. He took a deep breath and steadied himself against the wall with both feet before resuming his descent, more cautiously this time. There was another tear, and Filippo dangled precariously. "God have mercy," he said, closed his eyes, and jumped.

Miraculously, he landed on both feet. Standing upright, he checked all over and found that he was unhurt. More importantly, he was free. Filippo gave thanks to Mary for protecting him and strode off in the direction of the Swan's Neck Inn.

There Filippo enjoyed a bowl of stew and several cups of wine while he listened to a group of musicians play upon their lutes, pipes, and tabors. As the night grew long, he realized that there was no need to return to the palazzo. Indeed, he refused to be locked up like a caged animal. Was it not he, Cosimo, who wished something of Filippo? And why should he give it if he was not trusted to deliver? Being in need of a place to sleep that night, he continued on to the candle maker's shop to visit one of the prostitutes within the upstairs chambers.

The following morning, well after the sun had risen, Filippo made his way back to his bottega on Via Chiara. He threw open the shutters, pulled a cloth from a barely begun commission, and set to work. He was settling in when Giogante, Cosimo's secretary, burst through the doorway. "You are alive!" he cried.

"Alive and free!" Filippo retorted and turned back to his work.

"Please," Giogante continued, "Cosimo is in distress. When he saw the sheets ripped away and lying on the ground! We did not know. Were you injured? Had you wandered off in a daze? He set me to search both sides of the Arno for you. Cosimo begs you to return and promises never to lock you in again."

"Promises?" Filippo needed to be certain.

"Cosimo de' Medici is a man of his word."

Later that evening, after a light supper, Cosimo and Filippo retired to Cosimo's antechamber. "Why," Cosimo wanted to know, "would you do such a foolish thing? You might have been gravely injured."

"After hours of work," Filippo explained, "I must walk about. I must talk, eat, drink, listen to music, dance. It is the tide that sweeps far out to sea, gathering strength before returning to shore. I must be out among people." Cosimo did not appear convinced. How to explain it? "My soul strives," he added.

"Can your soul not strive through prayer?" Cosimo asked.

Reason would suggest this to be true. "No," he admitted.

"Well, that is a shame," Cosimo said. "You would be much less trouble." He smiled. "But it is I who have learned an important lesson. A gifted painter such as yourself must never be treated as a pack horse. Rare minds are like celestial beings, not asses for hire."

"I do not know about celestial, but to be respected, even by a great man such as yourself."

"Not great," Cosimo sighed. "The Florentines are a fickle lot. They will soon find reason to slander me. The wise man rides the wave of both adulation and derision, never gliding too comfortably on one, knowing too well that his path will soon dip into the other, and swell again, a new beast to ride."

"There is wisdom," Filippo said, with sincere admiration.

"Seneca," Cosimo said. "He writes: 'Away with the world's opinion of you—it is always unsettled and divided.' Seneca was wise. Aristotle was wise. I know men. That is my gift. In business, it is of great value. There are times, however, I wish I did not know men so well."

"It could prove disappointing," Filippo said.

"I wish my life were one of the mind, that I could take what I see and spin great theories from it, but I am left with knowledge of the raw product only, without the skill to weave anything from it. I envy philosophers, rhetoricians, artists such as yourself."

"Ah, but this knowledge you weave to great effect in trade and commerce is, I have found from watching you, also an art."

Cosimo's face softened, and his dark eyes lit up. "Do you think so?" he asked. The idea that he, too, was an artist brought him joy.

"Indeed," Filippo said.

"But the world of commerce is fraught with human frailty."

"My work," Filippo said, "unfolds in a place untouched by human frailty."

"Yours included?" Cosimo smiled.

"Mine most of all." Filippo held his glass out so that Cosimo could refill it.

We are not born for ourselves alone. Plato

"I, too, know that peaceful space," Cosimo said, pouring more Vermiglio into both glasses. "For me it is a place of study. I forget the world outside the walls of Santa Maria degli Angeli. When a student there as a boy, I did best with figures but struggled to learn languages. Niccolo, though, Niccolo soaked in languages like earth the rain, and they became a part of his very being." Cosimo spoke of his friend and mentor Niccolo Niccoli. "He spent his fortune on artifacts. What a collection! Coins from ancient Greece, urns, intaglios, vases, manuscripts. Each time he purchased a new manuscript and had it transcribed, we read it together. As young men, we had a dream of going to the Holy Land, of seeing it ourselves, of doing archaeological research." His eyes lit up in a way Filippo had never before seen.

"Why did you not go?"

"My father, may his soul rest in peace, would not allow it. 'You do not have time'," Cosimo intoned, imitating his father's stern voice, "'for frivolous pursuits. We have a business to run.' Of course he was right. That is where my gift lies. I had already, at that young age, done much to secure our bank's position in Rome." He had lost the light in his eyes.

"Is that when you began your own collection?" Filippo asked, hoping to again lift his spirits.

"Yes. A banker can collect. He cannot create as you can or go on great adventures like Niccolo. But he can acquire, appreciate."

"It takes knowledge to appreciate," Filippo reminded him.

"Yes. I was given an exceptional education. I cannot complain. But I was not able to utilize what I learned to great effect, rhetoric not being my gift. I am happiest, even today, in study groups at my old school, or poring over a newly discovered manuscript."

"Book learning was difficult for me," Filippo admitted. "The monks despaired at my stupidity. I found it impossible to read. I do not know why. When ideas are discussed, I understand and can follow arguments. However, the page holds a jumble of letters. And Latin. I, a friar, to this day know only a little. But, when I paint, I live and breathe inside my work. When I become aware, again, of the world around me, it looks new, as if much has changed since I last took notice. When I paint, I move forward in an attempt to do what I have not done before."

Every new painting, it was true, presented a challenge to outdo the last unless a patron held him back, specified with stultifying exactitude the limits of what was to be painted. Then, the result was static, the movement of creation stifled. But, when he had latitude, it was as if he were engulfed by the work, ran toward some elusive horizon beyond which lay a light he chased, a view to be newly discovered. Even now, dressed for the evening meal at Cosimo's palazzo, his hands told the story, never free from the evidence of his craft, no matter how thoroughly he washed them, traces of paint in the creases of his skin, darkening the pads of his fingertips, caked under his nails. Where did he end and his work begin? Even when he bent his head over his hands in prayer, he was aware of the faint odor of pigments.

"I sometimes experience what you speak of when I work with figures," Cosimo was saying. "I do not see figures before me, but the movement of goods from port to port, a client's holdings flowing like a river, first in one direction, then another, growing, diminishing. I move figures around, and I see it all play out. Time passes. I am unaware."

"Yes, that is it," Filippo said. "It is like that."

CHAPTER 35

The year of Our Lord 1438, Florence

Cosimo continued to provide Filippo with introductions that led to commissions. The year before, Filippo had painted a female member of the Este family. He was chosen for his ability to create exact likenesses and to realistically render fabric and jewels. As he worked, Filippo noticed that his subject's fiancé was always lurking about. This gave him an idea. He decided to create a narrative that placed her fiancé in the portrait as well, gazing in at her through an open window. Then he made another innovation that placed the work in even higher esteem. Through a second window, just behind the female sitter, he painted a view out toward the walls of Florence. Ingegno. No one in Florence had ever seen anything like it, and he was now flooded with requests for portraits. He did not mind because they paid well and helped with workshop expenses. Although his reputation was growing, it took many years to become established. This forced him to take on more commissions than he could manage. When unable to meet deadlines, he now sometimes found himself in litigation, but with Cosimo's advice he was able to win his cases.

It was an exciting time to be in Florence. Painters, sculptors, and architects often gathered at each other's botteghe to discuss their work. One day in the prolonged heat of September, a group of his friends gathered at Filippo's bottega, where he worked on a new panel. It was here that his brother Giovanni found him.

"Ah, it is good you are here," Filippo said as his brother walked through the door, "for I paint you in this commission, as one of the friars, and will now have more than memory to work from. Sit. Donatello is telling us about a dissatisfied customer. I, myself, had the pleasure of witnessing the event of which he speaks."

Donatello had just finished telling the story of the bust he had thrown from the roof and now complained, "This merchant thinks anyone can create? Perhaps even he can sculpt. Let him make it, then. If I can create it, I can destroy it."

Brunelleschi noted, "An artist willing to destroy his own work is the rarest of birds."

"Your anger," Giovanni said, whose own temperament was mild and steady, "will one day bring you more trouble than it is worth, Donatello." Then he turned to Filippo who, unable to concentrate, had put down his brush and was wiping his hands with a cloth. "And you, Filippo. Your passion for women will be the end of you." He rolled his eyes at the others, who laughed.

Filippo wished he could be as carefree as Giovanni, but the deep passions to which he had alluded, the passions that drove Filippo, were necessary. His brother reminded Filippo of their father, of whom he had a vague memory, alight with laughter, a spark in his eye. Giovanni never took anything too seriously, least of all himself. Filippo envied his brother this sense of ease but knew that his art required him to play the full range of notes of this earthly existence on his own heart. His gift, if he had one, was to be able to embrace the shadows and always find his way back to the light.

"You are ever lighthearted, brother. Therefore," Filippo retorted, "I am going to sink Pappa's butcher's clever into your head in this painting, and you will smile still." He picked up a charcoal stick and sketched the top of a clever sunk an inch into the top of

Giovanni's head. "There," he concluded, "you are no longer an insouciant friar inviting the viewer to have a look. You are the martyred Sant' Alberto looking as if the axe in your skull tickled rather than troubled you."

"See here, I smile for soon I will join God in heaven," Giovanni laughed.

"You may cleave him," Brunelleschi said, pointing to the likeness of Giovanni in the painting, "but with his words he has skewered you."

"It is good to see," Giovanni said, "that my little brother has discovered his sense of humor in this painting. Will you leave it? Where will it hang?"

Filippo considered. "I will leave it. It is for Cosimo and will hang above his bed."

"Perfect." Brunelleschi slapped his knee with delight. "As Cosimo lies there moaning with the gout, he can thank God he has not such a headache."

Just then, Michelozzo and Alberti walked in, Michelozzi saying, "I agree with you to a point, but not to line or plane."

"What is this nonsense?" Brunelleschi asked.

"We argue some points of his treatise on painting," Michelozzo explained. Two years earlier, Alberti had made available his treatise on painting, published in Latin, but this was the year that he made it available in Italian.

"There is some good instruction, Alberti, for young painters," Donatello said generously, "about the center line never being higher or lower than a man in a painting. About the proportions of a man being measured out in head lengths."

"Who would notice that," Brunelleschi asked, "but Alberti?" They all laughed. "Always in his own head, thinking, thinking, but paintings do not burst forth from mere thought."

"I could place the entire population of Florence in a painting," Filippo grumbled, "and it would be pleasing to the eye," arguing against Alberti's stipulation that there never be more than nine figures in a painting.

"I but meant," poor hounded Alberti explained, "that too many bodies in a painting creates confusion in the eye of the viewer."

"Once you have taken mathematics into account, precision, as you call it, what then?" Filippo continued. "Painting requires a leap to a place where there is no control, from beyond what we know or can speak of, a place where one is moved as if by divine hand. All who view the work are then likewise moved by it. Beauty cannot be manipulated. It arises spontaneously."

"And that is the most, at one time, on an erudite subject that our Filippo has spoken," Brunelleschi said. "See how your treatise troubles the mind. Stick to your mathematics, Alberti, at which you are a genius. Leave the painting to painters."

"And this pleasantness you speak of." Donatello shook his head with disgust. "Pah. All must be pleasant to look at? Too bad for my Zuccone. If a man has a broken nose, fix it? If his eye is missing, turn his head to reveal the side with the eye intact? If his chin recedes, build it up so that it juts forward?"

They all laughed at this obvious poke at Alberti's vanity, he himself turning red in the face at the mention of his receding chin.

"Not all of life is pleasant." Donatello raised his voice to add emphasis to these words. "And yet we must gaze upon it."

"A painting must breathe," Filippo agreed, repeating the lesson Masaccio had taught him so long ago. "At its best, it lives and breathes with its own life."

"But the soul of the viewer," Alberti argued, "must connect with the souls of those who are there portrayed. We are drawn to beauty."

"We can only connect with beauty?" Filippo scoffed.

"Spoken by the man who connects best with beautiful women," Brunelleschi said, drawing laughter.

Ignoring this jibe, Filippo continued his thought. "A soul is made up of both joy and misery. It is scarred by sorrow, but then toughened when it responds with courage and fortitude. Is there not beauty in that?"

But, here, Alberti warmed to his subject. "A soul is not subject to experience. It is eternal and eternally beautiful."

"Not so," Donatello contradicted him.

Filippo agreed. "It is gravely affected by life. The strength with which it overcomes all obstacles, all grief, does not diminish it but makes it all the more beautiful."

"Here! Here!," Filippo's friends shouted in unison. Poor Alberti could not win. Filippo felt sorry for him. "You did teach me the veil trick, which I found useful."

"Yes," Michelozzo agreed, "ingenious. To peer through the threads of a veil and thus mark out a composition."

"And," Filippo added, "to use the boxes made of threads to see where the shadow of a figure falls, where the highlight."

"Yes, you see," Brunelleschi said, "mathematics again."

Not wishing to reduce Alberti's contribution to mathematics alone, Filippo said, "I, too, through experiment have found that colors take their variations from light. And you taught me another valuable lesson. You advise to plan out a painting in one's head before ever putting pen to paper to sketch it. I do not know why, but when it is planned out in such a way the possibilities open, when work on it commences, to the accidents during the process of creating it that are leaps into uncharted seas."

"Another thing about which Lippi knows," Brunelleschi said, "derived from his days at sea."

"Still," Alberti told Filippo, "we do disagree fundamentally. Our understanding of painting, of the life of the soul, is diametrically opposed."

"And who is the greater painter?" Donatello wanted to know. "If we devote ourselves solely to the study of perspective, we forsake the substance for the shadow."

Alberti had walked over to Filippo's painting and was scrutinizing it. Although Filippo did use perspective in the planning of a composition, he understood that the manipulation of color played an even more important role in creating the illusion of depth. He felt the need to explain his method. "Intersecting lines help me to map out a scene, but figures and the space they move through are revealed through color and gradations from light to shadow. The simplistic color harmonies you recommend are not enough to accomplish this. We do not see in a continuous line. Our eyes move first in one direction, then the other. You know math, Alberti, but I know how to guide the eye of the viewer."

Alberti continued to stare at Filippo's painting, giving it serious consideration. "Yes. I see," he said. So he was open to refining his treatise.

Filippo decided to challenge him on the one stipulation he found most wanting. "I wager you a bet. I wager that I can place more than twenty figures in a painting, and it will be a work to marvel at."

Brunelleschi rubbed his hands together. "And what will the loser have to relinquish?"

Filippo thought for a moment. He knew what he wanted. "Alberti will remove that stipulation from his treatise in a revised edition."

"Done," Alberti said. "And Lippi will destroy his painting before all of us when he discovers the truth of my assertion."

"We have a deal," Filippo said. They shook on it.

"In the meantime, perhaps you should write a treatise on architecture, Alberti," Brunelleschi concluded.

CHAPTER 36

The year of Our Lord 1438, Florence

"Ferrara?" Cosimo fumed. He had just learned that the ecumenical council, which would negotiate the reunification of the Roman Church with that of Constantinople, would meet in that far-flung, inconsequential little city.

"The patriarch himself will be in attendance. The only city worthy of hosting such a delegation is Florence. How did tiny Ferarra usurp us?"

His secretary had no answer.

"And how do they intend to pay for it? There will be hundreds in the retinue. The lodgings alone. The food must be exquisite. These proceedings could last for months. Imagine the commerce it will bring. The scholarship. Well, Ferrara will not be able to sustain such a lavish undertaking. Keep your ears trained. When they falter, we will save them. What other business?"

"Niccolo's personal library," his secretary reminded him.

"Ah, yes. Niccolo left me his entire library. Apart from a few manuscripts that I will keep for my own use, I have decided to create a library in Niccolo's honor that will be open to all. He believed that any man who wanted to learn should be provided with the means to do so. There are at least eight hundred manuscripts, and I have commissioned Vespasiano to search the world for more. The library is to be made freely available to all those who wish to deepen their knowledge."

There is a bond of community that links every man in the world with every other. Cicero

"This has never before been done. Are you certain?"

"Ingegnue," Cosimo said. "It seems even I can create what has never before existed."

"Where is it to be located?"

"In San Marco," Cosimo said, "tucked away from the noise of the city, a place of quiet contemplation."

"A sound choice," his secretary agreed. "Now, another friend to honor. The painter Uccello is waiting to see you."

"Show him in." This painter had been recommended by Filippo, who was juggling several commissions at once. Uccello, a mathematician as well as a painter, was known for his command of perspective and his minute attention to detail.

"I wish to commemorate the battle of San Romano," Cosimo told the fidgety painter who stood before him. "I want every cavalryman, every foot soldier, each pennant and standard, every broken lance, down to the nails in the horses' shoes. The last great battle of the triumphant Niccolo da Tolentino. I am told you are the man to do it."

Uccello bowed his head. "I am honored."

Cosimo was busy. He had no time for false modesty. "I want to feel as if I am on the battlefield. Can you accomplish this?"

"Yes," Uccello assured him.

"Good. The contract is written. See my secretary on your way out."

It weighed heavily on Cosimo's conscience that he had not been able to free the great condottiere from the bastard Visconti.

Tolentino deserved a better end than to die in captivity. One day, he would see to it that the Visconti was paid back in full. Although they had brought Tolentino's body back from Milan to Florence, where he lay in state in the baptistery surrounded by enough candles to light up heaven itself, and he had been laid to rest in the duomo, Cosimo could find no rest. Had not Tolentino, when hearing of Cosimo's own imprisonment, immediately rallied an army in Pisa to storm Florence and rescue him? Cosimo had held him off, preferring less violent means, but Niccolo had not hesitated in coming to his aid.

Cosimo was reminded, too, of his own father's actions when his friend Pope John had been imprisoned in Germany. It was true that it had taken close to three years to accomplish, but Giovanni had procured his friend's release. Sadly, the once great man had been reduced to a broken, sickly shell of his former self, but he had died in comfort in Florence among friends, in the knowledge that Giovanni had not abandoned him.

Cosimo had been in the process of negotiating Tolentino's release when word came, little more than six months after his capture, that the great man was dead. Cosimo was certain he had been tortured. But did they also torture his soul with words? Did they tell him he had been forgotten? This was the thought that pained Cosimo most of all, that his friend might have perished in the mistaken belief that Cosimo had abandoned him.

What little was left to do Cosimo would accomplish. The last great battle undertaken for the Republic of Florence, in defense of its freedom, by the courageous Niccolo da Tolentino, would be commemorated for all time in a series of panel paintings. May it commend him to God and place him in heaven's good graces.

When the panels were completed, they did not disappoint. The perspective was expertly mastered. Every detail, down to the nails in the horses' hooves, was rendered, as Cosimo had requested. And yet, there was something lacking. One day he decided to show them off to Filippo.

"The scope is great," Cosimo said, "the perspective achieved to perfection, every detail rendered. It is a credit to its craftsman. And yet, there is a stiffness in it."

Filippo replied only, "Masterfully done."

"Come now. What is missing? You are a painter. What is it?"

"The eye does not perceive by order and measure alone," Filippo began.

"By what, then?"

"The eye seeks what it desires. A painting stirs the soul not by measure but by that which cannot be measured. The space between. The light and shadow. It is both that for which the hand reaches and that which it will never hold."

"That sounds like a description of God."

"'Eternity is present in time,'" Filippo said, quoting San Bernardino, "'immensity in measure, that which cannot be represented in the representation, the invisible in the vision.'"

CHAPTER 37

The year of Our Lord 1439, Florence

The council had brought hundreds of visitors from Constantinople, complaining of the uncomfortable accommodations and poor food in Ferrara, but it had been the re-emergence of pestilence that had finally convinced them to flee. Certainly, they were better provided for in Florence with Cosimo footing the bill. The city streets were filled with long-bearded foreigners who wore elaborate robes and exotic headdresses. They had brought with them all manner of exotic animals as well. Filippo and his fellow painters sketched many of them, looking for opportunities to include them in paintings. Cosimo took advantage of the scholarship offered. He sent his friend, Traversari, to take notes at the proceedings and later annotate the theological arguments. Cosimo was now able to acquire manuscripts from the source so that they could be translated for the first time directly from Greek into Latin.

Filippo was at work on a commission from the Company of Or San Michele for the Barbadori Chapel of Santo Spirito. He had learned that a new painter, Veneziano, had attempted to steal it out from under him. Veneziano had written a letter to Piero de' Medici, who would have satisfied him if not for Cosimo's intervention. Filippo would ensure that these commissions turned out to be works that solidified his stature among his peers and secured his reputation in Florence.

The Barbadori Chapel offered him a unique opportunity for experiment. Apart from the stipulation of which figures would be included, the Company of Or San Michele left all decisions to him, a rarity, requiring only that the sacristy in this important church be adorned with a work of truly outstanding beauty. Filippo decided that he would paint Mary in Majesty, not in the traditional iconic way, stiff before a flat gold background, but enthroned in a heaven that reflected the beauty of Earth. He would surpass himself, peopling the composition with saints and angels, fourteen in all, including Mary, in graceful movement. He would flood the scene with direct light, gradually leading it into deepest shadow in the far recesses of the background. His goal was to create a complex work both in composition and lighting without detracting from its beauty and grace.

Filippo began by scratching the basic conception into the gesso, but he would use this only as a guide. He would allow himself to make changes until the end, the act of creation a reflection of the movement, the energy of the work itself.

Immediately, Filippo struck on the idea of using a real woman to depict the Virgin Mary. His sister, Piera, a poor widow who earlier that year had languished for five days in a fever and then passed into God's hands, was surely herself now in heaven. She had been Filippo's caretaker after their mother's death, so that he felt her loss deeply. Piera would serve as his model. This turned out to be more of a helpful device than he had imagined, for once he created a Mary who reminded him of the sister he loved, the scene began to unfold in a space that he strove to round out and make real.

As he worked, he decided to engage all of the figures in movement. Even Mary, her hip supporting the baby Jesus, wrapped in a sling hung around her neck and over her shoulder, much as his sister might have carried her own daughters, now steps forward. The cloth swaddling Jesus is delicate, diaphanous, with a barely perceptible gold gilt border.

The istoria will move the soul of the beholder when each man painted there clearly shows the movement of his own soul...known by movements of the body. Alberti

Filippo changes Santo Frediano's pose in the process of creating it, catching him as he begins to genuflect, braced by his staff. The saints and angels have faces Filippo has seen on the streets of Florence. While painting the finials, he decides to form them into organic shapes, as if they, too, despite being made of stone, bloom like the lilies carried by the angels. Filippo works carefully from front to back, from direct light to deep shadow in gradations of color from warm to cool. He frames a distant landscape within a window and leaves the throne room open to the sky.

He creates pillars that appear to be made of marble with swirls, splotches, and dots of paint in green, lavender, red, and yellow. He employs unique combinations of colors. Architecture is not white but shot through with lavender and green. All of his whites he now tints with blue, lavender, green, grey, or yellow. Green draperies are green-violet and red are blue-vermillion. All of the gradations of colors he has studied in nature now pour forth from his hand, his brush, dripping with light.

The painting is nearing completion when Filippo has an idea. He places his brother, Giovanni, whose face and monk's hood are visible above a balustrade, peeking out from behind an angel. He next places his own face where it could easily be missed, on the opposite side, partially obscured by an angel's wing. The three siblings are together once again.

He traces the edge of Mary's mantle with fluid lines, his imitation of the Arabic language, a flow of characters like song, in gold gilt. Gold, the final touch, is a subtle addition throughout the work, but one that lights it as if with divine presence. Even the green band of marble cornice just behind Mary's halo is pierced with gold specks where the light falls, white specks in the shadows.

The work finished, Filippo stepped back to study the result. No one ever before created a painting like this one. He felt a light pass through his body like that he had experienced as a youth when he first saw Masaccio's work, a sense of being in the presence of something that transcends the merely earthbound, a reverence for the force, not of him but through him, that led to its creation.

As he stood taking in the finished work, Filippo's brother Giovanni entered the bottega. "We must provide," he told Filippo, "for Piera's daughters." Their sister had left behind six children, all girls, not in good health themselves.

Giovanni stopped before the painting, stunned into silence. "There is our dear sister herself. My brother, this is a new way of painting. Surely, God has had a hand in this."

"Do I not know it?"

After a silence during which Giovanni took in the details of the work before him, he placed his hand on his brother's shoulder. "You are truly gifted." He paused. "Which is good news for our nieces. You will command higher prices, and they are in need of dowries."

Having himself been forced by circumstance into the Carmine, Filippo knew too well the results of having a life of the cloth thrust upon one. No, he could not do this to another, and certainly not to his dear sister's children.

"I am a poor friar with no ability to support them," Giovanni continued, "but you. You must for the time being feed, clothe, and house them. If you agree to renew your associations with the Carmelites, I will be able to request that a benefice be bestowed on you."

Filippo cut him short. "Impossible. I have not lived as a friar of the order for ten years."

"But, Filippo. If I can procure a benefice for you, it will come with substantial income." Filippo lightened a shadow on Mary's nose. "Benefices are bought and sold," Giovanni argued. "Men own twelve at a time and do little to sustain them. They are treated as tokens."

"Not by me," Filippo said.

"There is little choice, Filippo. Two of Piera's daughters are already of marriageable age. If we do not find them husbands soon, they will be too old to wed."

Filippo put down his brush and turned toward his brother.

"Unless"—Giovanni hammered the final nail into his argument—"you are willing to force them to take the veil."

Filippo said nothing.

"The prior has spoken to the archbishop, who says he will see what he can do. What will you have me respond?"

With a sinking heart, Filippo said, "We must provide."

Giovanni was relieved. "That is where I will be able to help. There is a provision that allows for another friar to stand in for you. I, in fulfilling your duties, will earn the stipend. It will not interfere with your work. Between us, we will not only provide for our nieces but save dowries as well. After that, they will be their husbands' problem. But we will not have abandoned them to a life they did not choose. Until a benefice can be procured, will you be able to support them?"

Filippo was not sure he would be able to do so. But, not long after, by the grace of God, the Confraternity of Sant' Agnese took up a collection that provided a dowry for the oldest of Piera's daughters. A marriage was arranged with a carder, a lowly trade, but the man was from a good family. The confraternity decided to make this a regular practice, providing every three years a dowry for a girl from a family too poor, or one left an orphan. However, it was determined that, since there was such dire need in the community, no family would receive more than one. That left five girls in need of dowries.

Luckily, he received two large commissions. One was for a Coronation of the Virgin for Sant'Ambrogio. The other was for an Annunciation for the Martelli Chapel in San Lorenzo, the church of the Medici.

CHAPTER 38

The year of Our Lord 1439, Villa Medici at Carregi

Cosimo and his brother Lorenzo sat at a table on the upper loggia of their villa. A mild wind gently stirred the tendrils of vines hanging from the trellis above them. They had finished the mid-day meal, which had been cleared away save for a platter of fruit. Cosimo leaned over to refill their wine glasses. "Twice in two years Milan has advanced on Florentine territories and been pushed back by Sforza. I was right about the man," he mused.

"He is Italy's best condottiere," Lorenzo agreed. "Not even the Visconti's menace of a general Piccinino is able to encroach on our lands. We have not lost one hamlet in all of the fighting."

"More importantly," Cosimo continued, "he becomes as good a strategist off the field as on."

"How so?" Lorenzo asked.

"I had a letter from him not three months ago in which he takes on my question of Piccinino's loyalty to the Visconti and reasons it through admirably. He learns quickly under my tutelage." Sforza was an able and worthy student. Cosimo smiled and reached for a grape.

"What did he have to say about it?" Lorenzo pressed for more information.

"Sforza lists all of the reasons it is unlikely that Piccinino goes behind the duke's back. I am able to see his meaning. Then he tells me that he has made overtures of friendship toward Piccinino, as I requested, to no avail. But, he writes, this matters not since he does not need to go through the condottiere to make deals with the Visconti. Sforza has in his possession a document from the old bastard agreeing to his ownership of lands he stole from him, which he is certain the Visconti will honor. After Sforza fought against him on Florence's behalf. Remarkable."

"The Visconti honorable!" Lorenzo laughed. "Why, the crazy bastard murdered his own wife and her entire entourage for listening to a servant boy play the flute."

"He made the servant boy out to be her lover," Cosimo reminded him. "He was ready to be rid of his duchess."

"Could he not have sent her away?" Lorenzo countered. "Taken a mistress? The madman murdered every last maid."

"Ah, well. You need not convince me he is a madman. Sforza writes"—Cosimo laughed remembering— "he writes that all Piccinino's loud talk amounts to scarecrows, good for frightening kites and the like, but not him since he is not a bird of prey but the son of a Sforza. Ha. He ends by saying that anyone who attempts to take what belongs to him will find a thornier road than they do by simply demanding it."

"He is formidable," Lorenzo agreed.

"Then, just this month," Cosimo continued, "I have a letter from him advising that in the choice of alignment, it would be better for us to side with Piccinino than with Venice. There, you see, he does not allow his judgement to be clouded by emotion. Venice, he claims, cannot be counted on. Did I myself not recently discover this to be true? He also relays that the Visconti once again makes overtures to him regarding marriage to his daughter Bianca. Sforza plays both sides to the middle. I was right in my assessment. He is an astute politician."

"You trust him?"

"I know the man. He is someone you could play odds and evens with in the dark. He is not a cheat."

"Unlike the Venetians," Lorenzo noted.

"Damned Venetians," Cosimo grumbled. "They told me that Sforza is impudent and in need of a lesson lest he grow more demanding."

"There is something to that," Lorenzo interjected.

"They play a game, Lorenzo. We are allied, but they refuse to pay Sforza for defending against Milan's advance, although it places their own lands in jeopardy. But, if Florence, they said, out of fear of Sforza—ha!—wishes to pay him, that is her business."

If the loftiness of spirit that reveals itself amid danger and toil is empty of justice, if it fights not for the common safety but for its own advantages, it is a vice. Cicero

"What will you do?" Lorenzo asked.

"We will pay him, but not out of fear. And, we will never again place our trust in the Venetians. Sforza is an important ally, Lorenzo. He will help us achieve our ultimate goal."

"Which is?"

"Peace. Omina bona in tempore. All good things in time."

Now you are ready to learn how to blend the deepest shadows with the light, how to work them in together, how to achieve the most subtle layering on of gold.

(THE CRAFTSMAN'S HANDBOOK)

PART THREE

BLENDING THE DEEPEST SHADOWS

WITH LIGHT

CHAPTER 39

The year of Our Lord 1443, Florence

Lucrezia would always remember her eighth year of life as a rare one in which her mother was neither pregnant nor nursing. She luxuriated in her mother's attention and was excited to learn that her father, a silk merchant who often traveled for a year or more, would be returning home. At the end of Easter week, her parents decided to take their two eldest, Lucrezia and her sister Spinetta, to the sacra rappresentazione, the Ascension play, at Santa Maria 'del Carmine. She had heard about this wondrous pageant that people traveled from afar to see. Her sister, Isabetta, who was much older, had attended the play every year with her brother and grandmother.

Lucrezia was allowed to wear her best giornea. She could not keep from resting her eyes on its soft shade of blue, pure as the sky on a cloudless day, embroidered with tiny sprays of pink and yellow flowers. This blue was her favorite color of all. Her hands caressed the fabric, the finest of silks, slippery and cool to the touch. Its rustle reminded her of water rushing over rock. Her sister, whose blond hair cascaded down a giornea of the palest green silk, was a little pool of light on a spring meadow.

When they arrived, the basilica was teeming with people. Lucrezia had never seen so many in one place. All of Florence must have turned out for the event. She could barely sit still with anticipation.

Lucrezia leaned her head against her father's arm and listened to the story as it was recounted but, with so much to take in, she found it difficult to focus. Her eyes strayed to the many-colored lights that dotted the stage. The expanse of vermillion cloth that covered the mountain caught her eye. She knew it to be priceless. Her father had once explained the rarity of the red pigment that made any cloth dyed with it the most expensive of all. She realized that she had missed some of the story. Jesus was now speaking. She sensed the apostles' pain at losing their friend, but what did consolation mean? Truth. She knew truth, but how did that bring comfort? A clap of thunder made her jump. The lights went out. She gasped. Silence.

Lucrezia held her breath and tried to understand what was happening. Quite suddenly, Jesus flew up into the sky. It was a miracle. When He reached a cloud high above, there with a burst of light. The crowd exclaimed. The music rose, and one by one a multitude of tiny stars filled the heavens. Lucrezia was surrounded by a feeling of comfort, the kind that she experienced when curled up on her mother's lap. It was a dreamlike trance during which she was filled with wonder in a world where nothing can go wrong, a beautiful and perfect place.

And as, announcing dawn, the breeze of May stirs and exudes a fragrance filled with the scent of grass and flowers, just such a wind I felt stroking my brow. Dante

As they walked home from the Ascension play, Spinetta, who was holding both parents' hands, looked up and, with furrowed brow, asked, "Does Jesus come from heaven every year?"

Her mother gave her a puzzled look. "To be in the play," Spinetta explained, the frustration of not being understood evident in her voice.

Her father and mother exchanged glances that were filled with surprise and uncertainty, and then her father said, "Of course, my little rosebud. Jesus loves the people of Florence. He makes the trip every year." He smiled and winked at his wife, Caterina, who smiled lovingly back at her husband.

Spinetta nodded her head, satisfied. Lucrezia smiled along with her parents, knowingly, but was left to wonder, Who is this man who can fly?

CHAPTER 40

The year of Our Lord 1443, Florence

Filippo sat behind the rows of Carmelite friars and novices directly in front of the rood screen on top of which the play would unfold. He had worked each of the last nine years on its production. This year, he had repaired the giant copper star that hung high above the crowd, tipped with lanterns that were filled with fireworks. He had made additional parchment lanterns for the stage to replace those that had gone up in flame the year before, and had stitched fresh peacock feathers into the wings of the angels.

He now knew all of the tricks used to give the appearance of magic. Five hundred oil lamps shone through vases that were filled with a mixture of water and various colors of pigment. Other lamps shone through dyed parchment. The effect was of hundreds of colored lights that filled the stage with their glow. Brunelleschi had designed the machinery that allowed Jesus to rise from the earth and fly up into the sky. The lanterns hanging from the large star exploded with light when he passed before the cloud. Angels, robed in ochre, indigo, saffron, and cinnabar, wore wings made of ostrich and peacock feathers. They held real instruments, but the melodies were played by professional musicians assembled off stage.

None of these tricks were known to Filippo the year he entered the convent, a boy of eight, the first time he witnessed this glorious event. His aunt Mona Lapaccia never left the house except for provisions. She did not like to be among people. The night that he saw the Ascension play for the first time, he was, having just been placed in the convent, a malcontent among the young boys. His brother Giovanni assured him that he was in for a treat. Even so, as he sat among the others, jostling and cuffing, he could not have imagined the scene to come.

It began slowly enough, with music and a few simple instructive words to help the audience understand the story that was unfolding. A stone castle with high towers stood opposite a mountain that was draped in cloth of vermillion. High above both was another wooden structure painted gold, with a large round opening in its center covered by an azure curtain. Above this were the sun, the moon, and all of the stars.

The angels who surrounded Jesus as He walked to the city of Jerusalem each carried a real flowering branch. Once Jesus had left the city with His mother and Mary Magdelene, He returned to find Peter and the other apostles. They followed behind until He stopped at the bottom of the Mount of Olives. There, He blessed each apostle as they knelt at His feet. Jesus gave each one a gift. Andrew received a net: "You will be a fisher of men." Then Jesus told them, "Since everything that was ordained has been fulfilled, I go to my Father and yours." As He slowly rose above them, the apostles wept and pleaded, "Do not leave us, or we will be orphans."

They were speaking about him, Filippo. How did they know? Tears stung his eyes. Jesus answered them: "Weep not. I will not leave you like orphans." He wiped the tears from the corners of his eyes so that the other boys would not see. "I will ask my Father to send you the Spirit of Consolation, the Spirit of Truth, which will teach you everything. If I do not go, the Comforter will not come to you."

There was a peal of thunder. The music stopped. The lights went out. A hush fell upon the crowd. Filippo held his breath as Jesus ascended to heaven. A cloud drifted toward Him from the sky; He met it in mid-air with a burst of light, and the music rose once again. One by one, a multitude of stars lit the heavens. The azure drape lifted, and the light revealed God the Father, hovering in mid-air before the golden castle. Angels danced around Him, playing upon pipes, lutes and bells. Filippo leaned forward to take it all in. Jesus and the angels who traveled upward with Him raised their arms in praise. His ordeal was over. He was home.

The play had never lost its fascination for Filippo. Even though he now knew how the magic was created, he was drawn in as he had been the first time he saw it. His eyes still filled with tears when Jesus said, "I will not leave you orphans. I will ask my Father to send you the Spirit of Consolation." But, it also brought his mind back to that day long ago when control over his own fate had been wrested from him, a memory that left him feeling despondent.

And the darker you want to make the shadows in the accents, the more times you go back to them.... Cennini

When the play was over, Filippo, head bent, made his way slowly back over the Arno to his bottega on Via Chiara. Yes, he thought, Jesus said that he did not leave us orphans, that the comforter would come to us, and it was true that, as a child, the kindness of the monks had provided some solace. But, he had always been aware that he was an orphan. He was abandoned. This was the source of the dark space inside of him. He was brooding on this when the laughter of children up ahead drew his attention.

A small family, a mother, a father, and two little girls, crossed the bridge a few paces ahead of him. The youngest appeared to be five or six. She skipped along between her parents, holding both their hands, her long blonde hair trailing over a meadow-green dress.

The oldest, a girl of about eight, the age he had been when he first saw the Ascension play, held her father's hand and, at that moment, looked lovingly up at him. Her long blond hair swept back and forth across her dress as she walked, a lilt to her step, a charming little dancer in pale blue silk, all sky shot through with sunlight.

Filippo found himself walking faster. To what end? He slowed his pace. No matter how quickly he walked, he would never catch up. He was shut out, the light he perceived around them like the one he chased in his paintings. The bridge behind them now, he watched as the fortunate little family branched off onto a side street. He continued straight on, the light at his back throwing his shadow before him.

CHAPTER 41

The year of Our Lord 1443, Florence

The commission from the Martelli was for a panel painting to be placed in their chapel in the Medici church of San Lorenzo. It was to be an Annunciation. Filippo decided to venture a new way of representing the drama. He would, once again, use his sister Piera as the model for Mary, but not idealized, as she had been in the Barbodori chapel. He would paint her as she was. Her facial structure, softer in the previous painting, would be more angular, her forehead not as round, but more broad, higher, her nose less chiseled, flatter, and her eyes more deeply set.

Filippo would place as much emphasis on tree and vine, on anatomy and dress, as on the details of architecture. Figures turned and twisted in a way that demanded his close attention in order to maintain a truth of form and movement. He detailed the tucks in Gabriel's bodice, each individual layering of his collar, the studded leather belt that cinched Mary's robe.

Two angels behind Gabriel witnessed the drama, providing a new device. They looked out at the viewer, inviting them to participate, as dictated by Alberti. There was a precedent in the Bible for the angels, who added a layer to the narrative, as well as to the composition. Filippo placed a glass vessel filled with water on a step in the foreground of the painting, one that begged the viewer to touch it to be certain that it was not real. He framed the whole with arches and pillars that echoed those in San Lorenzo, creating the effect of a space inside the wall where the drama unfolded.

This was a painting to step into, a place where one could walk beyond Mary's chamber, out into the garden, and past this, further, into the city. To accomplish this, Filippo used a single vanishing point, but once established, he focused his attention on color, light, and shadow. As he had told Alberti, vision does not move in a straight line but wanders along the way.

Donatello was working in San Lorenzo at the same time, on the doors to the sacristy. When the painting had been put in place, and Filippo stood before it, Donatello joined him, saying, "The work praises its craftsman," throwing his arm around Filippo's shoulders. "No one understands light and color as you do."

"I am pleased," Filippo agreed. "The space in between where the subtle variations of light dance." His finger traced in the air the areas of empty space in the painting they now viewed. "The space in which the story takes place. Where before there was nothing, now a moment of intense meaning that will once again be gone, empty space. There, the time when it did not exist, and there the time when it does. Masaccio was not only telling me to breathe into my work but to allow my work to breathe."

"Ahh," Donatello said, winking, "and the boy becomes a man." They stood for a moment in silent contemplation of Filippo's Annunciation.

Then Donatello noted, "The framing pillars and arches are one with the architecture of San Lorenzo. As if we could step up, walk into the painting, careful not to topple the vessel of water." The glass was positioned on the step at the edge of the painting, leading into it, so that one would have to carefully place one's foot.

Filippo nodded.

"And Mary," Donatello said, "caught in a moment of surprise.

And yet, there is a trace of sorrow. You have chosen a real woman to represent the mother of God?"

"She is an angel in heaven," Filippo said. "One who suffered much in life, as Mary did."

"Yes. Yes. I see," Donatello mused, clearly thinking about something else now. "What fascinates me is that the vanishing point is held in the hand of the angel Gabriel. See there? So that our eye is drawn deepest into the painting just at the place where it is drawn back to the hand that invites us in, and to the surface."

O, glorious stars, O light made pregnant with a mighty power, all my talent, whatever it may be, has you as source.   Dante

Filippo smiled. It felt good to hear someone else recognize what he had achieved, understand how he had accomplished it. Then, Donatello went further with his analysis to a place that Filippo had not traveled, humbling him.

"It reminds us that, although we feel as if we can step into the painting and are invited to do so in order to better understand the drama taking place there, it is a spiritual space. Held in the hand of an angel. Only in our imagination can we truly step into this drama."

CHAPTER 42

The year of Our Lord 1443, Florence

Cosimo was happy to see Traversari walk through the doorway of his antechamber. It was always a great diversion to discuss philosophy with him. "Friend." He stood to welcome him.

"Cosimo," Traversari began, "there is something in particular about which I wish to speak."

"So, there is a reason for your visit."

"It is about Carlo. I feel it is advisable that, before the boy takes his vows, he should meet his mother. Meet Maddalena."

"That would be unwise."

"Cosimo, the boy is seventeen. He is about to make a vow that is all-encompassing. Before making such a commitment, do you not think, he must know who he is, from whom he comes?"

"He has no choice but to take the vow, and he knows from whom he comes."

"The story is not the same as direct knowledge of his mother. Would you keep him from her?"

"It would not be wise," Cosimo repeated.

"Not wise for you, perhaps," Traversari countered. "But, the boy? Cosimo, she is his mother."

"And, if upon meeting her, he decides he wishes to throw away his only chance of living a respectable, comfortable life?"

"It will be his choice. Not many have that opportunity."

"Nor does he," Cosimo grumbled. Traversari was right, of course, as much as Cosimo hated to admit it. "Fine. You have my assent." He gritted his teeth. "You will accompany him?"

"It is a journey I would not have him make alone," Traversari assured him.

After Traversari took his leave, Cosimo moodily reflected on their conversation. He was happy that his old friend and mentor was looking after Carlo. How long had it been since he had thought of Maddalena? At first, it had been as he had told her; he thought about her every day. But, this had been so painful that it was unsustainable. There was business to attend to, politics to navigate, building projects to supervise. So, he had locked the memory of her in an impenetrable chamber of his heart. Not even the sight of Carlo, with his dark hair and blue-grey eyes, rattled that door.

Yes, the boy looked like his mother, she would be pleased to see, apart from the long beak of a nose that he had inherited from his father. Cosimo smiled. Carlo alone had inherited his nose and his hawk-like gaze. There was a sadness about the boy, as well. Would meeting his mother ease his melancholy or worsen it? Ah, well, Traversari knew best. And, what of him? Would the carefully concealed chamber in his heart regain its pulse?

The second kind of pleasure involves memory, for it accompanies desire, a mental affection...[it] is therefore always mixed with pain. Plato

When he returned from Rome, Carlo did not mention his journey. Should Cosimo ask? Probably not. If the boy wished to speak of her, he would. But, then again, would he not be reluctant to bring it up? Oh, damnit, he wished to know. He sent for Carlo.

"How did you find your mother?" he asked as the boy entered his office.

"She is well."

"But, is she? Is she happy?"

Carlo hesitated. "She is not unhappy."

Cosimo focused in on his son. "How did the meeting go for you?"

"It was strange. At first. But, she dispelled the awkwardness. She is kind-hearted. And beautiful. It soon felt as if I had always known her."

"Ah," was all Cosimo could think to say.

"I look like her."

"But for my nose. I am sorry for that."

They laughed.

"She has learned to read and write," Carlo offered.

Cosimo raised an eyebrow.

"The bookseller," he explained. "The one you sent her to with lists of manuscripts."

"Ah, yes. Well, good for her."

"I hope that I may continue to visit with my mother?" Carlo asked, his hands balled into fists at his sides the only betrayal of what this meant to him.

So, this was not to be the end of it. Cosimo had assumed, but of course, having met his mother, the boy would wish to get to know her. He could deny him, but to what end? She was his mother, and God knows, he had no other. Contessina had made a point of looking past him as if he did not exist. Carlo had never caused him an ounce of trouble. "Of course you may visit with her." He hesitated. "You are a good boy, Carlo. She must have been proud."

"She did say."

"What will you do?"

"Do?" Carlo appeared to be confused.

"Will you take your vows?"

"Yes."

"Good boy. A wise decision."

Carlo bowed to take his leave. "Father."

"Carlo, I am proud of you as well." Cosimo gently placed his hand on the boy's shoulder.

"Thank you, Father."

It appeared that meeting his mother had made Carlo no more nor less melancholy.

CHAPTER 43

The year of Our Lord 1443, Florence

Lucrezia stood ready, the head cook, Angelina who was called Lina, at her side.

"You have learned all of the rudimentary skills," her mother was saying, "required to make nourishing meals for the family. Lina tells me that you have ably accomplished these tasks. Now it is time that you learn how one of the most important sources of sustenance is made. Remember, Lucrezia, if you have grain, oil, and wine, you will never experience want."

Lucrezia could hardly contain her excitement. Since she was a little girl she had loved sitting on a stool watching Lina knead bread, anticipating the day she herself would be allowed to do so. As a married woman she would not be called upon to cook or bake, but every young girl apprenticed at both in order to understand the needs of their servants and to appreciate the importance of the administration of their own duties. Unlike the careful measuring of ingredients by sight or the course chopping of vegetables, bread required the mastery of a technique. The more skillful the baker, the better the bread. She carefully measured out the ingredients in her palm.

"Bene. Molto bene," Lina applauded her. "The careful measurement of ingredients makes the difference. Only the kneading matters more. You have a good eye, little one. There is no one more precise at measurement. You are like a little merchant when in the storeroom as well. No one will go hungry in this household."

Lucrezia swelled with pride. It was true. She took her responsibilities seriously when weighing and measuring out supplies to determine the quantities that needed ordering. The family and servants all depended on her accuracy. Poor Spinetta was often scolded for yawning and for the occasional spillage of grain from the scoop, prompting mother to warn her, "Grain is God's gift, Spinetta. Not to be wasted. You taunt Fortuna to leave your family hungry." But, Lucrezia enjoyed plunging her scoop into the grain, carefully evening out the top, placing it on the scale, subtracting the weight of the scoop, and recording the measure over and over with attentive focus. At the end, her mother always said, "Leave a little at the bottom unmeasured to ensure that you never run short."

The time to knead had arrived. "Never knead with the wrists and hands," Lina advised. "Use your upper arms. Throw all of your strength into it. Push with the flat of your palms, then roll, punch, prod, fold, and then push it again," she demonstrated. "Now you."

Lucrezia took a deep breath and used the strength of her thin shoulders and upper arms to push against the dough. Its consistency was sticky and left pieces of itself stuck to her hands.

"Sprinkle a little flower, flop it over," Lina instructed, "and push it again."

Lucrezia did as she was told.

"Not like that," Lina stopped her. "Move your hands like this when you roll. Now punch it." Lucrezia giggled as she watched Lina take out all of her imaginary aggression on the poor lump of dough. But, the dough was slowly beginning to take on a soft, pliant yet intact consistency.

"Now you. Let me see you do the rolling technique." Lucrezia complied. "That's it. Now punch." Lucrezia battered away. "Bene.

You are a little warrior. Molto bene." Lina smiled with satisfaction. "You cannot knead enough. I will leave you to your work. Remember. Push, fold, turn over, flop, punch."

The light filtered through a nearby window, falling across the table as Lucrezia worked, warming her in its comforting glow. She giggled seeing that her arms up to her elbows were covered in flower. As she struggled with the dough, she and it were becoming one. From this formless lump she was determined to create a loaf of the proper consistency that would nourish the entire family. She smiled as she worked, lulled by the ceaseless activity, the creative struggle taking place in her hands. What a wondrous thing, this making of bread.

CHAPTER 44

The year of Our Lord 1443, Florence

Filippo soon regretted that he had done a friend a favor by taking on his nephew, Frediano da Ravenzano, as an apprentice. The boy was undisciplined and never failed to disappoint. Filippo would not have minded if he had worked hard to overcome his faults, but the boy lacked passion, and this Filippo could not forgive. Now here he was crowing about being given more responsibility. When, he demanded, would he be tasked with painting a panel?

In response, Filippo gently prodded him, "'Let not confidence be without knowledge,'" quoting Seneca as he had often heard Cosimo do. "You have read Alberti's treatise, have you not? 'Perfection in art will be found in diligence, application, and study.' You will never be any good as a painter if you do not apply yourself. 'He draws the bow in vain who has nowhere to point the arrow.'"

Leaning over Frediano to better see his most recent drawing, Filippo instructed, "Now then, where is the light source? From which direction does it flow?"

The boy was silent. He could never supply a simple answer. "It is a simple question," Filippo said, growing exasperated. "From which direction does the light fall upon the cast?" A window above his apprentice's left shoulder supplied all the light he needed. He did not even have to imagine a light source.

"Here." Filippo thrust his arm up toward the window. "Your light source. All that we perceive is light, Frediano. The shadows as well. See how you have all the light you need to model your figures. Study how it falls on your own arm and hand, onto the table. And, what is this?" He pointed to a stick with lines running down its length.

"A pillar," Frediano said.

Filippo smacked his own head with his hand. "A stick," he said. "Which pillar? Which cornice?"

Frediano's face took on the blank expression that infuriated Filippo. "You do not have to imagine a pillar," he said. "This is Florence. The streets are full of them. A viewer should feel as if he has turned the corner onto Via Bardi and is about to walk down it. Go. Look. Use your eyes," he urged. "They are your greatest tool."

Shaking his head and grumbling under his breath as he turned away, "like a deaf cow in a bell tower," Filippo moved on to Diamante, a young monk who had recently begun service in his workshop. At seventeen, he was a full five years younger than Frediano, but his passion for painting was such that he stayed behind every day long after the others had left. Barely a year in the workshop and Diamante was ready to assist in the painting of the background on a panel that was now being prepared. Francesco was at work sanding the poplar board for it, a task that Filippo could not entrust to Frediano.

"Well done, Diamante," he said. "You have mastered the consistency of a light source. Except here. Do you see?" Diamante did see and rubbed away the area indicated with a crumb of bread used for this purpose so that he might begin to rework it.

"Yes. That's it," Filippo said. "Your modeling creates figures of real weight. Work next on movement. We must feel that they not only stand upon the ground but that they move through space, that beneath these robes they have limbs, limbs caught in the moment when they are about to move forward or turn aside, as they twist to see, to reach out. Here." He grabbed the charcoal from Diamante's hand and with one swift movement drew a line that curved through the center of a figure, first one way and then the other. No sooner did he hand the charcoal back than Diamante was again at work, following the maestro's direction.

"You will assist me, Diamante, with the painting of the distant landscape on this panel. You must begin to learn the importance of color to richly deceive the eye."

No one can be envious and thankful at the same time. Seneca

When Filippo turned back toward Frediano to view his progress, he discerned a narrowing of the boy's eyes, a tightening of his lips.

CHAPTER 45

The year of Our Lord 1443, Florence

Cosimo had been hunched over his desk all morning. He settled back into his chair and allowed his eyes to rest on the rustling of leaves in the late summer breeze outside his window. Suddenly, it was not swaying leaves that he saw but Maddalena's eyes, a stormy blue. The breeze carried her voice to him, her laughter. He traced her soft white hand, knowing it as well as he knew his own. He would write to her. No, he must not. Why not? It was unreasonable. No good could come from it. Would she even want to hear from him? What was the point? To tell her he wished to visit? After what he had done, would she want to see him? His father had forbidden it, but his father was gone more than ten years now.

Affections that happen to the body sometimes expire before they reach the soul and leave her unaffected, at other times traverse both soul and body, and communicate a shock to both. Plato

He could not get her out of his mind, not since Carlo had spoken of her. There was nothing for it. Cosimo pulled out a piece of parchment, dipped his pen in ink, and stared down at the blank page. What, after all these years, could he say to her?

Just then the door burst open, startling him. "What in the name of God?" But, seeing his secretary's face, he stopped short.

"It is Lorenzo," his secretary said, out of breath from running. "Cosimo. Quite suddenly. May he rest in peace." He blessed himself.

Cosimo was stunned. He could not move. Not only he, but the world seemed paralyzed. He sat for what felt like an eternity. "Where is he?" he finally asked.

"At home."

Cosimo rose from his chair. Stiffly, perceiving only a blur of sights and sounds, he made his way to his brother's palazzo.

When Cosimo entered his brother's bedchamber, his breath caught in his throat. His brother lay on the bed where he had been placed, his hands folded on top of his chest. His wife, Ginevra, knelt beside the bed, prostrate, her arms thrown across his body, sobbing.

"Ginevra," he walked over and placed his hand on her shoulder. She looked up, tears streaming down her face. "Why? Why?"

Cosimo could only shake his head. His brother. His dear brother. Gone in a moment. While he was still so sorely needed in this life. Cosimo needed him, his wife, his two young sons, yet small boys. A good man, a far better man than Cosimo. Lorenzo was no political maneuverer. He was guileless, more straightforward. Even as a child he had had a purity about him, an honesty not often found. Standing there, the last member of the family, Cosimo felt so very alone, as if a part of his body had been ripped off, a jagged hole left open to the elements.

We are all bound by this oath: To bear the ills of mortal life, and to submit with good grace to what we cannot avoid. Seneca

Less than a month after Lorenzo's passing, Cosimo brought his brother's family into his own home so that his two young nephews would grow up with a male family member to look after them. Soon after, he went to San Lorenzo, the family church, and put into motion the massive renovation project that had long been on hold there. His tribute to his brother, it would be a classical revival accomplished by the great Brunelleschi.

After Cosimo reviewed the plans for the renovation, he settled back into his chair. It was a singular feat of measure and proportion, geometry informing art. Corinthian columns and entablature blocks supporting rounded arches. The pure white coffered ceiling that set off gilded rosettes. The stark white of the ceiling and walls contrasting with the grey stone of the arcades. It was simple in design and effortlessly elegant. This was a building project of which he was proud. Long after the Medici were exiled from Florence, for that day was sure to come, his buildings would survive, gifts to his city. There was a knock at the door. "Come."

His secretary delivered a letter. "From Rome," he said.

Cosimo glanced down and then waited for his secretary to leave. It was a woman's handwriting. He stared at it, discerning the strength of purpose in the steady hand and the forward thrust of the letters. His own hand shook as he ripped through the seal. Dear Sir, it began: I wish to thank you for allowing my dearest son to come to me. He is a fine boy. His renewed presence in my life is a gift for which I am eternally grateful. Maddalena

Cosimo traced the well-shaped letters with his finger. As he did so, she came clearly to mind, as if only yesterday he held her in his arms. He pulled a piece of parchment toward him and dipped his pen in ink. His heart was beating fast. He must be careful in his response, restrained. But, he hoped this correspondence would continue for a long time. He told her that Carlo was, indeed, a good boy, who had learned early that moderation, as Seneca teaches us, is contained in virtue.

It was not long before he had a response: If by this your meaning is more than abstemiousness, but also encompasses self-denial and forbearance, then yes. His heart was bound long ago. It barely troubles him now. This is the source of his melancholy.

She cut him to the quick. This was the Maddalena he remembered, with her incisive intellect. She pierced through his rhetoric with clear-eyed accuracy. He had missed her. Yes, he would keep his promise to his father. He would not see her, but he would converse with her. This relationship by correspondence must never be revealed, and most certainly not discovered some day when he was gone. To that end, he now pulled her first message from the drawer. With each new response, he would destroy the one previous. He crumpled it in his fist and threw it into the fire. He watched as it went up in flames.

CHAPTER 46

The year of Our Lord 1444, Florence

There was a chill in the early February air the morning Filippo began the portrait of a wool merchant's wife, Mona Lucia. Her husband decided that he wished to commemorate the astonishing beauty of his wife in a painting. It was a new but common practice among the merchant class to commission portraits of their wives dressed in their most luxurious attire and draped with their most precious jewels, all of which, after marriage, they were forbidden by sumptuary laws to wear in public. Since their husbands had spent much of their wealth on these items of dress and ornament, which evidenced their status, they commissioned portraits. For Filippo, portraits continued to provide easy money that paid his workshop expenses. Her husband was unable to wait to make the arrangements, so he left the contractual details to an agent. He was certain of one thing; he wanted Filippo Lippi, the most sought-after painter in Florence.

At this hour of the morning, the sun streamed through the window, illuminating her face. Her golden hair shone like a nimbus about her head. The sunlight caressed her delicate hands, the bones of which were like those of a songbird. The skin of her forearm was exposed where the sleeve of her cioppi had fallen back. Her profile, sweet in its innocence, was one that a painter might use as a model for an angel. Filippo had never seen a face so beautiful. He soaked it in, filled with admiration.

One day as he worked, she asked, "What is it like? Out there?" She looked longingly toward the window.

Filippo knew that the life of a highborn woman was restricted and carefully monitored. Best not to encourage a longing for that which she could not possess. "Crowded," he said. "Noisy. Dusty. Smelly. Muddy when it rains."

"There is so much to see," she said, as if she had not heard his answer. "Wares beautifully displayed. People to engage in conversation. Artists and artisans at work in their botteghe."

"I am an artist at work. What is so worth seeing?"

She disregarded his comment. "So much activity. Fruits and vegetables arrayed on tables with careful attention to color and texture. Baskets and crockery laid out. Cloth of many colors, silks and brocades." Here she stopped, lost in her imagination.

Filippo remembered the hardship of being ripped away from the streets as a boy when cloistered at the Carmine. He recalled how, after being on the ship for months, with what wonder, even chained together with his shipmates, he had taken in the markets of Tunis. He understood her longing to break free from the confines of the home, but ladies did not wander the streets. Servants purchased food. Men selected cloth and housewares. "People haggle," he said. "They swear and spit. Fights break out. Filth lines the streets. Animals wander. It is a rough and ugly path to negotiate."

"No place for a lady," she said. Her head drooped forward so that her chin nearly touched her chest.

Filippo could not work with her head bowed in resignation. He walked over to her and gently placed two fingertips beneath her chin, raising it, tilting it slightly upward, re-establishing pride of position in her bearing. She looked up at him, her eyes sad. "Do you think me beautiful?"

Filippo lost the objectivity of the painter and became a man, standing so close to her, asked such a question. He stared into her eyes, beheld her beauty shimmer like gold in the sunlight, and affirmed, "You are the most beautiful woman in all of Florence." He regretted the words the moment they left his mouth, words that hung between them with such weight that only with difficulty did he pull himself away and walk back to his easel.

During the following days, conversations between them grew more difficult. "I long to walk outside," she said. "Perhaps if I disguise myself. Would you take me?"

"Disguise yourself?" he asked, half listening. There was a translucent quality to her skin that he was working out.

"As an apprentice. As a boy who is your apprentice."

He stopped working. "No one would believe you a boy."

"A maidservant then."

"You are far too beautiful. It would be dangerous."

"A boy then," she persisted.

The time she spent alone had clearly forged an unparalleled imagination in her. As the days progressed, she continued to bring up the subject of playacting, of pretending to be his apprentice in order to walk the streets. The fantasy had taken hold in her.

"It is a fantasy," he reminded her.

"I have already worked out where to procure the necessary clothing. It will be easy enough to sneak out of the house. I only need you to escort me as I am unfamiliar with the city."

"You must give up this dream. It is unhealthy."

"How so?"

He sighed. "Mona Lucia. You are no longer a child. You are the wife of a merchant. You must know your role in the world."

"This has nothing to do with that."

"It most assuredly has."

"I will be disguised. I will no longer be the wife of a merchant."

"You are and always will be the very same." He put his brush down. "Do you not have occupation? A household to run?"

"The head maidservant has been with the family since my

husband was a boy. She takes care of the ordering and oversees the household chores. I follow behind and try to learn, but she forces me to wrest information from her. Even then, she gives a scant account, and misinformation I am sure. It is impossible."

Filippo was not surprised. The maidservant was, no doubt, jealous of her beauty and scornful of her youth. "You must demand her attention. It is your house."

"Room upon room," she said wearily, "grand, enclosed, dark empty spaces in which one's footsteps echo with such hollow sound."

So, it was also disinterest on her part that held her back. "Needlepoint," he suggested. Cosimo's wife Contessina was forever hunched over needlepoint.

"I disdain needlepoint," she scoffed. "Infinite tiny stitches. It is so dull. I fall into a sound sleep almost at once."

He knew nothing more about a fine lady's occupation. "Did your mother not guide you in the ways of a lady? Teach you the offices of your position?" he asked.

"My mother and my older sister are very close," she said. "They spent much of their time together when we were growing up. I believe my mother taught Giulia many things. Even today they spend time together. They are much alike, my mother and my sister."

"And you? Did your mother not teach you as well?"

She did not answer at once. "She was at all times engaged in activity with Giulia."

So, she was an orphan as much as he, one with a mother who lived but an orphan nonetheless. But she did have an older sister, as he had Giovanni. "And your sister? Did she tease you?" He got no response. "What did they say of you, your family? What kind of child were you?"

She thought. "I do not know."

"Oh, come now," he persisted. "Think on it. There must be one word that was used to describe you. Some little ones are sweet, others energetic, intelligent. Yet others are mischievous, generous. What child were you?"

"I do not know," she repeated.

She did seem to be telling the truth. How sad that was. Filippo had often seen how character was built on the foundation of these early familial observations.

"And you?" she asked. "What child were you?"

"A miscreant," he blurted, hearing his aunt's voice spit it out at him.

"In truth?" she asked, alarmed.

"I had neither mother nor father," he explained. "I was in the charge of an aunt. She did not like me."

"Nor my mother, me."

He looked deep into her eyes. There was a connection between them. "The word?" he asked again, knowing there must be one.

"Timid," she said, "pathetic."

"Feeling alone in the world," he said, "what child would not be frightened?"

After a long silence during which he studied her, he said, "Once. We go only once." He regretted his words the moment he spoke them.

She jumped from her chair and, with delight, danced around the room as if to release the pent-up energy of a lifetime. He had seen nothing yet of timidity in her.

The sun which first made my breast warm with love.... Dante

"What have I done?" he thought as he waited in the dark alley where goods were delivered to her house. He could lose his head for such foolishness. They would need to stay to pathways not travelled by his fellow artists. Their keen eyes would at once discern the truth. His heart beat rapidly. There she was, dressed in a young boy's attire, her legs covered only by tights beneath her brown homespun tunic. It was unseemly. He pulled the hat down low over her eyes. "I cannot see," she complained. "What is the point?"

"Do not allow anyone to see your eyes," he said. "They will know at once. Stay by my side at all times."

Filippo and his charge made their way through the narrow, crowded streets. They had to thread through a litter of pigs grunting its way through a pile of garbage and dodge donkeys laden with goods, until, finally, rounding a corner and dispersing a throng of pigeons high into the air, they reached the Mercato Vecchio, the place she most wanted to see. At this time of the morning, artists were in their botteghe, taking advantage of the good light. He raced through the market, aware that it was a district where he might nevertheless run into an associate. She stopped to watch a caged bird sing and again to take in piles of luxurious fabric, running her hand along the slippery silk, tracing the velvet patterns of the brocades. He grabbed her arm with a roughness he regretted, but it was his neck that was at stake. "Boys do not stroke cloth," he whispered.

Leaving the market behind, he breathed a sigh of relief and made his way at a more leisurely pace to Or San Michele. It was the one place that, when he was a boy with the same desire to wander, had left the greatest impression. It was also an unlikely spot in which to meet up with anyone. She stood a long time before the tabernacle, taking in the ivory carved like lace, the deeply saturated hues of sapphire and ruby shining in its depths. He took her to the back and showed her the beautiful relief carved there. She then knelt and prayed. What could be wrong with this, with allowing her a few moments of devotion at a holy shrine she might otherwise never have seen?

When they left, he headed away from the city center and out toward Santa Croce. In doing so, he skirted the Medici palazzo and the church of San Lorenzo. He would have liked to have shown her his Annunciation there, but it was best avoided. On their return from Santa Croce, her home and the end of their excursion drawing near, he veered and crossed to the Oltrarno. It was a dangerous move. The district that held his childhood home and the Carmine was another quarter where he might be recognized. He could not help himself. She might never otherwise see his work apart from the insignificant portrait he made of her. He headed to Santo Spirito and the Barbadori chapel there.

Standing before the altar, she sucked in her breath. "A work of which I am most proud," he whispered.

"Yours?" She looked up at him, the admiration in her eyes clear even in the shadow cast by her hat. He felt light, as if he might float.

"Maestro," a voice said behind him, "what brings you this side of the Arno?"

Frediano da Ravenzano, no friend. Thankfully, no keen eye either. But would he need one? Filippo pressed her to her knees to pray, then turned, placing himself between them, his wider girth hiding her from view.

"Ah, Frediano. Here to study, are you? Render columns, perhaps?"

Frediano blanched with anger. Not a time to poke him. Filippo softened his voice. "It is good to see you hard at work."

"You bring a new apprentice?" Frediano asked, craning his neck to see beyond Filippo.

"No. No. Not at all. A friend's nephew. From Pisa. Going home tomorrow. Well, I look forward to seeing the drawings you produce. Bring your renderings tomorrow morning and we will have a look at them."

He waited for Frediano to turn and walk away, which he seemed reluctant to do. He was ever suspicious. It was in his nature. When he was finally a safe distance, Filippo grabbed her arm and raced from the church. There they nearly ran into his dull apprentice again. How had he managed to intersect their path? Filippo pushed her head down from behind, nodded at Frediano, and rushed off.

Frightened now, Filippo took the long way around, back to Santa Croce and through deserted side streets until they reached her home. Short of breath, he left her at the entrance to the alley. "I must be off."

"Thank you," she said to his departing back.

CHAPTER 47

The year of Our Lord 1444, Florence

After their journey through the city, Mona Lucia was different. There was a glow of anticipation that radiated from her being, which he worked to capture. But, it soon faded. She began pressing him to take her once more; after all, no one had noticed. It had been a safe journey and was certain to be again. He reminded her of their agreement: one time only. She gave up. Her shoulders slouched, her head hung low. Filippo walked over, knelt before her, and took her hand in his. "It is not wise to rail against one's fate," he said, not sure that he entirely believed it. Had he not done so himself?

She grabbed his hand in her own, brought them to rest above her heart. "Do you think me beautiful?"

"I have already said as much."

"I am so alone." Her eyes held a well of sorrow.

Filippo felt his body melt. He struggled to hold himself in check. She was a wealthy merchant's wife. This was dangerous ground. He stood and quickly stepped away.

These exchanges continued until Filippo became loath to go

near her. And, then there was the lovebird she kept in a wooden cage at the window that was forever singing. Between her persistent goading and the birdsong, he was having difficulty concentrating. He also wasted much time instructing her from afar on her positioning. She seemed to take pleasure in his discomfort and one day absent-mindedly ran her index finger up and down along the space partially exposed above her bodice where her breasts pressed together.

Filippo swallowed to control his voice. "Mona Lucia, if you would please place the hand you have raised back atop the hand that lies in your lap...."

"You must come closer. Show me what you want of me," she teased.

"Mona Lucia, surely you know how to place one hand atop the other."

"And other things as well," she said.

"We are done for the day," Filippo said, abruptly.

She was up and across the room in one swift movement. "May I see?"

He placed a cloth over what was, at this point, only an underpainting without detail or color. "It is not ready to be seen. We are done for the day."

"Please do not go," she pleaded. The depth of despair in her eyes was matched by the dark well in his own soul. "Please," she repeated. Taking a step closer, she placed her hand, small and precise, on his chest. They gazed into each other's eyes. He read in hers, what? He read that which is familiar. It pulled him with such force toward her that his body quaked. It was too much. He grabbed her, pressing his lips to hers. They sank together to the floor. Amidst the frenzy of unlacing, her hair tumbled loose. He plunged his face into the waves of it.

Afterwards, running his fingers through her hair, Filippo whispered, "Two united," envisioning the combustive comingling of mercury and sulfur that produces the rare vermillion.

He was a fly ensnared in a spider's web or, perhaps more

accurately, the danger was such that he was a moth entranced by flame. Indeed, since the fly is snatched in the web by chance, he was more like the moth that is drawn to the flame and, although each dance with fire leaves it singed, willingly moves once again to the dance, until the final moment when it is wholly consumed.

This was a new experience for Filippo. Lovemaking built slowly, a swelling storm of sensation, clouds accumulating, the distant rumble of desire. Waves washed over him, slowly at first, then building, closer and closer, until the final, explosive crash, the obliterating release, a cry into the wind.

"Theopista," he whispered, stroking her silken hair.

She gave him a questioning look. "Theopista?"

"Theopista," he explained, "was a Greek saint who lived in ancient times. She was taken captive by a sea captain, her husband left stranded on a distant shore." She smiled. He never again called her by her real name. She was Theopista to him, and they lived together on a deserted island.

Up until that moment I had not been bound by chains so sweet and gentle.

Dante

When the portrait was completed, it remained draped so that no one would question Filippo's continued visits. But, seven months passed swiftly, and her husband was due to return in one day's time. He would want to see the painting.

"Tell me about your husband," he said, curious to know whose bed he slept in.

"He is small of stature," she began, "thin of bone," and then she stopped.

"Go on."

"He is a good man," she said. Filippo winced. "He is fragile, his manliness not so apparent." She stroked the hair on Filippo's chest with her hand.

"He is a eunuch, then?" Filippo asked unkindly.

"No. He seems"—she hesitated—"afraid to touch me."

"Afraid of your beauty," Filippo said, knowingly, and felt a pang of understanding, a feeling of kinship for this man he had never met. They shared the same woman, did they not? They, all three, were bound in the same knot of futility, he with a wife who did not love him, Filippo with a woman he could not have, and she with both. "When he returns," he ventured, hoping for her denial, "perhaps you will feel more kindly towards him."

"Perhaps," she agreed, absently, an admission that felled Filippo with the bluntness of its truth. This drew him to make love to her once more.

Afterwards, they lay facing each other in the bed, Filippo's fingers tracing the moon's journey across her hip and down her leg.

"What if my husband discovers us?" she asked.

This question pulled him out of his reverie. "Hmmmm?"

"My husband," she repeated, "if he should discover?"

Filippo grew fearful. "Is he likely to?"

The lovebird began to sing. She smiled at the sound. "Mmmm, only if the sweet bird sings will he know."

"From birdsong?" he asked.

"Ah," she replied, "she is a very clever bird."

Filippo swooped her tiny body beneath his own, kissing her all over.

"But," she persisted, "if a person should speak."

He propped himself up onto his side and looked at her. "Your maidservant. She sleeps soundly?"

"Snoringly so," she laughed.

"Ha! I see why she is banished to the opposite side of the house. Then we need not fear," Filippo assured her. "I am discreet." He noticed a change in the light. "I must leave." He ran his hand once more along her firm breast and down the center of her torso, resting it on her stomach, wishing he could make her his alone. For a moment, they stared into each other's eyes. The bird began to sing; the light changed still further.

"I see by the change of light that dawn draws near. I must leave or we will, indeed, be discovered." He stood and quickly dressed.

As he tuned to leave, she clasped him from behind. "When will I see you?"

"Your husband returns today," Filippo reminded her, "but he will soon be gone again. When he leaves, send word."

"It will be months," she groaned. "I cannot wait so long."

Filippo, leaning over her, traced the contours of her face with his thumb, committing it to memory. The rounded cheek, the pointed chin, the full, well-shaped mouth, the perfect line from brow to bridge of nose, and the eyes, round as moons, deep in color as the sea sparked by the fire of the sun. He was sunk on their shores.

He had never before known the love of a woman. He tethered to it like a ship to anchor, allowed it to seep into him like paint into plaster.

"My most beautiful pain," he said. And then, "I will paint you from memory."

"Can you?" she asked, delighted.

"Yes, I am at work on a commission for the church of Sant' Ambrogio."

"Am I to be the Virgin?" she asked.

Filippo shot her a sideways glance. "No," he said, "that would be improper, for men will recognize you. No. I will paint you as Sant' Theopista. As you are."

"Is that not an unusual saint to include in a painting? Will it bring you trouble, my portrait?"

He leaned in close and looked directly into her eyes. "Not nearly as much as your person." He grabbed her and kissed her hard on the lips. Then, quickly throwing on his mantello, for now it was indeed getting light and soon all of Florence would be throwing open its shutters, he turned to leave.

"Wait!" she yelled. Filippo stopped at the door. She knelt, perfect in her nakedness, at the edge of the bed. Day's first light, barely discernable, outlined her shoulders, traced her arms, outstretched. "I will miss you."

"And I, you," he said, kissing his palm and holding it out to her before turning to leave, his heart heavy in his breast, as he made his way quietly down the halls, the anchor having become a loadstone in the well of his being. She was, indeed, his most beautiful pain and, the portrait being completed long before, he did not know if he would ever see her again.

Night after night, he crept out after curfew. Like a thief, he risked arrest if found, or worse, having his throat cut by a genuine thief, risked it all to stare up at her shuttered bedchamber. He remembered the day he had led her through the streets of the city. He had been so consumed with thoughts of the risk he took that he had never considered the danger she embraced. Damage to a woman's reputation was irreparable, an egg once cracked that can never again be made whole. Her husband would surely have sent her back to her family, sought an annulment. Theopista, unmarriageable, would have been sent to a convent. She took the risk without fear, afterwards wished to take it again. Hers was a brave spirit.

Filippo wandered, restless, unable to sleep. He missed the slow, steady loss of himself, the fall into her, as if he flew from a great height, arms spread like wings, and dropped, a wind beneath him bracing him until the final blissful descent to Earth. Now, each night, he hid behind corners when he heard footsteps approaching, until he found himself beneath her windows, unable to enter, to drift, to land.

Months passed without word. When the room was dark, he imagined her asleep, his body pressed against hers, waking her. But then, a new thought began to seep into his consciousness. When he saw the dim glow of candlelight, he imagined her making love to her husband, and he was consumed with jealousy. Had she betrayed him? Used him? Did she care at all, or had he been a mere diversion while her husband was away? If she truly loved him, she would find some way to send for him. She was intelligent—devious, in fact. He had seen it. Why did she not send word? She had never loved him. Perhaps she loved her husband now, or no one at all. Perhaps she had taken a new lover. One thing was certain. She had abandoned him to his pain, a pain that rested in the dark familiar recesses of the space where he floated alone and lost.

CHAPTER 48

The year of Our Lord 1445, Florence

W hen the convent of San Marco was given over to the Dominicans, Archbishop Antoninus, who was a member of the order, suggested that Cosimo rebuild the twelfth-century structure. In this way, Antoninus instructed, he could begin to make reparations for his sins. The one Cosimo most worried about was the sin of usury. Was it possible for a banker to fully atone? Antoninus, one of the most devout men who had ever lived, would be able to guide him.

Cosimo set his favorite architect and friend, Michelozzo, to the task. He requested only that he be provided with his own cell in the convent, a space for contemplation and prayer. It soon became the place to which he often retired in search of peace. The time he spent at the convent helped to settle his soul. Shut away from the world in a cell without windows, he meditated on the meaning of sacrifice, and Antoninus soon became his personal confessor. Cosimo spent long hours discussing matters of doctrine with the monk, as well as the state of his own soul.

Of this one thing make sure against your dying day—that your faults die before you do. Seneca

One day Antoninus spoke at great length about the importance of forgiveness. It was something with which Cosimo struggled. "I hold myself to a high standard," he explained. "My father taught me from an early age how to live an honorable life. I expect the same of others. All men should strive to live an exemplary life. How is this expectation wrong-headed?"

"You yourself have provided the explanation," Antoninus instructed. "You who were fortunate to have had such a father. From childhood were taught by his example. This father continued to guide you since fortune favored him with advanced age. You are unique in having been so favored by God and are, therefore, called upon to guide others, especially those who, less fortunate, were not so well instructed. This leads me to a corollary. If another has not enjoyed the same advantages as you have, must you not meet that individual with an understanding heart? Is it not cruel to judge their behavior? Cosimo, judging not is a prerequisite to forgiveness. Can you now find forgiveness in your heart?"

Cosimo realized the truth in Antoninus's words. "I feel a fool."

"No one is a fool in God's eyes," Antoninus assured him. "Think of those whose actions you have not forgiven. Who are they?"

"Well," he thought, "there is Chiari, who is a blockhead and useless as a prior."

"Cosimo," Antoninus cautioned.

"His father, it is true, was a blockhead as well, poor man. He means no harm." As he pictured Chiari in his mind's eye, Cosimo felt a shift, his derision subsiding. Although limited in ability, the man did try. He felt a sudden tenderness for the fennel head. This new experience of succumbing to compassion left him with a sense of calm.

"Who else?" Antoninus persisted.

There were so many. There were men he had encountered in business. Those he employed at the bank. But, in light of the gravity of the lesson he was learning, his judgement of them seemed petty. And, he did not really know them. Then, quite suddenly, a deeply held revulsion clutched his heart. The men who had wanted him dead, those who had called for his head on a pike. He would begin with the easiest of these. "Strozzi," he said. "Supplying Albizzi with the funds to usurp me. An old fool. I say that with affection. I do not believe he understood their intentions. He was duped and thought, no doubt, that he acted in the best interests of Florence. I forgive Strozzi." A sense of peace again swept over him.

"Good," Antoninus said, smiling. "And the others? Albizzi? Filelfo?"

Cosimo knew the answer too well. His soul was not pure. Whose was? "Return to me on that point," he answered, "when I am no longer a man, but have become a saint."

CHAPTER 49

The year of Our Lord 1446, Buti Villa outside of Florence

In order to escape the heat, Lucrezia, her mother, and siblings were staying at the family's small villa in the country for the summer months. Her father stayed on in the city to work but joined them at the end of each week. They had just recently arrived, and the heat was not yet oppressive. Clouds tumbled through the sky. A light breeze blew through the meadows, ruffling a tapestry of wildflowers. Lucrezia's mother was busy once again with a new baby. Her half-sister, Isabetta, newly married and with a baby of her own, was visiting for the week. The two women rested beneath the shade of a chestnut tree. The babies were asleep, nestled in cradles covered over with a light netting.

They watched as Lucrezia gathered her siblings, instructing them to stand in a circle and hold hands. Then they danced around and around, singing a song. Lucrezia picked up the pace of the song, and along with it the speed of the dance. Faster and faster they twirled until, dizzy, they fell to the ground, rolling and laughing.

When they had caught their breath and stood again, the two youngest wrapped their arms around Lucrezia's legs in a crushing hug. She loved these spontaneous displays of affection and held them to her for a moment. Then, seeing that the older boys were growing restless, she said, "Take the ball and stick out beyond the trees. Play fairly. No fighting."

Then, Lucrezia turned to the girls. "We will gather wildflowers. Pick a beautiful bunch, and I will teach you how to make a wreath for your hair. But, first, we will make one for Mama and one for Isabetta."

Watching them, Isabetta said, "Lucrezia is so good with the children. It is remarkable in one so young."

"I could not do without her," Caterina agreed. "She will make a wonderful mother one day."

When he visited, her father found more time than usual, during the long quiet days of summer, to read to Lucrezia from Dante. She was twelve years of age, bright and inquisitive, with a delving mind. Today, he had decided to read to her from the Purgatorio:

The sun, its rays like red flame at my back, was cut off by my body and threw the shadow of my shape before me. Dante

"You see, Lucrezia, how Dante, throughout the Purgatorio, brings us back to the image of his shadow. The shades of those who have died are insubstantial and, therefore, do not cast shadow. Dante, who is yet alive and traversing the realms of the dead, does cast a shadow. In this way, those who are dead identify him as a living being."

Lucrezia understood the literal interpretation but knew by now that there was more to be deciphered. She began, aloud, to puzzle it out. "To cast a shadow over something is thought to be a bad thing. A shadow blocks the light. It also conceals. A shadow falling over something can be a bad portent. So, why then do our bodies cast shadow?"

Her father smiled. "Indeed. Dante does not, however, describe the shadow as falling over any other object. He speaks of the shadow cast by our body, extending out before us. Here again, you see, later on in the same canto: 'This is a human body you see, which now divides the sun's light on the ground.' Our bodies divide the sun's light, block it. There is great responsibility in this. You see, Lucrezia, Dante is telling us that you cannot hide from yourself. The sun at your back will at all times throw your shadow before you—for you and for all others to see. The question is: What shape do you want your shadow to take? What person do you want to be?"

CHAPTER 50

The year of Our Lord 1445, Florence

It was difficult to wrest his mind from thoughts of her, but once Filippo focused in on his work, all else disappeared. This commission was the most challenging yet. It was the Coronation of the Virgin for Sant' Ambrogio. Massive in size, it would include more than twenty figures, and was certain to best Alberti on his rule of nine. Filippo set them into groupings to provide the eye a pathway. He would use color gradation, moving outward from sharp contrast of light, shadow, and pure hues at the center to diffuse, blended colors at the edges. Mapping it out had taken some time. As he was conceiving the drawings from which it would be rendered, he did not hear his brother Giovanni enter the bottega. Giovanni stood before him and waved his arms about to get his brother's attention. Filippo, looking up from the drawing, blinked, not realizing why the blank panel he expected to see did not meet his eye.

"Ah, brother." And then, the sight of Giovanni reminded him of Piera's daughters. "I am sorry. I have no money for you this month. This commission proves expensive, and it drags on." Filippo sighed. It weighed heavily on his mind. It had been years, and they had been able only to marry off two more girls, leaving three still in need of dowries. "I should not have challenged Alberti on the number of figures in a work. The project is massive."

"You are enjoying the challenge," Giovanni contradicted him.

"I am," Filippo admitted, "but I will not save the price of another dowry for at least a year at this pace."

"That is just what I have come to talk to you about," Giovanni said. "I have good news. A rectorship has opened up in a wealthy parish just outside of Florence, San Quirico. Pope Eugenius himself has bestowed it upon you."

"They know that I cannot fulfill my obligations to a parish and paint at the same time?" Filippo had not forgotten their previous conversation but felt a twinge of foreboding.

"I know, brother. We spoke of this. You are able to have others fulfill those duties for you. Because of your fame as a great painter, the Bostichi family will accept you for the position. Once you are formally instated, I will fulfill your duties to the parish."

"And the members of this wealthy parish, the Bostichis you say, will not mind?"

"You will only have to show up six, seven times a year, say Mass once a year so all can see you. It comes with a stipend of sixty florins a year. Between this and your commissions, we will be able to save dowries for all three of our nieces."

"So, they have been told," Filippo asked, doubtfully, "that I must paint?"

"Would they have such a great painter wasting his time in tending to landholdings and hearing confessions?" Giovanni pushed his point. "It was with Cosimo's intervention, of course."

"Well, if Cosimo thinks it a good idea." Filippo hesitated, but what other choice was there? "Between us," he decided, "we will save our dear Piera's children. That is what she would have wanted." What could be wrong with that?

"It is settled then. You must do one thing in the coming years. Keep better records of your transactions so that no shadow of doubt falls upon you. You are not the most able-minded record keeper. All the more reason to allow me to handle the parish transactions."

"I am capable," Filippo protested, "but I cannot do the two at once. When I am caught up in a project, nothing else exists. It is a world unto itself that swallows me whole."

"It must be another world that produces such miracles. It is as if one could step through a wall into this separate world, one analogous to our own, only more beautiful."

Therefore, we ought to give our every care to discovering and learning beauty.

Alberti

Filippo enjoyed the making of art and life as one, but then he enjoyed all the more taking it further away once again, into a world of impossible beauty. This desire had come late to him, after long and patient study. He realized that if he could create a peopled landscape with life-like detail, he could also create one that pushed far past this, one that pulsed and breathed in the ideal.

CHAPTER 51

The year of Our Lord 1445, Florence

Filippo's apprentice Frediano da Rovenzano belonged to a powerful family, but to a branch of it that had fallen on hard times. Frediano's cousin, Michele, a wealthy and influential man, was Filippo's friend and had talked him into taking Frediano on as an apprentice. The Rovenzanos were also allied with Leonardo dei Bostichi. Bostichi was a member of the landed nobility whose family had been patrons of the church of San Quirico, where Filippo held his benefice, since the eleventh century.

When he had been gifted the benefice, Cosimo told him that Leonardo had expected to make the decision, as his forefathers had done for more than four hundred years. "But times are changing. Benefices are bought and sold. One person can hold many. Benefices have come to be seen as a guaranteed source of income rather than as a holy office to administer. Not that I condone such conduct. But, Leonardo will choke with anger, no doubt, when he discovers the privilege has been wrested from him. Choosing a new rector is one of a handful of honors left to the nobility. He has no recourse, however, since Pope Eugenius himself has gifted it."

"It is disquieting that I benefit from my association with you at the expense of another," Filippo confessed.

"Do not waste tears on the nobility. They have had power stripped from them because they abused it. It will certainly stanch his wound to learn that you are fast becoming a famous painter. Their association with you will bring honor to the parish."

And let it stand for a day or so, until the heat goes out of it: for when it is so hot, the plaster which you put on cracks afterward. Cennini

Within a fortnight of Filippo's decision to allow Diamante to help in the painting of the Sant' Ambrogio panel, Frediano da Rovenzano's esteemed cousin, Michele, to whom he had complained, strolled into the bottega and begged a moment of the maestro's time.

"Frediano has been with you for nearly three years," Michele began. "There is less than a year left to his contract, and he has yet to paint anything, not a twig."

"Which is, indeed, what he draws," Filippo complained, "sticks for pillars."

If he were more forthright, he would admit that, even more than Frediano's lack of passion or ability, it was his character that posed the greatest problem. At first, his obsequiousness had merely irritated Filippo. But, over time, Filippo saw that he was disingenuous. What Frediano said was calculated. What were his true thoughts and feelings about anything? And, if one did not know a man's heart, how could he be trusted? Filippo avoided him. It was wrong of him, he knew, to avoid an apprentice whom he had been commissioned to teach. But, damn it, Filippo thought, he had work to do.

"May I remind you," Michele continued, as if reading Filippo's thoughts, "that you were contracted to teach him to paint?"

"Paint?" Filippo's voice rose in agitation. "He cannot even properly prepare a panel to be painted upon."

"He was not contracted to prepare panels," Michele argued.

Filippo grew exasperated. "Michele, a painter must know how to prepare a panel or he has nothing upon which to paint. 'Those who have never learned do not want to learn,'" Filippo finished, quoting Seneca.

"What you say may be true, Filippo." Michele tried to reason with him. "But I promised his mother, whose husband, may he rest in peace, was my father's brother. I promised that Frediano would have a profession to sustain him when he completed his contract here."

Filippo sighed. He understood the pressure of family obligation. His friend was in a bind. He needed to fulfill his promise. "All right. All right. I will allow him to paint the predella. God help me."

"Thank you, Filippo." Michele seemed much relieved. "I will never forget the help you have provided."

"Frediano," Filippo called out, his voice gruff with anger. "You will paint the predella."

"Thank you, Maestro."

"Try not to make a complete mess of it, will you?"

CHAPTER 52

The year of Our Lord 1446, Florence

After the first two terse communications, Cosimo wrote Maddalena a long letter about his life, confiding his thoughts. He rambled on. She responded with one sentence: What legacy will you leave?

It was something about which he had not given much thought since that day years ago when he had sat with Lorenzo discussing Sforza—when Sforza had seemed a means to an end. Since then, his time each day had been divided up like so many small investments. Maddalena was holding him to account. What legacy? His sons? His buildings? He was the wealthiest man in all of Italy. Was that all he could manage to leave? One day, when the Medici name was dragged through the dirt, as it inevitably would be, what did he wish to remain, apart from his buildings?

I will consider, he wrote back.

Later that evening, Cosimo, accompanied by his three sons and two nephews, attended a gathering of scholars hosted by Archbishop Bessarion. He was particularly interested in hearing what Genisthos Plethon had to say. It was widely accepted that

Plethon was the world's leading authority on Plato. More of the Greek philosopher's works were being rediscovered in Italy since the Ecumenical Council, which had brought more than trade to Florence, as Cosimo knew it would. Many of the Greek scholars had stayed behind when it ended.

The measure of a man is what he does with power. Plato

Plethon spoke about Plato's myth of the cave. We are all chained, he said, bound at the ankles and neck, so that we can only see the wall of the cave before us, where shadows move to and fro. These shadows are the world as we know it—an illusion cast by the light of a fire that burns behind us. But we cannot turn our heads, so we do not know this. Truth exists outside the cave, illuminated by the light of the sun. But, most never venture outside the dark cave. Most are content to live in the shadows. Plato put forth that one should spend one's youth and middle age studying, and only in old age should one go back to the cave to become a ruler, using the wisdom acquired to guide others. This choice to return, Plato asserted, would necessarily be a reluctant one. Who would wish to leave the place of truth illuminated by the sun?

Cosimo listened as Plethon explained Plato's meaning. It was not knowledge of ideas alone upon which the sun cast its light, but the truths about oneself that one chooses to ignore. These are laid bare by the sunlight, allowing us to learn, to change our natures. It was then that a disturbing truth about himself surfaced. He was not a reluctant ruler. He enjoyed the intrigue, relished besting others. He was not a wise man who had reluctantly reentered the world of illusions. Acceptance of this truth about himself evidenced his ability to look into the light without turning away, but it did not diminish the flaw he found in himself by doing so. He was also, although carefully calculating in order to obey the church's laws, a usurer. He must atone for these flaws. One never knew when one's reckoning might arrive. Maddalena was right. He must, without delay, determine his legacy and make the necessary arrangements to bring it to fruition.

But, what would have happened to Florence, Cosimo wondered, had he gone off to study, returning only in old age to guide it? Throughout his life he had searched out lost manuscripts, had studied philosophy. He had, through study, been able to turn his head a little to see the fire, perhaps even to discern some of the light filtering into the cave from above. But, most of his time was spent among the shadows, arranging and rearranging them. It is all well and good, he thought, for the man who has no civic, no business obligations to retire to the quiet of the country in order to seek out the truth. Someone must stay among the shadows.

CHAPTER 53

The year of Our Lord 1445 – 1446, Florence

Later that day, after struggling to return to work, Filippo could bear it no longer. He made his way to Theopista's home and requested entry. Once inside the courtyard, he grew fearful of his recklessness. He paced back and forth for what seemed an eternity before deciding to leave. Then he saw her at the top of the landing, on the upper loggia. The weight of indecision drained from him, and light as the wind he raced up the stairs. As he drew near, she raised her hand as if to stop him. It was then that he noticed she was pregnant. He proceeded more slowly until he stood by her side. They were alone, out of view of the street, the servants busy inside. Their eyes locked, and as they did he knew he should never have doubted her. He reached out, grasped both her hands, and brought them to his lips.

They stood without speaking, and then, looking furtively round, she pulled him inside. Hugging close to the walls, stopping now and then to listen to distant voices to discern their direction, they made their way to her bedchamber, where she threw herself into his arms.

"You tremble," he said, stroking her hair and kissing the top of her head as one comforts a child.

She pulled away, bringing his hand to rest on the swell of her belly. "It is yours."

He was startled. "Are you certain?"

"Do you not remember remarking on the plumpness of my belly?" He did. "We are fortunate that my husband returned when he did. Any longer and it would have been impossible." She did not finish. "Oh, Filippo. I am so frightened."

"Of your husband?"

"Of the birth."

Filippo understood. Most women did not live to see their first child. If they survived one birth, they often succumbed during another. Had his own mother not perished with his? "I will protect you," he said, his will stronger than his reason.

"You are my strength and my comfort," she said, her eyes burning brightly. "But it is impossible. We cannot see each other."

Filippo picked her up in his arms and placed her gently on the bed. Then he lay down beside her. He stroked her face, kissing it all over, each touch, each kiss imparting a memory. He felt a tenderness so deep and yet terrible that it pained as much as it thrilled him. They lay together, fully clothed, gazing into each other's eyes until the fading of the light.

...gazing into the beautiful eyes which Love had made into the snare that caught me.   Dante

They must have fallen asleep because they were awakened by the sound of voices moving toward her door. "My husband," she whispered, jumping up. "You must leave."

He stood, cupped her face in his hands, and pressed his lips against hers in a long, lingering kiss.

"You must not return," she said, "if you love me. Go now."

Pain made him numb. "I will never love again," he said, feeling the truth of it.

"Nor I," she answered.

Filippo ran to the window, looked out to be sure no one saw him, and climbed onto the balcony. As he did, he turned to look at her one last time. By the light of a single candle, Theopista held a mirror up and smoothed her hair into place, a gesture that moved him outside of her life, a life settled into uniformity, certainty. The door opened, her husband saying, "Ah, there you are."

Filippo raced down the stairs and out into the night.

Pilotless ship in a fierce tempest tossed   Dante

Filippo was unable to work. His brooding led to occasional outbursts. Diamante found him one day browbeating an apprentice. "How do you expect me to work with paints not properly ground?" Filippo yelled. "Here, give it to me." He grabbed the glass pestle from the shaking hand of the boy.

"He will not learn how to put handle to shovel," Diamante scolded, "if you rip the tool from his grasp at every mistake."

A vision of Antonio, the gardener, cowed by his aunt passed through Filippo's mind, but he brushed it aside. "I must do everything," he retorted, "even grind paints."

"No," Diamante said, "you need to grind."

Filippo was silenced by the truth of Diamante's words.

"If you wish to grind away at your pain," Diamante said, lowering his voice, "paint her, inconspicuously, as a devotee of the Virgin, in the background, amidst the crowd. You will paint your heart, and no one will ever know."

Filippo took half his advice. He painted Theopista as he had promised her he would, her beauty preserved for all eternity. She gazed directly into the viewer's eyes, inviting them into the narrative of the painting. So as not to arouse suspicion, he painted her husband as well, whom he had seen coming and going from the house when he stood, concealed, staring up at her bedchamber. He painted the man as Sant' Eustace, the husband of Theopista.

The project was nearly completed. Filippo had accomplished

his goal; he had bested Alberti. He smiled at the thought of the haughty mathematician having to amend his beloved treatise. Filippo's apprentice Andrea offered him some bread and cheese as they sat together during a break from work.

"Did you not recently complete a portrait of this saint?" Andrea asked, pointing to Theopista. "Of the real woman?"

"Yes," Filippo said, trying to keep any evidence of emotion from his voice.

"It is sad, is it not?"

"Sad? What is sad?"

"Did you not hear? She has passed into the great sea. In childbirth."

Filippo did not know how long he sat, stunned into silence, when suddenly he grabbed brush and paint and, in a frenzy of activity, only half aware of what he was doing, painted himself, on the other side of Eustace, as San Martino. Already having rendered the saint's back, Filippo now turned his head around to meet the viewer's gaze, as Theopista did, his hand gesturing toward her. To add more injury, Filippo could not help depicting her oldest son kneeling before her with a baby's version of his own face, Theopista's hand cupped beneath it, turning it toward the viewer. "See whose child," one could almost hear her say.

The congregation would see the altarpiece from a distance and at an angle. They would discern it as a whole, its monumental size, the focus for them the coronation of the Virgin at the apex. Only the nuns, who would kneel in front of the painting, near to it, would be drawn in by the direct gaze of the saints, Martino and Theopista. Who knew what they would make of it? Perhaps they would not notice at all. As women, they were taught to lower their gaze and as nuns, in prayer, to raise it. Lost in prayer, they would raise their eyes upward in a gesture of devotion, thus also resting their gaze upon Mary's coronation. If they did notice, they were cloistered, his secret safe with them.

One day, the painting done and the apprentices gone, Filippo stood before it, studying it. He was having difficulty letting it go.

But, with the donors growing restless, he had agreed to install it the following day.

Lost in thought, he heard voices and turned. Alberti and Donatello entered the bottega. Alberti, feigning reverence, dropped to one knee before Filippo and lowered his head. "I submit to you, Maestro Lippi. I am beaten."

Donatello threw his head back and laughed. "A wager that will be spoken of for all eternity."

"I do not care about how long it lives on," Filippo said, "only that you are prepared to uphold your end of the bargain, Alberti. Will you rescind that preposterous rule of nine?"

Alberti surprised him. "It has already been stricken from the text."

"The project is well worth it then," Filippo said.

Alberti stared at the painting. "I see. You have collected figures in groups and positioned them on different planes."

"More importantly," Filippo explained, "the colors are as they appear in real light. You see." He pointed. "The purest of hues at the center where light and shadow clash, the gradual transition to blended tones at the outer edges."

"Ah," Alberti said, rubbing his chin, "I was skeptical when you attempted to explain this to me earlier, but yes, I see it. You win, Lippi. And now, I must be off. I wished to honor our wager before I left for Mantua."

When Alberti was gone, Donatello turned to Filippo and asked, "Will you leave yourself so prominently exposed in this painting?"

"No," Filippo answered.

When Donatello had left, he rounded out the nose of the saint, made his lips fuller. It took so little to change one man's face to that of another. He darkened the eyes, but he left in them the pained expression of loss. A viewer would now need to closely scrutinize the saint to realize that it had once been a portrait of Filippo. He had made sure to leave the faint trace of himself in San Martino's visage, a reminder.

Then Filippo wrote the words "My most perfect work" in Latin on a banner held by an angel. People would assume it meant the monumental work, the painting or, since the angel knelt before the donor, the work he had commissioned. Only Filippo knew that it meant his love, his child. This was something about which he must never speak.

He reached out and traced her face with his thumb, as he had that morning before he left her bed, in order to commit it to memory, to carry it with him. Now, here alone she breathed.

CHAPTER 54

The year of Our Lord 1446, Florence

A t the start of the day, Filippo, the contract fulfilled, decided to rid himself of Frediano da Ravenzano, who had arrived uncharacteristically early. "There. The last of it," he said, pouring a handful of coins into Frediano's outstretched hand. "Our contract is satisfied. Be off with you."

"It is not enough," Frediano complained. "Many other apprentices have been paid more."

"That is a gross exaggeration," Filippo growled. "A handful only. Apprentices who have done more. The predela you painted! Bodies with no definition, no form, legs like sticks, drapery without folds. And, I shall have to leave it as is to fulfill the date of contract. The price I pay is the one agreed upon in the contract." Could he not rid himself of this boy? "You are fortunate that your cousin is a good friend, or I would have given you the boot long ago."

Reason wishes to pass a fair judgement; anger wishes the judgement it has already passed to seem fair. Seneca

"That is unfair. I have worked long and hard," Frediano protested.

"And have been of little use to me."

"I will take it to court," he threatened.

"Join the rest who do," Filippo said, not feeling at all threatened. Then, he thought it wise, as Cosimo would have, to gain proof of payment. "You will write on the contract the date, the amount received, and the fact that you are satisfied with payment, and you will sign to it." He held out the contract.

Frediano did not take it. "If I refuse?"

"I will have words with your cousin, who drew up the terms of the contract and who, I believe, continues to support you."

Frediano did as Filippo instructed, huffing with anger, and strode out the door. Filippo threw the signed contract onto a table just inside the entrance to the bottega where they had stood. Then he turned and walked to the opposite end of the room, gathered his remaining apprentices, and dove into a demonstration of a technique.

At the close of the workday, Diamante, who had become Filippo's unofficial secretary and was also now his confidante, searched for the signed contract, in order to file it away, but could not find it.

"I had hoped to do the wise thing for once, Diamante." Filippo sighed. "Ah, well, some are not meant for wisdom."

"But, Maestro, where could it have gone? Frediano must have stolen it."

"Perhaps he did, Diamante. Let him have it. Where will he go to complain? Who will believe him? All one must do is view his work. We have more important things to attend to."

CHAPTER 55

The year of Our Lord 1447, Florence

Filippo often wondered what made Cosimo, so short in stature, such a commanding presence. Was it his penetrating intellect? That was certainly a factor. There was his vision that always placed him several steps ahead of other men. And there was something more elusive, greater than mere confidence, for many men have that, deserved or not, although undeserved it was merely arrogance. Even when sitting, Cosimo held his energy in check with great difficulty. It burst forth with the sudden thrust of an arm, the bang of a fist, as when he had jumped up suddenly on that day long ago, saying, "Walk with me." Cosimo had a way of curving back into his chair, at complete ease, then quite suddenly springing into action, startling everyone as he rushed forward, shouting commands, setting things in motion. Perhaps it was the sheer energy of the man, restless and unpredictable.

Having shared a light supper, the two retired to Cosimo's antechamber, where he poured them both a glass of Vermiglio, saying, "You must try to stay out of the courts, Filippo. You are gaining a reputation for being difficult."

"Impatient donors are to blame. Do they think the work is birthed fully formed from my head? That all it takes is a few strokes of the brush to complete?"

"They do not believe you to be Zeus birthing Athena. Filippo, I understand, but do try to be more punctual in meeting deadlines. Set completion dates that you can meet when drawing up the terms of the contract."

"I cannot. They want the work before it is begun. Was Brunelleschi's dome built in a year?"

"A poor comparison. All of Florence was vexed with Brunelleschi."

"Until it was completed. Now he is a genius."

"Well, at the very least, do the work yourself. Do not have some workshop apprentice do it and pass it off as your own."

"One time only," Filippo admitted. "I regret having done it. A useless apprentice. A favor to a friend. It was while I worked on the project for Sant' Ambrogio. It took all my effort."

"Ah, Sant' Ambrogio. Why do you always give them more than they ask? Can you not be satisfied to follow specifications? Done by you, the work will surpass all others. Is that not enough?"

"What is the point of giving what is expected? It is the threshold of what is not yet possible that I seek. I cannot constrain myself." Within, he knew, there was also a desire to please beyond measure that drove him with its indomitable force.

"Perhaps I taught you too well how to litigate," Cosimo was saying. "It has become a habit with you."

"It has proven useful to have learned from the man who never loses."

"Yes. Well. Winning hinges on anticipating an opponent's next move. A man's decisions are not determined from an examination of his reasoning but of his passions and fears. I often wonder how it is that they cannot discern my next move."

"You keep your passions in check. I can attest to that, having played chess with you."

"Self-discipline makes a man difficult to read. It is a subtle war."

"In that," Filippo said, "you share something with the pirate leader."

"We are all pirates who survive the game, those most of all, who flourish."

"I saw Carlo on the way in," Filippo said, changing the subject. He had become good friends with Cosimo's illegitimate son.

Cosimo smiled. "Carlo. It is a shame that he is a man of the cloth. He would have made a fine banker."

"Did he not want to pursue that course?"

"The priesthood was the best I could offer him. It provides protection. And status," Cosimo explained.

"And abstinence." Filippo thought of his own struggles with it.

"Celibacy? He has a will of iron. One of the reasons he would make a good banker."

"Celibacy is an extreme hardship," Filippo said, "if you do not have the calling."

"Even if you do, I imagine," Cosimo said. He stared out the window. "How do you think all of these men embrace a life of abstinence? Are there so many who are able? It seems unnatural. A man's impulse. And you. What of this woman in the painting?"

"I am no longer a man of the cloth," Filippo reminded him.

Cosimo raised an eyebrow. "You are, and you are not."

"She was not mine to have," Filippo admitted for the first time.

"Adultery is a grave sin," Cosimo said, leaning forward, fixing Filippo with a steady gaze. "You are without her. Surely that is punishment. But remember, there is punishment in this world, and there is eternal punishment. Do not wait to make your peace with God."

Although it seemed impossible that something as beautiful as his love for Theopista could be wrong, Filippo knew that adultery was a grave sin. Having committed it, he needed to search his soul. What if he died before he found the time to do so? He could not make amends directly to the person he had wronged. And, his workshop full, commissions in progress, how to repent? He decided to fast for six months, to forego the mid-day meal, and to eat only soup and bread for supper. He would donate the money he saved to the confraternity to provide alms for the poor.

The following day, he began by going to confession. The priest asked, "Do you feel remorse for your sin?"

"I know it was wrong, but I do not feel remorse, Frate," he confessed. "What then?"

"Then you will not find forgiveness in the eyes of God. Penance and prayer," the priest suggested. "We pray they will lead you to sincere remorse."

That is what his aunt had said all those years ago when she had left him at the Carmine. Was it a failing in him, this ability to do wrong and not feel remorse? No. What had he to feel remorse for then, just a boy? He had felt it when he had wished for the malicious Jacopo to be taken by the pestilence and it came to pass. But perhaps that was more fear and guilt than remorse. He felt it when he had not been able to save Matteo. And, again, when, in the rage that followed Matteo's death, he might have killed a man. But this? How could something that had felt so right, so loving, leave him remorseful? And yet, he knew it was wrong. He had wronged another man. He would need to pray for Theopista's husband. It would not be easy.

Filippo continued to fast beyond the six months, each night praying for Theopista's soul, as well as for that of her husband, the most difficult of prayers to say. Then he turned his prayers inward, where he searched for remorse. In time, he fell gravely ill. Faint and burning up with fever, he was taken by Diamante to the infirmary at the Carmine. Lying in bed, Filippo prepared himself for death.

But the good friars nursed him and he began to regain his strength. When his fever broke, exhausted, Filippo searched his soul once again for remorse. Had he not lost Theopista? Had he not paid for his sin? Was the pain of loss itself not evidence of this?

It seemed his soul swirled around him, blurred by motion. How to compose a pure penitence from this, unsteady and fragmented? It would not hold still. He could not grab on, wrest it into place, bring order to its chaos. Thoughts swirled, objects, people, places.

Then, there it was, and all was still, the image of her in her husband's arms caused Filippo such pain that, although only imagined, it brought him into intimate contact with this man he had never met. In his own heart, Filippo felt the other man's pain. In his anguish, Sant' Augustine's words came to him unbidden. He had learned them as a boy in the convent. "Mercy cannot exist apart from suffering."

He had wronged this man with casual disregard. Why? What man understands why he commits a wrong? Filippo did not. But lying there sick and alone, it came to him. His relationship with Theopista went back, far back. It was Sant' Augustine whose confessions again gave him the answer. Although Augustine was not himself an orphan, Filippo knew that his own reason was the same: "The single desire that dominated his search for delight was simply to love and to be loved," to fill that deep empty well inside of himself: "This was the arena in which he wrestled."

Filippo thought of all those he had lost—his mother, his father, his friend and defender Poultray, his mentor Masaccio, Matteo, Theopista. He again sank into the abyss, Augustine's words echoing in his mind, "Where should my heart flee to in escaping my heart?" The answer was nowhere. The only path was through the fire of pain and remorse. Any other left one fleeing the pain but always carrying it. He needed to turn toward it. To embrace the full force of it. To find the courage. It was only by walking through the fire that he would be able to come out of it, on the other side, ready to move forward.

He had traversed the abyss. Remorse brought repentance. "Faith first, and then hope," Matteo had said. As a young apprentice grinding pigment, his eyes had followed the changing light, how it illuminated curves and edges, cast shadows, altered colors, all the while the pigment beneath his hands growing deeper, more radiant in hue. The changing light of day was like the continuous flow of circumstance that fell across one's form, that altered it, but the soul, like the pigment, ground away at by self-reflection, also formed one in a way that was within grasp. The more one worked it, the more pure and luminous its color grew. Now it was time to use the marteloio of his soul to return to the place he had begun, to find what had been lost.

Inside clings truth's seed, submerged in the soul. Boethius

When Filippo was ready to leave, he discovered that during his stay there, Diamante had delivered a wooden trunk. A gift from Cosimo, it was elaborately painted and filled with luxurious linens. As Filippo was preparing to leave, Fra Bartolomeo reminded him of this possession. "Do not forget to take your trunk."

Filippo offered it as a gift to the infirmary, but the friar refused it as too fine an object for such a place. They were, Filippo reminded him, in need of a large trunk for storage, and the linens were thick and finely stitched so that they would last a long time. Fra Bartolomeo offered to purchase it, and Filippo, seeing that he had no choice, agreed to accept the smallest fraction of its worth. He then donated this sum back to the Carmine.

Before he left, the prior asked for a word. "I am concerned, Fra Filippo, with your many cases of litigation over the course of these past few years."

"Ah, well," Filippo sighed, "the less I have to do with courts, the better. But when I must…"

"Must you?" the prior asked. "It is unusual for a man of the cloth to be involved in lawsuits."

"But if I am cheated," Filippo explained, "and I know how to defend myself, should I not do so? I have a workshop to support."

"It is unusual," the prior insisted. "Fra Angelico, for example, would not find reason."

Filippo, held in comparison to this devout monk and painter, would always be found wanting. "Indeed," he said, "Fra Angelico does not have to pay for his own workshop. As a practicing monk, he is provided with one."

The prior acquiesced. "Well," he said, "if you think it necessary."

"These are times in which everyone brings suit," Filippo

reminded him. "Not only bankers and merchants, but painters, apothecaries, goldsmiths. It is, unfortunately, the only way to settle differences. We live in a litigious society."

"That is sad, indeed." The prior shared Filippo's exasperation with this state of affairs. "They do say," he continued, "do they not, 'May God preserve you from sorrows, evil, and lawyers'? Try, my son, to keep your contribution to this unfortunate business to a minimum. Now go, and God be with you."

Later that year, when the prior entered the names of the friars in the convent register, he hesitated, and then deciding that Filippo was now more a man of the world than a man of God, he entered "Fra Filippo, painter, former Friar of Santa Maria del Carmine."

CHAPTER 56

The year of Our Lord 1450, Florence

Sforza had managed, finally, to marry the Visconti's bastard daughter, Bianca, but when the devil at long last decided to take the duke, he died without naming an heir. In addition to Sforza, both Naples and the Duke of Orleans laid claim to Milan. For three years after the Visconti's death, Milan, resisting all, had existed as a republic.

Cosimo sat back in his chair. "And how does your wife fare?"

"She is well," Sforza responded. "Bianca and I are well suited."

"Fortuna has favored you," Cosimo said. Then, leaning forward and piercing Sforza with his gaze, he told him, "It is time. Much longer and the Milanese will become accustomed to life as a republic. But, as they are a people without the stomach for it, they will end up submitting to the first strong power that promises to keep them safe from themselves and from others. Better you than Venice or France."

"I will need backing," Sforza responded.

"The funds are at your disposal. You need only march in. On one condition."

Sforza narrowed his eyes. "Yes?"

"It is a strange request of a condotierre."

Sflorza noticeably stiffened.

"War is your business," Cosimo continued. "What are your feelings about it?"

"War should be avoided," Sforza said. "As a good tactician, I am able to circumvent unnecessary harm to my men, but I have seen what war does. I have seen too many battles. I do what I must."

"Italy," Cosimo said, "has been forever at war with herself. She is tired. I want to put together a league of city states and kingdoms. I want to realize an Italy at peace."

Sforza raised an eyebrow. "You have a vision."

"I once had a vision of peace for Florence. I now envision peace for all Italy. Will you support me in this?"

"I will."

"Then you shall have your funds," Cosimo concluded.

Later that night, he wrote to Maddalena: It has begun.

Just as in music...a certain harmony of the different tones must be maintained...so also a state is made harmonious by agreement among dissimilar elements. This is brought about by a fair and reasonable blending of the upper, middle, and lower classes....What musicians call harmony in song is concord in a state. Cicero

When Sforza marched into Milan, he did not meet with resistance. Where there had been riots and famine before his entry, he brought peace and plenty. With Cosimo's guidance, he immediately improved the system of taxation, making it fair to all and more efficient. The large sums of money collected helped him not only run the kingdom and fund public projects, but invest in works of art and architecture. He would make it a city of culture, one its inhabitants would be proud to call their own.

He has learned under my tutelage, Cosimo thought. His actions will hold him in high esteem among the Milanese and will maintain peace within. Milan, once an enemy within fifty miles of Florence's border, was now a trusted ally. It was time to put the rest of his plan in motion. Sforza, a friend who had benefited from his mentoring and his money, had been easily persuaded. Of the other rulers, only the pope might prove amenable. He would begin with him.

CHAPTER 57

The year of Our Lord 1452, Florence

L ucrezia's father called for her and her sister Spinetta to join him in his antechamber. Lucrezia was now nearing eighteen years of age and excelled at the fine arts of needlepoint and managing a household. She had also spent the last six years reading great works and discussing them with her father. She was especially well versed in Dante. Her uncle, her father's brother, was a Dante scholar at the university in Pisa. Together, she and her father read his commentaries. Lucrezia was happy. She loved her life. It was perfect.

"My dearest daughters," her father began, "I am in the process of finding husbands for you. Lucrezia, I have already begun negotiations with a family of good standing. You will marry within the year."

Both fear and excitement seized her heart. This was what she had been waiting for, to be a wife and mother. But now that it was imminent, she felt unsure, unsteady. "Father, so soon? May we not wait? One additional year, perhaps?"

"Ah, do not knit your brow with worry, my sweet Lucrezia."

"My wish is that he be kind," she pleaded. "That he be like you."

Her father laughed, pleased. "I have chosen well for you. I see integrity in his soul, kindness in his eyes. And you, my dearest Lucrezia. You will make a splendid wife, beautiful, intelligent, of generous heart. No man could ask for more."

Excitement began to push aside her fear. "I trust, Father, that he is as you say."

His eyes wandered to the gardens outside the window. "You will wear the finest silk. What color? Blue? Yes, blue. You will have roses woven through your hair, festoons of roses draped upon your horse."

"And..." She hesitated, not wanting to seem demanding.

"Come now. And?"

She confided, "Lavender. I love lavender best."

"Ahhh, lavender. A fitting flower for my Lucrezia's wedding. Simple, like her, modest, and inestimably beautiful, with a scent that is unforgettable. Yes, indeed, you shall have your lavender."

Your will is free, upright, and sound. Dante

Lucrezia pictured the white horse, herself astride it, dressed in blue silk interwoven with golden threads, embroidered with tiny pearls. Her hair crowned with roses and lavender, her horse festooned with them. Her father's voice cut into her dream.

"A meeting has been arranged for the week following the feast of San Giovanni."

That was less than a month away. Lucrezia placed her hand over her breast, trying to still the flutter she felt there. She could not wait to meet this young man with integrity in his soul and kindness in his eyes.

CHAPTER 58

The year of Our Lord 1452, Florence

For the remainder of the day, Lucrezia walked about in a daze, questions swirling in her head. Her needlepoint now dropped into her lap, her hands idle, she stared off into the distance, chasing her thoughts. Would he have light hair or dark? Blue eyes or brown? Would he be tall, short, thin, broad? Then she realized that every picture of him she conjured presented a smooth face, one upon which the features could be clearly discerned, the mood and inclination easily deciphered. But what if he possessed a beard?

"Lucrezia." Her mother's voice broke into her thoughts.

"Yes, Mama?" Lucrezia hastily picked up her needlepoint and forced herself to focus on the endless pattern of rosebuds. Although she did not enjoy needlepoint, this was something over which she had complete control. But her life was about to change in ways over which she had none.

He mother had walked over and now sat beside her, gently placing her hand over the one Lucrezia was using to pick at fabric with needle and thread. She looked up from her work.

"You must not dwell on what you do not yet know," her mother advised.

"Mother, what of his appearance, my betrothed?"

"Your father has chosen a good man, one who will treat you with kindness. That is all that matters."

Lucrezia was disappointed. Now that she knew of his existence, she wanted to be able to think of him.

Sensing this, her mother said, "I will meet him the day that you, too, first set eyes upon him, the day that both your families gather. But I do know that he is, although several years your senior, a young man. Your father thought this important to the growth of companionship between you."

"Like that you have with Pappa?"

"Like that between your father and myself." Her mother reached out and stroked her face, then cupped her chin in her hand. Lucrezia was her eldest, the first of her children to wed.

A sudden thought startled Lucrezia. What if she found him distasteful? "Mother, what if?" She did not know how to phrase her concern.

"What troubles you, my dearest Lucrezia?"

"What if, when I meet him? Mother, what if he is not to my liking?"

"We will not force you to marry against you wishes, Lucrezia. But, I implore you to meet this young man with an open heart. It will be his kindness toward you that will bathe every feature of his face in the light of love and tender affection, no matter what those features. You will want no other. I wish for you to know the same ease of love and companionship that your father and I have been blessed with all these years. Given your sweet disposition and the care with which your father has chosen, I have no doubt that you will. Now, take this certainty, tuck it into your heart, and give it no further thought, for it will soon come to pass."

Lucrezia felt suddenly like a small child in the cradle of her mother's soothing voice, her calming words. She dropped her head onto her mother's shoulder and found herself encircled in her embrace.

The fortunate she [Fortune] prostrates—in one hour. Boethius

    That night Lucrezia had a fitful sleep. Men's faces loomed, one with thick eyebrows, another with thin lips. Would any features, as her mother had said, come to be cherished through the simple act of kindness?

CHAPTER 59

The years of Our Lord 1450 – 1452, Florence

Filippo lived on Via Chiara, the "street of light." His bottega, on the ground floor, was flooded with it each day. This was what he had dreamed of long ago when he had stood this side of the Arno and told Giuseppe that he would one day live and work here. A few times a year he visited San Quirico, where once a year he said mass. Giovanni was doing a fine job of administering his duties. Through their combined efforts they had already provided all but one dowry for their nieces.

It was at this time that the rector of San Niccolo de' Frieri, a kind old man named Giovanni da Foligno, passed into the great sea. Several of the friars were called upon to perform his duties until a replacement could be found. Now that Filippo was the recipient of a benefice, he was included among the group. There was mass to be said three times a week and the nuns' confessions to be heard, an amusing affair, the order being composed of sweet and innocent women who ministered to the sick at their hospital.

The nuns gave tirelessly of themselves, and their transgressions were trifling. Filippo would always remember one young nun whose sin was typical of those confessed to him. "Fra Filippo," she began, "I was on night duty and, shamelessly succumbing to fatigue, I fell asleep when someone might have been in need of me. God forgive me."

"Sister," Filippo said, stifling a smile, "a merciful God forgives you such a mild transgression."

"But," she began, then stopped, realizing, no doubt, that she was about to contradict him.

"But?" He gently urged her to continue. She was silent. "What troubles you, Sister?"

"Fra Giovanni always chastised me for my slothfulness. He said it was one of life's major sins, and that it displeased God greatly."

I am satisfied if every day I take something from my vices and correct my faults. Seneca

How to answer and not say anything ill of Fra Giovanni? Filippo chose his words carefully. "Fra Giovanni, in his great wisdom, knew God's displeasure with such things. But God knows what is in your heart, which only means well and always tries to do what is best. Is that not so?"

"Oh, yes."

"Well, there, you see? God knows your heart and, therefore, forgives you. Say one rosary in praise of God's love and understanding. In nominee Patris, et Filii, et Spiritus Sancti. Amen."

Surprisingly, the nuns requested that Filippo succeed their former rector. He fulfilled his duties to them, including the keeping of careful accounts of expenditures and the handling of dealings with the outside world on their behalf. They paid him a modest stipend, all of which he used to buy supplies, such as oil and wine, and to pay their taxes.

CHAPTER 60

The year of Our Lord 1452, Florence

A fortnight after learning of her imminent betrothal, Lucrezia sat together with Spinetta on the bed they shared. Since they were of marriageable age, they had been given their own bedroom. The sisters, only two years apart in age, had always been close and served as each other's confidante. Lucrezia needed to speak about the conflicting feelings in her heart.

"Spinetta, this is what I have always dreamed of, being a wife and mother, but now it is upon me, I am plagued with feelings of doubt. Oh, sister, there is so much I do not know. So much that is uncertain."

"Yes," Spinetta agreed. "It is frightening when one does not know what is to come."

"I know how to run a household," Lucrezia reasoned, "and how to care for children. But, how does that all come about? What leads me to it? What do I walk into?"

"Mother will tell you all," Spinetta assured her.

"Yes, there is much information she can provide. But, how does this man, this stranger, in one day become my most intimate friend and family?"

Spinetta grabbed her sister's hand in both of hers. "Do not fret, Lucrezia. It must be possible. Look at mother and father."

"Oh, I know it must," Lucrezia said. "I am but one person. So many before me have done the same. And, Spinetta, I know that I cannot leave this life without being a mother. I must steel myself, dispel these doubts, and meet this man with an open heart."

The door opened and Anna, the maidservant, walked into the room. She wagged her finger at them. "It grows late," she whispered. "Time for talk is over. To bed with you. Your mother will be here any moment to check on you. If she discovers you are not abed...."

The two quickly slid beneath the covers, but Lucrezia was restless. She stared into the warm glow of the banked fire. She must leave all that she knew, all that was comfortable. Depart from the bosom of her loving family to enter a stranger's house. As she watched the dancing flames, she suddenly saw children twirling, dancing, laughing. Were they her future children? To be a mother. The door clicked open. It was her own mother. Lucrezia closed her eyes. Beneath her closed eyelids, she could still see the warm glow cast by the flames. This was her destiny. Comforted, she drifted off to sleep.

In the middle of the night, the fire now embers, a sudden pounding woke her, making her heart jump. What was it? Someone's fist drummed on a door. There were heavy footsteps on the stairs. A scream. Lucrezia jumped from bed, threw on her mantel, and, Spinetta at her heals, rushed to the top of the stairs, where they were met by a servant. "All is well," the servant assured them. "There has been a small accident. The doctor has been sent for. Back to your room now."

"I heard a scream. Who screamed?" Lucrezia asked, shivering at the memory.

"A silly servant." They were led back down the hallway to their room. "All is well. Back to sleep now."

How could she sleep? Lucrezia dutifully crawled back under the covers. In the darkness, she listened for voices, footsteps, anything that would tell her what had happened.

The next morning, when Anna came in to help them dress, she had to be awakened. Why was she so sleepy? Then she remembered. "Anna, what happened last night? I heard voices. A scream. The doctor. The doctor was sent for."

"I do not know anything of that," Anna said, helping them dress. "You must hurry. It is late."

Anna did not take time, as she normally did, in the preparation of their hair. She did not crisscross small sections of it in braids, nor did she weave a diaphanous silk cloth through it. She brushed it out and bound it with a simple cloth.

"Will we be working in the storeroom today?" Lucrezia asked, assuming this meant that it was to be a work day and that she and Spinetta would be helping her mother take stock of supplies for the kitchen.

"Oh, no, miss. Come. Your mother awaits you."

When Lucrezia entered the camera, she noticed that her mother's hands were fidgeting. She had never seen her in a nervous state. They awaited her sister, Margherita. What could this mean? Why were they all assembling? And why was her half-brother, Antonio, here? Once Margherita arrived and was seated, Antonio stood and looked them over.

"This is a sad day," he began, but Lucrezia noticed that he did not sound as if he were sad.

"Our father," he continued, "passed into God's hands last night."

Lucrezia did not hear another word that was said.

CHAPTER 61

The year of Our Lord 1452, Florence

Cosimo was calling upon his friend Agnolo Acciaiuoli to perform a service for Florence. "I will tell you my thinking," he began. "As you know, since Sforza marched into Milan, Venice, threatened by our alliance, has banned Florentine banks from doing business and has kicked out all of our merchants. Alfonso, out of hatred for Sforza, has done the same in Naples. We must counterbalance the two, who are now aligned against us, before we can bring them to negotiation. This is why we send you to France."

Acciaiuoli nodded. "I understand. But is it not dangerous, this proposed alliance with France?"

"We must never see French soldiers on Italian soil," Cosimo agreed. "This is why we ask you to use your considerable rhetorical gifts. It is for this reason you have been chosen. Obtain for us the best possible arrangement. A limited alliance is preferable—two years, say, to be revisited at that time. By then, we may no longer need them. This move will also open up a new and lucrative market while we wait to be invited back into Venice and Naples."

"I see," Acciaiuoli said. He held up one hand. "I do not know that my skills in rhetoric will garner us a deal that does not include giving way to French troops."

"Naples, yes," Cosimo agreed. "France's claim there. At the moment France remains occupied by England to the north. She does not yet set her sights south. If you cannot make a deal without giving way on this point, compromise on Naples. Alfonso stole Naples from France. Let France try to gain it back. Alfonso will not be easily defeated, and the situation may well force him to the table."

Great deeds are not done by strength or speed or physique: they are the products of thought and character and judgement. Cicero

Cosimo had known that he chose well in Acciaiuoli. Agnolo made a good deal with France for the duration of two years, as Cosimo had suggested, the alliance to be revisited at that time. They had had to compromise on Naples, as predicted, agreeing to allow French troops to cross Florentine lands if ever they decided to attack Alfonso. Now new troubles festered. Although unaware of the exact terms of the alliance, Alfonso was livid. Cosimo was banking on the fact that the threat of a French invasion would induce Alfonso to see benefit in joining an Italian league.

The other problem was Venice, which had appealed to the Holy Roman Emperor Frederick to intercede and bring an end to the alliance between Florence and Milan. Cosimo was ready to play his next card. Frederick was in Rome to be crowned by the pope, a symbolic gesture. Cosimo wrote, inviting the emperor to stop in Florence on his way home. It would mean footing the bill for the fifteen hundred drunken Austrian knights in the emperor's entourage, but that was a small price to pay, and the Medici bank could well afford it.

The emperor would leave for home disinclined to interfere in Italy's affairs. France's attention continued to be dominated by war with England, but after nearly one hundred years, the people of both countries were growing tired of conflict and the expense it incurred. Cosimo needed to act quickly before France's attention turned south.

He pulled out a piece of parchment, dipped his pen in ink, and wrote: My dearest Maddalena, The plan unfolds as expected.

He who chooses the life of Reason and Wisdom must forego every Pleasure, great and small. Plato

He did not tell her the particulars. A personal letter could easily fall into the wrong hands. So, instead he wrote to her about one of Plato's dialogues.

She had asked in her last letter: What of love? Does Plato speak of love?

He now wrote: Yes. Love, Plato teaches, begins with love for one person, but higher than this is love of the many. Through our pursuits we are able to benefit many people. Higher still is learning. This highest form of love, like that which you and I share, of philosophy, of knowledge, leads us to "the colorless, formless, intangible, visible only to mind," to "the great ocean of beauty," that we contemplate, giving "birth to many beautiful speeches and thoughts."

Her response was soon in coming: Why then are we given body, mind, and soul? Are they not all of equal importance? Plato places philosophy as the highest love. As Plato is a philosopher, is this not self-referential? I propose that our ability to perceive another's soul is the greatest gift, the highest love.

She had pierced through yet again. Cosimo, himself, had been engaged in the very pursuits about which Plato spoke—government, the crafting of laws. He had not found much beauty or love there. Perhaps that was the lowest form of love. Learning was, ultimately, a solitary pursuit, although rhetoric could enlighten others with the knowledge one had learned. But, how dry and dusty it all felt. He had only touched another's soul once. The memory of this connection still moved him deeply.

He responded: When I read your letters I sense you here beside me. I see you. I hear your voice. I feel I can almost touch you.

She responded: It is a sad embrace that touches naught.

Her words thrust like a rapier.

CHAPTER 62

The year of Our Lord 1452, Florence

Lucrezia sat in the wide expanse of the sala with her mother and seven siblings. Silence shrouded the room like a thick fog. In a house that had always been filled with the laughter of children there was an eerie quality to this silence. The youngest boy, not yet three, was playing quietly with some toys on the floor, and the baby was asleep in a cradle. The others sat stiffly, eyes downcast. Her mother stared out the window, hands folded in her lap. Then, there was the hollow echo of footsteps. Isabetta entered. Lucrezia's mother stood and held out her arms in greeting. But, as they embraced, she slumped in Isabetta's arms momentarily, letting out a small sharp cry like that of a baby bird.

Just after they were seated Lorenzo asked, "Can we go outside to play now?"

Her mother's face, when she turned toward him, held a blank expression. Lucrezia, normally attuned to all of their needs, did not stir. She sat, hands side by side on her lap, palms down, and stared straight ahead.

"Can we? Please. Can we play?"

Spinetta rose. "Come," she said, "you must change first." She laid a hand on Lucrezia's shoulder to stay her, but there was no need. Lucrezia could not move. She was weighted down by the sea of sorrow inside her.

Our stern reared up, the prow went down...until the sea closed over us.

Dante

Three of the boys left with Spinetta. Margherita slid closer to Lucrezia and timidly placed her hand on top of her sister's. Lucrezia took her sister's hand in hers.

Isabetta and her mother spoke in low tones. After a short time, Isabetta excused herself, saying that she wanted to speak with her brother. She promised to say farewell before she departed.

Shortly after she left, Lucrezia's mother seemed to come to herself. "Lucrezia," she said, "see if you can catch up with Isabetta. Ask her if she would like to join us for the mid-day meal. And, if she would, let Jacopa know there will be one more."

Lucrezia did not move.

"Bestir yourself," her mother coaxed. "Go now."

Lucrezia stood and moved slowly to the door. What did food matter? They ate none of it. As she approached, she heard the door to Antonio's office shut. She would wait. Jacopa would need to know as soon as possible. Quite suddenly, she heard Antonio's voice raised. It startled her.

He was complaining, "more numerous than rats. Even the pestilence has not decreased their number."

Lucrezia moved closer to the door, placing her ear against it, her hand pressed to the thick wood.

Isabetta had let out a cry of surprise. "How can you speak so of children?"

"A litter," he repeated.

"Your own brothers and sisters."

"You are my sister."

"And they," Isabetta insisted.

"By half," he countered.

"Let not God hear that thought," Isabetta warned him.

"It is unjust. When am I to marry?"

"I understand, Antonio, but they must be provided for."

"I will send the first two off to a convent at once."

Lucrezia's heart drummed unsteadily inside of her. She turned, resting her back against the door so that she would not fall to the ground.

"Oh, brother, no! They are of an age to marry this very year. Plans have been made. Lucrezia will make a fine match. A political alliance, Antonio. Beneficial to family and business."

"With a hefty dowry to pay," Antonio reminded her. "No. It is settled."

"Do not do this, I beg of you."

"It will be done while they grieve, before they have time to protest."

"You are cruel. Father would be displeased."

"Father should not have bred like a rabbit."

"Antonio, you speak ill of the dead. Of our father."

"He did not have a thought for me."

There was a shuffling of papers. "I have work."

Isabetta's footsteps approached.

Lucrezia drew away from the door.

Isabetta started when she saw Lucrezia standing there. "What have you heard?" she whispered, pulling her down the hallway.

"Everything," was all Lucrezia could think to say.

"I will speak with my husband," Isabetta promised. "He will be able to make Antonio see reason."

CHAPTER 63

The year of Our Lord 1452, Villa Medici at Careggi

I t was infuriating. Cosimo had just learned of the plans for his son Giovanni's villa in the country, an elaborate design, built into the side of a cliff without farmland to give it purpose. Moreover, its brilliant white walls would be visible against the cliff from every vantage point in Florence. This went against the grain of every lesson Cosimo had taught him, and he told Giovanni as much. "You must draw up a new set of plans. I will send Michelozzo around to you within a day's time. He understands the importance of restraint."

"It was Michelozzo who drew up the plans that I now possess," Giovanni reminded his father.

"Yes, well," Cosimo grumbled, "he was evidently forced to comply with your specifications."

"As he does with yours when he works for you," Giovanni said. "It is my money. I will spend it as I see fit."

"Waste it," Cosimo countered. "You will bring envy upon this house."

"I am sick of hearing it," Giovanni retorted. "My grandfather did not possess the wealth we do, or he, too, would have used it to live in greater luxury."

"Do not tell me what your grandfather would have done," Cosimo warned. "Do not be so presumptuous. I grew up in his house, learned firsthand his lessons."

"He was full of lessons," Giovanni scoffed.

"And sons grateful to learn them!" Cosimo slammed his fist upon the table. "Envy is a weed."

"A weed that should never be allowed to grow in one's garden."

"Should never be watered," Cosimo corrected him. "There is a difference."

"Let them be jealous," Giovanni said. "Perhaps it will compel them to be more industrious in order to attain their own luxuries."

"'People court and loathe the prosperous,'" Cosimo said, quoting Seneca. "It is easier to take what belongs to another man."

"A fault of theirs, not of mine," Giovanni said.

"Until you hang from the gallows in the Piazza della Signoria," Cosimo warned. "Men such as you 'whom success has made unbridled and over-confident...' You remember what Cicero said. '...should be led into the training-ring of reason and learning so that they perceive the frailty of human affairs, the variability of fortune.' Frailty, Giovanni, variability. Has nothing I taught you taken hold? Must you build this villa of yours on a hillside within full view of all Florence?"

"It is precisely for the view of the city it provides that I build it there," Giovanni said.

"On the side of a cliff so that the land cannot produce a single bale of wheat? What is its purpose, this villa?"

"Pleasure," Giovanni said, his chin jutting out defiantly.

"Pleasure," Cosimo scoffed. "The vainglorious pursuit of a rooster." Seeing that the insult had hit its mark, he continued, "Humility is the most important of the virtues for a leader to learn precisely because, from his height, it is the most difficult to cultivate."

His words did not have the desired effect. Giovanni turned and walked swiftly to the door. "You disappoint," Cosimo said to his back.

"Good," Giovanni retorted without turning, and he stormed out through the door, slamming it behind him.

Cosimo's own father had been disappointed in him only once that he knew of, and he had felt the sting of it deeply. It had caused him to stop and reflect on his actions and motivations. His father's disapproval had helped him to become a better man, one who would be more careful next time, who would consider how his actions affected those around him. Cosimo's disappointment in his two sons was not new. Giovanni especially displeased him. The boy had been more foppish in his youth and was, as a man, more vulgar in his display of wealth than his brother. Both sons were men of large appetite—for food, drink, material possessions, and women. Both had mistresses, he knew, although they were married. No moderation there.

Cosimo grunted as he dropped into a chair. He held his head between his hands and rubbed his face. If only he could wash away what had just transpired. He was getting too old for this. Had he not that very year turned sixty-five? Very few men saw the passing of more than fifty years. He had been expanding the family business for well over forty and had been guiding Florence for nearly twenty. He was tired.

But Cosimo dared not give up the reins. Who would take them? Giovanni? He was self-centered, disrespectful, and ungrateful. Cosimo's eldest son, Piero, had been in poor health since he was born. No one had expected him to live past childhood. It was Giovanni who, since he was a child, had been groomed to take over the business and the stewardship of Florence. Giovanni was not fit to guide a horse. What would happen to all that Cosimo had built so carefully throughout the years? What of his legacy? It made his heart sick to think of it.

It was with an appreciation for the irony of the truth that he acknowledged, of all his sons, Carlo was the most fit to take the reins. Carlo listened, and he had his mother's innate intelligence, her good sense. How unfortunate for Florence that he was a bastard, his abilities wasted on the clergy.

There was a knock at the door. Who was bothering him now? "Enter!" he yelled out, intending to give whomever it was a good thrashing with his tongue.

"Cosimo." Filippo greeted him cheerily. "I hope you are not in too bad a temper. I passed Giovanni on the way in."

"Ah, Filippo, I had forgotten you were coming. I have good news. Sit. I have a commission for you. An important one, and one that you have need of at this time in your career. When was the last time you worked on a fresco?"

Filippo's eyes lit up. "Not since I was a young man."

"That time set sail long ago," Cosimo said.

Filippo, who was now forty-six years old and in need of a major fresco project, ignored the good-humored insult, and asked, "Where? For whom?"

"It is in Prato."

"Prato?" Disappointment crept into Filippo's voice. "Not Florence?"

"Prato is a pilgrimage site," Cosimo reminded him. "Your work will be seen by pilgrims from all over the world. And the compensation is more than twice that provided any other painter for comparable work. They wish for you to begin immediately. They are keen for its completion."

"Anxious for its completion before it is begun," Filippo grumbled.

"Fra Angelico is held up with work in Rome, or he would have taken the project. Well."

"I was not their first choice?"

"It will be your best work yet," Cosimo prophesized, "goaded not a little by this feeling of competition that I detect." He trained his hawk's eye on Filippo.

"Fra Angelico," Filippo said contritely, "is deserving of his acclaim as a painter. And he is a man pure of heart."

"You speak the truth. As to this commission, it is for a series of frescoes in the main apse of Santo Stefano."

When Filippo left, Cosimo again rubbed his eyes. There was always enough complaining to go around. No matter how much he tried to help. And Giovanni. What would Maddalena have said? Leave him alone? Allow him some freedom while he is yet young and able to enjoy it? Seneca is a stiff old rooster, and Cicero puts one to sleep? The problem was that he was too old. Too old. Ah, well, at least there was Cosimino. Never did a boy possess such a singular intellect, such a straightforward zest for life. His hopes were bound up in his grandson. The boy would be capable of taking the reins from his grandfather; indeed, he would far outpace him. It was a shame he would not be alive to see it. The only trouble was that Giovanni might allow everything to crumble, all that he had spent his life building up, brick by brick, before Cosimino had the chance to succeed him. There was another knock on the door.

"Enter!" he growled.

The door opened and his daughter-in-law, Ginevra, came through, holding her son by the hand. "Cosimino wished to visit with you, but if this is not an acceptable time—."

"It is the very best of times," Cosimo said, smiling. "I am delighted."

"Poppy!" Cosimino raced across the room, jumped onto his grandfather's lap, and gave him a crushing hug.

Cosimo laughed aloud. "And what have you been up to today, my boy?"

"I saw a bird," Cosimino said, eyes widening.

"A bird? And what was it that made this particular little bird so different from all others?"

CHAPTER 64

The year of Our Lord 1452, Florence and Prato

Before he left for Prato, Filippo decided to visit Sant' Ambrogio. He told himself that it was to contemplate his most monumental work before undertaking the massive fresco project. He had not been inside the place in years. As he stood in the hushed interior, his eyes took in the whole of the work, settling finally on Theopista.

At first, he had thought of her every day. When he thought of her now it was with affection, what was left of his great passion. He reached up to gently trace her face with his thumb. She was all memory now, memory and this painting. He turned abruptly and left.

The first layer of plaster needs to be rough and uneven or the smoothest layers on top will not adhere.   Cennini

When Filippo arrived in Prato the deep chill of winter had already settled in, the cold and damp making it impossible to begin work on the frescoes. Filippo would have time to plan them out as well as to work on other commissions, but his first stop was Santo Stefano. He strode past the Chapel of the Holy Cintola, frescoed by Gaddi, and along the narrow nave lined with massive green marble pillars until he reached the main altar.

There he and Diamante viewed the walls of the apse. "I have not worked on a fresco for a long time, Diamante," he said, warming to the prospect. "When last I worked on one, I myself prepared the wall." He reached out and caressed the rough wall, and then patted it as if to congratulate it on being a fine and sturdy one.

Filippo turned and pointed toward the north wall. "There, where the light of late day falls upon the wall, the colors, warm, will burn in its flame." He turned abruptly, gesturing toward the south wall. "And there, ethereal tones, cool as air, will breathe in the vaporous light of morning."

The pragmatist in Diamante noted, "The sole window is bricked up. How will you illuminate objects? Cast shadows?"

"Do you not know how an object appears in early morning light? In the last light of day?"

"Yes, but—"

"Well, then," Filippo said, as if that settled it, and rubbed his hands together with anticipation. "We have work to do, Diamante. We have work." He stepped back to better view the wide empty expanse before him.

Filippo stood without moving for so long that Diamante's stomach growled out into the apse in its demand for the mid-day meal. Filippo ignored Diamante's protests of hunger. He stared, every so often raising his arms to peer through a box shaped by his fingers as he mapped out sections of the wall. Diamante dropped heavily onto a nearby bench.

Donatello often spoke about the figure within, how he could see it encased, awaiting release. Filippo could not pierce through wood with his gaze, but when he looked at a smoothed wooden surface, a smear of thick plaster, he heard the swell of the wind, the rustle of silver leaves, smelled the recently tilled earth flush with new growth. He saw all suffused in light. In this way, he felt peace like a wave rising from the depths of the sea that swept across the empty space of panel or wall.

Some time later, punctuated by the sudden clap of his hands, Filippo's voice echoed up into the rafters, "I must begin to sketch." He swiftly turned and rushed from the church. He looked back on his way out the door to see Diamante, rubbing his eyes and his poor empty stomach, lumbering after him.

Filippo worked at a feverish pace, sketching page after page of scenes from the lives of Santo Stefano and San Giovanni. When he stopped, it was already dark. He had been working by candlelight without noticing the change. He lifted his head and looked around. He felt as if he was waking from a dream, and slowly became aware of a pang in his stomach. "I am hungry. Why did you not tell me it was night?"

Diamante, a look of shock and then anger crossing his face, was about to protest when Filippo threw his head back and laughed. "I can always pull the tail of your goat, Diamante," he said. "Come. You must be famished."

While they sat at the inn, savoring a pheasant stew and soaking up gravy with hunks of bread, Filippo said, "Frescoes, Diamante, yes, but they will glow with the brilliant light of panel paintings, with their full range of colors. Never before in such a massive work, the figures larger than life, the detail, the subtleties, the shades and tones of a panel."

"But will that not take many years to complete?" Diamante asked, frightened by the prospect of fending off yet more patrons as Filippo labored, oblivious.

"When they see what I have created for them, for their little town of Prato...." Diamante groaned. Wishing to cut off his complaints, Filippo changed the subject. "We have much work to do before we begin the frescoes. I have received a commission here from Provost Inghirami, but we must first return to Florence, where more work awaits us."

Diamante had become indispensable. He managed things when Filippo was away. Filippo remembered him as a boy of seventeen.

He had shown such promise. He was now a painter who was more than capable, although his promise had never quite found fulfillment. It was his stubborn need for perfection that undermined him, leaving his figures static and overwrought. He was too fond, as well, of decoration. He weighed figures down so with jewels, Filippo often told him, that they could not have moved if they wanted to.

One day Diamante had explained, "I work and work at one detail to reach perfection, and still it eludes me."

"No. No. No," Filippo had yelled out, equally exasperated. "There is the detail, yes. I, too, work at it, but then I am stretched across the whole, the vision in its entirely. My focus narrows, then expands. It is as if I see through an opening that adjusts, closes in, opens up. All the while, I am engulfed. I am inside the work. When I step away, view it from afar, I see what needs doing. Then, I am sucked in once more, surrounded. I chip away at it until, from its center, both I and it emerge."

Filippo could see that his explanation had not helped. It had only left Diamante feeling more perplexed. How to explain that when Filippo painted he was, at once, aware and unaware? There was no memory, no desire, no beginning or end; there was, solely, the process of becoming.

He tried again. "You do not need to fill a painting with all that you know, Diamante. It is not to prove yourself a maestro that you paint. Hold back in order to allow the truth of the scene to emerge. Only then will it speak. Only then will it breathe."

He wished he had a better way with words, could have helped Diamante find his stride, his personal vision. Still, the young man was proficient, the best assistant any painter in Florence could boast of, and he was dependable. Trustworthy to a fault, he served as Filippo's confidante.

CHAPTER 65

The year of Our Lord 1452, Prato

I t was the cold that hurt more than the dark, seeping through her skin and into her bones like death. Lucrezia remembered, with longing, the crackling fire banked in the hearth of her bedchamber, how she curled up in bed to sleep in the circle of its warmth. Each morning now, awakened for matins, her teeth chattered, her body shook. Where was she inside this shivering husk? Where did she reside? There was no more Lucrezia. She quickly dressed; if she was late, she would be made to kneel on the cold stone floor of the chapel, in prayer, for hours, discipline being the God worshipped here. The birds outside were chirping with delight. What had they to be so happy about? As the novices hurried along the loggia, hunched over with the cold, Lucrezia noticed a thin blanket of snow on the ground, glowing in the light of the moon. Its beauty found no answer inside of her, where there was only darkness.

You harvest darkness from the light itself. Dante

Later that day, just before nones, Lucrezia made her way to the kitchen. She was in a rush to get there, not because she enjoyed pealing and chopping turnips, but because it was one of the few times she and Spinetta were able to spend time together. They shared kitchen duties with another of the novices, a plain and entertaining girl whose company they enjoyed.

Simona did not have the delicate features of Lucrezia and her sister, or the slender, graceful body. Her nose was wide, her eyes close set, and her body fleshy. Her thick arms were made for scrubbing floors, washing clothes, and kneading bread. In contrast to her features, she possessed a finely tuned heart. She also knew a thing or two about the streets, being a carder's daughter and allowed to walk in them. Her ear was sharp, her eye aware. She befriended Lucrezia as soon as the latter arrived at the convent, taking a protective, even a proprietary attitude toward her. Although she was not educated like Lucrezia, she was more knowledgeable about the world. When her father had passed away, and his debts were paid, there was nothing left. Family possessions had been sold to pay the small dowry to the convent.

As they peeled and chopped, Lucrezia explained that her brother, Antonio, had also been unable to supply a dowry large enough for marriage. Simona stopped peeling, the turnip slipping from her hands. "Your father was a silk merchant," she said. "You would have had Monte shares. He would have bought in when you had lived through the first year."

Lucrezia stopped working. "Monte shares?"

"You know nothing of the Monte delle Doti?" Simona asked, surprised. "It is an investment for a dowry. Even if your father put in a small sum, say one hundred florins, only ten years later it would have been worth five hundred florins, a good sum. A chest full of clothes, linens, some ready cash were all that your brother needed to provide. Mind you, clothing is expensive, but he would have gotten a merchant's price on the silk."

This news crushed Lucrezia, and then a thought occurred to her. "The money in the Monte is mine, is it not?"

"He will have confiscated it."

"Then there is no hope."

"What of Isabetta? What of Mother?" Spinetta asked. "Will she not come?"

Simona was not easily persuaded. "One thing is certain. He did not place you in a convent in Florence, of which there are more than there are pigeons on a piazza. He wanted you well out of the way, out of contact with family members."

"Mother is nursing the baby to save the expense of a wet nurse."

"Then she cannot travel," Simona said. "That is why you are in Prato. How many children younger than Spinetta?"

"Six."

"God help us," Simona crossed herself, "and all yet live?"
Lucrezia nodded.

"The worse for you. How many are girls?"

"The three after Spinetta are boys."

"How old?"

"The youngest is ten."

"They will have been sent away. Apprenticed," Simona said with certainty. "Cast out into the world to make their way."

"Lorenzo is but a boy," Lucrezia protested.

"What of the others?"

"Two girls and a boy."

"Convents will not take a girl before the age of eight," Simona informed them.

With an involuntary gasp, Lucrezia brought her hand to her mouth. "Margherita is eight. Surely not."

"Look at it this way," Simona tried to comfort her. "She will not know what it is that she misses." She was a person who believed that it is better to know the truth, whatever it was. "Lucrezia"—she placed her hand gently on her friend's shoulder—"you must accept the possibility that no one is coming for you."

That was not possible. Lucrezia was meant to be a wife and mother. Not only that, but her father had shared texts with her. Together they had pored over her uncle's commentary on the great poet Dante. She felt so much larger than the confines of the space she now inhabited. She felt a sudden need to break free.

Wiping her hands on her apron, Lucrezia grabbed Spinetta and began to dance. Around they whirled, stifling laughter, as Simona looked on. "Come. Join us," Lucrezia said, holding out her hand.

Simona's head drooped. "I do not know how."

The sisters stopped. "You do not know how to dance?" Lucrezia asked, stunned. "Well, then, we must teach you!"

Step by step, they taught Simona until, exhilarated and exhausted, they stopped to catch their breath. "Oh," Simona cried out. "Our work. We must hurry or there will be no mid-day meal."

Rapidly they peeled and chopped. "I so enjoy dancing," Spinetta said.

"Yes," Lucrezia agreed. "What if? What if we were to teach everyone to dance?"

"During our free time," Simona said, quickening to the idea, "when the prioress and the older nuns take a nap."

Their eyes met, and they laughed. "She need never know," Spinetta said.

"It is settled then," Lucrezia said, but the dance had given her such a feeling of freedom in contrast to her situation that she soon drooped back into sorrow.

While they worked, Simona and Spinetta tore off small pieces of bread and ate them. Spinetta held one out to Lucrezia, who refused it.

"You do not eat, Lucrezia. You waste away," Spinetta admonished.

"Then there will be nothing left of me to torment."

"Please, dear sister, do not say such things. It frightens me."

"I am sorry." Lucrezia placed her hand on Spinetta's. "You, as well, do not belong here. I think only of myself."

"In truth," Spinetta began hesitantly, "in truth, I like it here."

"That cannot be true," Lucrezia said.

"I love the solitude," Spinetta explained, "the peaceful flow from one devotional hour to the next. Once I reconciled never to marry, it has not been so difficult. I do miss Mother. But, Lucrezia, I do not think I could manage a household like you could. And I do not, like you, desire so very much to be a mother." She cast her eyes downward.

Lucrezia's little sister had always seemed such an extension of herself. She saw Spinetta for the first time, standing apart, a person in her own right. But, what woman does not want to have a child? Does not wish to be a mother? "What then?" Lucrezia asked. "You would have wished to grow old alone? To be the one to care for aging relatives?" What a circumspect and sad existence, she thought.

"In truth," Spinetta admitted, "I am afraid of childbirth, Lucrezia. And, how many stories have we heard of women trapped in loveless marriages? Or worse, mistreated. From marriage, there is no escape."

"Father would have chosen well for us."

"Father is no longer here to choose."

"So, you are contented in this place?"

"It is surprising, I know. But, yes."

"God has blessed you with an accepting nature. I am too prideful."

"It is not pride, sister. God has blessed you with intelligence and strength of purpose suited best to the world, not to the convent."

"Oh, Spinetta, what shall I do?" Lucrezia cried. "I will never reconcile to this place."

Spinetta drew her sister to her and held her close as she wept. There was nothing to say, no consoling words to apply like a salve to her sister's wounds. Lucrezia was misplaced, and there was nothing for it.

CHAPTER 66

The year of Our Lord 1453, Florence

his was a disaster, a turn of events Cosimo had not fore-
seen. That it was a surprise frightened him. Perhaps his
faculties were weakening. Had he grown too old to lead?

Venice had overrun lands belonging to Sforza, tying him up at
home, and Alfonso had sent his son Ferrante to attack Florence.
The Neapolitans were on the march across Florentine territory.
The people of Florence, still smarting over their dismissal from
Venice and Naples, were furious and blamed Cosimo. Crowds
gathered every day outside the doors of his palazzo. When Rencine
fell, fear raced through the streets.

Cosimo tried to remain steady. He gave reassurances. But he
knew the situation was volatile, the results uncertain. Long ago,
Lorenzo had warned him that he risked everything by playing this
game. Now, at the most precarious moment in his plan, while all
of the balls he had put in motion were suspended in mid-air, an
unforeseen turn of events threatened to bring them all tumbling
down. If this happened, the people would blame the Medici. Exile
would be the best they could hope for. Florence sent reinforcements

to every village. They would also have to depend on the loyalty and courage of the residents.

An image flashed through Cosimo's mind. On that day long ago when he had crossed the piazza on his way to the Signoria, had the vision of himself hanging from the gallows been a premonition of what was to come rather than what might take place imminently? His hands shook. Was he to lose at the game for the first time? He felt ill. His nerve was failing him.

Worldly fame is nothing but a gust of wind, first blowing from one quarter, then another, changing name with every new direction.   Dante

He pulled a piece of parchment out. Whenever he grew close, Maddalena pulled away. He rubbed his eyes. You cannot force someone to love you. Nor can you prevent them from loving you. He dipped his pen in ink and wrote: You cannot prevent my love for you.

This was the first time since he had left Rome that he had declared it. A lost love. A memory. A few lines written on a page.

Cosimo had always grappled with the idea of a life after death, was inclined to disbelieve in it. Each time he had been close to death it had felt final. But, he was also close to men who created. Fra Angelico, Filippo, even the irascible, crusty old Donatello worked in the spiritual realm. Through their works, he himself had come close to perceiving it. Perhaps this speculation was only because he grew old. Was he frightened of disappearing? Was he growing feeble-minded?

One thing was certain. His love for Maddalena, as illusory as it had become in the earthly world, felt more real than anything he had ever experienced. Did this not prove that his love for her stretched beyond the mere confines of time? He sealed his letter, slowly rose and, mid-day, made his way to his bedchamber.

Days passed during which Cosimo remained in bed under his physician's care. At one point, Ferrante's men pillaged within six miles of the city itself. But, the villages all around proved obstinate in the face of his army, and Ferrante could not gain a foothold. Florentines did not easily succumb to domination.

Then word arrived that René of Anjou and the French army had entered Italy. He had come to aid Sforza and, together, they soon had the Venetians on the run. Sforza was able to send his brother Alessandro along with two thousand cavalry to Florence, which together with the Florentines quickly regained all the land that had been taken. Ferrante gave up and returned to Naples. Disaster had been avoided.

At the same time, the unimaginable happened. Constantinople fell to the Turks.

CHAPTER 67

The year of Our Lord 1453, Prato

The young nuns gathered in a small area behind the garden, farthest from the living quarters. Those from Florence who knew the dance had instructed those from the countryside in the Saltarello. Before long, dancing had become a daily activity. Now, Lucrezia and Spinetta in the lead, they began a series of kicks to dance forward, skips to dance back, twirls around each other, and then the final dizzying whirl arm in arm, around and around.

"What are you up to?" A figure came toward them from out of the shadows of the loggia. It was Sister Agnese, the prioress's assistant. Where the prioress was kind and compassionate, Sister Agnese was severe and punitive. She had taken an instant disliking to Lucrezia, saying, "You are not a silk merchant's daughter here. It will take much hard work and penance to rid yourself of your airs." The smallest infraction led to punishment. Lucrezia often found herself on her hands and knees, scrubbing the stone floors. She had asked Spinetta and Simona why Sister Agnese hated her so. "Because," Simona had explained, "she is jealous. You are beautiful and kind, and she is neither." And now, here she was marching toward them.

The prioress was sympathetic when Lucrezia, singled out, was brought before her. She gave the dancer a gentle reprimand and was about to dismiss her when Sister Agnese insisted, "They must be punished. Dancing now. What next? Where will it lead?"

The prioress hesitated. "Not too harsh. I leave it to you, Sister Agnese."

While scrubbing the floors, Lucrezia stopped every so often to stretch her back and rub her knees. When she did, she reminisced about the dance and the laughter, the buoyant feeling, body and soul, the joy of movement. It was worth it.

Later that day, as Lucrezia cooked the meager broth, Spinetta and Simona filled baskets with bread. Spinetta stopped suddenly, holding a piece of bread aloft. She stared out the window, her head cocked to one side as if she were awaiting the approach of someone whose arrival was imminent. "I thought I heard something, but no. It is soon two years, and no one has come. We shall be forced to profess."

"Dear Spinetta, no one is going to rescue us. We are forgotten." Lucrezia's face, once filled with light, was in this place perpetually set in sadness. But deep down she was angry. "If we were men, we could walk out of here. But we cannot walk out because we have no money and no means of obtaining it."

"It is more than that."

"What then?" Lucrezia challenged her sister.

"Well," Spinetta faltered, "if attacked, a man can defend himself."

"How often," Lucrezia retorted, "does a man face attack?"

"But if he did. That is why, in or out of the convent, we are protected. We are secluded, but we are safe."

"A high price to pay for safety. I think there is more to it than that. Only the women of wealthy families are kept indoors. Are the women of families with less wealth worth less? They move about freely."

"They have work to do. It takes them out of the house, but even they must keep to themselves and be careful in their dealings with others."

"No. It is that women provide male heirs. Men have endless choices. We must join a man's household. If no man will have us, we have two options only, to become a prostitute or a nun. Odd, do you not think? One makes her living from intimate contact with men, while the other is barred from having any at all. It is this single physical ability we have that defines us. We are either the one who belongs to all men, the good wife who belongs to one, or the solitary prisoner who spends her life in prayer for the sins of all the others. Not one has her own life."

"She who chooses has her own life," Spinetta said.

"Yes," Lucrezia agreed, "she who chooses."

"Sister, you dwell too much on questions of fate that are not in our hands but in God's alone."

"More in some people's hands than in others." Lucrezia sighed. "But perhaps you are right. I am sorry, dear Spinetta. What else is there to do in this prison but think?"

"I shall go tomorrow. Ask the prioress to give us more occupation. Or you will surely go mad."

[S]he hears a bell ringing in the distance, which seems to mourn the dying day. Dante

The following day, Spinetta made her way to the prioress's office. When she entered, the prioress smiled. "Ah, there you are, my child. Please take a seat. We will await your sister."

Spinetta was confused. Had the prioress read her mind? Had someone, another novice, overheard her conversation with Lucrezia the night before and spoken with the prioress about it?

Lucrezia entered. Once she was seated, the prioress stood before them and took each of their hands in hers. "My dear children, I have sad news," she said. "Your mother, may God bless her soul, has been taken into God's heavenly kingdom."

CHAPTER 68

The year of Our Lord 1454, Florence

"Of what good is prosperity without peace?" Cosimo demanded.

"Yes, indeed," Dietisalvi Neroni, ambassador to Milan agreed, "but prosperity may be enough to satisfy Sforza."

"Sforza grows old and wearies of war," Cosimo contradicted. "He will take my guidance either way."

"He reveres you," Neroni agreed. "He has learned how to rule from you. In fact, he has much improved the kingdom he conquered. The people of Milan have grown to love him."

"Ha!" Cosimo laughed. "Perhaps I should declare myself Duke of Florence. In order to allow for the people to love me."

"Freedom makes a republic fickle," Neroni agreed. "But freedom is worth the price."

"Florence's greatest gift is its freedom, including its freedom from foreign influence, which is why we need to make peace with each other. Sforza is with us. The recent fall of Constantinople occupies Venice to the east, the bulk of its trade relying on the Levant. This is greatly to our advantage. The Venetians would otherwise prove impossible. Lying thieves. Then there is the pope. The pope wishes for peace."

"The pope," Neroni retorted, "wishes to expand his lands into territory unable to resist his armies and to do so without the interference of any of Italy's major city states."

"Yes, well, let us hope he moves quickly so that we may soon see peace throughout all of Italy. The only obstacle is Naples. Alfonso."

"Alfonso has always been an obstacle. And his son Ferrante. A strange and vile creature. Even less inclined toward peace."

"Nevertheless, Alfonso fears France and its claim to his throne. It is there that we can be of help to him."

"But what of France? Florence has at all times sided with France against him. How will they be appeased?"

"It is always a matter of balance, just as when it made sense to shift alliance from Venice to Milan, assuring Florence a true and loyal ally. We can rely on Milan to protect us from Venice, and on France to protect us from Naples. But split alliances do not bring peace. If all of Italy is to remain safe, we must unify. You are right, however. I must tread lightly. I cannot jeopardize Florence's alliance with France but must also give assurances to Alfonso or he will not join the league. And, above all, we do not want the French marching into Italy."

"This is a tricky business," Neroni agreed. "What will you do?"

Governments cannot do without a splendid reputation and the good will of their allies. Cicero

Cosimo sat in contemplation, his hands tented, the tips of his fingers tapping his long nose. Quite suddenly, he grabbed the arms of his chair and leaned forward, startling Neroni. "I will downplay the strength of the French League, strongly hint that there is a crushing lack of funds. That will appease Alfonso. As for the French, they are a pragmatic people. They will understand that we are forced by current circumstances to join this quite temporary peace deal in order to recover financially. There is truth in it, apart from the characterization of it as temporary."

"That seems a good plan."

"I have a rare manuscript of Livy that I will gift to Alfonso as well. That will sweeten the deal."

CHAPTER 69

The year of Our Lord 1455, Prato and Florence

The preliminary sketches for the frescoes were completed. Filippo knew they would change as he worked, but he always envisioned a project as a whole before he began. Now he was working on a commission for Inghirami, provost of Santo Stefano. It was of the death of San Girolamo. Filippo would pay homage to his mentor Masaccio by placing a crippled beggar among the mourners. He would honor Giotto and his frescoes in Padua with a realistic portrayal of grief. It was difficult to paint a face contorted by anguish. He thrilled to the challenge. This would be the most lifelike portrayal of grief ever yet painted, imbued with dignity.

Filippo was working on the face of the cripple when a messenger arrived. "Nuisance," he thought. "What the devil can he want?" He continued to work, but then there was Diamante's voice breaking through, a frightened tone giving it an edge. Filippo threw down his brush. "What is it?"

"They request your immediate presence," Diamante said.

"Who? Where? Speak."

"The Archiepiscopal Curia. In Florence. Filippo, you have been charged with breach of contract."

"Breach of contract?" Filippo stormed. "Nonsense! Who brings this charge?"

"Frediano da Ravenzano."

"Son of a whore!" Filippo banged his fist on the table.

"He claims he was never paid."

"Never?" Filippo stuttered. "You saw me give final payment, did you not?"

"I did," Diamante confirmed.

"And afterwards, I entrusted my Giotto to his care. Ungrateful rodent. Well, I am happy to have taken the precaution of having him sign the contract. Do you remember? Admitting to satisfaction with payment? Find that for me, will you, Diamante?"

Filippo picked up his brush and continued to work.

Diamante said, "Filippo, do you not remember? It disappeared."

"Hmmmm?" Filippo was lost in his work.

"It is not here," Diamante said.

He threw the brush down. "And they wonder why I cannot deliver work on time. What do you mean it is not here?" Filippo asked, stalking over to Diamante's desk and flinging loose papers in all directions. Many had not yet made it as entries into ledgers, so Diamante was chasing after and scooping them up. "I remember, Diamante. I remember because it made my blood boil to pay him. He calls himself a painter. He is no painter. I paid him for nothing. Now he swindles payment from me again? I refuse to pay him one more soldi. He is not worth even one of the forty florins already paid."

"Filippo, the contract disappeared. Do you not remember?"

"Ah, yes."

"Perhaps you should pay him and be done. We have much work to do."

"He thinks that because I receive large commissions he can swindle me? I have a bottega to run, real apprentices to pay, not to mention supplies, rent. He is not worth, Diamante, your little finger." Filippo held up his to demonstrate.

"Filippo, please. It is not worth the trouble."

"We will have to create one. His signature was, well, how else would I know his signature? It was like that of a child, no character in it." Filippo pulled out a contract waiting to be signed by the next new apprentice and signed it. "There. That should do it. Now, I will write my satisfaction with payment. Date it."

"Filippo, this is ill advised. This is forgery. Your word against his, surely."

"I do not have time, Diamante. I begin my commission. This should settle it." He blew on the ink to dry it.

The following day, having arrived in Florence, Filippo made his way to the Badia, where the Curia awaited him. He was aggravated and mumbling to himself when, as he turned a corner, he nearly collided with Donatello.

"Lippi," Donatello greeted him, clapping him on both arms and leaving a trace of sawdust. "I heard you were in Prato."

"Prato, yes," Filippo said. "But I have been called, an annoying business, to the Archiepiscopal Curia."

"The Curia?"

"Charged with breach of contract. That imbecile Frediano da Ravenzanno. An apprentice of mine, you remember? Nonsense, of course."

"He was always trouble. But the Curia? Why is it not being handled in civil court?"

"I do not know, but I must be on my way. They await me at the Badia. Get this damned business over with. I will meet you at the Silver Swan for supper?"

"Until then."

Filippo rounded the corner of Via Santa Margherita and made his way to the main entrance to the Badia. The caretaker responded to the loud banging of Filippo's fist upon the outer door, scowling as he opened it to allow him to enter. Filippo walked along the loggia, making his way to a room in the farthest northwest corner of the monastic enclosure.

The Badia was one of the oldest structures in all of Florence. It had been built in the 900s and had always played an integral role in the workings of the city. In the 1200s, while the Bargello was being built, the Podesta met there, and again, while the Palazzo della Signoria was being built, government leaders met there. Its bells rang along with those of the communal prior and the Podesta. No other bells were given that privilege. Now the Archiepiscopal Curia held court within its enclosure. Filippo noted that the orange trees in the courtyard were beginning to bear fruit.

The sword has been joined together with the crook, and linked by force they inevitably proceed badly. Dante

"In the name of the Lord, Amen. Here begin the proceedings in the matter of breach of contract against Fra Filippo Lippi, dipainture. The proceedings will be recorded by the esteemed notary Ser Filippo Mazzei."

"Fra Lippi." The older of the two judges, the vicar Raffael da Bologna, addressed Filippo directly. "You have been summoned to answer the interrogations regarding the matter of breach of contract in order to avoid payment stipulated by contract. Will you now take an oath to tell the truth?"

Filippo took an oath to speak the truth with regard to all questions put to him.

"Certain information," the judge continued, "has been obtained by our command." Here, the vicar held up a piece of paper that looked familiar to Filippo. It was the contract he had forged.

"Frediano da Ravenzanno has claimed that he has never received payment for services rendered as your apprentice and that he never signed a contract accepting said payment. How do you respond to this charge?"

"Preposterous. He received regular payments, the final one of which is signed to on the paper you now have in your possession."

Filippo looked over at Frediano, who did not blanch. In fact, he did not appear to be at all concerned with this piece of evidence.

"Why," Filippo continued, "did it take nearly seven years for my former apprentice to bring suit against me? If he was not paid, as he claims, why did he not come forward at once?" This was a point of fact that would be difficult to wiggle out of.

"Fra Filippo Lippi," Frediano said, "is one of the most prominent maestros in all of Florence. I was but a lowly apprentice. I am now also a maestro but at the time had no standing. I was frightened."

Filippo laughed. He could not help himself. Frediano afraid? He was devious, malicious, but never afraid.

"Fra Lippi, we remind you that this is a serious matter being presided over in a solemn court. Perhaps not like those in which you are accustomed to litigate. We ask that you behave with respect for this court."

"I will bear that in mind," Filippo said, bowing his head, but the reprimand had taken him by surprise. And why were they referencing his suits in civil court?

The younger judge, whom Filippo did not recognize, scolded, "Archbishop Antoninus reminds us that the Archiepiscopal Curia does not make distinction between the lowliest of citizens and the highest."

"Fra Lippi," the vicar continued, "you have provided the court with a document that you claim to be the contract drawn up between yourself and Frediano da Ravenzanno seven years ago, and yet the paper on which it is written does not appear to be old."

Filippo prevented himself from blurting out, "Not as old as you, surely." Instead, he explained, "My records are neatly and carefully preserved."

Frediano laughed aloud. The judges did not seem to notice.

"Will the court not reprimand Frediano da Ravenzanno for his disrespectful behavior?" Filippo asked.

The dour vicar fixed him with a withering stare. "Do you sit as a judge in this case, Fra Filippo?"

Why was he being reprimanded and Frediano not? The judges were exhibiting bias. They asked Frediano if he had signed the contract to the effect that he was satisfied with payment. Filippo tried to stare him down, but Frediano, fidgeting nervously, would not meet his eye. He looked straight ahead. "I never signed a receipt of payment," he said.

"Ah!" Filippo jumped to attack, wishing for a quick end to the proceedings. "So, you admit that you received payment. What you deny is that you signed a receipt."

The younger judge said, "Then you, Fra Filippo, admit that, although, as you claim, the defendant was paid, this document is a forgery."

"I do not." Filippo wondered how, if at all, he had slipped up. "I contend that Frediano lies. He has not the talent to sketch a pillar, but he was paid—for nothing—and signed a receipt to that effect."

"If you felt," this fennel-head continued, "that he had not earned his wages, why did you pay him?"

Filippo felt his blood begin to boil. He hated judges with their tricky language and well-laid traps and believed sincerely that the whole lot of them should be strung up in the public square. "What I have provided is the receipt," he insisted, "drawn up for the purpose of recording a payment of wages, wages not earned, in fulfillment of the contract. Although nothing produced by Frediano da Ravenzanno was of use to me. He set me back in my labors. If he had any decency at all, he would admit to his ineptitude and not demand payment at all."

"So, you admit," the vicar continued, leaning forward and looking down his nose at Filippo, "that you did not pay him."

"I admit no such thing."

"Your wording gives you away. You said, and I quote, 'He would not demand payment,' which does not place the act in the past, but rather in the future."

Filippo, growing irritable, waved his hand as if to wipe away all that had preceded. "The fact remains that he did not earn his wages, but he was paid them."

The younger learned ass then held the receipt up in one hand, shaking it. He squinted down at Filippo. "This document is newly written. Surely, the defendant, in the course of bringing charges, did not agree to sign a receipt."

"It is not newly written," Filippo repeated, exasperated. "The document clearly states that Frediano da Ravenzanno was paid, and he signed it to that effect seven years ago," he added with emphasis, glaring at the judge.

"Then you will not object," continued this judge with the long, beaked nose on which spectacles balanced precariously, "if we ask the defendant to produce his signature for comparison."

Filippo glanced over and saw that Frediano was smiling like an imbecile. "He will not sign his signature as he normally would do," he protested.

"We will ask," the judge explained, "that a legal document, one signed in the past, be produced for comparison."

Filippo bowed his head in acquiescence. What else could he do? His goose was cooked. Surely, he could not have remembered Frediano's signature from so long ago.

The document, when produced, was sufficient to close the case. Frediano would be paid—again—but the Archiepiscopal Curia was not satisfied.

"Fra Filippo Lippi, do you admit to the grave and immoral sin of forgery?"

"I do not," Filippo said beyond all reason.

"We, the judges, according to our office, desirous of promoting Christian morality and speaking on behalf of the Archiepiscopal seat, do hereby decree that Fra Filippo Lippi be imprisoned and tortured until he confess."

Torture? Had he heard the judge say "torture"? Filippo was certain that he must not have heard the judge's words correctly. He did, however, find himself being roughly handled as he was led into an adjoining room. It was a large, dark storeroom of some sort containing jugs of oil and wine and bags of grain. A door at the far end was opened, and he was pushed into a dark, dank tunnel, so narrow that one guard was forced to walk ahead, the other behind. Filippo held his hands out at his sides to feel his way along.

It seemed they walked forever, and then another door opened, and he found himself in a basement where he was shoved into a cell, the door locked behind him.

Once his eyes had adjusted to the dim light, his cell being filled with more light than the tunnel had been, Filippo estimated the direction and the distance of his journey. The cell must be located in the basement of the Bargello. There was no other explanation than that there was a connecting tunnel between the Bargello and the Badia. He was a prisoner, but whether of the church or the state, he did not know.

CHAPTER 70

The year of Our Lord 1455, Florence

"This time he has made a mistake that I do not know I can fix," Cosimo said. "Deceit after the fact makes a man appear guilty of the deed of which he stands accused. What was he thinking?"

"Lippi is stubborn," Donatello said, "and he does not always think ahead."

"Stubbornness," Cosimo grumbled. "A habit among painters and sculptors."

Donatello ignored this obvious reference to himself. "Painting is Lippi's life. He has no patience for idlers who seek the glory without the courage to perfect the craft."

"I will send a dispatch to Antoninus this day. As you know, however, he is embroiled in a dispute with the Podesta. The Curia oversees a trivial matter regarding a question of marriage. Giovanni della Casa and a woman of low birth, his mistress. He was foolish enough to have made promises. Hmm." Cosimo shook his head. "But the archbishop is impeccably fair minded. And the podesta, arrogant son of a whore, treats Antoninus, who made a reasonable request of him, with disdain. Antoninus asks only that the civil courts hold off with their investigation until his own trial, in which this same woman, this mistress, is also a litigant, has been resolved. In order to avoid prejudicing the case, you see."

"There are rumors," Donatello interrupted, "that they torture Lippi."

"Torture? Credible rumors?" Cosimo asked.

"Yes."

"The greatest painter in all of Florence? Are they mad? I will bring the full force of what power I yet possess. Pray God it will be enough."

I come to take you to the other shore, into eternal darkness, into heat and into chill. Dante

"He was paid!" Filippo shouted, indignant. The rack turned. He screamed out in pain. It was unbearable, but he would not relent. How could he? "I cannot confess what I did not do. He was paid, the filthy beggar!"

The wheel turned. "Do you confess?"

"No," he cried out. Was he awake? No, he dreamt he was asleep. Then they woke him, or did they? He lost track of his bursts into consciousness, his descent into darkness. He was wet and shivering. Where was he? He tried to sit up and found that his feet and wrists were shackled. He was on the ship. He groaned, "No." And then, the stench of breath, the black leather mask with slits for eyes. It all came back. He heard a creaking sound, like rigging stretched taut. His arms and legs felt as if they would split from his body. There was something in him that was fixed, inflexible, a metal beneath the thin veneer of skin that had been forged in captivity.

Filippo passed out. When he awoke he found himself curled up on the hard, stone floor. Cradling his stomach, he shivered with the cold. Then he felt a surge and rushed to the corner of the cell, where he retched. Afterwards, leaning his back against the stone wall, his mind drifted and he fell asleep.

The following day, as his jailor led him once again to the chamber, he whispered in Filippo's ear, "Confess. You must confess, or they will kill you." Passing through the entryway, he whispered a final warning. "Do you want to die here?"

Filippo did not want to die, but the jailor must be mistaken. They would not murder a prominent painter, Cosimo's friend. He again protested his innocence. The rack turned, and he cried out in pain.

The torturer bellowed through his mask, "Confess!" Filippo thought of his work. It loomed above in his imagination, his first monumental commission in its early stages. He must complete it. As he uttered the first words of his confession, the rack turned several times in succession. He felt a snap in his gut and cried out. A jolt of pain shot through his body from his feet to his head, where it exploded, stealing his breath. He lost consciousness.

Filippo was awakened by a splash of cold water. He wanted nothing more than to curl up around the searing pain in his gut. Then he remembered. His torturer grabbed him by the hair and yelled into his face, "You forged the document. Confess!" Filippo's stomach convulsed. He tried to turn his head away.

"Yes," he whispered.

"I cannot hear you," the torturer yelled. "Do you confess?"

"Yes." Filippo pushed the word out as loudly as he could, and then he lost consciousness once more.

When he awoke, Filippo was back in his cell. He slowly became aware of a searing pain in his abdomen. As the shadow passed from his memory, he pulled his robe apart and saw, as he had feared, a bulging mass beneath his skin. He groaned. He would die here. Shivering, he curled up on the stone floor of the cell. He drifted in and out of consciousness, his mind traveling down corridors where it roamed the streets of Florence, the shadowy interior of his childhood home, Cosimo's palazzo. Where was Cosimo? There was Matteo's smiling face. "Escape," he had said. Escape? What had Filippo learned long ago? Ah, yes. That he had it within himself to escape. There all along. He forced himself awake and crawled, holding his stomach as he did, to a wall, the only place on which to draw.

The sole implement he could find was a loose chunk of crumbled stone. He honed it against the wall and, filing it to a sharp point, lifted his arm. He yelled out in pain. It would have to be a sketch low to the ground, on a level with where he sprawled.

He began with the judges. Would they have been surprised to see the supercilious sneers etched into their features, the smug disregard, the arrogant disdain that had hardened their faces? Then he began on the torturer, in whose eyes, the only visible part of his face, he captured base cruelty, the same joy of inflicting pain that had sparked in Jacopo's eyes, the boy who had taunted and shamed him, the boy who had died in the pestilence. The torturer shared Jacopo's love of another's suffering.

As he was finishing, the door of the cell opened and Diamante— oh, thank the Lord, Diamante—entered. He lifted Filippo with great effort to his feet and walked him out of the prison. Filippo wrapped his arm around his apprentice's broad shoulders. Diamante had nearly to lift Filippo off his feet, he was so weak with pain. Once outside the Bargello where Filippo had been imprisoned, Diamante paused. "You are badly injured," he said. Filippo could only nod. "We must get you to the Carmine."

CHAPTER 71

The year of Our Lord 1455, Florence and Villa Medici at Careggi

The friars kept Filippo warm while he slept through several days. They fed him a few spoonsful of broth when they were able. They had tied a heavy piece of cloth around his midsection, unwinding it each day to determine its effectiveness.

"Rest," Fra Bartolomeo said. "Allow your body to heal."

But what of my soul? Filippo wondered. Tortured by my church. When the pain subsided, he tried to sit up, but moaned with the effort and fell back down.

"Give it time," Fra Bartolomeo said.

"Time," Filippo repeated. All those years ago, when he was just a boy and the pestilence had swept through the Carmine, Fra Paulo had told him that time would be forever altered. Filippo was at first perplexed by this, but he had soon discovered its meaning. Here was another experience that would alter time forever.

The friars were tireless in their work, and Filippo was soon able to sit up, to eat soup with some vegetables in it and a hunk of bread. Now awake but immobile, he had time to think. When had the church begun to use torture as punishment? And for such an insignificant infraction. It was a sin, to be sure, but so many sins were far worse. He had not believed it even as it took place, not until the very end when he realized he might die at their hands. Had the archbishop known? Antoninus was a devout and humble man. Surely, he would not sanction torture. And why had Cosimo, the archbishop's close friend, not come to his aid? The world, it seemed, had turned upside down, or, he thought, looking at the cloth truss he wore, inside out. But, this was not laughable. His church had transformed before his eyes. And he had confessed to forgery. What of his benefice? His commission?

When Filippo felt well enough to travel, he left the Carmine and stayed for a time at Careggi, the Medici villa, where he was looked after by Cosimo's personal physician. Filippo was angry. Although his family at the Carmine was not changed, he could not reconcile what he had experienced with his faith. His faith had sustained him in times of distress, from the Sacra Rapresentazzione when he first entered the convent, a comfort to him; to the ship, where he had learned from Matteo first faith, then hope; and during his pain at the loss of Theopista, his guilt over their illicit love, finding understanding in the words of Sant' Augustine. His faith had been a support, soothing him in times of need.

His was a faith grounded in the teachings of Jesus, in compassion and mercy even for sinners, especially for sinners, who needed it most. It was a faith that recognized the shortcomings of all, not only their light, but their shadow, that gave them the time to learn, to become better. It was a faith that poured down on one like the light of the sun on the flowers in the courtyard, warm and sustaining.

Later that day he and Cosimo sat together on the upper loggia, quietly contemplating the river. "Does Archbishop Antoninus know that they use torture?" Filippo asked.

"The archbishop is a wise and devout man," Cosimo snapped. "He was at the time deeply engaged with the civil courts. Fighting them to ensure that a woman of low birth was being treated with equal justice to the high-born fool she sued. Now that he is aware, he will take measures, but I fear this is only the beginning, Filippo. From the church there comes a dangerous shift. Its days of benign good will toward its flock are fast being replaced with judgment. Punishment. Not here, not in our local places of worship where our good monks are compassionate and devoted to learning. But there is a focal point of power that will sweep even them someday, unwilling, into its surge. Wherever there is a center of power, and especially where one man holds it, we no longer have a field of worship. We have a state."

"I see darkness where before I saw only light," Filippo said.

"You and I, old now, will not see the worst of it," Cosimo mused. "Where men claim that they alone know God's will, their license is unbounded. What did Dante say? 'Rome used to have two suns, which illuminated the two paths...but now, the sword has been joined with the crook.' I fear the one sun will extinguish the other." As he spoke, Cosimo stared out past the river, to the dark forest that rose up behind it. Then he turned toward Filippo. "What possessed you to be so obstinate?"

Filippo protested, "Frediano is a liar and a cheat."

"And now," Cosimo countered, "he has cheated you beyond what he had hoped. You will suffer from this, my physician tells me, for the remainder of your days."

"I will be trussed," Filippo agreed. "Should I have confessed? Was I to lie before God?"

Cosimo turned a jaundiced eye. "That was the intention."

"I could not confess what I did not do. It took courage to hold out under torture."

"Yes," Cosimo said, "too bad your gut does not appreciate your courage."

Filippo laughed but stopped abruptly and, groaning, bent over to wrap his arms around his belly.

Cosimo leaned forward, a serious expression in his eyes. "I know, Filippo, who was behind this. You look surprised. Did you think that a painter of little worth had the power to inflict such harm? Did you not wonder why you were called to the Curia? He used your benefice as reason to have the case heard there instead of civil court, where no doubt you would have won."

It was true that as a man of the cloth, any case brought against Filippo should be heard in ecclesiastical court. But the lines of his position were so blurred that his cases had always been tried in civil court. "Who brought it to the Curia?"

"I am afraid," Cosimo said, "that it is your association with me that has led to your mistreatment. Do you know the Bosticchi? Friends of Ravenzanno."

"Is that not the noble family associated with San Querica?"

"Yes. You have lost your benefice."

"Ah, well," Filippo conceded, "I will no longer have to pretend to be a man of the cloth. There is comfort in that."

"You will make a better man than you did a man of the cloth. I am sure it rankled when the archbishop appointed you. The Bosticchi had always chosen. He is a member of the political faction that currently, quite successfully, opposes me. After this business with the farm workers revolt, his allies have gained ground in the Signoria. My power has been much diminished. Well, there is nothing like incentive to gain it back. You have given me that."

Anger is useless…. With its wish to bring others into danger, it lowers its own guard. Seneca

Cosimo called for his bank manager. When the manager arrived, Cosimo said, "I wish to call in some debts. Does not Bosticchi owe a large sum? Borrowed to the hilt of his noble sword?"

"He does, sir," the manager concurred.

"Let us begin with him. And find out which of my fellow bankers owns the bulk of his debt."

"How much must he repay, and in what time frame?" the manager asked.

"All of it. At once." The manager raised an eyebrow and started to respond but hesitated. Cosimo continued, "And there are ten or twelve other families who have been grossly overextended for some time now."

Filippo had never before seen how dispassionate Cosimo could be in taking revenge. He also witnessed for the first time the extent of Cosimo's power, how he could ruin a man, an entire family, with a single command.

"Bring me a list," Cosimo demanded, "and I will decide. Begin with Bosticchi." He waved his hand in dismissal.

His manager hesitated. "May I ask for what the funds will be used?"

"Projects. First, the new convent chapel I had built for the novices of Santa Croce is in dire need of an altarpiece. Fra Lippi has been commissioned to paint it."

As his manager turned to leave, Cosimo winked at Filippo, who felt for the first time the sweet taste of revenge but soon thought of the families who would be ruined. "What will happen to the families?"

"I do not execute them," Cosimo said. "I do not banish them. Bosticchi and his faction believe they can better rule, but they are wrong. They will only manage to tear down what we have built, and what then? The Republic in ruins."

"But without money," Filippo persisted, "how will the families survive?"

"I take away Bosticchi's means of doing us further harm." Filippo remembered Cosimo applying the same reasoning when he banished Strozzi upon his return from exile. "As for the others, it is their debt, is it not? They knew the risk."

After a brief pause, Cosimo assured him, "They have recourse. And if they do not, there is the Buonuomini."

The Buonuomini, a group initiated by Archbishop Antoninus, were the twelve good men who provided alms for those who had fallen on hard times. The good men saw to it that those in need received clothing, wood, food, and wine each week.

"The archbishop," Filippo said, "is a generous man. The poor of the city owe him much."

"Ha," Cosimo responded, "the archbishop has often said that he created the Buonuomini because Cosimo de' Medici ruined men faster than God could save them. Who do you think provides the bulk of the alms?"

Of course, Filippo realized. How had he not seen? The magnitude of funds required to do such work could not possibly be raised one soldi at a time. So Cosimo ruined men, and then he saved them. Although, admittedly, the shame of having to accept alms broke a man's spirit—another form of revenge.

"Do not reveal my secret," Cosimo said, fixing Filippo with his gaze.

"I will not," Filippo assured him.

"My soul depends on it," Cosimo said, this time not in jest.

And ruining twelve families will require substantial penance, Filippo thought.

Since Cosimo had business in Florence, he left early the next morning. Filippo was to remain at Careggi for as long as it took to regain his strength. As he sat in the gardens, his gut slowly mending, he thought about the ease with which the church had decided to torture him. Was even the church bound, like Cosimo, to the exercise of power? The church he had grown up knowing was outside the world of men. But then, he had known it only through the kind monks of the Carmine, monks who were cloistered. They lived and prayed in a kind of spiritual paradise on earth. The church was becoming more of a player in the world of men. Was it subject, then, to the same laws of survival? Was it bound, like Cosimo, to exercise its power or risk losing it?

CHAPTER 72

The year of Our Lord 1455, Prato

One day in late spring, the scent of flowering linden trees carried on the breeze, the prioress led the novices through the streets to Santo Stefano where, in a small side chapel, a private service was being held for them in honor of Mary's cintola, the church's sacred relic. Along the way, they passed through the mercato, where Lucrezia smiled at the children of a vegetable seller. They circled around her, singing and dancing. She laughed and danced with them and for a moment felt light-hearted.

Afterwards, kneeling in prayer, she was split, one part of her filled with the joy sparked by the encounter, like seeds of light, the other encased in the tough skin of longing and despair. As she watched the merchant's ease with her children, she appreciated their joy, but at the same time she felt an aching desire to experience it herself. Her body and soul cried out for it.

Lucrezia possessed the right temperament for motherhood. Where Spinetta was often impatient with the herding of children, whose focus was scattered, or was distracted by her own needs and desires, Lucrezia was filled with energy when attending to them.

She took pleasure in the simplest duties, saw the humor in every foible. When she soothed them, played games with them, or arbitrated between them, she did so with a gentle touch, a desire to better understand them.

It was difficult to concentrate inside the church with all of the work going on there. A famous Florentine painter had arrived to create frescoes in the main apse. Scaffolding filled the immense space where apprentices moved about, busy in their work. Boards clattered, voices murmured. The painter, she knew, was focused on a section of wall high above. The sounds of industry, of purpose, echoed up into the vaulted ceiling, awakening her spirit, piquing her curiosity. As she left the church, she wished to stay, to continue to listen to this life-affirming activity.

That night, their kitchen duties completed early, Spinetta stopped in Lucrezia's cell on the way to her own.

"God is cruel," Lucrezia said, thinking of the children earlier in the day. "My longing for a child is unbearable."

"Of all people, Lucrezia, you should be a mother. God intended for you to be one."

"God has turned His back on me. What did I do, dear sister, to anger Him so?" Lucrezia pleaded.

"You, Lucrezia? You have never wronged anyone."

"Then, why? Do you think, Spinetta, that it was my doubts about marriage that brought me to this? That I did not trust?"

"No," Spinetta assured her. "It was only natural to have had questions."

Lucrezia looked around at the walls of the tiny cell, blackened with age and damp, the small window, high up, meant to give meagre light but not distraction, the narrow bed, a kneeling bench, a single candle, a crucifix on the wall above it. "Do you remember, Spinetta, the doll we shared? It had belonged to Mother. The one with gold brocade dress and green silk ribbons in her hair?"

"Yes, Santa Margherita."

"Do you remember her significance?" Spinetta looked puzzled. "She is given to brides. She is the patron saint of fertility. Spinetta, we are imprisoned in the convent of Santa Margherita." Lucrezia gave out a cry, half laughter, half despair, and began to sob.

Spinetta put her arms around her sister. "Keep faith, dear sister. I pray every day for our release. It is our fate to be rescued. Our brother will have a change of heart."

"I fear not."

"Isabetta, then." The bell sounded. Now that the weather had turned colder, they were allowed to say matins and lauds in their cells. Before she left, Spinetta squeezed her sister's hand. "Do not lose heart."

But Lucrezia knew that they would soon be asked to take their vows. They had been spared by the devastating news of their mother's passing. She and Spinetta had been left in peace to grieve, but now each morning when she awoke Lucrezia feared it would be the day of reckoning, the day she dreaded.

For of all the adversities of Fortune the saddest is this: to have once been happy. Boethius

Shortly before the feast of Mary's Assumption, the prioress called for her. "You must decide," she said. "You cannot remain a novice forever. Are you ready to commit your life to God?"

At Lucrezia's hesitation, she continued, "If you choose not to take vows, your brother has made clear that he will not provide for you. There is no one in Florence with whom I now have contact, but I will be happy to find you a position in a household here in Prato. It is a hard life. Consider well whether you are not better suited to a life of quiet contemplation and of light and pleasurable work in the garden."

When Lucrezia spoke to Spinetta later that day, she discovered that her sister had made up her mind. "I know well what life is here but know not a life of drudgery. We might end up in a good home with a kind family. But, as easily, we might find ourselves among people who treat servants with disdain, or worse, abuse them."

"But we also might find a position in which we are allowed to save a dowry and one day marry," Lucrezia argued.

"Lucrezia, servants came to Father and Mother's house as young girls of seven or eight to save dowries. It takes years. I am nineteen. You are twenty. Several years from now, perhaps an old widower of low birth would consider us. But, more importantly, think on this, Lucrezia. If we leave this place, we will be separated."

Protests she had been preparing died on Lucrezia's lips. "You are my only comfort," she said, disheartened. She could not be separated from Spinetta. She had no one else in the world.

That night Lucrezia could not sleep. It was not the station in life that she had wanted, not the lavish dresses and jewels, or the villa in the countryside. She had grown up feasting her eyes on her parents' love. She saw how their faces lit up when they looked at each other. She took in the small tender gestures they made toward one another. Lucrezia did not hunger for faith; she hungered for love.

CHAPTER 73

The year of Our Lord 1455, Prato

Back in Prato, Filippo took up work on the frescoes. He picked up his brush, the tip made of fine hog bristle, and brushed it back and forth across his fingers, feeling it firm yet soft against his skin. When he dipped it in the pot of paint, his thoughts disappearing into a well of darkness, reemerging with the light found in its depths, his brush glistening with its color.

Filippo was painting the final section of plaster that had been prepared for the day when his assistant Andrea interrupted him. The prioress of Santa Margherita wished to speak with him. His concentration disrupted, Filippo's sigh echoed throughout the apse. Diamante, sitting beside him, said, "I will see to it."

Filippo surveyed the swath of wet plaster yet to be painted and slowly focused back in on the small section upon which he had been working. This was the late hour when the plaster became ravenous for color, the pigment penetrating deep into its skin. Filippo worked at a feverish pace in order to take advantage, applying coat upon coat with the tiniest of brushes. When the faintest remnant of light had vanished, his nose nearly scraping the plaster to see by the candlelight Andrea held, Filippo put down his brush. He stretched his arms and his back, turned to Andrea, and said, "We are done." Then, he leaned back to view the work he had completed, a calm spreading through him, skin and bone, like the dawning of early light.

As Filippo climbed down from the scaffolding, he was surprised to see in the dimming light the prioress, her head bent in prayer. Ah, yes, he had forgotten. "She wishes a word with you," Diamante said, "a favor."

At the sound of his voice, the prioress blessed herself, stood, and, bent with arthritis, slowly approached.

"I apologize, Prioress," Filippo began, "but at the start of each day wet plaster is laid. It must be painted before the waning of the light."

"Fra Diamante has explained," the prioress said. "I am so sorry to disturb you, Fra Filippo."

"Not at all, not at all," he assured her. Prioress Bartholomea de' Bovacchiesi was from a good Florentine family. She was a kind woman who was well respected in Prato. "How may I be of help?"

"We are in need of a chaplain, Fra Filippo. We would be so honored," she began.

He had given up the life of the cloth, had been relieved to do so. At the look of hesitation on his face, she quickly added, "The duties are minimal. To hear confession, to say mass three times a week. That is all."

Filippo did not have the time for this, and it had been years since he had performed such duties. He was about to decline when the pleading look in her eyes stopped him.

"We also wish," she continued, "to have a painting executed in honor of the Virgin Mary's cintola. If you agree to the commission, we will of course compensate you as you are accustomed."

Filippo softened. He was the most highly paid painter in Florence. He could not accept payment from the poor sisters of Santa Margherita. He would charge only the price of materials. "Mass will need to be said before prime and the first light of day," he said.

"Of course," the prioress agreed.

And it will interrupt my coveted sleep, he thought, adding aloud, "And if I may share these duties with Fra Diamante?"

"Of course, Fra Filippo."

"Well, then, we have an arrangement. As to the painting, what are your needs in that regard?"

Diamante fulfilled most of the duties of chaplain for the nuns at Santa Margherita. Filippo offered their services free of charge. His commissions had long brought him enough money to be comfortable. His work now brought such high prices, in fact, that he had purchased a fine house in Prato directly across from the duomo. In addition to this, he rented a house and workshop in Florence and owned two houses there that had belonged to his father. He even thought of seeking a small house in the countryside, on the outskirts of Prato, where he might retire in the event of an outbreak of the pestilence, and from which he might procure vegetables and fruits. In any event, he never took payment from nuns, who truly lived a life of poverty in adherence to their vows.

Do not wonder if I cast no shadow.   Dante

Not long after they had taken their vows, words that fell numb from Lucrezia's lips, a sound as meaningless as the drone of a bee, the famous Florentine painter, who had been away on a trip for some time, appeared at the convent to say mass. They called him the "jolly monk," and he was, indeed, the happiest monk she had ever seen. The energy of his movements and his booming voice seemed to define, in contrast, the dead weight inside of her.

He was a curiosity, for who could find fulfillment in this constricted life? Was it his painting that filled the great void? She wished that she, too, had some occupation to pass the time, to bring her joy. Her every gesture mechanical, she took the communion wafer on her tongue with the usual lack of conviction. God had not answered her prayers. He had abandoned her. She had taken her vows because there was nothing left to do. Where did God reside in all of this? Surely not in a wafer, rough as parchment, that dissolved on her tongue, swiftly disappearing, as indifferent and elusive as the God whose flesh it was supposed to be.

CHAPTER 74

The year of Our Lord 1455, Villa Medici at Careggi

It was a mild early winter day, but with a slight chill in the air. "An invigorating day to work outdoors, do you not think?" Cosimo asked his grandson Cosimino.

"Yes, Poppy," the boy agreed.

Cosimo was teaching him how to prune grape vines.

"But, why, Poppy, do you cut so many of his arms off?" Cosimino asked, pointing to the ground littered with twigs.

Cosimo looked where he pointed and then back at the bulb that formed the top of the main trunk, branches trailing off of it from either side. "It does look like a man, does it not?" Cosimo laughed. "Well, Cosimino, I cut many of the arms away so that the roots may better nourish the fruit of those that are left."

"So many, Poppy," the boy said, still looking at the littered ground. Then he looked up at the vine. "How do you know which arms to leave?"

"Ah, an astute question," Cosimo said, reaching out to tousle the boy's head. Cosimino, at the age of five, always intuited the most important question to pose. "Well, it is in agriculture as it is in life. Here. Feel this." He picked up one of the discarded branches and handed it to the boy. "Weak wood does not support growth. Do you understand?"

His grandson, a grave look in his eyes as he pondered this, said, "Yes, Poppy."

"Now," Cosimo continued, placing the boy's small hand around a branch that had been left attached. "Grasp it. A fine, sturdy branch. Good wood is critical to the cultivation of fruit." As he said this he thought about how his grandson was the strong wood upon which the fruits of his labor would be carried forward. But, the boy was asking another question.

"Poppy, why then are there weak arms at all?"

Cosimo did not have a ready answer. "Hmm," he thought. "Perhaps it is to give us an example that we can see with our eyes. We must prune our own weaknesses as we prune the vine. If left unchecked, they will prevent us from bearing good fruit. Once they are lopped off, our strengths will be fed by the full pulse of our roots."

In every product of earth there is inborn power.   Cicero

His eyes fell on his grandson's upper arm. At this tender age, it was thin as the wing of a newborn bird, untried in flight. They would need to protect him until he gathered the strength to soar.

CHAPTER 75

The year of Our Lord 1455, Prato

Lucrezia had not attended to the weeds, and they had taken hold. Grabbing one close to the earth, she shook it, loosening its grip, and yanked it out whole. It made a ripping sound as its roots gave way. After much coaxing, the next weed held fast, so she stabbed at the ground around it, careful not to chop roots where they entered the earth. It would only grow back again. It must be rooted out whole.

Then she moved on to a vine that, having already choked and killed several plants, had begun to spread. Lucrezia stood to gain leverage and pulled with all her might. It only dug into her palms where it slipped through her grasp. Anger rose in her like a flame. She would not allow this sinister growth to murder her vegetables and herbs. She chopped at the earth around its base, making deep gashes, then grabbed several strands and yanked. She almost laughed with joy when she felt it give way, rip out in one long line, its secondary roots not nearly as deep. Some plants had been lost in the battle with the vine, but it had been defeated. They were now piled together in a heap where, no longer sustained, the vine's once vibrant leaves lay limp and wilting in the sun.

Satisfied with her work, Lucrezia sat on the nearby bench to rest. The sun felt so warm on her skin that she closed her eyes, leaned her head to one side, and soaked it in. She breathed deeply, feeling it caress her face and neck.

Life was going well, Filippo thought, as he made his way from Santa Margherita to Santo Stefano. He had stayed late after saying mass in order to further discuss the panel painting with the prioress. Winter would soon be upon them, the fresco abandoned until warmer weather. The sun this morning shone brightly in the sky, where only two or three small wisps of cloud drifted. The air was sharp and crisp. He decided to cross through the garden on his way to the gate.

The herbs were nearly done for the season. Only the winter vegetables would remain, leeks and tubers. Filippo imagined them floating in a thick gravy with some meat, steaming with warmth on a cold winter's night. He could almost smell the stew when his thoughts were distracted by a figure sitting on a small bench surrounded by baskets. A young nun sat motionless, her head tilted to one side, eyes closed, the light falling gently along the curve of her cheek and down her slender neck. A high stone wall stood at her back.

"Good morning, Sister," he called out joyfully as he approached.

Startled by the sudden sound of his voice in the quiet of the walled enclosure, Lucrezia jumped. Recovering herself, she smoothed her habit and nodded her head in greeting. Their eyes met.

Filippo knew deep pain and could recognize it in another. This nun was too young and beautiful to know such anguish. Old and calloused as he himself was, pain was sewn into his being. But this young nun had surely been created by God for joy. She was beautiful, of that there was no question but, at the same time, so bereft, so filled with despair. What was its source?

Filippo sat beside her. "Sister, you appear downcast, and this such a glorious day. What is it that troubles you?"

He imagined some small transgression over which she need-lessly tormented herself.

"It is nothing, Fra Filippo. It is, as you say, a beautiful day."

Her voice held no conviction. Her head was lowered and her eyes cast downward so that she could not see the day. Filippo would not be put off. "You may confide in me, Sister, for something troubles you."

"I am ungrateful," she blurted. Ah, he had been right. "The sisters are so kind, the prioress one of the kindest of women."

"Indeed, she is," he agreed. She did not offer anything more. Filippo decided to try another approach. "Where are you from, Sister? What are you called?"

"I am Lucrezia Buti," she said, her back straightening, her chin tilting upward. "I am from Florence."

"Ah." Filippo let out a cry of delight. "My home as well. Are you also from the Oltrarno district?" He himself had grown up on the other side of the Arno. He assumed she must have as well since such a beautiful woman would otherwise have been married off with a handsome dowry.

"No," she said.

"Ah, well. What does your father do, then?"

"He was a silk merchant," Lucrezia said, her head drooping once again.

"I see," he said, sympathetically. "Your father has joined God in his heaven. I am sorry for your loss, Sister, and now understand the source of your grief."

A single tear had made its way from the corner of her eye, which she quickly wiped away. Filippo resisted the urge to pull her to him, to allow her to cry in his arms, this child. It would be un-seemly. He patted her hand. "It is difficult, I know."

Her eyes moved back and forth beneath her partly closed lids as if she searched the ground for something. She was agitated. There was more.

"Having chosen the life of the cloth must, at this particular time, bring you much comfort," he ventured.

"I did not," she blurted, but then caught herself. So, that was it.

"When you father passed on, when was that?"

"Three years now, just prior to the feast of San Giovanni," she said. "My half-brother."

"Ahhhh, I see," Filippo said. Had he not, himself, provided dowries for his six nieces? Her brother had been unwilling to do the same. This practice of imprisoning young women against their will because of the inability or unwillingness to pay the price of a dowry was barbaric. She was so young, so beautiful. An idea occurred to him. "Sister, have you professed?"

"Yes," she said, and his heart sank. "Just after the feast of the Assumption."

That was only three months hence. How cruel Fortuna was. Filippo had been prepared to provide her a dowry. "Well, we must make the most of it then," he said. What else was there to say? "Is it your duty to tend the garden?"

She nodded. "The prioress has given me a devotional book to read. It uses the garden as a metaphor. Tending to the garden: tending to one's soul. It likens pruning plants that are overgrown to confessing sins and doing penance. It speaks of pulling weeds from soil as pulling sinful thoughts from one's mind. And, of course, cultivating flower and fruit is prayer, which cultivates the soul. The soul is illuminated by God's divine love as the plants are by the sun."

Filippo detected skepticism in her voice. Sister Lucrezia recited the platitudes in her book of devotion as if they held no meaning.

"You do not find the book helpful to the cultivation of your devotion?"

She studied his face for a moment, thinking of her battle with the vine, not unaware of the feeling in her heart as she had fought it, the anger there that needed excising. "I do not like being told in a deceptive way to accept my fate, to turn away from the things of this world in order to dwell in the garden of the soul."

Others might have found this confession shocking. Filippo was mildly surprised by it. There was more to this nun than ethereal beauty and grace. "Well, perhaps you should put aside the book for now. Concentrate on the earthly garden you tend. A joyful occupation. In a garden, there is life and growth," he began, trying to cheer her, but her head drooped, and she creased her brow. What had he said? "You do not enjoy the work? Perhaps I could have a word." But that was not it.

"Oh, no, Fra Filippo. I love the work. It is only that…"

"Only that…?"

"I so wanted to be a mother." There was a catch in her throat as she shared, finally, the deepest source of her grief.

"I am sorry, Sister Lucrezia," he said. "That is, indeed, a hardship." They sat in silence in the quiet of the cloistered enclosure.

He was sharing in her sadness, without thought, when suddenly an idea came to him. Why not? She was from Florence, after all, the daughter of a merchant, a woman of culture. "Sister, I have been given a commission to paint the Virgin Mary handing down her cintola to Sant' Tommaso. Would it interest you to be my assistant? It is unconventional, I know." To his knowledge, no woman had ever apprenticed, certainly not one who was cloistered. She looked up expectantly. There was a glimmer of light in her eyes.

He explained, "You would help to prepare the panel, mix the paints for me each day." The light in her eyes grew. "I will need to obtain the prioress's permission, of course," he hastened to add. "If you are amenable."

"Yes," she said, and the faint hint of a smile played around her mouth. "Very much so. Thank you, Fra Filippo. I am honored."

"Well, then," he concluded, "I will speak with the prioress when I return in a few days' time with the sketches for her approval. Until then, tend well to your garden, and look up every so often so as not to miss this glorious day God has made for us."

He was delighted to have brought some small joy into her life. As he bade her farewell and continued on to the gate, the bell rang, calling the nuns to prayer. Ah, well, he thought as he exited through the gate, so much for the beautiful day.

Dawn was overtaking the darkness of the hour, which fled before it. Dante

Lucrezia was unable to concentrate. Now that she had met him, this jolly monk, she could see that there was more to him, much more. She had shocked herself when she admitted her deep desire to have a child. There had been something in his eyes, more than mere kindness, encouragement, compassion that had pierced her reserve, sharp and clear as rays emanating from the sun. The odd thing was, now that she had spoken of it, she felt lighter. The deep pain was still there, but the pressure surrounding it had been relieved. Of course, she had often spoken to Spinetta about her desire, had lamented her situation, but confiding in her sister was like speaking to herself. This was different.

A sharp glance from the prioress, a rarity, shook Lucrezia from her reverie. She had fallen far behind the others in the saying of her rosary, the incessant prayers that mocked her with their devotion to a God who had abandoned her. She was surprised to recognize the rebellion in her soul. Rebellion against God? The all-powerful, the all-knowing? That surely would not end well—and yet...

He, this well-meaning monk, had proposed a new occupation. Thinking of it, her heart lifted with joy. To be of use. To help in the making of a painting, one that would hang above the altar for years to come. To be industrious. To see her contribution to a beautiful painting—for she had heard that he and Fra Angelico were the greatest painters in all of Italy—to see it every day as she knelt in prayer. She could not be a mother, that was denied her, a pain as deep as the fathomless sea, but this monk had given her a purpose, a gift that lifted her heart ever so slightly on the tides, a murmur of joy.

CHAPTER 76

The year of Our Lord 1455, Prato

Filippo was on his way to Santa Margherita with the sketch for the panel painting tucked beneath his arm. In order to teach Sister Lucrezia to be an apprentice, he would need to work inside the convent walls. There was a chance that the prioress would balk at the idea. It would also be more practical to have his apprentices prepare the panel and carry it to Santa Margherita for him. However, if he were to need a model to sit for him, well, once sequestered in a room, he could also teach her how to mix paints.

The prioress was overjoyed with the sketch. "Your painting will be of great aid in our reflection upon the mystery of the Virgin's cintola, Fra Filippo. It will be like a candle lit in the heart and the soul."

He had not known that the prioress possessed such a gift for the poetic. He was grateful for her praise. "Thank you, Prioress. You are too kind. I am humbled."

"We cannot thank you enough, Fra Filippo. Now, I am sure you have much work."

"There is one more thing, Prioress, if I might. Would it be

possible to have one of the nuns sit in position to help with the painting of Mother Mary?"

"Oh, Fra Filippo, a nun as God's holy mother?"

"There will be no resemblance, Prioress. Do not misunderstand me. It is simply an aid, so that I may represent the proportions, the posture, her most chaste gestures correctly."

"I see. But where would this take place? My nuns do not leave the cloister."

"Oh, no. I would not think of suggesting it. No. I was thinking that my apprentices could prepare the panel and set it up in a room here in the convent. Somewhere out of the way so as not to create a disturbance."

"I cannot think of where. We have so few rooms, and I do not want your apprentices to cross the paths of the young nuns in my care."

"Which is why I was thinking that the perfect place would be the sacristy. There is enough room, and it is away from the areas where the nuns perform their daily duties."

"Well, I cannot think of an objection. You must coordinate your work around the canonical hours, of course." Filippo concurred with a nod of his head. "We will discuss amongst ourselves," the prioress continued, "who might take on the task."

"May I suggest the young sister who is so sad, the one I told you about. I spoke with her in the garden?"

"Ah, Sister Lucrezia." The prioress sighed and shook her head.

"Perhaps it would lift her spirits to have additional occupation. Other than her duties in the garden, of course."

"A sound suggestion, Fra Filippo. We will discuss it, and when you return to begin work, we will be ready for you."

Filippo knew he could press it no further and left that day without knowing if he would be able to fulfill his promise to Sister Lucrezia. But, when he arrived to begin the commission, Sister Lucrezia and a wrinkled, arthritic old nun entered the room.

"Sister Lucrezia," he greeted her, "and?"

"Sister Domenica, this is Fra Filippo, who will be painting the altarpiece for us."

The little nun, no larger than a ten-year-old child, bowed her head.

"It is a pleasure to meet you, Sister. Please. Have a seat." Filippo indicated one of two chairs that had been brought in for their use. He had placed it far off to the side in the shadows. The old nun squinted up at him and then settled herself into the chair with a groan.

"This wet weather must make things difficult for you," he said. "Arthritis?"

"Arthritis, yes," she agreed. "It is not for us to complain, however, given the Lord's great suffering."

"Indeed. Well, make yourself comfortable, Sister, while we commence work."

He walked back to a small table upon which the pigments, jars, eggs, and blotting paper had been arranged. "Now, Sister Lucrezia, are you ready to learn how to mix paints?"

She smiled, her eyes gleaming. Yes, he thought, this is how she should look every day.

Lucrezia, it turned out, was quick to learn and fastidious in her work.

"If you keep this up, I will make you a real apprentice, for you mix paints better than any I have."

She smiled with delight at his praise. "Please, take a seat so that I may begin," he said, indicating the armchair that had been put in place to represent the throne upon which Mary would sit.

As the days progressed, it became apparent that Lucrezia's favorite part of the process was the mixing of paints. When she sat, which she needed to do at length without moving, she had time to think. It was then that, when he was not concentrating on the work before him, Filippo saw the dark veil of sorrow fall across her face and settle in her eyes.

"There is sadness in your eyes, Sister," he began, hoping to draw her into conversation, to take her mind off her troubles.

"'Fortuna turns her sphere and, blessed, she rejoices,'" Lucrezia said, sharing her thoughts.

Filippo's mouth dropped open. "Dante."

"You drip paint," Lucrezia said. Seeing that, indeed, his brush suspended in mid-air, dripped, Filippo put it down.

"My father and I read Dante together," Lucrezia explained. "We shared my uncle's commentary on his work."

That was why he had recognized her name. Her uncle was the eminent scholar whose work on Dante was widely discussed at Careggi. "I am not so certain I understand Dante's meaning in this," he ventured. "What is it he is saying about Fortuna?"

"It is not dissimilar to what the devotional books teach. Fortuna is fickle. Dante tells us not to place great store in earthly things, for in a moment they can be lost." She hesitated, thinking, Filippo was sure, of her own fate. "We should place our trust instead in what is eternal."

There was more to this nun than he had realized.

Dawn was overtaking the darkness of the hour which fled before it, and I saw and knew the distant trembling of the sea. Dante

One day while Filippo was deep in contemplation of the composition of the painting, he was startled by a loud noise. Pulling himself from focused attention, he looked up to see Lucrezia, lips pursed as if to hold something back, the corners of her mouth twitching. Had she made the noise? No. There it was again, one long, sustained drone followed by several snorts. Sister Domenica, head thrown back, mouth opened wide, had fallen asleep and was snoring like an old drunk.

Filippo's eyes met those of Lucrezia. She covered her mouth with her hand to stifle her laughter. His entire body shook with the effort to hold back. At seeing him overcome, Lucrezia's shoulders shook, tears filling her eyes. Filippo had to turn his back to her before they were able to contain themselves.

Their sniffling and long sighs to relieve tension woke the old nun, who, looking about, said, "I must have fallen asleep."

Filippo and Lucrezia were saved from a new struggle with

laughter by the sudden ringing of the bells. The faithful were being called to terce. Filippo composed himself. "Well, we have accomplished much this day. Thank you for your patience, Sister Lucrezia. Sister Domenica." His voice broke in the saying of the old nun's name.

Afraid she would burst into open laughter, Lucrezia rushed out through the doorway.

"I have never seen Sister Lucrezia in such a hurry to attend prayers," Sister Domenica remarked. "This activity begins to improve her moral character." She bowed slowly, supporting her back with her hand. "Fra Filippo."

"Good day, Sister Domenica. Until tomorrow, then."

CHAPTER 77

The year of Our Lord 1456, Villa Medici at Careggi

osimo sat at a table on Careggi's upper loggia with a delegation from Lucca. A light breeze gently lifted the vines that hung from the latticework above while they discussed affairs of state. Since negotiating the peace of Lodi for all of Italy, Cosimo had lost interest in matters of state. He was old, had been at it a long time, and nothing would ever again be so challenging. With that accomplishment he had also improved his image in Maddalena's eyes. Her tone had grown softer.

Cosimo grew bored with the young men who made up the delegation—they had much to learn—so when his grandson ran out through the doorway, he commanded his grandfather's immediate attention. Cosimino held a blade of grass aloft in one hand.

"Poppy," he said, panting, "Poppy, he does not believe me."

"What is this?" Cosimo asked. "Who does not believe? What is it they doubt?"

"Lorenzo," Cosimino said, indicating his older cousin. "He does not believe that a blade of grass can sing." Cosimo laughed. "Please, Poppy. Show me again. Show me how you make it sing."

The ministers shuffled in their seats, impatient to get on with business. Cosimo ignored them. "Come here, Cosimino. Come here, child." He took the blade of grass and demonstrated how, by holding it between his fingers and blowing on it, the grass was made to give out a loud whistle. His grandson, delighted, clapped his hands. The ministers leaned forward, expecting Cosimo to dismiss his grandson.

Instead, Cosimo handed the blade of grass back to the little boy. "Now you try."

Cosimino failed at the attempt. He handed the grass back to his grandfather for yet another demonstration. This time Cosimo took his time, explaining in detail.

The ministers cleared their throats. Back and forth Cosimo went with his grandson, pressing the boy's fingers up against either side of the grass, teaching him how to place his lips up against it, the proper amount of pressure to be applied by the exhalation of his breath. The ministers shuffled their feet and moved about in their chairs. They exchanged glances, coughed, and sighed. When a sharp whistle pierced the air, several of them jumped.

"You are a magician," Cosimo said. "Now off with you. Prove Lorenzo wrong. Ha!"

The boy ran back out through the doorway, holding the grass aloft between his fingers so as not to lose the proper grip. Cosimo, watching him go, smiled. Only when Cosimino had disappeared from view did Cosimo turn back to the ministers. "Now," he said, ready to proceed. He was met with angry stares.

The most officious of the ministers decided to speak for all present. "One must wonder how a great man discussing matters of grave importance can leave ministers waiting while he teaches a boy to blow on a blade of grass."

"A blade of grass," Cosimo said, "to a small boy is all there is in the world. That, sir, is wonder! Do you not remember?"

Philosophy begins in wonder. Plato

Cosimino was not only intelligent and curious about the world, he was a good, kind-hearted boy as well. He was like his mother, a decent and intelligent woman, one blessed with common sense. Cosimino had inherited the best of them. He would continue his grandfather's legacy.

As for the ministers, they were young and impatient. Strategy, he mused, comes more easily with experience. These men, hot-blooded, rushed ahead like horses let loose on a hillside. Was there no one who was capable? Cosimino, now only six years of age, would need to grow up quickly.

CHAPTER 78

The year of Our Lord 1456, Prato

Diamante woke with a stomach ailment and could not hear the nun's confessions. "Blast!" Filippo said to himself as he made his way to the convent. It was March, and a wet snow had fallen during the night that now soaked his stockinged feet. He shivered with the cold and damp. At least the frescoes were progressing at a steady pace. He was realizing his vision in them. But this would also now be a day that he could not work on the panel painting, and he had looked forward to spending time with Lucrezia.

Filippo settled himself into the seat behind the rood work. He was no longer a man of the cloth. What had he to do with hearing confessions? Thank the Lord nuns were in no dire need of absolution. He heard footsteps approaching. A nun knelt on the other side of the rood work and made the sign of the cross. "Bless me, Frater, for I have sinned." It was Lucrezia.

Head bowed, eyes closed, she began, "I do not give attention to the saying of prayers. I take the sacrament without proper reverence. Oh, Frate, is it a sin to pray for death?"

He was taken aback by her plaintive tone, the sincerity of her words. He tried to comfort her. "It is a pleading for deliverance only."

She started when she realized who it was, but then decided to confide in him. "I feel that I live not in this world, or in the next. I live in a place of shadow."

"Shadow is made of light," he said. "Without both, there is no form, no life."

"Is it life? I think at times I must have passed into the great sea," she confided. "The world and everyone in it moves about, but I stand still. This is the purgatory of which Dante wrote."

"I knew that feeling as a boy until the time when I began to paint. I knew it again when enslaved, but I escaped. When God does not seem to answer our prayers, it is time to take action."

"There is no action within a woman's grasp." Lucrezia's head tilted downward, so that Filippo had to bend forward to hear her. "I have neither family who remembers nor dowry. No man will take me as wife."

"I will," Filippo blurted, "I meant. What I mean to say is that I will take you away from here. I will help you escape."

Lucrezia lifted her head to look at him. There was just enough light in the confessional for him to discern the hope in her eyes.

As little flowers, bent and closed with chill of night, when the sun lights them, stand all open on their stems...did I become. Dante

"In one week's time," he said, "I will hear confession again. Think on it. We will release you from this bondage. But we must have a plan."

She made the sign of the cross and stood. "Thank you, Fra Filippo," she whispered and disappeared through the heavy curtain.

What had he done? Surely this was the most outrageous risk he had ever taken. Just as his life had settled into a comfortable routine, his work going well, his fame secured, he had blundered his way into danger yet again. Had he lost his senses? But he could not stand by and watch her suffer.

At her next confession with him, Lucrezia unfolded her plan. "Spinetta," she said, "will come with me, for she will follow me wherever I go. But there are three others."

"God help us." Filippo made the sign of the cross. A harem was forming. "Must they all leave? At once?"

"They are desperate," she explained. "I cannot abandon them." She saw the hesitation on his face. "Sister Simona has given birth to a daughter."

Filippo coughed loudly. "How do I not know of this? I am her confessor." He was astounded. What else did he not know of this place?

"One evening," Lucrezia continued, "she was handed through a hole in the convent wall so that she might be baptized. She lives with relatives. If Simona could go to her…"

What had he gotten himself into?

"And," she continued. Filippo blanched. "Sister Piera had, long ago, a son, who lives with her cousin in Prato. It would be so wonderful, Fra Filippo, if she could see her little boy."

Perspiration broke out on Filippo's forehead. Was he to save the world? He was a naïve fool. This was not at all like San Niccolo de' Friere, where the nuns were innocents, devoted to caring for the sick. People lamented the evils of big cities like Florence, but little Prato was teaming with vices if even the young nuns in the convent hid such secrets.

It suddenly dawned on him to ask, "And how does this happen, Sister? How are these children conceived?" He lowered his voice so as not to release sensitive information to echo into the high, vaulted ceiling. "Where?" he whispered.

"Sister Simona and the mason fell in love. No one in this place has chosen to be here."

"But where?" Filippo persisted. "You are never alone."

"At night," she revealed. "In the bell tower."

"God have mercy." Filippo again crossed himself. "And," he wondered aloud, "how do they give birth?"

"There is a midwife who is discreet."

"No doubt of that." He did not try to hide his sarcasm.

"Do not think ill of her, Fra Filippo. She was in despair when she found love, and—"

"And you?" He thought suddenly that she was taking advantage of his good nature in order to cavort with a lover. "Have you, Sister?" She looked puzzled. "Had relations? With a man?"

"Oh, no!" she exclaimed. And then, "No," sadness falling across her face, such a dark shadow that Filippo was sure she told the truth.

CHAPTER 79

The year of Our Lord 1456, Prato

Gemignano Inghirami, distinguished papal jurist and provost of Santo Stefano, had arrived to view the progress of Filippo's work. A kindly old man, older in fact than any other man in Florence and its provinces, Inghirami, now well into his eighties, was still able to walk, though his gait was excruciatingly slow, bent as he was nearly horizontal at the waist. Leaning on a staff, he made his way to the main apse where Filippo and Diamante climbed down from the scaffolding to join him.

Inghirami peered up at the top tiers, now completed. On the north wall, the birth and childhood of Santo Stefano. On the south wall, the birth and naming of Sant' Giovanni. Inghirami contemplated one and then the other. Finally, he turned to Filippo. "This day I am blessed to retain my good sight, for these frescoes are beyond compare. Such detail. One is pulled into the narratives of each birth. And the brilliance! They have the brilliance of panel paintings. Remarkable. This work will serve to aid the spiritual contemplation of multitudes for all time to come. We made the right choice in you, Fra Filippo."

Filippo had realized his vision. Ingegno. Something never done before. After the plaster had dried, he had applied infinite details a secco, on dry plaster, and then illuminated the whole, sparingly, with gold.

Experiment, the source that feeds the streams of all your arts. Dante

"Thank you, Provost." Filippo bowed, humbled by the great man's words.

"The governors press you to quicken your pace," Inghirami said.

Filippo was about to protest, to explain that such work required time, but Inghirami held up his hand. "I will hold them off. Continue to do what you do so well."

"Thank you," Filippo said, sincerely grateful for his understanding.

The scaffolding had been lowered to the middle tier of the north wall. Filippo's apprentices were busy measuring, tracing angles, and checking accuracy with levels.

"It begins like this," Inghirami said, watching them, "and ends with this." He raised his arm to indicate the finished mural above. He looked at Filippo and smiled warmly. "Carry on," he said, and then turned and began to make his way back up the aisle.

"Poor man," Diamante said. "At that pace, he will be home by nightfall."

"He is a great man. It matters not how quickly he travels on Earth. One day he will ascend swiftly to heaven," Filippo said. Apart from Cosimo, he was not used to being understood by patrons.

The will to act and the power to carry through have wings that are not feathered equally. Dante

As he mapped out the scene of Santo Stefano's mission, Filippo remembered that the very next day he was to hear the nuns' confessions. He had thought much about his proposal to help Sister Lucrezia escape and had decided it was too risky. He would need to tell her. He wished he had never raised her hopes since now he would need to crush them.

CHAPTER 80

The year of Our Lord 1456, Prato

On their way back from vespers, Lucrezia pulled her sister into her cell. "Spinetta," she whispered, "I have found an escape."

"Escape?" Spinetta asked, confused, eyes widening with fear. "What have you done, Lucrezia? Your mood has been much improved of late. It is this monk!"

"Shhhh," Lucrezia hushed her. "He is kind, not amorous. It is he who will help us."

She was not convinced. "At what price?"

"Nothing has happened. Sister Domenica is with us at all times. Fra Filippo offered to help, then changed his mind. But my pleading was more than he could bear. He is sincere in his wish to aid us in our flight. Listen." Lucrezia proceeded to lay out the plan. "In little more than a fortnight we will be free."

"One or two, perhaps, but five?" Spinetta asked. "This is dangerous, Lucrezia, and if we are caught we will most certainly be separated."

"We will not be caught," Lucrezia said with firm resolve.

"You are determined, then?"

"Determined to be free of this place."

Spinetta hesitated, lowering her head as if in prayer. When she raised it, she held Lucrezia's gaze, "I cannot abandon you in the face of such danger. God help us, I will accompany you."

When Spinetta had gone, Lucrezia spread her arms wide. She could have cried out with joy. Instead, she danced around and around the tiny strip of open space within her cell. There was a fire in the friar. When he worked, there was intensity in his eyes, his movements quick and decisive. He became one with his purpose. It was infectious. Lucrezia, dancing, felt a flame rise in her, the torch of life.

And, having set our stern to sunrise, in our mad flight we turned our oars to wings.   Dante

It was May 1, the first of the five days on the liturgical calendar when Mary's cintola was to be celebrated, not only by the devout within Prato itself, but by pilgrims who arrived from near and far. The bells of Santo Stefano rang out, calling the faithful to the duomo. Prato was so filled with people that one could not walk through the streets. Slowly and ceremoniously, a procession wound its way through the narrow streets in time to the rhythmic pounding of drums.

Standing outside of his house, on the fringe of the piazza across from the duomo, Filippo awaited its arrival. The deep sonorous beat of the drums seemed to pound within his own chest. What he was about to do was dangerous. If he were caught, he would lose all standing within the church. Not even Cosimo would be able to help him. That he might lose the fresco commission filled him with dread. Perhaps kind old Inghirami would come to his aid. Filippo wiped his sweaty palms across the cloth of his robe.

Rounding the corner, close behind the prioress, Lucrezia kept her eyes trained on the deep crimson banners at the head of the procession and the sky beyond. They had left Via Santa Margherita and were making their way along Via San Georgio. They would soon arrive at the Piazza del Duomo. Since they were of no standing, the group of nuns were at the tail end of the procession. This would aid them when the time came. In spite of the regular rhythm of the drum beats, her heart fluttered. She had anticipated this moment since the day she had arrived at the convent, but now that it was here, she was losing her nerve. The hair on her scalp tingled, and her breathing grew shallow. Lucrezia steadied herself. She could not draw attention to their little band of runaways. She looked around at the others, who were all fidgeting nervously. Piera pulled at her habit. Bridgitta cleared her throat several times. Simona clenched and unclenched her hands. The only one who appeared to be calm was Spinetta. Lucrezia could not let them down, not now that she had raised their hopes. She took a deep breath and steeled herself for what was to come.

The trumpeters at the head of the procession had reached the entrance to the duomo and now blew their horns to announce the beginning of the ceremony. First, there would be a mass within. The crowd pressed forward so that the entire group of nuns was separated from the rest of the procession and pushed backward. As the throngs surged, carrying the prioress and two other nuns, Lucrezia drew back further. As if connected to her by invisible strings, her fellow escapees receded with her as a group. A gulf soon widened between them and the multitude. The prioress and two other nuns were now lost in the crowd, being pushed forward. By the time they realized the others were gone, they would believe only that they had been separated in the crush of the crowd.

Quickly, Lucrezia turned and took the final few steps to the side entrance of Filippo's house. He was there waiting for her. He held the door open, and one by one the nuns ducked inside. When the door slammed shut, they gave out a collective sigh of relief.

Lucrezia reached up and removed her habit, swinging her hair free. The others did the same. They looked at each other and laughed nervously. "We are free," Lucrezia said.

"We are free!" they all said in unison.

"There is no time to waste," Filippo warned. "When the mass is over, and the crowd makes its way to the piazza for the showing of the sacred cintola, the prioress will surely discover you are missing."

Fear descended on the room with a hush. The nuns looked from one to the other.

"Come," Filippo said, "A cart awaits you behind the house. It will take you to your final destinations."

Three of the nuns made to follow him, but Lucrezia and Spinetta stood perfectly still, looking lost.

"Will you not come?" Filippo asked.

"We have not yet made arrangements," Lucrezia said.

There was no time to waste in argument. Filippo quickly dispatched the three nuns out the back door to their chosen fates.

This is no easy voyage for a little bark, the stretch of sea the daring prow now cleaves. Dante

Several days after the nuns escaped from the convent, Prato was full of the news. Where could they be? They seemed to have disappeared in the air like a puff of smoke from a snuffed candle. Had they been abducted? Had they run away? Were they hiding within the city walls, or had they left Prato altogether? By then, Filippo was beginning to worry about the two nuns left in his house. What was he to do with them?

That night, he asked to speak with them. "Sister Piera is back with family in the Prato countryside. Sister Simona and Sister Brigida have been spirited away to villages in the Mugello, where they too are in hiding with relatives. Is there someone in Florence, a cousin perhaps, to whom you might appeal for help?"

Lucrezia and Spinetta gave him blank stares.

"Think now. You cannot stay in this house forever. It is on the piazza. You will be discovered before long. Returned to the convent, or to one far worse."

He detected fear in Lucrezia's eyes. Surely, she had known she could not stay. Did she not have a plan?

Spinetta reached out and took her sister's hand. "We thought only to escape, the rest to be dealt with once we were free." With calm, steady voice she added, "We have no one."

The impact of the four words pierced his heart. They had no one in the world who cared for their welfare. He could not abandon them. "I will think on it."

Later that night after a light supper, Filippo sat alone at the inn sipping wine. He could provide each of them with a dowry, but they were still married to the church. No man would, indeed no man could take them as wife. There was no one in Prato to hide them, save himself. Did he know of anyone in Florence? Given that they had no familial protection there, that might prove more danger-ous. Their half-brother was a wealthy citizen. If word got out as to their whereabouts, and gossip abounded, he well knew, they would be placed in a convent far worse than the relatively pleasant Santa Margherita. Why was his house situated on the piazza of all places, directly across from the duomo? To make it easy for him to roll out of bed and across to work, and of course when he'd chosen the place he had no thought of harboring fugitive nuns. What would Cosimo say to that? He shuddered to think of it. He was on danger-ous ground. Ground. It was the ground he lived on that presented the greatest obstacle. Had he not thought of purchasing a small house in the countryside, one to which he and Diamante might retire in case of pestilence? If ever there was a time to do so, it was now. He would begin his search in the morning.

Diamante, frantic to get this business over with, sat down across from Filippo. "We must rid ourselves of these nuns before they are discovered," he whispered. "The town is full of the news."

"We are doing so. Where there were five, there are two."

"And these two, if they have nowhere to go, must be placed with a family in the countryside. Labor on a farm will provide occupa-tion, and it will be unlikely that they will be noticed in such a place."

"The countryside. It is precisely that about which I have been thinking."

Diamante let out a sigh of relief.

CHAPTER 81

The year of Our Lord 1456, outside of Prato

Filippo had managed to find a house in the country that was surrounded by seven hectares of land. There was a large vegetable garden at the rear of the house, and a beautiful view out over its orchards and olive groves. The house itself was not overly large, but it had been well built and maintained. In the middle of the night, he spirited the sisters out of his house in town and brought them to their new home.

As summer grew into autumn, Lucrezia gardened and cooked, while Spinetta cleaned and mended. This was not why Filippo had helped them escape the convent. The other three nuns, he knew, lived in much the same way. All had been freed from their bonds to the church, their cloistered lives, but was this any better? When he was a young man, he had been able to walk out the front doors of the convent with his prior's blessing. He had traveled, seen great works of art, found employment as a painter. It did not matter that, when he left, he had only a few soldis to his name, a loaf of bread, and some wine. But a woman without a dowry could be either a nun or someone's lifelong servant. Which was better? He could not say. He watched as Lucrezia knelt at the fireplace, stirring an aromatic soup with a large wooden spoon. His heart ached for her. She had insisted on doing her part in the household as payment for his help. But she deserved to be dressed in silks, this daughter of a silk merchant, and fine brocades. She deserved to be cherished. Compassionate in nature, she was born to be a mother. The tenderness he felt for her at times overwhelmed him, but he fought these feelings. His wish to help her had been genuine, not tinged with self-interest.

He walked over and pulled her to her feet. "Lucrezia, I am sorry for the life I have led you to. Please allow me to hire a woman to do these household chores. I can well afford it."

"And how will I spend my time while she labors?" Lucrezia smiled. "In idleness? I do not mind. I enjoy the occupation, and I feel it is my small way, our small way"—she nodded toward her sister, who sat in a chair before the fire mending stockings—"to repay you for your kindness."

"But you owe me nothing. I had six orphaned nieces who I supported and provided with dowries, so that they might not end as I had, forced into a life I did not choose. I would not, by my life, deny aid to any living being."

"You are too kind a man, and too generous," Lucrezia said, placing her small hand over his heart. Her touch startled him, and her as well it seemed, for she pulled it back quickly, but the intimacy of the spontaneous gesture held them for a moment in its grip, and their eyes locked. Filippo reached out and took her hand in both of his—his coarse, roughened with paint and plaster, hers soft and warm. It aroused something in him.

"I must go," he said. In one swift movement, letting her hand drop, he turned and rushed through the doorway, leaving Lucrezia behind, bewildered by his sudden departure.

We made our way into a forest not marked by any path.   Dante

Filippo waited a full week before returning to the house in the country, but he could wait no longer. Although he had left them with enough firewood, they needed supplies. After carrying in the sack of grain and the jugs of oil and wine, he washed his hands at the basin. Lucrezia had made a stew. He breathed in the savory aroma of thyme and sage with a hint of cinnamon. When she served him, he thanked her, careful not to look up.

"Fra Filippo." She sat beside him. "I must apologize for being so forward the other day. It was not my intent to offend you. I reached out to you without thought, moved by your kindness. Please, do not be angry with me."

He looked at her. Angry with her? She should be angry with him for the feelings that her small gesture had aroused in him. As he looked at her, it dawned on him that, in this circumscribed world in which she lived, he was a friend to her, that, apart from her sister, he was her only friend. While he had been trying so desperately to control his feelings, he had not considered hers. He was her friend, first and foremost. He would never again be so selfish.

"Lucrezia, do not be upset. It was myself with whom I was angry, not you." He left it at that; he dared not be forthright about his feelings. "Here. Here. Stand up, please." Pulling her to her feet, he decided at that moment, "I have a surprise."

The childlike gleam in her eyes at the idea of a surprise reminded him of how little joy she had experienced in the past five years. He placed a small purse on the table. "For you and Spinetta. Enough to purchase the finest wool with which to have dresses made."

Lucrezia's eyes glowed with excitement, but then she frowned. "Thank you, Fra Filippo, but we cannot accept."

"Please, call me Filippo. Both of you."

She had picked up the little bag and held it out to him.

"It is a little something only, not enough to clothe the two most beautiful women in all of Prato as they deserve."

"We cannot accept such generosity."

"Nonsense. It is in payment for all of your labor. It is only fair. Tomorrow I will arrange for Mona Antonia, a fine and discreet

seamstress, to come for a fitting. Provide her with all of the specifications regarding your needs for cloth and ornament."

"Fra Filippo."

"It is nothing. You cannot wear nun's robes forever. Is there
something else you need? Anything at all."

"No. You are most kind."

"There must be something. A spice for cooking, perhaps. Some
rose water?" She shook her head. His eyes rested on her beautiful
hair. That was it. Women adorned their hair. "An ornament for
your hair."

She touched it self-consciously. "There is one thing."

"Anything."

"If you have scraps of paper that you no longer need. A writing
implement."

Of course. Why had he not thought of it himself? Later that
day, Filippo set about making Lucrezia a ricordanze. He bound
leaves of the finest paper in leather. Then he painted a flowering
woodland scene on its cover in which the graces danced to the music of Apollo's lyre.

CHAPTER 82

The year of Our Lord 1456, countryside of Prato

It had been a good day. Molding his figures from shadow and light, Filippo was achieving his vision. Today he had, as well, employed ingegno and had realized fantasia, his imagination made real through invention. While he was working on San Giovanni's mission, he came to the place in the narrative when the saint knelt in prayer in the rocky desert. Envisioning an angel, Filippo decided to paint it a secco, on dry plaster. The resulting angel shimmered and hovered as if unattached to the fresco, suspended in mid-air, a vision from the spiritual realm.

Uplifted by the success of his day's work, Filippo decided to make an unexpected visit to the house in the country. When he arrived, Lucrezia was working in the herb garden just outside the kitchen door, which had been left ajar. When Filippo had bought the house, it stood empty, all sharp angles and cold lines, corners filled with shadow and dust. Lucrezia had filled it. Wooden bowls smoothed by wear stood ready on the tabletop. Select pieces of crockery in blue, white, and yellow were scattered on shelves. Earthenware jars held oil and wine. A wooden rack was suspended from the ceiling where herbs had been hung to dry. The corners were swept clean. Lucrezia had pressed every angle into a graceful curve, inviting in the light and air.

A gentle breeze blew in through the doorway, rifling the pages of the ricordanze he had made for her, which lay open on the table. Curious, he glanced down at it. She wrote of the cycles that passed in her herb garden, about the blooming of the orchards, the recognition of birds by their song, where they had nested. Halfway down the second page, she had written, in a beautiful hand: "The sun-drenched butterfly floats in still air, in time to the music of a wind I cannot hear. Her movements speak of joy in life I crave, but do not bear." Filippo was right in assuming that she was not happy here. He walked outside to join her.

Lucrezia knelt in the garden. There was sage, oregano, rosemary, thyme, and basil for cooking. Garlic, leeks, chard, cabbage, and parsnips abounded. Slender silvery stems of chamomile turned their white-petalled, yellow-faced flowers to the sun. These were dried and brewed in a tea, useful for stomach upsets. There were onions for rheumatism, watercress for insect bites, and parsley for bad dreams. Lavender was used to calm the nerves, placed under the pillow to ease headache. It was the lavender that Lucrezia was now tending to, snipping off the withered flowers to allow for new growth. Apart from the lavender she deftly trimmed, there would all too soon be only winter vegetables to be tended.

Did I not find you thus, Filippo thought, in the convent garden?

When Lucrezia heard him step through the doorway, she looked up. Although she smiled upon seeing him, sadness rested in her eyes. They soon settled together on a nearby bench beneath a beech tree. Filippo ventured, "I am sorry that you are not happy." He held his hand up to stop her protest. "It is much the same as the cloister, is it not?"

"It is not," she said with such conviction that she surprised him. "I am not bound to a cycle of prayer, to endless routine that drives me, whatever else I might want to do. Here, I am free." She paused, and a smile played around the corner of her mouth. "Free to enjoy the glorious days God has given us."

"You mock me," he said, with a sigh, remembering his admonishment the first time they had met.

"No," she hastened to assure him, "I do not mock. Tease, perhaps. You did, after all, speak the truth. Each day we are given is a beautiful day. Only I could not see it then. In that place."

"I remember feeling much the same as a boy in the Carmine. This is not all you had hoped for, however. In life."

Her eyes looked off into the distance, settling on a row of trees in the orchard as if she were seeing something that existed only in her imagination. "No," she admitted.

He had made her sad. "What can I do?" he asked, feeling desperate to make her happy.

"If I were only able to go into Prato," she said. "But that is not possible. And…"

"And?"

"I long for a child," she admitted, the sadness in her eyes deepening.

"Ah," he said. What else was there to say? The source of her despondency was the same as it had always been. "So, I have taken you out of the convent but to a small patch of earth only."

"Oh, I am happy to be free of the convent. I felt as if dead and dwelling in Dante's purgatory."

"I know the feeling."

"Does this lack of devotion make us bad people?"

"No, dearest Lucrezia. Someone once told me that I was a good man, not a devout man, but a good one. That is not such a bad thing, is it?"

"You are always able to lighten my mood," she confessed. "When you have been to visit, I feel uplifted for a long time after." She looked at Filippo as if deciding whether to reveal something, and then continued, "I was angry with you when first I saw you."

Filippo was shaken. "What had I done to provoke such strong feeling?"

There was a hint of a smile in her eyes. "They call you the 'jolly monk,'" she said as explanation.

He was perplexed. "And, this joviality angered you?"

"I thought, 'What has he to be so happy about?' Your joy stabbed at the center of my discontent. Shone a harsh light on it. I saw that it was not sadness that I felt, but anger. The contrast between us revealed my innermost feelings."

"Ah, perhaps it is only that I have had more practice in the hiding of my discontent."

"You?" she asked, scrutinizing Filippo, as if seeing him for the first time. Then, her voice softer, she said, "Please. Tell me." The compassion in her voice moved him to tell his story.

"You and I, Lucrezia," he finished, "have been abandoned by our families. We were given up, forfeited, so that others might have an easier life."

"I never imagined that one day I might be abandoned. I was so cared for within the circle of my family."

"For you, a hard blow." Filippo tried to offer hope. "And yet," he began, and she looked up at him as if to hold on to every word, "there are children in Maria della Scala, and places like it who, by the hundreds, die from disease, and of loneliness, too, God knows. How many give up? Children of servants and slaves, orphans like myself, too many to name. They are like the waves of the sea that roll onto shore, a great mass that stretches briefly the expanse of the sand but does not hold, and then is pulled back to whence it came. What is God's purpose in this?"

Filippo had lost himself in imagining the sad fate of so many, but aware again of Lucrezia's presence, he realized that the comparison of her loss with that of children who perished did not provide hope. He made a feeble attempt to lighten her load. "You were well cared for at Santa Margherita, were you not? As I was at the Carmine. And my brother Giovanni was there, just as you have Spinetta."

"Spinetta," she concurred. "What would I do without her? Oh, Filippo. I have not been able to speak of my troubles to anyone for so long. Spinetta loses patience. And who else would understand?"

They sat in silence. Bitterns gave out their lilting song. Bees, slowed by the cooling air, drifted past. Spinetta was far off tending to the olive grove. "At the convent," Lucrezia said, "I would lie awake at night and wonder, 'Why has our mother not come for us?' I missed her so. Sometimes, when the novices were allowed out, to walk to the duomo for special services, we might pass a mother, a woman selling fruit at market, with the freedom to be out in public, her children around her. The pain of seeing what I could not have. But then, seeing them laugh and dance, I would laugh along with them just as my own mother had." Lucrezia's eyes lit up now. "At such times, I experienced an odd sensation, as if for a brief moment I were my mother. I could feel myself smiling out from her face, hear her laughter in my own, feel her very joy."

Filippo understood. "At being a mother." Lucrezia turned toward him.

"I did not know a mother's love," he continued, "and have only a vague memory of my father. Not much, a sense of happiness when I recall his face. He laughed often, and when he did his eyes lit up. He was never angry. He took great joy in the smallest of things. He was a jovial man."

Filippo stopped. His eyes met hers. "The jolly monk," she said.

The ice that had confined my heart was turned to breath and water. Dante

Lucrezia placed her hand gently over his where it rested on the bench between them. Her light touch sent a jolt like a spark up his arm and down through his body. He grabbed her hand in his, and with his other pulled her to him. Pressing her against his chest, he kissed the top of her head. It was a tender kiss, like that one might plant on a child. He was surprised when her body seemed to melt into his. He wrapped his arms around her. A warm sensation that he had all but forgotten filled him, moved him. She yielded to his kiss, and then met it full on. In that moment, they traveled far from shore.

Filippo lifted Lucrezia in his arms and carried her inside. She buried her face in his chest. He made his way to the bedchamber and placed her down gently beside the bed. He unbuttoned her sleeves, one by one, slipping them from her arms. Then he slowly unlaced the bodice of her giornea. When she stood in her white linen camicia, he kissed the back of her neck where the lace brushed her skin. She shivered. Filippo swelled with desire. He pulled her to him.

As he did so, he had the strange sensation that they had known each other long ago, had spent a lifetime together and were reunited in that moment. "Welcome home," he whispered in her ear. She smiled knowingly. She felt it too, then. He lifted her and, placing her gently on the bed, he lay down next to her and ran his hand along her sun-drenched shape, through the strands of her hair, golden threads, each caress prolonged, each breath an eternity.

CHAPTER 83

The year of Our Lord 1456, countryside of Prato

Afterwards, Filippo lay on his back, arms thrust upward, surrendered to sleep. Lucrezia ran her hand over his chest, the rough patch of hair there, and down the slope from his ribs to his stomach. She traced the concave space, the skin smooth, and then placed her hand gently on his abdomen and the ugly mass bulging there just beneath his skin, the proof of his torture. She bent and kissed it, then ran her hand back up to his chest, laying her palm flat against it. His hand dropped across his chest on top of hers. She laced her fingers through his and studied his face. His eyes were closed, a smile resting on his lips. Had she been a painter, she would have painted him like this, abandoned of all desire, free of all memory, given up whole to sleep.

Lucrezia lay her head down in the crook of his arm. She felt her body as never before, every part of it, as if she had been sheathed in a new skin, one that tingled with life. She lived. This was no mere chance. God had blessed her.

Filippo, opening his eyes, turned to look at her. She had fallen asleep. The dim light threw a soft veil over her beauty. Just as the long summer days were exchanging place with the lengthening shadows of autumn, the fields of his life bloomed with light. Lying on his back, staring up at the ceiling, he wondered at the mysteries of life, that he, a man of advanced age, should be lying beside Lucrezia at this moment. He had drifted, drifted, drifted and, without warning, had been washed ashore. She was so ethereal in her beauty and yet provided this solid ground beneath his feet, a new and welcome feeling. Her head nestled into his side. He could feel the light touch of her breath on his skin. The contentment he felt was as alive with sensuality as their lovemaking had been. In the past, he would have turned to her, insatiable, made love to her again. Instead he lay, eyes closed, suspended in fulfilled desire, the moment after the flare of passion's flame, the moment of prolonged bliss. If this was aging, he embraced it wholeheartedly.

Once again, Filippo turned slowly so that he could gaze upon her. She was an undiscovered country, one that, since she was a woman, ran underground most of all, unexposed to light, a place where it was a challenge to discern colors and shapes. He knew that he would never discover every mystery of its landscape, but he would never stop trying. Her eyelids fluttered and opened. As he gazed into her amber eyes, their warm brown splashed with gold as if awash with sunlight, a flood of tender feeling swept through him. He pressed up against her and whispered, "The stars awaken in you."

O Lady who give strength to all my hope.   Dante

With morning drawing near, unable to sleep, Filippo stole out of bed and made his way to the window. This house in the country afforded more freedom than one in the city, where inhabitants needed to be off the streets by sundown, shuttered within by nightfall for fear of thieves who lurked without. In the country, shutters could be opened at night, when the moon climbed the chambers of the sky. He threw them open now.

There in the first awakening of light before dawn, a full moon hung, visible above the branches of the oak trees beyond the orchard, a moon like a lantern floating on a bank of clouds in an indigo sky. As Filippo stood immersed in the sight, he heard an owl hoot in a distant wood, its call confident in measure, soft in tone. The steady beat of his heart felt at one with God's world in all of its beauty. If painting was his passion, Lucrezia was his solace. His love for Theopista had been like the sun piercing through a fast-moving cloud. His love for Lucrezia encompassed every gradation of shadow to light, the sun's full palette, every tint and hue.

Now you are ready to learn how to blend the deepest shadows with the light, how to work them in together, how to achieve the most subtle layering on of gold. Cennini

They had met late, and only God knew how long they had together. Within each moment they must live a lifetime. It was like a kernel, no, like the seed of a pomegranate, in which seed and flesh are one. Perhaps this is what was meant when they said that one seed in each comes directly from heaven, and he who eats of it is filled with the light of paradise. To live each moment, seed and flesh of it one, is to live as if in paradise.

Lucrezia had taught him this, the sweetest of all life's lessons.

CHAPTER 84

The year of Our Lord 1457, Florence

Filippo had left Lucrezia in Prato since Giovanni de' Medici could wait no longer for the commission for King Alfonso of Naples to be completed. If Filippo did not finish it soon, the gift to the king, in gratitude for his signing of the peace agreement of Lodi, would be too late in coming and would miss its mark. Filippo worked quickly. He needed to be home for the birth of their child. He knew too well the dangers of childbirth. He must be there to will her to hold on.

"You have outdone yourself," Donatello told him. "This is a work that greatly honors its craftsman. Wasted on the king of Naples."

"Politics," Filippo scoffed. "Was it not you who said when first we met that you gave no heed to it? You had too much work to do. I agree."

"Cosimo asked after you. I believe the gouty old goat misses you."

Filippo sighed. It was difficult to stop work once it was in progress. Each time he did it took far too long to find his way back in.

But he knew Cosimo too well and knew that he was using Donatello to deliver a directive.

He finished work for the day and made his way to Via Larga. As he crossed through the first-floor sala, he admired the intricate designs of the intarsia that decorated the furniture scattered there. He was directed to Cosimo's personal chapel, where his friend awaited him. No expense had been spared in its decoration. The coffered ceiling alone, glazed terracotta done by Luca della Robbia, must have cost a fortune. He wondered how much Gozzoli had been paid for the frescoes decorating the three walls. Filippo was vexed that he had not received the commission, but then, with the monumental project in Prato still underway, who knew when he would have been free to begin?

"I have not seen you in some time," Cosimo complained as he approached.

"I work on the gift for King Alfonso."

"Ahh, yes. I hear you have outdone yourself. Excellent. I have another commission for you."

Filippo tensed. Did people not understand that working on many projects at once holds up all? He was about to protest, but Cosimo was saying, "I want you to paint an altarpiece for my chapel."

"I would be honored," Filippo said. One thing was certain. He would not allow his altarpiece to be the mere culmination of the procession of the magi that adorned the walls. It would stand alone.

"And how are the frescoes coming?" Cosimo asked.

"I have been busy in Prato."

"So I have heard." Cosimo raised an eyebrow and focused his eagle eyes on Filippo. "The frescoes, however, move along slowly."

"The project is an immense undertaking."

"Not so grand as your other project. Abducting a nun?"

"Rescuing," he corrected.

"She was promised to God."

"So was I," Filippo countered.

"You were released by your prior."

"A woman has no such recourse."

"For good reason."

"What reason justifies imprisonment for one who is innocent?"

"It is a woman's lot. She is born to suffer."

"Is that what you said of Maddalena?"

"Watch yourself, Filippo. Do not use your knowledge of me."

"In argument only."

"Well, then. For the sake of argument, you must stop seeing her at once, as I did Maddalena. Make the sacrifice for both your sakes. Send her back to the convent."

"I cannot."

"Take your feelings in hand, Filippo."

"She is pregnant."

Cosimo sucked in his breath. "And so the argument is extended. It is true then. You abducted her to satisfy your lust. You have defiled a nun."

"No. Not lust. That was not the reason. We came, over time, to know one another. It was only then that intimacy grew between us."

"As did your loins."

"It is not to be mocked."

Cosimo studied him closely. "This nun. You love her?"

"Yes."

"That is too bad. It is a carnal sin to allow your desire to overwhelm reason."

"To end in Dante's second circle. But I do not desire alone. I place Lucrezia above all others, as Dante placed Beatrice. The love that I have encompasses not her physical form alone, but all that she is. I would not have guessed that from a feeling so mundane as mutual sympathy, the deepest love grows."

Great fire leaps from the smallest spark.   Dante

"I fear for you, Filippo. A measured love is not possible. Remember this. In monks the people will allow for some transgression. But they will not tolerate a fall from grace in a nun. Now, let us speak of the commission. It is of great importance to me. I wish to contemplate Christ's great sacrifice as I kneel in prayer. A crucifixion scene."

"May I suggest?"

"You have a different plan for the focal point of my chapel? Should it not be Christ's suffering? His life given for all men's, for my own sins?"

"I suggest this," Filippo said, taking in the cavernous darkness of the room, lit only by candles and torches, "I will paint a dark wood. 'Midway along the road of our life, we find ourselves lost, alone in a dark wood.'"

"Ahhh, Dante. We are further along in life than half, you and I."

"Indeed, we are older than we deserve. All the more reason to search for the light in the darkness, to contemplate its beauty. Not the penance for sins of the past, but reflection on salvation, the light itself for which Christ sacrificed. All three faces of God, the father, the son, and the Holy Spirit."

This met well with the equal importance of the holy spirit, the belief that Cosimo, Traversari, and the Roman church upheld, and thereby piqued Cosimo's interest. "Go on."

"It will not be a narrative. It will be a dream, a vision. The dark wood will be the Mugello, painted in such a way that you will recognize your family's birthplace. It will bear evidence of the industry of the Cistercian monks. Penitence will be brought to mind by the figure of San Bernardo, who tells us that 'woods and stones teach us what we can never hear from any master.' Did he not say that we can be rescued from the deep pit of ignorance through love of God and plunged into a place bright with eternal light? Mary, bathed in light, will kneel in adoration of the Christ child. God the father and the Holy Spirit above radiating rays of heavenly light that swirl around them."

"It sounds a work unparalleled in beauty. And the darkness represented only by the surrounding wood?"

"Shadow is created by light. Light and shadow together create form."

Filippo could see from the expression of appreciation that crossed Cosimo's face that he understood the connection between the light and shadow of the proposed painting and the light and shadow of his own life—its form.

CHAPTER 85

The year of Our Lord 1457, Florence, and the countryside of Prato

osimo's son, Giovanni, was up to his old tricks. He refused to pay Filippo for the extra ultramarine and gold leaf necessary to make this a painting worthy of a king. Filippo could not continue without additional funds. Not only that, but the pestilence had arrived once again in Florence. If he stayed, he risked never seeing his child. Giovanni, himself, had already escaped to safety in the countryside. There was nothing for it. Filippo knew what price the pestilence exacted. The memory of its visit to the Carmine gave him a sense of urgency. He must leave Florence immediately.

He skirted the city, avoiding the crowds gathered at street-corner shrines where masses were now being held. It was thought since the last contagion had swept through the city that congregating in enclosed spaces aided the spread of the disease. Perhaps, Filippo conjectured, it was congregating at all. He was not taking chances. He must make it to Prato. Lucrezia was depending on him.

I am one who, when love breathes within me, takes note.   Dante

Giovanni was livid. Lippi had done it this time. He burst into his father's inner sanctuary. "He has absconded once again."

"Who?" Cosimo, studying Gozzoli's fresco, did not turn around.

"Lippi. He has left Florence, rent on his bottega past due, the painting for Alfonso yet unfinished."

"He will return."

"When? And what would possess him to leave so suddenly, the painting nearly completed?"

"He has gone back to Prato."

"To the frescoes?"

"I predict he will return within a fortnight. In the meantime, you must cover the rent so as not to leave the contents, to which the painting belongs, susceptible to confiscation."

"Why do you never grow angry with him?" Giovanni asked, exasperated. "Why do you never cut him off?"

"Cut him off? He is one of the greatest painters in all of Italy."

"One who cannot be counted on. One who leaves commissions unfinished."

"I think of the many years that I benefitted from my father's good counsel. Filippo, an orphan, an unknowing child, a foolish youth, had only himself to depend upon. I cannot imagine an entire lifetime without father or mother." Cosimo turned to give Giovanni a withering stare. "And neither can you. You are uncharitable."

Giovanni ignored his father's criticism. "Well, let us hope he decides to return before the years have left the great peace accord no more than dust in the memory, new troubles festering."

Cosimo turned his back to his son once again. Giovanni was always too dramatic for his taste. "Lippi will return. He always does."

"It had better be a work of unparalleled beauty," Giovanni ranted.

"Think of all he has made of his misfortunes. The work will praise its craftsman," Cosimo assured him.

How many sweet thoughts, what great desire, have brought them to this woeful pass. Dante

Lucrezia lightly stroked the soft skin of his cheek so as not to wake him, this baby boy, this beautiful child. God had blessed her. He curved to her shape, his small head nestled on her shoulder, his face turned toward hers, fists curled beneath his chin, eyes closed in perfect slumber. The warmth of his small body pressed against her like an extension of her own. She cupped his head in her hand. He breathed in and out through slightly parted lips; his breath, unspoiled, smelled of newness.

There was a commotion just outside her bedchamber, and the door flew open. Filippo had arrived. He had kept his promise, returning for the birth, only missing it by a few hours. He stood in the doorway as if in a trance. She smiled, waiting for him to move, to say something.

Filippo had not anticipated this moment. Thoughts rushed through his head. She was a vision. She was Mary. She was every mother and child. She was his mother. This struck him to the heart. Surely his own mother had held him in her arms once, if only once?

Coming to himself, he rushed forward, fell to his knee beside her, grabbed her hand and kissed it.

"Filippo," she said, the saying of his name holding within it, like a clear drop of water, the place he held in her life. "We shall name him Filippo."

CHAPTER 86

The year of Our Lord 1458, Florence

Having finished the painting for King Alfonso, Filippo now set to work on the painting for Cosimo's chapel. Once the drawing was fixed, he laid down a translucent layer of paint that would shine from beneath, irradiating the luminous skin of Mary and the baby Jesus. Since egg tempera was fast drying, he needed to use infinite fine strokes of the brush. Some colors he bound in linseed oil. He had decided to use a small range of colors, which subdued the tone, creating a mood for contemplation, but also allowing for greater luminosity where the light fell.

Filippo built the background up slowly, then carefully defined forms and added details. There was depth in the darkness; like sorrow, it possessed layers. A viewer would move through it, further and further into its interior, traveling into the landscape. An oil layer of copper resinate provided greater depth, making necessary the further enhancement of the highlights. Filippo tried new inventions to get the effect he was looking for, learning as he went.

The ultramarine used for Mary's robe was ground more finely than it had ever been for any painting. Filippo used five different shades of it. The layers were so thin that he applied them over and over again to maintain translucence. He used five shades in thin layers for Mary's skin tone as well.

Then, he was ready to create the heavenly light. This would set the painting apart. Filippo utilized every possible means to create light in a painting. He used water gilding for Mary's halo on top of eight shades of Armenian bole, applying three layers of gold leaf. The rays were incised and then stippled to create iridescence.

Filippo decided to use bole once again as a ground for the heavenly rays. It made for a smoother surface. The timing of the application needed to be exact, the mordant sticky enough to be gilded. Besides the gilding, he painted tiny dots that swirled around and through the threads of light and spattered across Mary's mantel. The variation in the means of creating light made it appear real.

The confluence of various ways to portray light revealed the essence of light itself, present but ephemeral, beyond our reach yet a part of our very being. Divine light spilled from the hands of God the father above, and then separated into thin threads of gold. One thread attached to each living soul. Had he not felt it on the ship tug at him, will him to hold on? Light, God's grace, shadow, our struggle. Yet, without shadow, no form. He had spent his life exploring this gradual progression from shadow to light, this earthbound existence.

Our imagination is too crude…to paint the subtler colors of the folds of bliss.   Dante

It fell short, he knew, as all paintings did, but it was the best he had to offer. When it was finished, he knew Cosimo would be pleased.

CHAPTER 87

The year of Our Lord 1459, countryside of Prato

As the months passed, Lucrezia spent much of her time watching Filippino interact with the world. Sometimes, lying on his back, he kicked his feet in the air, then reached out to catch them. Failing, he erupted into peels of laughter and tried again. When he had finished with that game, she would pick him up and carry him through the orchard, handing him a peach or a pear to examine. Filippino would poke it with his finger, lick it, try to stuff it whole into his tiny mouth.

By the time he was two, he was an explorer, the property surrounding the house his domain. When he ran down an incline, Lucrezia chasing after, his tiny foot suddenly coming down where the land dipped far below his footfall, before she could utter a cry of alarm, his little body lurching forward, he would throw his arms out, recover his balance, and continue without slowing pace. He was sure-footed, she told Filippo. A good thing to be in an ever-shifting world.

Today she sat comfortably, her eyes drinking their fill of him as he slept. This is all she had wanted. The hum of insects, an occasional bird call, the serenity of a sun-drenched day interrupted now and then by the sweep of an autumnal breeze.

Simona would be visiting later on with her daughter. Lucrezia could not wait to introduce her friend to Filippino who, fresh from his nap, was sure to entertain them. They both owed it all to Filippo. Her mother had been right all those years ago, although as a sheltered girl of seventeen she had not understood. "His kindness will make him beautiful in your eyes, and you will want no other." She smiled. Filippo was a handsome man in spite of his years.

Filippino stirred and stretched, his little mouth forming an O as he yawned. She gently stroked his face, his fat little cheek. Eyes still closed, he reached up and grasped her finger tightly in his little fist, then settled. He would drift for a few more peaceful moments before waking. Then, his energy, unleashed, would flood every corner of her life with light.

By following your star, you cannot fail to reach a glorious port. Dante

Lucrezia had missed her fellow sisters from the convent. Since it was a beautiful day, she, Spinetta, and Simona decided to take their refreshment at the outdoor table that had been set under the trees. After they ate, Simona's daughter, now six years of age, floated among the trees in the orchard beyond, her arms spread, face uplifted.

"She is beautiful," Lucrezia said. "What a blessing for you to be a part of her life again."

"For now," Simona said, her eyes cast downward.

Startled, Lucrezia asked, "For now? Surely you are happy to be with your little girl."

"That is what I have come to tell you. To warn you. When I first arrived at my cousin's house, the servants treated me with scorn. I cared not. What did it matter? I had my Teressa. Later, visitors acted as if I did not exist. Even this I could bear. But when my sweet little girl tried to play with the children of the servants, they taunted her with vulgar slurs. About me. About her. Prostituto! Bastardina!"

"Oh!" Lucrezia reached out and placed her hand on her friend's shoulder. "Cannot your cousin intervene on your behalf?"

"I spoke with my cousin's wife," Simona continued. "She asked me what I would have her do when it was my presence in her house that was the source of this new trouble. She told me it would only grow worse with time. Who, she asked, would take my daughter as wife, knowing who her mother is? 'You will see her locked behind the walls of the very convent you escaped,' she informed me. 'Your sin will be her shame and her undoing.'"

Lucrezia and Spinetta exchanged glances.

CHAPTER 88

The year of Our Lord 1459, Florence

It had begun with a bad cough that progressed until the conges-
tion sat like a stone in his chest. Cosimino, not yet eight years
of age, burned with fever. The family's physician was called in,
who immediately closed all of the windows and curtains against
the bad air. He bled the boy, hoping to rebalance his humors. But
the boy only grew worse. His parents were terrified. Giovanni sat
by his son's bed through the long nights, every so often reaching out
to take hold of his only child's limp little hand, to will him to revive.
His wife took over at daybreak.

Ginevra pressed a cool cloth to Cosimino's cheeks, kissed his
forehead, and prayed, "God, dear God, please protect my sweet
boy. Make him well again." When she knelt to say her rosary, she
pressed the beads so hard between her fingers, she thought she
might snap them from the chain. "So hard, so hard, little seeds of
onyx, break open with my prayers and bring forth life."

When Cosimo arrived, he asked for some time alone with his
grandson. He had already bargained with God, promised to pay
back any gains he might have achieved dishonestly, offered to build

new convents for every mendicant order. But what were money, buildings, to this? To this small life? This perfect spark of light?

Cosimo knelt at the side of the bed and bowed his head in prayer, his forehead pressed into his clasped hands. "Take me, God. Take me." He looked up beseechingly. "Leave this boy. This beautiful child." Cosimo's heart pressed against his ribs. "Strike me down," he pleaded. "I will endure anything."

Days passed like this until one chill November morning when, clouds stacked in the sky like lead, the blustery winds of autumn swept up the boy's soul and delivered it to heaven.

I have come to lead you to the other shore; into eternal darkness; into fire and into ice. Dante

It was a cave in which Cosimo dwelt. Plato's cave? If only it were. Then, all he would have to do was walk out of it to find the light. In this cave, sound was muffled as if a giant had clapped its hands over his ears. There was no light to see by, its thread having been stolen. What kind of day was it? Did the sun roll out from behind the clouds? Was it cold? Did the scent of linden fill the spring air, or that of smoke, the final vestiges of the year's harvest now burning? He did not know. He had left his dark cell at San Marco more than a month earlier, but it seemed he had carried it with him to Careggi. He was no longer able to sit out on the upper loggia caressed by a wafting breeze, because when he did he saw Cosimino, hands held high, grasping a blade of grass, running toward him, smiling. The only place was the garden, where his vines were now tended by others.

There were times when he awoke in the night with a vision of Cosimino's small white hands crossed over his tiny chest, delicate bone and flesh, lifeless as marble, fragile as death. He had thought that at San Marco, lost in prayer, he would find comfort. But he had found that for some things there is no comfort.

CHAPTER 89

The year of Our Lord 1459, Florence

Filippo had come to pay his respects. What does one say to a man who has lost a grandson only seven years of age? Cosimino, his namesake, a baby still, had grown ill and passed into God's hands within days. Such a terrible thing, the loss of a child, a grandchild, not much more than a baby. Cosimo, he had heard, was taking it hard and, inconsolable, had withdrawn into himself.

"I am sorry that I did not come sooner," Filippo said. "The painting." He was working on a painting for the Martelli.

"The painting. Yes. I wish to speak about," Cosimo said, thinking of Filippo's Adoration above the altar in his chapel.

"How does it go with you?" Filippo asked.

After a brief silence, Cosimo said, "Giovanni's grief knows no bounds. He eats more than ever. He will eat himself." He stopped abruptly.

"And you?" Filippo asked.

"I hold up," Cosimo said, without conviction. "The painting. Before all of." He stopped short of finishing, moving his hand back and forth in front of him to indicate all that had come after. A distracted look, something new, crossed his face, and then he found the words. "You were right about the painting for my chapel. Contemplating beauty does bring me closer to God. From the shadows of deep despair. Divine light. No one understands light as you do, Lippo."

"It is good to know that my painting brings comfort."

There has to come a time of withering, of readiness to fall, like the ripeness which comes to the fruits of the trees and of the earth. Cicero

"Each time I contemplate it," Cosimo continued, "I see something new. I see the axe and think, 'The axe is laid unto the root of the trees. Every tree therefore which bringeth not forth good fruit is hewn down and cast into the fire,'" quoting Luke. "This brings me, old and flawed, to repentance. But what of a child? Innocence ready to bear good fruit. Well. There is no means to understand." He sat in silence, and then continued, "The painting," as if remembering what he had begun, "is beautiful and yet contains within it such sorrow. We know what is in store for this mother and child. The very flora and fauna speak of it. The red titmouse in the grass, Christ's passion. The five-petaled red flowers, his five wounds. Yet, in the darkest landscape of our soul, a clearing, threads of golden light."

"The breath of light. God's divine mercy." Filippo finished his thought.

CHAPTER 90

The year of Our Lord 1459, countryside of Prato

Filippo had never expected to dwell within such a nesting calm. Each morning he awoke in Lucrezia's arms, each night he settled down in them. Just as she had curved the angles and corners of the house, she now smoothed out his very being. It was as if they dwelt in timelessness: He was a child. He was a man. He was spread beyond his own flesh and bone. They dovetailed, feathering together with ease, embracing the strength of flight. They embodied the fire of light.

He had never imagined his life would take such a turn. At first, he was frightened of being a father. Who was he to take on such a task? A man who had not known his parents or the habits of family life. But, as he watched Lucrezia interact with Filippino, he began to learn, and soon he found his own way with him. Whenever he looked at the boy, whose blond curls and tender brown eyes were so like those of his mother, he felt an ache in his heart, a need to protect coupled with the knowledge that this would not always be possible. It was with a great sense of wonder that he reencountered his son each morning. Who was this child? He wished to learn.

When Filippino was two years of age, he began teaching the boy how to play a little with paper and charcoal. One day he walked into the kitchen, having left Filippino drawing circles and lines, to find that the boy had placed his little toy horse on the table and rendered it, down to the platform and wheels it stood on and its rope for pulling. When Filippo examined the drawing, he found it to be, although inexact, in perfect proportion and with everything correctly placed, including its little painted on eye. Lucrezia had laughed at his astonishment. "Do you think you are the only painter in the family?" she had asked.

It was late afternoon, Filippino sweetly napping, his little fist curled up under his chin. Filippo breathed in the crisp early winter air and pulled Lucrezia closer. The frescoes moved along more rapidly now. He had completed the second tier and would, come spring, begin the final bottom tier, where he had planned a painting like no other. It was to be the feast of Herod, a tribute to Donatello, whose bronze relief in Siena he had copied as a young friar. But he would put his own stamp on it. Lucrezia would be the model both for the queen and for Salome, caught in the midst of dance. He had already moved her to distraction with his drawings of her as she danced. She complained she would be dizzy for all eternity. He smiled. Never before had a figure danced through a painting.

"Teressa is six years of age," Lucrezia was saying.

"Who?" Filippo asked.

"Simona's daughter."

"Ahhh, yes." Lucrezia had not said much after their visit and had been in a pensive mood ever since.

"Filippo, it is heartbreaking. Children fling insults at her."

"Who?"

"Teressa. Adults stare and whisper as she passes. What will her life be?"

"People can be cruel," he agreed.

"Simona has decided to take her daughter to relatives in Florence and she, herself, will return to the convent."

"What?" Filippo could not believe what he was hearing.

"Piera's son," Lucrezia continued, "was sent away from her cousin's house to an uncle in the Mugello. At first, they would not allow her to see him. She persisted so they relented but afterward told her she was not to come again. If she did, her son would be placed in a convent. It would have been better, they told her, had he not known who his mother is." Lucrezia's voice broke with these last words.

"What kind of a place is this"— Filippo shuddered—"where it is better for a child not to know his mother? What have we come to?"

"They are nuns who have spurned the rules of conduct, which I have also disobeyed," Lucrezia said solemnly. "We have all sinned."

"Lucrezia. Lucrezia." Filippo pulled her close to comfort her. "Dear, dear Lucrezia." He stroked her hair. "You are good and better, far better than most." He felt her shake her head back and forth against his chest in disagreement. "Did you choose the life of a nun?"

She lifted her head to look at him. "No."

"A slave must endure," Filippo told her, remembering long days at sea, "but if he should glimpse the chance for freedom, should he not take it? If God provides such a gift, are we to turn our backs on it?"

"No," she conceded, doubtfully. "Oh, I do not know."

"Lucrezia." He held her face cupped in his hand. "Love is God's greatest gift. I know I have not been the noblest of men. But is this not a blessing for all we have endured? I accept this gift graciously."

"Filippo," she said gravely, and his heart sank. "Filippino will suffer. I love our son too much to see him bear the scorn of others because of who I am."

"You would send him away from us?"

"There is nowhere to send him. My family will not take him. They cast me out long ago with little care. What use would they have now for my son?"

"What, then?"

"Filippo. I have given it much thought. I must return to the convent. Spinetta and I both."

"No! I will not allow it!" he cried, then winced, for he had never spoken to her in this way before.

She reached out and placed her hand on his heart. "I must. It is the only way. If I am repentant, then people will not append my guilt upon our son. He will have you. He will be your apprentice. A great painter one day, like his father." She tried to sound encouraging, even though her heart ached with every word.

"And, you?"

"I never imagined there could be a fate more cruel than mine was when you found me. But that despair was nothing as compared to this."

"You cannot leave us. You cannot abandon your child. And, what of me?"

"You will live and work. You will have Filippino to love. When you look at him, you will see me." A sob escaped that she could not suppress.

"You cannot abandon us," he said.

"What shape do I wish my shadow to take?" she asked, the firmness returning to her voice, the resolve to her face. "Do I wish to make every choice for myself alone? Choices that do not place even my son's welfare ahead of my own? Could I live with such a shadow? Oh, Filippo, is there a heaven to aspire to, a hell to fear? I am not certain. But, I do know that I cannot stand by and watch my sweet Filippino suffer. Suffer because of choices I have made. I cannot. I cannot bear it."

"Lucrezia," he said, reaching for her, the saying of her name melting all of his defenses, and yet even as that boundary between them disappeared, he felt her slipping away.

He pulled her close, but with little comfort. He hated small, provincial Prato. But, even if they were to move to Florence, they could not disappear amidst the crowds. People would notice. Why could they not keep busy with their own lives? What business was it of theirs? People looked too much at others, judging, and not enough at themselves. There was evil in this. See what damage it did.

"When will you go?" he asked.

"When Filippino is weaned. Just after Christmas."

That was in less than two months. Had he not learned long ago that God makes the most beautiful days of our lives prelude to the most painful? This might not be everyone's experience, but it was his own.

How from sweet seed may come a bitter fruit? Dante

Since Spinetta and Lucrezia were both leaving, Filippo employed a nurse. Lucrezia chose carefully, a young girl, Josephina, of tender heart, from a poor family in a nearby village, not from Prato's center. Her family needed the money, and she could be trusted to be discreet. Not wanting to take all he knew away from Filippino at once, Spinetta left first, and Lucrezia followed a month later. She had waited until the last possible moment. By the time she left, Flippino was chubby with health and eating almost as much solid food as a boy twice his age.

Filippo stood helpless as Lucrezia held Filippino in her arms, pressed her forehead against his, looked into his eyes and said, "Mama must leave, but my heart stays with my Filippino. Whenever you think of me, you will feel me here." She placed her hand on his little chest. "You and Pappa will visit me soon." Then her body swayed back and forth as she sang him a little song, the thinness of her voice painful to hear. She buried her head in his little chest, his chubby arms encircling it, giving it a big, bold hug.

She placed Filippino in Josephina's arms, turned swiftly, clutching her mantel at her breast, and rushed out the door.

This was not right. Filippo followed, stopping her just outside. "Lucrezia, please."

She turned toward him. "I cannot stay." Then, she pulled her hood up over her head and climbed into the waiting cart. He watched until she was swallowed up in the darkness.

CHAPTER 91

The year of Our Lord 1460, Prato

"Before you profess," the new prioress said, arms folded across her chest, "you must know that Fra Filippo has been forbidden to enter within the convent walls. You will not be permitted to see him, or"—she hesitated, casting her eyes downward—"or your son."

Lucrezia let out a small cry, the sound of which, like the sharp chirp of a baby bird, startled the prioress, who jumped. Lucrezia felt dizzy and swayed where she stood. The prioress, recovering herself, grabbed Lucrezia's arm and led her to a chair. "Sit," she commanded.

Lucrezia, now seated, composed herself and looked up into the prioress's eyes. "Please," she pleaded.

The prioress held firm. "There is no other way. God will not accept half-hearted penance." In truth, she blamed her dear sister Bartholomea for her leniency with the young nuns in her care. How had that ended for her, after all? In disillusionment and early death, only six months after the incident of their escape. She herself would not make the same mistake.

It was a crushing blow when Filippo arrived a few days later, Filippino in his arms, at the gates of Santa Margerita, and they were turned away. Lucrezia was now locked inside, out of reach.

"A cruel blow, Diamante," Filippo grumbled to his friend. "Why does love not prevail? Why does God not intervene on our behalf?"

"It is sad, Filippo. But you knew the risk. You are, after all, a monk, and she, a nun."

Filippo did not need to be chastised. "I have not lived as a monk these twenty-five years," he reminded Diamante.

"Yet..." Filippo detected exasperation in Diamante's voice. "You enjoy the benefit of close relations with the order."

"They are my family, Diamante. Would you have me abandon my family?" Was even Filippo's loyal companion unable to understand?

"I am sorry. I forget," Diamante said, remembering that he himself, with a large and loving family, had chosen to join the order. "And yet." Diamante held up his hand as if he were about to give a blessing but instead heaped on more criticism. "Lucrezia is a professed nun. Is it not a grave sin for her to leave the order? To enjoy the pleasures of the flesh? Even you, Filippo, cannot get away with such sacrilege."

"But she is a wife and mother now. Would the church take her away from her family?"

It was six months since Lucrezia had returned to the convent, and the scaffolding in the duomo sat silent. All work had ceased. This conversation was the most Filippo had spoken since Lucrezia's departure. Since being turned away at the gate to the convent, he had sat in a chair by the fire, his attention lost somewhere in its dancing flames.

Then she and sleep, as one, departed. Dante

Diamante rode to Careggi. "I worry for his health," he told Cosimo. "He does not eat. He does not drink. All work has come to a standstill. I continued on to the extent that I was able but dare not move forward without him. The duomo stands idle. The governors grow restless, but I cannot rouse him."

"Yes, the guests from Venice mentioned something of this. They said they were unable to meet with him, as he was ill. They had the highest praise for the work underway. Tell him I wish to see him."

Diamante looked down at the floor.

"You do not mean to imply that he will not respond?"

"I cannot predict."

"Very well. I will summon him." Cosimo quickly penned something, sealed it, and handed it to Diamante. "Tell him, tell him I very much wish to see him," he said, softening the command.

In the silence that followed, Cosimo realized that his very command might be disregarded. "Perhaps there is something we can do to mitigate the situation," he said, although this was not what he had intended.

"This will rouse him," Diamante said.

"I leave it to you, then, to persuade him."

"Hope will persuade better than I," Diamante said, bowing and taking his leave.

From the first day within this life I saw her face...pursuit of her in song has never been cut off. Dante

Upon Diamante's return to Prato with news of Cosimo's intervention, Filippo immediately took up work again on a tondo for his friend Bartholomeo Martelli. It was of Mary enthroned, with her child on her lap, the scene of her own birth in the background beyond her right shoulder, visitors, women and children, arriving with gifts. Above and receding from this scene, a ladder led Joachim to Anna's doorway, symbolizing Mary's conception.

Diamante peered over his shoulder as he worked. Filippo was executing the tondo with more geometrical precision than usual. The combination of various scenes within an oval demanded some observance of mathematical rules, but Filippo would normally, after a nod to geometry, move quickly to the use of color and light to trick the eye.

Diamante pondered aloud, "I have never seen you give such detailed attention to geometrical exactitude."

"Do not distract me," Filippo blustered uncharacteristically.

Lost in the minutiae of lines and angles, Filippo was able to forget. He became absorbed in lighting the figure of the baby Jesus, who held one pomegranate seed between his tiny fingers. He held it up to his mother, to Lucrezia, who was the model for Mary. One seed comes directly from heaven. Who deserved heaven more than his beloved Lucrezia? She had suffered much, had she not? One could see it here in her eyes, eyes Filippo had painted as he last remembered them, the depth of pain in them that of a mother who has lost her son. Lucrezia had suffered, but remained kind and generous of heart. Was that not life's greatest challenge, and had she not met it? Filippo looked into the eyes that stared out at him from the panel. "It is wrong!" he shouted, slamming his fist on the table where pots of paint clanked against each other and brushes scattered. "Wrong."

Diamante jumped from his seat, fearful that Filippo would lift the tondo from its easel and destroy it. But he would not destroy her, so lovingly created. "I leave for Padua at daybreak," Filippo said. "I have a commission to value there. I will stop in Careggi to see Cosimo. Do not, Diamante, do not allow Martelli to take her away"—he indicated the finished tondo—"before my return."

The following morning, as he prepared to leave, Filippo instructed Josephina, "If you are in need of anything during my absence, see Fra Diamante." He threw on his mantello and buckled his satchel.

"I will take good care of the boy," Josephina said.

Coming to himself, Filippo realized that he had nearly left without saying good-bye to his son. He was far too preoccupied these days. He knelt and held out his arms to Filippino, who was sitting on the floor playing with his toy horse, moving it up and down in a gallop and making horsey noises. "Filippino, come here, my son.

Come give Pappa a hug."

The little boy toddled over and threw his arms around his father's neck. Filippo held him close. Then, placing his hands on the boy's shoulders, he said, "Now. I go away for a short time only in order to value a painting."

"Way, way, Pappa way," Filippino said.

The boy did not understand. "I must go away to work. I will stand." And here Filippo crossed his arms over his chest, then cupping one elbow, he raised the opposite hand to rub his chin, nodded his head, and said, "Hmmmmm."

Filippino laughed. He mimicked his father's movements, and repeated, "Hmmmm."

"Exactly so," Filippo laughed. "You will make a great valuer of paintings one day. Be good for Josephina and do everything she asks. I will return soon."

He hugged the boy again, stood and turned to leave. Diamante, forever the worrier, yelled after him, "What shall I tell the governors?"

On his way through the doorway, Filippo raised his hand in farewell and said, "Tell them to pray that all goes well."

CHAPTER 92

The year of Our Lord 1460, Prato

The bones of Lucrezia's knees pressed into the stone floor, her back stiff and aching. She ran through the saying of the rosary over and over in a mechanical drone. She was elsewhere, transported to the house with the orchard, holding her baby boy, singing to him, feeling his chubby hand touch her face, the love in his eyes locked with that in hers, like the petals of a flower, all one. She was able to conjure so clearly, to smell his sweet, new scent, to feel his baby heft bounce on her knee, to hear the pure jingle of his laugh, its infectious, unfettered, joyous ring. With a sudden jolt, she found herself reaching, reaching out in an empty stone chapel, and released a wrenching cry of recognition. The prioress took it for the soul's repentance when, in fact, it was the echo of loss, and the regret she felt for her decision.

After several hours, Lucrezia's knees were so bruised from pressing into the stone she feared she might never walk again. Exhausted, she lay on her stomach on the cold stone floor, arms spread wide. She wished to melt into the stone, become one with it. "God, take me," she prayed. "Take me now."

There is no greater sorrow than to remember happy times in misery. Dante

It had only been a fortnight since their return to the convent when the five runaways had renewed their vows, repeating, "He has placed his seal upon me that I may prefer no love to Him." The thin tinkle of a bell punctuated every actor's part in the little drama. Such a feeble sound to designate the devastating event. It mocked Lucrezia's pain. The first time she had recited her vows, there had been no feeling attached to the words. This time she heard her voice as if it were being carried from a faraway place on the wings of the wind, to drift for a moment, barely discernable, and then fade away.

The last time she had taken her vows there were yet stirrings of life in her soul. Today, she dared not admit such light, dared not allow it to shine within. All of her feelings must be locked away in a dark chamber, for otherwise she would be driven mad. This was what her God demanded of her. These feelings then, this life God had given and then taken away, must be crushed into dust and buried for all eternity.

A veil of darkness fell before her eyes. There was nothing within to respond to the world without. She was buried alive.

CHAPTER 93

The year of Our Lord 1460, Villa Medici at Careggi

When he arrived at Careggie, Filippo found Cosimo in his antechamber. "So, you are once again in trouble," Cosimo complained, sounding weary. He motioned for Filippo to sit and poured two glasses of wine.

Filippo was tired of needing Cosimo's help. "I want a peaceful life, that is all. That is what Lucrezia and I have together."

"A mistake, Filippo. Ah well, people make mistakes."

"I have a son, Cosimo. I never expected. Filippino needs his mother."

"Something about which you should have given thought before now."

"Have you not loved?" Filippo asked.

"Well," Cosimo replied, "Contessina. She is a competent mother. And she does dote on me. One cannot go wrong with that, can one?"

Filippo ventured, "If she were no longer here, would you feel as if a part of you, body and soul, had been ripped away?"

"I do not know how I would feel," Cosimo answered cagily.

"Is there passion in your feelings for her?" Filippo was curious to know.

"Passion," Cosimo scoffed, revealing himself to be a man without passion in his life. "Passion is not all it is made out to be." Then he gazed off and smiled. "I am fond of her, Contessina."

"And Maddalena?" Filippo asked.

Cosimo started visibly at the sound of her name and calculated how to answer but finally, with genuine sadness in his voice, said, "I sent her away because I had no choice. She is a woman. Alas, one must do what one must. One cannot love in a measured way, Lippo. By God, if you had wanted to substantiate the rumors against you, this was a most well-calculated way to do so."

"Would not the pope, if appealed to, intervene?" Filippo pleaded. "Lucrezia and I have made a verbal commitment to one another. We have consummated our relationship. In the eyes of God and of the church, Antoninus himself confirms, this is a marriage. The boy needs his mother!"

Cosimo leaned forward. "This little nun is cunning. She has taken advantage of your good nature and kind heart."

"No!" Filippo protested. "That is not true."

"You are in love with her then?"

Filippo bent his head in ascent. "She is gentle and kind, and has known much sorrow."

"A dangerous combination." Cosimo wearily rubbed his eyes. "I warned you, if you remember, that people would not tolerate a fall from grace in a nun. 'Let not mortals take vows lightly,' Dante warns us."

"God did not mean for me a holy path," Filippo reminded him. "You have said so yourself. Neither did he mean one for Lucrezia."

"I will speak with the pope." Cosimo relented, but seeing the light of hope in Filippo's eyes, he added, "I cannot promise anything. In fact, it is more likely that he will be unwilling to help. Thank the Lord, Antoninus is not pope. Although he would agree you are married, he would have you adhere to your previous vows. Pius, of all popes, may be sympathetic to your plight. Did you know that before he professed, which came late in his life, he fathered at least two sons?"

"I did not."

"No. Well. He wished to provide for them. The first of his sons perished before one year had passed and also before Pius had roused himself to action on his behalf. The second son, along with his mother, vanished. He does not know if they are alive. He did not act swiftly then either, you see. There is regret."

Later that day, Cosimo sent a dispatch off to Pope Pius. My God, he thought, once again rubbing his eyes with weariness, why cannot Filippo be more like Donatello? Donatello's stink may rise all the way to heaven, where angels, no doubt, must hold their noses, for he washes not and he dresses in rags, but his love is his Muse, his sustenance his art.

CHAPTER 94

The year of Our Lord 1460, Prato

As he approached Prato, Filippo wished he could rush straight to the convent. He could barely contain himself, but he realized that he must prepare Filippino, not to mention Josephina and Diamante. Pius had decided on their behalf. He had released them from their vows. Filippo carried the document in his satchel. The whole world was about to change. A feast must be prepared. Perhaps he could, as well, convince two or three of his musician friends to play some tunes for the occasion. They must dance, he and Lucrezia, they most certainly must dance. Filippo wanted to jump from his horse, pick him up, and carry him in order to travel faster. When he, at long last, arrived at his house, he burst through the door, startling Josephina, who dropped a newly made loaf of bread to the floor. The bread knocked Filippino in the head, who was playing on the floor below, and now elicited cries of distress.

Filippo apologized, whipped off his mantello, and pulled Filippino onto his lap to quiet him. When the boy had calmed down, Filippo gave Josephina the news and sent her off to find

Diamante, as well as to buy pheasant and lamb, apricots and figs, and almonds, yes, salted almonds. It was to be a celebration.

Filippino quickly fell asleep in his arms. Tired himself from his long journey, Filippo rested his eyes and soon joined him. A full hour later, a loud obnoxious noise filtered through Filippo's dreams, along with peels of childish laughter. He awoke to find Filippino pointing at him and laughing. "Pappa, you snore," he said, and he proceeded to imitate the sound with fair accomplishment.

Filippo laughed and said, "It was not me."

Filippino, surprised, insisted, "It was you."

"No, no," Filippo corrected. "See how well you make the sound. Well, then." Filippino looked puzzled. "Well, it must have been you," Filippo concluded.

"Not me," Filippino again insisted, now indignant, "you." He pointed his finger at his father, then crossed his arms resolutely over his tiny chest.

"But," Filippo explained, "I was asleep the whole time. How could I possibly have made such melodious music?" Filippino now understood and laughed.

Suddenly, Diamante burst through the door. "Is it true?" he cried out.

"Yes, yes," Filippo concurred, as it all flooded back. "I have sent Josephina to buy food for a feast. And I will hire Tommaso and Francesco to play music. It is a celebration."

"Well," Diamante reminded Filippo, "good luck finding musicians awake at this time of day."

"Ah, well." Filippo realized the truth of this. "But we shall have a feast. I must change. I am full of dust from the road. And I must take a dress and mantel from the chest for Lucrezia. I wish to stop, too, at the lender for Josephina's dowry. She will receive it early, as we will have no need of her services. We all shall benefit from this happy circumstance."

"Hold off," Diamante advised. "You will need Josephina for a while yet, to help ease the transition."

This reminded Filippo of his son, who sat quietly listening.

"Filippino," he said, looking into the boy's eyes to discern his emotions. "Your mama is returning home." Filippo suddenly feared that it had been so long that Filippino might not remember her. "You remember Mama?"

Filippino nodded his head vigorously up and down. Filippo, relieved, laughed at his exuberance. "Of course you do. How could you not? The most beautiful woman on God's earth. I must delay no longer. All this time we have been planning, and she has been sadly going about her business, with no knowledge of this happy turn of events."

Filippo went to the bedchamber to wash his face and hands and to change from his dusty clothes. Then, he opened the chest. The scent of lavender rose from Lucrezia's dress. He hugged it to him, tears filling his eyes. "You are coming home," he said aloud.

Filippo kissed Filippino on the head, bade Diamante await their return, and rushed out the door, only to realize, halfway to the convent, that the precious document, the one he needed in order to obtain Lucrezia's release, had been left behind. He burst into the house, procured the document, and set off once again.

When he arrived at Santa Margherita, he had much trouble convincing the gatekeeper of his need to enter. He had, after all, been barred from the convent forever. He sent a message through the tiny opening to be taken to the prioress and, after what seemed like several hours but was surely only minutes, he was admitted.

The sun which first made warm my breast with love. Dante

The prioress, with a stern old stone face, was very unlike her sister and seemed reluctant to believe Filippo's story. He thrust the document under her nose and bade her read it. Finally, she looked over her glasses at him and said, "If the pope decrees, I have no choice but to obey."

"Is that not obvious?" Filippo asked impatiently.

She left and, again, an interminable wait followed. Finally, Filippo heard the door open and turned to see Lucrezia standing motionless in a pool of dark shadow that flooded the far end of the room. He could barely make her out, dressed in black, by the faint shimmer of white, the veil that covered her hair. A single shaft of light streamed in through one narrow window high up in the wall. Filippo walked into the light so that she might see him.

Lucrezia brought her hand to her breast. "No, no, you mustn't."

He walked closer. She was much thinner and the color had drained from her face, but she was as beautiful as ever. "Hurry," he said. "I have brought your clothes." He thrust them toward her. Lucrezia did not seem to understand. Confusion clouded her eyes. Filippo felt as if he must pull her from a deep well with great effort, out into the light. Had she not been told?

"Lucrezia," he said, "Filippino awaits. You are coming home."

She blinked, searched about the room, and still did not seem to comprehend. Uncertainty in her voice, she pushed at the air. "No. No. You must go. God will punish us."

"You have been released from your vows," Filippo told her, with the tenderness in his voice that he might use with a child. "Lucrezia. The pope himself. Look here." He thrust the document toward her. "The pope has released us from our vows. We are married. By the hand of Pope Pius."

Lucrezia at last grasped the situation. She walked into the light and collapsed in his arms.

CHAPTER 95

The year of Our Lord 1463, Florence

Cosimo must have fallen asleep in his chair because he was awakened with a start. Was that a scream he had heard? Someone had screamed. The gout rooted him in place. What had happened? He heard footsteps rushing to and fro. Why was no one arriving to inform him about what had happened? They disturbed him soon enough over trifles. He tried to stand, but it was no use. He would not be able to walk anywhere.

After what seemed an eternity, Piero entered the room, his face stern, blanched.

"What is it?" Cosimo demanded. "What has happened?"

Piero sat down across from him. "Mother. She fainted and has been helped to her bedchamber. The physician has arrived."

"Whatever for?" Cosimo was growing irritated. "Is she unwell? I thought I heard someone scream out."

"It is Giovanni, Father," Piero said. "He is gone."

"Gone?" Cosimo asked. What was wrong with Piero? What was he not saying? "Gone where? Speak up."

"God has taken him," Piero said, as if the saying of it might make it seem more real.

"No," Cosimo contradicted. "No. You are mistaken."

"Quite suddenly," Piero assured him. "His heart seized. He is gone."

They sat for some time in silence. Then, Piero stood and said, "I must go to his palazzo. Console Ginevra, who has now lost all."

So was I in the midst of that dark land.   Dante

Yes, Cosimo thought, first her young son, little Cosimino, her only child, and now this. He did not move. He remained in his chair throughout the night. He yet grieved the boy. So soon after. But this time there had been no warning, no illness. No kneeling beside his bed. No praying to God to save him. Like his brother Lorenzo, Giovanni had simply vanished. Here. Not here. Breath. No breath. How long would it take for him to comprehend the truth of this loss?

CHAPTER 96

The year of Our Lord 1463, Prato

Lucrezia had emerged from the convent a mere shadow of herself. It took months for her to regain her former strength, but her love for Filippo and Filippino gradually filled her with light, recreating contours, banishing the deepest shadows. Soon she was with child, swelling with new life. Laughter and joy filled the small house.

But it was not to last. The child, a boy, lived only three days. Lucrezia fell into a deep silence, broken one day when her sister Spinetta visited. "Spinetta, for months I have walked under a heavy weight, the burden of guilt. I believed I was being punished for my sins, for not remaining in the convent. I swallowed whole what I imagined were the prioress's words, and I choked on them. But then a small voice inside asked: What kind of God metes out punishment? What kind of God takes retribution against a child? What God is devoid of compassion? Of mercy? No. It was not my fault. But why? Why bring a child into this life only to take him back?"

Spinetta spoke haltingly, carefully choosing her words. "Many babies do not thrive, my dear sister."

"Oh, I know I am not alone," Lucrezia said. "But why?"

"It may be that their gentle souls are not made strong enough to withstand the harshness of this world."

"Then why do they arrive at all?"

"Perhaps, although they have not succeeded, they have tried."

I hope to write of her that which has never been written of any other woman.   Dante

Lucrezia picked up the ultramarine velvet cloth and draped it around Spinetta, over top of her black robes. "It is like the blue of the sun-drenched sea," Filippo had said when he gave it to her. Lucrezia gathered it here and there as Spinetta, unused for so long to such luxury, pressed it to her cheek and ran it through her fingers.

"Here," Lucrezia said, "gather the cloth just here, below the shoulders, and here again above the elbow." Then she drew a line with her finger. "A tracing of pearls lengthwise down the shoulder."

"Bellissimo," the tailor confirmed.

"Tiny pearl buttons," she continued, "two and two on each side for the clasps and continuing up along the neckline."

"Yes, yes," the tailor agreed, nodding his head with approval.

Lucrezia felt confident enough now to design her own clothing. Filippo praised her eye for design and color. This meant much to her because fabric was to her what paint was to him. She loved the feel of it in her hand, the crush of velvet, the cool slip of silk, the weft and hues, the brocaded designs, detailed embroideries, delicate stitchwork with fine gold and silver threads, a tuft of lace at the bust, a detailing of tiny pearls.

The sleeves on this giornea would have a unique design. She was to wear it over the rose-colored, brocaded velvet dress that Filippo had given her when their relationship began, the fabric he had chosen because it was the color Dante's Beatrice had worn when Dante first set eyes on her. It would have to be taken out at the waist since she was once again with child.

She was to wear the giornea in a painting Filippo planned of Mary in adoration of the Christ child. He had presented Lucrezia with a long strand of tiny pearls to weave through her hair and one large pearl to fasten onto her veil. The Mary in this painting would not wear a mantle, but a giornea. It was to be a portrait of a finely dressed woman like the many Filippo had painted for the wealthiest Florentine families. As much as it was a painting of Mary and the Christ child, it was a portrait to commemorate the union of Lucrezia and Filippo, with Filippino portrayed as the baby Jesus. Now a healthy, growing boy of six years, his chubby baby self was still fresh in Filippo's memory, he told her.

When Lucrezia had protested, saying that they took liberties, Filippo had cupped her chin in his hand, looked into her eyes, and said, "Do not all babies come to us from heaven?" This man always had his way. There was no dissuading him, and so Lucrezia made peace with the idea.

When completed, it breathed with tenderness. "Oh, Filippo, this painting is beautiful."

"It is you who are beautiful," he said, "and now contented." He remembered the unbearable sadness in her eyes that he had captured in the tondo just after she had returned to the convent. This, at long last, was what he had wished for her, a peaceful and contented life. In this painting, he had captured the breath of her light.

CHAPTER 97

The year of Our Lord 1464, Florence

osimo, suffering more and more from gout, now had to be carried everywhere. As Filippo arrived for a visit, just before the feast of San Giovanni, he heard a commotion and saw that Cosimo's chair, being carried by two servants, was fast approaching a doorway. "You draw me toward danger," Cosimo yelled out. "Do you not see? Careful. Careful."

"Why do you yell out so?" Contessina, trudging behind, grumbled. "Nothing has happened."

"If something had already happened," Cosimo retorted, "what use, then, to yell out?"

Filippo smiled. Cosimo had retained his wry wit.

After washing the dust off his face and hands, Filippo made his way to Cosimo's antechamber. There, Contessina sat engaged in some handiwork with needle and thread, chirping away delightedly, to no apparent end. Cosimo sat, eyes closed, in deep and distant meditation. She shook him by the shoulder to rouse him at Filippo's approach. "Why do you always sit with your eyes closed?"

"To get them used to it," Cosimo snapped.

Contessina tisked and shook her head.

Cosimo opened one eye, rolling it in her direction. "Do you not have something to attend to?"

She lifted her needlework as if to offer it to him, but then, with an exaggerated sigh, she rolled it up and placed it in a bag at her feet. As she rose and walked toward the door, she said, "Call a servant should you sink into your death throes. I will be attending to business downstairs."

When she had closed the door behind her, Cosimo laughed, "The older I get, the more annoying her chatter, and even more so her barbs. Contessina, bless her, has become quite a bossy old hen." He pulled himself up in his chair with difficulty, but when Filippo jumped up to help, he was shoed away with a firm hand.

"I grow old," Cosimo grumbled, "not feeble."

His face was like a fabric that had worn thin, faint remnants of the original design now barely visible. His skin sagged with age, making the sharp jutting line of his nose more pronounced. His eyes had yellowed, and he was thinner than ever. His movements, which had always been quick and decisive, were slowed, making him appear fragile, as did the almost imperceptible shake in his hand. Cosimo's eyes, however, remained as sharp as those of a hawk.

"You have a family to provide for," he began, "a second child. I have procured a commission for you. It may well be the best I have negotiated since Prato. This commission will pay 1,000 florins. Not as much as Prato, but a good sum. They want the dormition of Mary, her coronation on the ceiling of the duomo," Cosimo said, pointing upward and raising his eyes as if the dome rose above them. "Who else to accomplish this but you? You will have to travel to Spoleto. It is the final commission I negotiate for you."

He waved away Filippo's protests with a dismissive swipe of his hand. "This commission will take years to complete. I do not have years, Lippo."

Now that my race is run, I have no desire to be called back from the finish to the starting point. Cicero

Their eyes met, Cosimo's direct gaze emphasizing his understanding of this fact. Not many men faced death with such strength. "I have made my reparations with God. I have negotiated peace for all Italy. I have kept my promise to my jailor, Federigo Malavolti, by providing every year another hundred popolo minuto voting rights and eligibility for public office. I have created a library open to all that adds hundreds of manuscripts each year. I have filled the city with fine architecture, sculptures, and paintings. I give Florence the Platonic Academy. Philosopher rulers—the only thing to save them from the vicious cycle of rebellion and decay. I have done all that I am able. It will have to be enough. God has been good to me."

Filippo saw that, as Cosimo looked off into the distance, his eyes moistened. "You think of Giovanni and Cosimino."

Cosimo appeared startled to have had his own mind read as he had so often read those of others, but he assented. After a short pause, he added, "What of my legacy?"

"Piero will carry it on," Filippo offered, although he himself had never thought much of this son.

"Piero is not much longer for this world either," Cosimo said, "although Fortuna did take good care of him after all."

"Lorenzo, then." Filippo offered the name of the likely next of kin, though he was yet a boy.

"It is not the same," Cosimo said. "Not how I had imagined it would play out."

"No," Filippo said.

"God has allowed me to live so long because he knows I am a slow learner," Cosimo continued, raising a shaky hand to rub his eyes. "We may think we control events, but in the end it is all in God's hands. About His running of things on Earth, however, I will have much to say to Him. Ha! There is room for improvement." He smiled, but then grew serious. "Do not let the end catch you unprepared, my friend. Your spontaneity." Cosimo left the rest unsaid. He had done all he could for Filippo, for everyone, and now he was weary.

"It is time that you leave me to contemplate the inside of my eyelids," Cosimo said, and with this he shut his eyes.

Filippo looked around, nervous to leave Cosimo alone. "Shall I call for Contessina?"

Without opening his eyes, Cosimo said, "No, I want peace." He settled further back into the plush cushions on which he rested. "Not bad. Not bad at all." A smile settled on his face, all worldly care drained from it.

The divine is beauty, wisdom, goodness…and by these the wing of the soul is nourished. Plato

Later that evening, Cosimo received a letter from Maddalena. He tore it open. It said only: I grow weak.

He traced and retraced the letters with his finger. Could she fade away yet more? What did she mean, weak? Would she be unable to write? He must receive word of her. He sent a message off to Carlo, asking him how his mother fared.

Several days later, in the early morning hours, Cosimo awoke with a start. When he opened his eyes, he saw her standing before him, as real as the last day he had held her in his arms, kissed her, and pushed her away. He sat up, not daring to drop his gaze lest she disappear. She was older but still beautiful. Her face had filled out and was covered with a tracing of fine lines, but her eyes were unchanged. She wore a gown of deep emerald velvet. "Maddalena," he said, "how is it that you come to me?"

He heard words in his mind, softly spoken: "Worry not. I watch over you." And, then she was gone. A shiver passed through him. What was he to make of it?

The following day as he sat at his desk, he thought about the vision he had had the night before. It had been the early morning hour, he reasoned. The heat and humidity had been oppressive. He had been worrying about her and, half asleep, had seen her as he hoped she appeared, fit and healthy. His mind had played tricks on him. A tired mind, conjuring.

A sudden knock on the door startled him. He composed himself. "Enter."

The servant who handed him a letter said, "The messenger rode through the night."

Cosimo recognized the hand. He was afraid to open it. He took a deep breath to steady himself and tore open the seal. It read: I write to inform you that, in the early evening hours, my mother passed, peacefully, into God's hands. May the Lord protect and preserve her. Yours faithfully, Carlo

CHAPTER 98

The year of Our Lord 1464, Florence

Filippo made haste when the news arrived, traveling from Prato to attend the funeral. No expense had been spared. Although Cosimo had wanted, like his father before him, to be given a modest burial, Piero would not hear of it. A man who was called Pater Patriae, father of his country, while yet alive deserved a fitting farewell.

Filippo could not imagine the world as a place without Cosimo, who had been the one constant in his life. It was thirty years since he had swept into Squarccione's makeshift school in Padua, an exile with the air of an emperor. Filippo smiled to think of it. Cosimo was as much a part of his life as breath.

His son and grandsons headed the procession, followed by members of the mendicant orders, and then Ficino and other members of the Platonic Academy. Next came the painters, sculptors, and architects, Filippo included. Each held a taper. It was a solemn procession that wound its way to San Lorenzo, the sound of their footsteps, like that of an army, thundering up into the night sky—the sound, Filippo thought, of all that Cosimo had put into motion, the projects, the revolution of thought, the stampede of innovation. This was the sound that echoed up to heaven.

As I approach death, I feel like a man nearing harbor after a long voyage: I seem to be catching sight of land. Cicero

When they entered San Lorenzo, the interior glowed with amber light, the entire length of the nave lined with tapers. Cosimo had been more than a patron or a friend. He had been like a father to him. Filippo wept as the mass ended and Cosimo's body was lifted and lowered, upright, down into the floor of the church before the main altar. It was so like him. He would not lie supine in death, but would stand, ready if called upon, to step forward and do his part.

CHAPTER 99

The year of Our Lord 1466, Spoleto

Accompanied by Diamante, Filippo made his way to Spoleto to inspect the apse of the duomo. They would come away with completed drawings, mapping out the project that was scheduled to begin the following spring. An early morning mist was now thrown off like a mantello from the mountains' broad shoulders, revealing the black earth of plowed fields and green hills, not here the malachite of the Euganians, but shot through with gold. As he rode, Filippo watched the shadow of clouds deepen the colors of the hills and move on, leaving the sun free to soak them in its light until the next bank of clouds sped northward.

When they arrived in Spoleto, they undertook the arduous climb to the top of the mountain where Santa Maria dell' Assunta stood. "They have named it well," Filippo called out to Diamante, who rode ahead of him. "Mary of the Assumption. They could not have placed her closer to the clouds and to heaven itself to ease her ascent." Hearing Diamante's laughter, he added, "And perhaps, old man that I am, if we do not reach the summit soon, I will join her."

Diamante turned around. "If ascent is what you will experience."

"I do not appreciate being mocked when I am in extremis."

After eating a hearty mid-day meal, Filippo and Diamante followed behind the bishop, whose brisk pace was difficult to match. Filippo looked all around, admiring the magnificent Romanesque architecture. He was struck by the intricacy of the mosaic floor tiles, so much so that he nearly crashed into the bishop, who had stopped abruptly and now threw up his arms. "And here you will create an unparalleled work of art dedicated to the glory of the Virgin Mary, mother of God." He pointed to the wall behind the altar. "Her ascension into heaven." He pointed to the dome above. "Her coronation."

Filippo and Diamante stood together in the center of the space, surrounded on all sides and above by blank walls and dome.

"It is circular," Diamante said, not to state the obvious but to voice his concern. How did one paint on a curved surface as if it were flat, manage to flesh subjects out, to create proper distances and proportion?

Filippo rubbed his hands together and smiled. "A challenge. We have much work ahead, Diamante."

O glorious stars, O light made pregnant with a mighty power, all my talent, whatever it may be, has you as source. Dante

In no time at all, Filippo had figured out how to master this obstacle. The drawings completed, Diamante expected to return to Prato without delay. He knew Filippo missed Lucrezia and the children. Filippo, however, announced that they would stay on until after the feast of the Assumption. On the morning of the feast day, they joined in with the town of Spoleto at the services in honor of Mary's assumption into heaven. After the mid-day meal, the duomo now empty, Filippo spread out the sheets of paper on which the designs for the project had been laid. "From which direction did the sunlight enter through the windows this morning, Diamante?"

Diamante hesitated. "I believe…" He was about to point. "No. It shone from there. No." He turned and pointed to the rear of the duomo. "From there."

Filippo smiled, pleased with himself. "The sun shone down upon the altar from this direction." He drew a line with his extended arm from the windows behind and to the left across, directing it at the blank walls before them. "We will light every fresco, including that on the dome, from the same direction. On Assumption day, when the congregation assembles for mass, the very light of the sun will fall on each exactly so."

CHAPTER 100

The year of Our Lord 1469, Spoleto

Filippino, now twelve years of age, was working as an apprentice on the fresco project. It was evident from her letters that Lucrezia, staying on in Prato, missed her son terribly. But, she wrote, their daughter, Alessandra, eased the pain of separation. Filippo now stood and considered his son as the boy painted some distant mountains. He had, since that day long ago when he drew his little wooden horse, grown in promise. A careful and inspired draughtsman, he was particularly gifted in metalpoint renderings.

Filippo was pleased with another of his apprentices as well. Botticelli, who had first studied for a few years in the goldsmith shop owned by his father and brother, had come to him as a boy of seventeen. Only seven years under his tutelage, indispensable during the final stages of the fresco project in Prato, he was more than ready to run his own bottega.

Called Botticelli because he was round about the middle like a barrel, he offered a clear contrast in form to that of Filippo's spare and lanky son. It was comical to watch the two work the board that smoothed the plaster from one end of wall to the other. Antonio, a middle-aged apprentice who rendered architecture with facility, was needed as a counterbalance to the broad Botticelli or poor Filippino would have found himself dangling precariously from his end of the board.

Filippino idolized the older apprentice just as Filippo had once lionized Masaccio. It was deeply gratifying to watch his young son approach painting with such diligence, exuberance, and reverence. He would be a great painter one day.

Filippo slowly climbed the scaffolding to work the final layering on of gold across Mary's white mantle. His gut was troubling him, causing him an excruciating pain that came and went, so he paused often during his ascent. But, as he worked, he lost touch with the pain. When he had finished, he sat back to view her completed form, her face modeled after that of Lucrezia. "Is she not magnificent?"

"She is beautiful," Diamante agreed.

"The sun, the moon, and all of the stars," Filippo said. He picked up his brush and moved to another section of the scaffolding.

"We must stop to eat," Diamante protested.

Filippo was not listening. He was painting the sun, the moon, and all of the stars.

To the highest circles raise your eyes so that you may behold the queen enthroned. Dante

The following morning, as a summer rain shower ended, Filippo and Diamante made their way to the top of the steps that led down to the broad, sloping piazza, the duomo at its far end. When they reached the final step, the clouds hovering above the duomo, so close that one might touch them from the rooftop, suddenly parted. The sun shot through, and a rainbow spread from one end of the structure to the other. They stood, awe-struck.

"She is well pleased with our work," Filippo said.

So that above us blazed in steaks the seven bands in all the hues the sun takes for his bow. Dante

The apprentices were milling about when they entered the duomo. Filippo gave hurried instructions for the mixing of paints, climbed the scaffolding, and contemplated his vision of Mary being crowned until the paints were assembled. The ceiling beneath the scene made ready, he painted there the very rainbow they had witnessed.

Though he did not like to contradict Filippo, Diamante asked, "Are you sure? There is no precedent."

Filippo did not answer. When he was done, there was no question. He descended the scaffolding, stood beneath, and gazed up at the completed dome. Then he called Botticelli and Filippino to his side. They approached, the first lumbering, the second a gangly waif, trailing behind. Filippo swept his arms wide to take in the whole. "It comes together in the end, does it not? Contemplate. The invisible that is present in the vision. You will never touch, but you must reach."

"I have never known you to be so philosophical," Diamante laughed.

"I grow old, Diamante, I grow old."

At the last moment, Filippo changed the design for Mary's dormition. "I place all of us," he explained, indicating the assembled workshop, "at Mary's feet where we pay homage. The apostles, their lives a pure reflection of God's love, at her head where, in greatness of spirit, they look upon us, mere men, painters who through the act of painting hope in our small way to offer our work in gratitude—we, who can only hope for mercy in return." He turned aside and, in a low voice, said for Diamante's ears alone, "I hope through my work to have won more than I have lost by my mistakes."

Filippo had fulfilled the prior's exhortation to him all those years ago when, as a young man, he had left the Carmine. He had painted for the glory of God. He, of all living painters, had portrayed real people, revealing saints as ordinary souls who had become extraordinary. He had tried, always, to bridge the gap between the sacred and the profane so that all who looked upon his works could understand that the people written about, those whose stories could so easily become rote, lose meaning, had walked the earth. He did this in order to give hope. All could strive. It was not the attainment but the attempt. At least, he hoped so, for his paintings were all he had to offer. God, he thought, has mercy for us, poor men who fall and rise, then fall and rise again. It is not what happens to you, after all, but what you bring inside yourself to meet with it, what you take away.

After the first year had passed in Spoleto, Filippo had gone home to Prato just after the harvest season, his favorite time of the year, when the sun seemed to climb down from the sky to rest in the Tuscan hills and the heat lifted. He had had business to attend to, the purchase of another property, this one for his daughter Alessandra. But, not this year. He must work until the frescoes were finished.

Old age comes unsought.   Boethius

Lucrezia snipped away at the lavender, placing handfuls of the slender silver stems that were lined with deep purple flowers in the basket draped over Alessandra's baby arms. Her daughter watched intently as Lucrezia worked. Only four years old and already she displayed a preference for industry. Later on, Lucrezia would teach her how to hang them in bunches to dry and, later still, how to stuff little silk bags with the fragrant stems and sew them shut.

The sun was beginning to slant across the orchard. It was autumn, the harvest already in for the year. On a nearby farm, the workers had cleared the land and were burning piles of debris. She could smell the sharp, dusky scent of the smoke, see it billowing up into the sky. This was Filippo's favorite time of the year. Wherever he was working, he always made the journey home in autumn.

But his recent letter had informed her that he would be staying on in Spoleto. He was working at a feverish pace, he wrote, to complete the frescoes so that he could be home by Christmas for good. He was getting too old to travel, he explained, and his poor wounded gut bothered him more and more, especially when climbing scaffolding. He would settle in Prato and take smaller commissions close to home.

Lucrezia missed him, with his broad shoulders and large, rough hands that caressed her face as gently as the brush of a feathered wing. And Filippino. Lucrezia missed her sweet son terribly. But, as apprentice to his father, he would learn all he needed to know in order to be a great painter one day himself. He was where he needed to be. Filippo wrote that Filippino grew, it seemed, an inch taller each day. At the age of twelve boys changed so quickly. Soon he would be a man. She needed more time with him.

The scent of the fires, grown stronger, now permeated the air around them. Lucrezia looked skyward, where the smoke hung, a grey film that slightly obscured and, at the same time, deepened the final golden light of the day.

CHAPTER 101

The year of Our Lord 1469, Spoleto

There was a chill in the air. Filippo shivered as he swung his legs over the side of the bed. The chill would soon creep further into each morning and finally eat into the day so that they would no longer be able to work. With a sense of urgency, he threw water on his face, dressed, and entered the kitchen where a fire blazed. Filippo stood before it, rubbing his hands together, thinking about the frescoes. In his mind, he slowly scanned what had been completed, well satisfied. He imagined the compositions yet to be realized coming to life under his gaze. He smiled. They must complete the commission this season. It was a race against not only the creeping cold but the pain in his gut.

Filippo turned his attention to the table, where Stephanina had laid a meal of cured meats, cheeses, and hunks of bread. Diamante, always ravenous, was filling his plate a second time. The light had only just begun to round out shapes, differentiate forms. Before it slipped away, Filippo and his apprentices would themselves honor God's creation by rounding forms, picking out subtle details of tone and shade, with as much reverence as the sun's rays themselves.

And I saw light that flows as flows a river.   Dante

That night, in the early morning hours, Filippo was awoken by a sharp pain. It did not subside as it usually did but grew worse. He could stand it no longer. "My gut," he yelled out, bringing Diamante running from his own bedchamber. "Diamante, it is over."

"Nonsense," Diamante said. "Indigestion."

Filippo groaned.

"You have pushed yourself too hard. You must rest, that is all. In a day or two you will be up, ornery as ever."

Filippo soon fell into a fever, from which he passed in and out of consciousness. Then suddenly he awoke. The fever had passed, for he no longer felt as if he boiled in a pot, and those around him were not obscured in a blur of vision. He recognized Diamante, grave concern etched into his face. The doctor bled him, but it did not ease the pain or reverse his condition. He continued to worsen. "I am spent, Diamante."

"No, Filippo. You must fight."

"Diamante," he said, at which his friend leaned in closer to better hear. "I place Filippino in your care."

"You will rise from this," Diamante affirmed. "You will work once more." The doctor placed his hand on Diamante's shoulder, the grave look that passed across his face belying these words.

Filippo tried to sit up. "Lucrezia," he said, and collapsed back onto the bed.

Diamante assured him, "She will be well cared for."

Filippo tried to master the pain for Filippino's sake. There was fear written across his son's face. He wanted to hold the boy in his arms, but he was too weak. With his hand, he gestured to Filippino to draw near. "My son," he whispered, and his eyes took their fill of him. The boy seemed to radiate a pure white light. This comforted Filippo, but he felt compelled to instruct him, struggled to leave him some words, to give him assurance, in the event that he should slip once more into a fever from which he might not return. Filippo was again seized with a violent spasm of pain. Diamante wiped the sweat from his face with a damp cloth. Filippo saw, as from a great distance, Filippino reaching out to him, fear rising in his eyes. Filippo willed the pain to subside and swallowed hard. He reached out his hand for Filippino, whose small, delicate, not yet manly hand clasped his own, warm and sweaty with the sweetness of life.

What words to leave? And then he remembered the gift that he, himself, had received at the most difficult times of his own life, delivered through many different voices, and he gave this gift to his son. "You will be a great painter one day," he told him and, in truth, believed it to be so. He looked into his son's eyes and smiled, smiled all the love he felt for him, all the appreciation for his existence, the only other gift he could muster. He held his son's gaze for as long as he was able until, weary, he felt his eyelids descend.

Feeling weak from the strain of too much thought, too many words, Filippo rested. He fell into a beautiful dream. He had entered one of his own paintings, the Adoration of the Christ child, flowers spread across the forest floor, and the Virgin Mary, gazing down upon her infant, her face filled with light, light swirling around her. And then, Filippo realized that he was the baby, and it was he who was looking up at her. And then, the place changed, and he was in the loggia of the Carmine, the sun streaming down, his face pressed into a yellow rose, and then he was the rose, filling up, like a vessel, with sun.

An opening parted in Filippo's chest. He dipped his brush into it, a deep, dark well. At the very bottom of it he found a luminous seed of light. He was sinking his brush into this light when, once again, the scene changed. Cosimo was standing beside him. Filippo said, "You are alive!" and was full of joy to see him.

"Remember, Filippo," Cosimo was saying, "a painter paints who he is."

They were in a garden. "You are happy," Filippo said, for he could see that it was so. Cosimo waved his arm to take in their surroundings. "Look at this," he said, "an entire kingdom. Run without our help. Imagine that!" Cosimo smiled, and Filippo followed his gaze as it moved to a place not far away where Cosimino, his grandson, sat building a little town that was surrounded by stone walls, all constructed of pebbles and sticks.

The scene changed yet again, and Filippo was looking through the casement window at a moon like a lantern, floating in a bank of clouds in an indigo sky, when he heard Lucrezia call to him and turned. She was sitting with Filippino on her lap, and Filippo realized that he had been in the process of painting a portrait of them. He walked back to the panel and took up his brush. Lucrezia bounced their son, young again, up and down on her lap, laughing. Filippo was laughing too, and saying, "Now, a little decorum. You are the Virgin Mary, after all." Lucrezia stood and danced around the room with Filippino in her arms. When she stooped down to hand him to the nurse, Filippo felt a wave of despair wash through him, but Lucrezia took him by the hand and led him into the orchard behind their house.

A light surrounded her where she stood, the sky at her back, the light a rose gold as if filtered through the skin of a pomegranate, and he heard al-Basir's voice saying, "One seed in each comes directly from heaven, and he who eats of it is filled with the light of paradise." Each moment, flesh and seed as one. He could hear himself saying her name, over and over.

In this rare temple of the angels, which has but light and love for boundaries.

Dante

Then he was sucked into a vast darkness. He lost his footing. Fear seized him. He struggled, gasping for air, reaching out, when suddenly he saw, far away, a scattering of tiny lights. As he grew closer, he discovered that the lights were interconnected, like a wide net cast over the sea. Suddenly, he was in the sea, surrounded by people, some of whose lives were interwoven with his own. He was not alone, had never been alone. All of humanity swam together in this sea, the others moving through the waves of their own troubles and joys, rippling outward, each feeling the wake of one another's movements, all buffeted by the continuous flow of circumstance, the forces that churned far out at sea, the greater troubles, pestilence, war, against which each seed of light had only the marteloio of its own soul.

The continuous thread of his own existence filled him, the beat and thrum of it, the color and hue, shadow and light, the breath of its light.

Slowly, its contours began to fade. The seed burst open. He found himself submerged in rivers of light.

EPILOGUE

The year of Our Lord, 1469 and 1484, Florence and Spoleto

He was more trouble than he was worth in life, and now even more so in death. "Is there no end to the trouble he brings?" Piero blurted as the messenger waited. "My father would want him home, or I would relent at once." He quickly wrote a cryptic message, "A Florentine artist must be put to rest in Florence," and handed it to the messenger.

It did not take long for Piero to receive a response. Florence, the note read, was full of great artists. So many were buried within its walls, in fact, that it could not keep count. Spoleto had but one, the one whose last work in life was the splendid decoration of the apse in its duomo.

Piero sent off another dispatch, explaining that Lippi was a Florentine citizen and, as such, must be interred in Florence, where his family, his fellow artists, and all of the citizens of Florence could gather to pay their respects.

Spoleto stubbornly refused to give him up. Lippi would be buried with honor, they wrote, in a manner reserved for only the most eminent of archbishops, in a marble tomb placed at the very center of the main aisle of the duomo, before the altar. It was more than he deserved, Piero reasoned, and gave up the fight. He himself had been ailing for several months. His strength fading, the effort to hold together all that his father had built was a severe strain.

Two months later, Piero passed into the great sea, and his son, Lorenzo, at the age of twenty-one, took over the reins of power. He was young, but he had been carefully groomed for the role and proved to be up to the challenge. He also took over the Platonic Academy and became as great a patron of the arts as his grandfather had been.

One of the artists he supported was Filippino Lippi. In the year of our Lord 1484, Filippino was a young man of twenty-seven, a maestro whose work was much sought after. He had been able to broker a good marriage for his sister, Alessandra, with a silk merchant of Prato. His dear mother was still with them, more than fifty years old now, ancient for a woman, but she was ailing.

Sitting at her bedside, he placed his hand over hers. She smiled up at him. "I am so proud of you, my son. You are the great painter your father knew you would become. You have taken good care of your sister. Now you must think of yourself. A wife. Children of your own."

"I will, Mother. My finances do not yet allow for the taking on of such responsibility."

"You are a good man. I want to see you happy."

"I am happy, Mother."

"I fear I will not live to see you married."

"You will," he assured her, although he was not certain.

"My forever sweet Filippino. You will make a woman a dear and loving husband." Lucrezia tried to sit up, winced, and fell back down.

"What can I get for you, Mother? What do you need?"

"Only to look on you." She smiled. "Your father would be so proud." She looked away, sadness clouding her face.

"You miss him still."

"I miss the simple things. How he would take me in his arms and dance me around the room. Around and around. Your father." She stopped. "He is so far away. He would want to rest here. Here in his beloved Florence. Not in some foreign land."

Within a fortnight, Filippino took the subject up with Lorenzo. Just as his father had had an easy relationship with Cosimo, Filippino was on comfortable terms with Lorenzo. "It is my mother's wish," he told him.

"Nothing more need be said," Lorenzo did not hesitate to answer, as he had the greatest respect for Mona Lucrezia. "I will think on it."

Lorenzo would rectify the situation. He fixed things; that was what he did best. He would do so to honor Lucrezia's wishes but also to do what his grandfather would have wanted. Not only that, but the Republic had never been bested. Florence would have its way. He, Lorenzo, would see to it.

With the enthusiasm of a young man not far from boyhood, although he was well into his thirties, Lorenzo began to hatch a plan. They would need to have tools at hand, so a fresco was out of the question. A monument, however, would provide the proper pretext. Who could object to the citizens of Florence wishing to honor the great painter at long last? He would commission Filippino, Lippi's son, and a great maestro himself, to design it and to oversee the project. This would allow them the necessary privacy. Filippino would be left alone much of the time out of respect. Lorenzo's grandfather would have appreciated the ingenuity of the plan. Lippi himself, from what Lorenzo had heard, would also be game for the ruse about to be played out. And no one would ever know, so where was the harm?

Filippino chose his two most trustworthy apprentices. They swore an oath of secrecy before Filippino and Lorenzo himself. Lorenzo told them that the consequences would be dire should word ever get out. After paying them a handsome sum for their part in the plan, his last words to them were, "If you should break your oath and utter a word of this to anyone, I will destroy you."

This was not the first time Filippino had returned to Spoleto. Although his mother had come as soon as she received the news, his sister Alessandra had been too young to make the journey. Years later, the entire family had made their way to his father's resting place. Afterwards, his mother and sister had returned home, and Filippino had continued to Rome where he had an important commission waiting. He had stopped again on his way back home from Rome. Now, here he was to supervise the construction of the monument before continuing once again to Rome where another commission awaited him. This time, it was his father himself who would be returning home.

Filippino sat near his father's tomb, the chink and clunk of chisel and hammer stilled for the day. As the natural light faded, the glow of candles all about shone with greater intensity. The tomb was an elaborate one, constructed of white and pink marble. They had done a fine job of honoring him, the Spoletans, but he belonged to Florence. Filippino remembered him saying, "There is no city in the world as perfect, even in its imperfections, as Florence. A man could be no more blessed than to be born a Florentine." Filippino wished that they could bring him home to a proper welcome, but secreting him back inside the walls of the city was better than leaving him so far away.

The monument having been completed, it was time to load the tools back into the large wooden crates. They had worked late into the evening to complete the project. Shutters were closed throughout Spoleto. They used the tools to lift the lid and, as silently as possible, straining against its weight, pushed the lid aside. They gently lifted his father's body, wrapping it in a tapestry and placing it in a wooden crate that stood ready. They nailed the top securely shut and slid the great stone of the tomb back into place.

Once outside, they placed the crate onto a cart. Filippino said farewell to his two apprentices, who would join him later in Rome. He watched as they made their way cautiously down the side of the mountain. The next time he would visit his father, it would be in Florence, where he would be interred in the Martelli chapel of San Lorenzo, beneath his Annunciation scene, across from his friend Donatello, and near to Cosimo.

THANK YOU

Thank you for reading *Where the Light Gathers*. If you enjoyed it, please take a moment to leave a review on Amazon, Barnes and Noble, Goodreads, or your preferred online retailer.

Reviews are the best way to show your support for an author and to help new readers discover their books.

To find out more about D Kathryn Pressman, please visit:

dkathrynpressman.com

ABOUT THE AUTHOR

A longtime lover of books and art, D Kathryn Pressman has combined her two passions in *Where the Light Gathers*, a work of historical fiction about the legendary Renaissance painter Filippo Lippi. Pressman has worked for more than thirty years as an editor, writer, and writing instructor. She has published magazine articles about artists and other topics of cultural interest, and poetry in literary journals. She now devotes herself full time to writing novels. Pressman received an MFA in fiction writing from Vermont College of Fine Arts. She lives in New England, where she, her husband, and their two dogs enjoy hikes together.

Made in the USA
Middletown, DE
15 July 2022